THE COPPER BEECH

THE
COPPER
BEECH

Maeve Binchy

ORION

The right of Maeve Binchy to be identified as the
author of this work has been asserted by her in accordance
with the Copyright, Designs and Patents Act 1988.

First published in Great Britain in 1992 by
Orion
An imprint of Orion Books Ltd
Orion House, 5 Upper St Martin's Lane, London WC2H 9EA

A CIP catalogue record for this book is
available from the British Library

Printed in England by
Clays Ltd, St Ives plc

*For Gordon, who has made my life so good and happy,
with all my gratitude and love.*

SHANCARRIG SCHOOL

Father Gunn knew that their housekeeper Mrs Kennedy could have done it all much better than he would do it. Mrs Kennedy would have done *everything* better in fact, heard Confessions, forgiven sins, sung the *Tantum Ergo* at Benediction, buried the dead. Mrs Kennedy would have looked the part too, tall and angular like the Bishop, not round and small like Father Gunn. Mrs Kennedy's eyes were soulful and looked as if they understood the sadness of the world.

Most of the time he was very happy in Shancarrig, a peaceful place in the midlands. Most people only knew it because of the huge rock that stood high on a hill over Barna Woods. There had once been great speculation about this rock. Had it been part of something greater? Was it of great geological interest? But experts had come and decided while there may well have been a house built around it once all traces must have been washed away with the rains and storms of centuries. It had never been mentioned in any history book. All that was there was one great rock. And since Carrig was the Irish word for rock that was how the place was named – Shancarrig, the Old Rock.

Life was good at the Church of the Holy Redeemer in Shancarrig. The parish priest, Monsignor O'Toole, was a courteous, frail man who let the curate run things his own way. Father Gunn wished that more could be done for the people of the parish so that they didn't have to stand at the railway station waving goodbye to sons and daughters emigrating to England and America. He wished that there were fewer damp cottages where tuberculosis could flourish, filling the graveyard with people too young to die. He wished that tired women did not have to bear so many children, children for whom there was often scant living. But he knew that all the young men who had been in the seminary with him were in similar parishes wishing the same thing. He didn't think he was a man who could change the world. For one thing he didn't *look* like a man who could change the world. Father Gunn's eyes were like two currants in a bun.

There had been a Mr Kennedy long ago, long before Father Gunn's time, but he had died of pneumonia. Every year he was prayed for at mass on the anniversary of his death, and every year Mrs Kennedy's sad face achieved what seemed to be an impossible feat, which was a still more sorrowful appearance. But even though it was nowhere near her late husband's anniversary now she was pretty gloomy, and it was all to do with Shancarrig school.

Mrs Kennedy would have thought since it was a question of a visit from the Bishop that *she*, as the priests' housekeeper, should have been in charge of everything. She didn't want to impose, she said many a time, but really had Father Gunn got it quite clear? Was it really expected that those teachers, those lay teachers above at the schoolhouse and the children that were taught in it, were really in charge of the ceremony?

'They're not used to bishops,' said Mrs Kennedy, implying that she had her breakfast, dinner and tea with the higher orders.

But Father Gunn had been adamant. The occasion was the dedication of the school, a bishop's blessing, a ceremony to add to the legion of ceremonies for Holy Year, but it was to involve the children, the teachers. It wasn't something run by the presbytery.

'But Monsignor O'Toole is the manager,' Mrs Kennedy protested. The elderly frail parish priest played little part in the events of the parish, it was all done by his bustling energetic curate, Father Gunn.

In many ways, of course, it would have been much easier to let Mrs Kennedy take charge, to have allowed her to get her machine into motion and organise the tired sponge cases, the heavy pastries, the big pots of tea that characterised so many church functions. But Father Gunn had stood firm. This event was for the school and the school would run it.

Thinking of Mrs Kennedy standing there hatted and gloved and sorrowfully disapproving, he asked God to let the thing be done right, to inspire young Jim and Nora Kelly, the teachers, to set it up properly. And to keep that mob of young savages that they taught in some kind of control.

After all, God had an interest in the whole thing too, and making the Holy Year meaningful in the parish was important. God must want it to be a success, not just to impress the Bishop but so that the children would remember their school and all the values they learned there. He was very fond of the school, the little stone building under the huge copper beech. He loved going up there on visits and watching the little heads bent over their copy books.

'Procrastination is the thief of time' they copied diligently.

'What does that mean, do you think?' he had asked once.

'We don't know what it means, Father. We only have to copy it out,' explained one of the children helpfully.

They weren't too bad really, the children of Shancarrig – he heard their Confessions regularly. The most terrible sin, and the one for which he had to remember to apportion a heavy penance, was scutting

4

on the back of a lorry. As far as Father Gunn could work out this was holding on to the back of a moving vehicle and being borne along without the driver's knowledge. It not unnaturally drew huge rage and disapproval from parents and passers-by, so he had to reflect the evilness of it by a decade of the Rosary, which was almost unheard of in the canon of children's penances. But scutting apart they were good children, weren't they? They'd do the school and Shancarrig credit when the Bishop came, wouldn't they?

The children talked of little else all term. The teachers told them over and over what an honour it was. The Bishop didn't normally go to small schools like this. They would have the chance to see him on their own ground, unlike so many children in the country who had never seen him until they were confirmed in the big town.

They had spent days cleaning the place up. The windows had been painted, and the door. The bicycle shed had been tidied so that you wouldn't recognise it. The classrooms had been polished till they gleamed. Perhaps His Grace would tour the school. It wasn't certain, but every eventuality had to be allowed for.

Long trestle tables would be arranged under the copper beech tree which dominated the school yard. Clean white sheets would cover them and Mrs Barton, the local dressmaker, had embroidered some lovely edging so that they wouldn't look like sheets. There would be jars of flowers, bunches of lilac and the wonderful purple orchids that grow wild in Barna Woods in the month of June.

A special table with Holy Water and a really good white cloth would be there so that His Grace could take the silver spoon and sprinkle the Water, dedicating the school again to God. The children would sing 'Faith of Our Fathers', and because it was near to the Feast of Corpus Christi they would also sing 'Sweet Sacrament Divine'. They rehearsed it every single day, they were word perfect now.

Whether or not the children were going to be allowed to partake of the feast itself was a somewhat grey area. Some of the braver ones had inquired but the answers were always unsatisfactory.

'We'll see,' Mrs Kelly had said.

'Don't always think of your bellies,' Mr Kelly had said.

It didn't look terribly hopeful.

Even though it was all going to take place at the school they knew that it wasn't really centred around the children. It was for the parish.

There would be something, of course, they knew that. But only when the grown-ups were properly served. There might be just plain bits of bread and butter with a little scraping of sandwich paste on them, or the duller biscuits when all the iced and chocolate-sided ones had gone.

The feast was going to be a communal effort from Shancarrig and so they each knew some aspect of it. There was hardly a household that wouldn't be contributing.

'There are going to be bowls of jelly and cream with strawberries on top,' Nessa Ryan was able to tell.

'That's for grown-ups!' Eddie Barton felt this was unfair.

'Well, my mother is making the jellies and giving the cream. Mrs Kelly said it would be whipped in the school and the decorations put on at the last moment in case they ran.'

'And chocolate cake. Two whole ones,' Leo Murphy said.

It seemed very unfair that this should all be for the Bishop and priests and great crowds of multifarious adults in front of whom they had all been instructed, or ordered, to behave well.

Sergeant Keane would be there, they had been told, as if he was about to take them all personally to the gaol in the big town if there was a word astray.

'They'll have to give some to us,' Maura Brennan said. 'It wouldn't be fair otherwise.'

Father Gunn heard her say this and marvelled at the innocence of children. For a child like young Maura, daughter of Paudie who drank every penny that came his way, to believe still in fairness was touching.

'There'll be bound to be *something* left over for you and your friends, Maura,' he said to her, hoping to spread comfort, but Maura's face reddened. It was bad to be overheard by the priest wanting food on a holy occasion. She hung back and let her hair fall over her face.

But Father Gunn had other worries.

The Bishop was a thin silent man. He didn't walk to places but was more inclined to glide. Under his long soutane or his regal-style vestments he might well have had wheels rather than feet. He had already said he would like to process rather than drive from the railway station to the school. Very nice if you were a gliding person and it was a cool day. Not so good however if it was a hot day, and the Bishop would notice the unattractive features of Shancarrig.

Like Johnny Finn's pub where Johnny had said that out of deference to the occasion he would close his doors but he was not going to dislodge the sitters.

'They'll sing. They'll be disrespectful,' Father Gunn had pleaded.

'Think what they'd be like if they were out on the streets, Father.' The publican had been firm.

So much was spoken about the day and so much was made of the numbers that would attend that the children grew increasingly nervous.

'There's no proof at all that we'll get *any* jelly and cream,' Niall Hayes said.

'I heard no talk of special bowls or plates or forks.'

'And if they let people like Nellie Dunne loose they'll eat all before them.' Nessa Ryan bit her lip with anxiety.

'We'll help ourselves,' said Foxy Dunne.

They looked at him round-eyed. Everything would be counted, they'd be murdered, he must be mad.

'I'll sort it out on the day,' he said.

Father Gunn was not sleeping well for the days preceding the ceremony. It was a great kindness that he hadn't heard Foxy's plans.

Mrs Kennedy said that she would have some basic emergency supplies ready in the kitchen of the presbytery, just in case. Just in case. She said it several times.

Father Gunn would not give her the satisfaction of asking just in case *what*. He knew only too well. She meant in case his foolish confidence in allowing lay people up at a small schoolhouse to run a huge public religious ceremony was misplaced. She shook her head and dressed in black from head to foot, in honour of the occasion.

There had been three days of volunteer work trying to beautify the station. No money had been allotted by CIE, the railways company, for repainting. The stationmaster, Jack Kerr, had been most unwilling to allow a party of amateur painters loose on it. His instructions did not include playing fast and loose with company property, painting it all the colours of the rainbow.

'We'll paint it grey,' Father Gunn had begged.

But no. Jack Kerr wouldn't hear of it, and he was greatly insulted at the weeding and slashing down of dandelions that took place.

'The Bishop likes flowers,' Father Gunn said sadly.

'Let him bring his own bunch of them to wear with his frock then,' said Mattie the postman, the one man in Shancarrig foolhardy enough to say publicly that he did not believe in God and wouldn't therefore be hypocritical enough to attend mass, or the sacraments.

'Mattie, this is not the time to get me into a theological discussion,' implored Father Gunn.

'We'll have it whenever you're feeling yourself again, Father.' Mattie was unfailingly courteous and rather too patronising for Father Gunn's liking.

But he had a good heart. He transported clumps of flowers from Barna Woods and planted them in the station beds. 'Tell Jack they grew when the earth was disturbed,' he advised. He had correctly judged the stationmaster to be unsound about nature and uninterested in gardening.

'I think the place is perfectly all right,' Jack Kerr was heard to grumble as they all stood waiting for the Bishop's train. He looked around his transformed railway station and saw nothing different.

The Bishop emerged from the train gracefully. He was shaped like an S hook, Father Gunn thought sadly. He was graceful, straightening or bending as he talked to each person. He was extraordinarily gracious, he didn't fuss or fumble, he remembered everyone's name, unlike Father Gunn who had immediately forgotten the names of the two self-important clerics who accompanied the Bishop.

Some of the younger children, dressed in the little white surplices of altar boys, stood ready to lead the procession up the town.

The sun shone mercilessly. Father Gunn had prayed unsuccessfully for one of the wet summer days they had been having recently. Even that would be better than this oppressive heat.

The Bishop seemed interested in everything he saw. They left the station and walked the narrow road to what might be called the centre of town had Shancarrig been a larger place. They paused at the Church of the Holy Redeemer for His Grace to say a silent prayer at the foot of the altar. Then they walked past the bus stop, the little line of shops, Ryan's Commercial Hotel and The Terrace where the doctor, the solicitor and other people of importance lived.

The Bishop seemed to nod approvingly when places looked well, and to frown slightly as he passed the poorer cottages. But perhaps that was all in Father Gunn's mind. Maybe His Grace was unaware of his surroundings and was merely saying his prayers. As they walked along Father Gunn was only too conscious of the smell from the River Grane, low and muddy. As they crossed the bridge he saw out of the corner of his eye a few faces at the window of Johnny Finn Noted for Best Drinks. He prayed they wouldn't find it necessary to open the window.

Mattie the postman sat laconically on an upturned barrel. He was one of the only spectators since almost every other citizen of Shancarrig was waiting at the school.

The Bishop stretched out his hand very slightly as if offering his ring to be kissed.

Mattie inclined his head very slightly and touched his cap. The gesture was not offensive, but neither was it exactly respectful. If the Bishop understood it he said nothing. He smiled to the right and the left, his thin aristocratic face impervious to the heat. Father Gunn's face was a red round puddle of sweat.

The first sign of the schoolhouse was the huge ancient beech tree, a copper beech that shaded the playground. Then you saw the little stone schoolhouse that had been built at the turn of the century. The dedication ceremony had been carefully written out in advance and scrutinised by these bureaucratic clerics who seemed to swarm around the Bishop. They had checked every word in case Father Gunn might have included a major heresy or sacrilege. The purpose of it all was to consecrate the school, and the future of all the young people it would educate, to God in this Holy Year. Father Gunn failed to understand why this should be considered some kind of doctrinal minefield. All he was trying to do was to involve the community at the right level, to make them see that their children were their hope and their future.

For almost three months the event had been heralded from the altar at mass. And the pious hope expressed that the whole village would be present for the prayers and the dedication. The prayers, hymns and short discourse should take forty-five minutes, and then there would be an hour for tea.

As they plodded up the hill Father Gunn saw that everything was in place.

A crowd of almost two hundred people stood around the school yard. Some of the men leaned against the school walls but the women stood chatting to each other. They were dressed in their Sunday best. The group would part to let the little procession through and then the Bishop would see the children of Shancarrig.

All neat and shining – he had been on a tour of inspection already this morning. There wasn't a hair out of place, a dirty nose or a bare foot to be seen. Even the Brennans and the Dunnes had been made respectable. They stood, all forty-eight of them, outside the school. They were in six rows of eight; those at the back were on benches so that they could be seen. They looked like little angels, Father Gunn thought. It was always a great surprise the difference a little cleaning and polishing could make.

Father Gunn relaxed, they were nearly there. Only a few more moments then the ceremony would begin. It would be all right after all.

The school looked magnificent. Not even Mrs Kennedy could have complained about its appearance, Father Gunn thought. And the tables were arranged under the spreading shade of the copper beech.

The master and the mistress had the children beautifully arranged, great emphasis having been laid on looking neat and tidy. Father Gunn began to relax a little. This was as fine a gathering as the Bishop would find anywhere in the diocese.

The ceremony went like clockwork. The chair for Monsignor O'Toole, the elderly parish priest, was discreetly placed. The singing, if not strictly tuneful, was at least in the right area. No huge discordancies were evident.

It was almost time for tea – the most splendid tea that had ever been served in Shancarrig. All the eatables were kept inside the school building, out of the heat and away from the flies. When the last notes of the last hymn died away Mr and Mrs Kelly withdrew indoors.

There was something about the set line of Mrs Kennedy's face that made Father Gunn decide to go and help them. He couldn't bear it if a tray of sandwiches fell to the ground or the cream slid from the top of a trifle. Quietly he moved in, to find a scene of total confusion. Mr and Mrs Kelly and Mrs Barton, who had offered to help with carrying plates to tables, stood frozen in a tableau, their faces expressing different degrees of horror.

'What is it?' he asked, barely able to speak.

'Every single queen cake!' Mrs Kelly held up what looked from the top a perfectly acceptable tea cake with white icing on it, but underneath the sign of tooth marks showed that the innards had been eaten away.

'And the chocolate cake!' gasped Una Barton, who was white as a sheet. The front of the big cake as you saw it looked delectable, but the back had been propped up with a piece of bark, a good third of the cake having been eaten away.

'It's the same with the apple tarts!' Mrs Kelly's tears were now openly flowing down her cheeks. 'Some of the children, I suppose.'

'That Foxy Dunne and his gang! I should have known. I should have bloody known.' Jim Kelly's face was working itself into a terrible anger.

'How did he get in?'

'The little bastard said he'd help with the chairs, brought a whole gang in with him. I said to him, "All those cakes are counted very carefully." And I did bloody count them when they went out.'

'Stop saying bloody and bastard to Father Gunn,' said Nora Kelly.

'I think it's called for.' Father Gunn was grim.

'If only they could have just eaten half a dozen. They've wrecked the whole thing.'

'Maybe I shouldn't have gone on about counting them.' Jim Kelly's big face was full of regret.

'It's all ruined,' Mrs Barton said. 'It's ruined.' Her voice held the high tinge of hysteria that Father Gunn needed to bring him to his senses.

'Of course it's not ruined. Mrs Barton, get the teapots out, call Mrs Kennedy to help you. She's wonderful at pouring tea and she'd like to be invited. Get Conor Ryan from the hotel to start pouring the lemonade and send Dr Jims in here to me quick as lightning.'

His words were so firm that Mrs Barton was out the door in a flash. Through the small window he saw the tea pouring begin and Conor Ryan happy to be doing something he was familiar with, pouring the lemonade.

The doctor arrived, worried in case someone had been taken ill.

'It's your surgical skills we need, Doctor. You take one knife, I'll take another and we'll cut up all these cakes and put out a small selection.'

'In the name of God, Father Gunn, what do you want to do that for?' asked the doctor.

'Because these lighting devils that go by the wrong name of innocent children have torn most of the cakes apart with their teeth,' said Father Gunn.

Triumphantly they arrived out with the plates full of cake selections.

'Plenty more where that came from!' Father Gunn beamed as he pressed the assortments into their hands. Since most people might not have felt bold enough to choose such a wide selection they were pleased rather than distressed to see so much coming their way.

Out of the corner of his mouth Father Gunn kept asking Mr Kelly, the master, for the names of those likely to have been involved. He kept repeating them to himself, as someone might repeat the names of tribal leaders who had brought havoc and destruction on his ancestors. Smiling as he served people and bustled to and fro, he repeated as an incantation – 'Leo Murphy, Eddie Barton, Niall Hayes, Maura Brennan, Nessa Ryan, and Foxy Bloody Dunne.'

He saw that Mattie the postman had consented to join the gathering, and was dangerously near the Bishop.

'Willing to eat the food of the Opium of the People, I see,' he hissed out of the corner of his mouth.

'That's a bit harsh from you, Father,' Mattie said, halfway through a plate of cake.

'Speak to the Bishop on any subject whatsoever and you'll never deliver a letter in this parish again,' Father Gunn warned.

The gathering was nearing its end. Soon it would be time to return to the station.

This time the journey would be made by car. Dr Jims and Mr Hayes, the solicitor, would drive the Bishop and the two clerics, whose names had never been ascertained.

Father Gunn assembled the criminals together in the school. 'Correct me if I have made an error in identifying any of the most evil people it has ever been my misfortune to meet,' he said in a terrible tone.

Their faces told him that his information had been mainly correct.

'Well?' he thundered.

'Niall wasn't in on it,' Leo Murphy said. She was a small wiry ten-year-old with red hair. She came from The Glen, the big house on the hill. She could have had cake for tea seven days a week.

'I did have a bit, though,' Niall Hayes said.

'Mr Kelly is a man with large hands. He has declared his intention of using them to break your necks, one after the other. I told him that I would check with the Vatican, but I was sure he would get absolution. Maybe even a *medal*.' Father Gunn roared the last word. They all jumped back in fright. 'However, I told Mr Kelly not to waste the Holy Father's time with all these dispensations and pardons, instead I would handle it. I told him that you had all volunteered to wash every dish and plate and cup and glass. That it was your contribution. That you would pick up every single piece of litter that has fallen around the school. That you would come to report to Mr and Mrs Kelly when it is all completed.'

They looked at each other in dismay. This was a long job. This was something that the ladies of the parish might have been expected to do.

'What about people like Mrs Kennedy? Wouldn't they want to . . . ?' Foxy began.

'No, they wouldn't want to, and people like Mrs Kennedy are *delighted* to know that you volunteered to do this. Because those kinds of people haven't seen into your black souls.'

There was silence.

'This day will never be forgotten. I want you to know that. When other bad deeds are hard to remember this one will always be to the forefront of the mind. This June day in 1950 will be etched there for ever.' He could see that Eddie Barton's and Maura Brennan's faces were beginning to pucker; he mustn't frighten them to death. 'So now. You will join the guard of honour to say farewell to the Bishop, to wave goodbye with your hypocritical hearts to His Grace whose visit you did your best to undermine and destroy. *Out.*' He glared at them. '*Out* this minute.'

Outside, the Bishop's party was about to depart. Gracefully he was moving from person to person, thanking them, praising them, admiring the lovely rural part of Ireland they lived in, saying that it did the heart good to get out to see God's beautiful nature from time to time rather than being always in a bishop's palace in a city.

'What a wonderful tree this is, and what great shade it gave us today.' He looked up at the copper beech as if to thank it, although it was obvious that he was the kind of man who could stand for hours in the Sahara desert without noticing anything amiss in the climate. It was the boiling Father Gunn who owed thanks to the leafy shade.

'And what's all this writing on the trunk?' He peered at it, his face alive with its well-bred interest and curiosity. Father Gunn heard the Kellys' intake of breath. This was the tree where the children always inscribed their initials, complete with hearts and messages saying who was loved by whom. Too secular, too racy, too sexual to be admired by a bishop. Possibly even a hint of vandalism about it.

But no.

The Bishop seemed by some miracle to be admiring it.

'It's good to see the children mark their being here and leaving here,' he said to the group who stood around straining for his last words. 'Like this tree has been here for decades, maybe even centuries back, so will there always be a school in Shancarrig to open the minds of its children and to send them out into the world.'

He looked back lingeringly at the little stone schoolhouse and the huge tree as the car swept him down the hill and towards the station.

As Father Gunn got into the second car to follow him and make the final farewells at the station he turned to look once more at the criminals. Because his heart was big and the day hadn't been ruined he gave them half a smile. They didn't dare to believe it.

MADDY

W hen Madeleine Ross was brought to the church in Shancarrig to be baptised she wore an old christening robe that had belonged to her grandmother. Such lace was rarely seen in the Church of the Holy Redeemer – it would have been more at home in St Matthew's parish church, the ivy-covered Protestant church eleven miles away. But this was 1932, the year of the Eucharistic Congress in Ireland. Catholic fervour was at its highest and everyone would expect fine lace on a baby who was being christened.

The old priest did say to someone that this was a baby girl not likely to be lacking in anything, considering the life she was born into.

But parish priests don't know everything.

Madeleine's father died when she was eight. He was killed in the War. Her only brother went out to Rhodesia to live with an uncle who had a farm the size of Munster.

When Maddy Ross was eighteen years old in 1950 there were a great many things lacking in her life: like any plan of what she was going to do – like any freedom to go away and do it.

Her mother needed somebody at home and her brother had gone, so Maddy would be the one to stay.

Maddy also thought she needed a man friend, but Shancarrig was not the place to find one.

It wasn't even a question of being a big fish in a small pond. The Ross family were not rich landowners – people of class and distinction. If they had been then there might have been some society that Maddy could have moved in and hunted for a husband.

It was a matter of such fine degree.

Maddy and her mother were both too well off and not well enough off to fit into the pattern of small-town life. It was fortunate for Maddy that she was a girl who liked her own company, since so little of anyone else's company was offered to her.

Or perhaps she became this way because of circumstances.

But ever since she was a child people remembered her gathering armfuls of bluebells all on her own in the Barna Woods, or bringing home funny-shaped stones from around the big rock of Shancarrig.

The Rosses had a small house on the bank of the River Grane, not near the rundown cottages, but further on towards Barna Woods which led up to the Old Rock. Almost anywhere you walked from Maddy Ross's house was full of interest, whether it was up a side road to the school, or past the cottages to the bridge and into the heart of town, where The Terrace, Ryan's Commercial Hotel and the row of shops all stood. But her favourite walk was to head out through the woods, which changed so much in each season they were like different woods altogether. She loved them most in autumn when everything was golden, when the ground was a carpet of leaves.

You could imagine the trees were people, kind big people about to embrace you with their branches, or that there was a world of tiny people living in the roots, people who couldn't really be seen by humans.

She would tell stories, half wanting to be listened to and half to herself – stories about where she found golden and scarlet branches in autumn and the eyes of an old woman watching her through the trees, or of how children in bare feet played by the big rock that overlooked the town and ran away when anyone approached.

They were harmless stories, the Imaginary Friend stories of all children. Nobody took any notice, especially since it all died down when she went off to boarding school at the age of eleven. Shancarrig school was much too rough a place for little Madeleine Ross. She was sent to a convent two counties away.

Then they saw her growing up, her long pale hair in plaits hanging down her back and when she got to seventeen the plaits were wound around her head.

She was slim and willowy like her mother but she had these curious pale eyes. Had Maddy had good strong eyes of any colour she would have been beautiful. The lightness somehow gave her a colourless quality, a wispy appearance, as if she wasn't a proper person.

And if anyone in Shancarrig had thought much about her they might have come to the conclusion that she was a weak girl who had few views of her own.

A more determined young woman might have made a decision about finding work for herself, or friends. No matter how complex the social structure of Shancarrig you'd have thought that young Maddy Ross would have had some friends.

There were cousins of course, aunts and uncles to visit. Maddy and her mother went to see families in four counties, always her mother's relations. Her father's people lived in England.

But at home she was really only on the fringe of things. Like the day they had the dedication of the school, the day the Bishop came.

Maddy Ross stood on the edge with her straw sunhat to keep the rays of the sun from her fair skin. She watched Father Gunn bowing his way up the hill towards the school. She watched the elderly Monsignor O'Toole in his wheelchair. But she stood slightly apart from the rest of Shancarrig as they waited for the procession to arrive.

The Kellys with their little niece Maria, all of them dressed to kill. Nora Kelly should have worn a hat like Maddy had, not a hopeless lank mantilla that made her look out of place in the Irish countryside.

Still it would be nice to belong somewhere, like the Kellys did. They had come to that school and made it their own. They were the centre of the community now while Maddy, who had lived here all her life, was still on the outside.

She accepted her plate of cakes, all served for some reason sliced and on a plate, rather than letting people choose what they wished.

Mrs Kelly looked at her speculatively.

'I think the time has come to get a JAM,' she said.

Maddy was mystified. 'I hardly think you need any more,' she said, looking at her plate.

'A Junior Assistant Mistress,' Mrs Kelly explained, as if to a five-year-old.

'Oh, sorry.'

'Well, do you think we should talk to your mother about it?'

Maddy began to wonder was the heat affecting all of them.

'I ... think she's a bit set in her ways now ... she mightn't be able to teach,' she explained kindly.

'I meant you, Miss Ross.'

'Oh. Of course. Yes, well ...' Maddy said.

It proved how little she must have been planning her life. She had *no* immediate plans.

There had been much talk that year of visiting Rome. It was the Holy Year. It would be a special time. Aunty Peggy had been, the pictures were endless, the stories often repeated, the lack of good strong tea regretted over and over.

But Mother could never make up her mind about little things like whether to have strawberry jam or gooseberry jam for tea, so how could she make up her mind about something huge like a visit to Rome? The autumn came, the evenings started to get cooler, and everyone agreed that there would be grave danger of catching a chill.

It was just as well they hadn't gone to all the trouble of getting passports and booking tickets. And as Mother often said, you could love God just as well from Shancarrig as you could from a city in Italy.

Maddy Ross had been disappointed at first when the often discussed plans looked as if they were coming to nothing. But then she didn't think about it any more. She was good at putting disappointments behind her, there had been many of them even by the time she was eighteen.

Her best friend at school, Kathleen White, hadn't even told Maddy when she decided to enter the convent and become a nun. Everyone else in the school knew first. Maddy had been shaking with emotion when she challenged Kathleen with the news.

Kathleen had become unhealthily calm, too serene for her own good.

'I didn't tell you because you're so intense about everything,' Kathleen said simply. 'You'd either have wanted to join with me or you'd have been too dramatic about it. It's just what I want to do. That's all.'

Maddy decided to forgive Kathleen after a while. After all, a Vocation was a huge step. Obviously Kathleen had too much on her mind to care about the sensibilities of her friend. Maddy wrote her long letters forgiving her and talking about the commitment to religious life. Kathleen had written one short note. In two months' time she would be a postulant at the convent. She could neither write nor receive letters then. Perhaps it would be better to get ready for that by not beginning a very emotional correspondence now.

And there had been other disappointments that summer. At the tennis club dance Maddy had thought she looked well and that a young man had admired her. He had danced with her for longer than anyone else. He had been particularly attentive about glasses of fruit punch. They had sat in the swinging seat and talked easily about every subject. But nothing had come of it. She had gone to great trouble to let him know where she lived and even found two occasions to call at his house. But it was as if she had never existed.

Sometimes when Maddy Ross went for her long lonely walks up the tree-covered hill to the Old Rock that stood guarding the town she felt that she handled everything wrong. It was all so different to things that happened to girls in the pictures.

Maddy had always known that there wouldn't be the money to send her to university, so she had thought it just as well that she didn't have any burning desire to be a professor, or a doctor or lawyer. But there was nothing else that fired her either. Other girls had gone to train as nurses, some of them had done secretarial courses and gone into the bank or big insurance offices. There were others who went to be radiographers, or physiotherapists.

Maddy, the girl with the long pale hair and the slow smile that went all over her face once it began, thought that sooner or later something would turn up.

Probably at the end of the holidays.

Mrs Kelly had been serious on that hot day, and in the very first week of September Mr and Mrs Kelly from the school came to see Mother.

Shancarrig's small stone schoolhouse was a little way out of the town. That was to make it easier for the children of the farmers, it had been said. Mr and Mrs Kelly had come as newly marrieds to the school in answer to Father Gunn's appeal. The last teachers had left in some disarray. Maddy had heard stories about drinking and dismissals, but as usual, only a very edited version of events, filtered through her mother. Mother never seemed to grasp the full end of any stick.

Mr and Mrs Kelly were a strange couple. He was big and innocent-looking, like a farmer's boy. She was small and taut-looking, her mouth often in a narrow line of disapproval.

Maddy Ross had looked at her more than once, wondering what it was about Mrs Kelly that had attracted the big, simple, good-natured man by her side. They were only about ten years older than she was.

She wondered if Mrs Kelly had looked about her and then, finding nobody more suitable, settled for the teacher. She certainly looked as if something had displeased her. Even when they came uninvited to see Mother they both looked as if they were going to issue some complaint.

Maddy found nothing odd about their asking Mother rather than asking her. After all, it was the kind of thing Mrs Ross would have a view on. Perhaps she thought her daughter Madeleine was intended for something more elevated than working in Shancarrig school. It was better to sound out the opinions before making a direct approach.

But Mother thought it would be an excellent idea. 'Fallen straight into their laps' was the way she described it when the cousins came to supper the following day.

'And won't Madeleine need to be trained to teach?' the cousins asked.

'Nonsense,' said Mother. 'What training would anyone need to put manners on unfortunates like the young Brennans or the young Dunnes?'

They agreed. It wasn't a real career like the cousins' children were embarking on: one in a bank, one doing a very advanced secretarial course, with Commercial French thrown in, which could lead to any kind of a position almost anywhere in the world.

To her surprise Maddy loved it.

She had neither the roar of Mr Kelly nor the confident firm voice of his wife. She spoke gently and almost hesitantly but the children responded to her. Even the bold Brennan children, whose father was Paudie Brennan, drunk and layabout, seemed easy to handle. And the Dunnes, whose faces were smeared with jam, agreed quite meekly to having their mouths wiped before class began.

There were three classsrooms in the little schoolhouse, one for Mrs Kelly's class, one for Mr Kelly's, and the biggest one for Maddy Ross. It was called Mixed Infants and it was here that she started the young minds of Shancarrig off on what might be a limited kind of educational journey. There would be some, of course, who would advance to a far greater education than she had herself. The young Hayes girls, whose father was a solicitor, might well get professions, as might little Nuala Ryan from the hotel. But it was only too obvious that the Dunnes and Brennans would say goodbye to any hopes of education once they left this school. They would be on the boat abroad or into the town to get whatever was on offer for children of fourteen years of age.

They all looked the same at five, however. There was nothing except the difference of clothing to mark out those who would have the money to go further and those who would not.

Before she had gone into the school Maddy Ross barely noticed the children of her own place. Now she knew everything about them, the ones that sniffled and seemed upset, the ones who thought they could run the place, those that had the doorsteps of sandwiches for their lunch, those who had nothing at all. There were children who clung to her and told her everything about themselves and their families, and there were those who hung back.

She had never known that there would be a great joy in seeing a child work out for himself the letters of a simple sentence and read it aloud, or in watching a girl who had bitten her pencil to a stub suddenly realise how you did the great long tots or the subtraction sums. Each day it was a pleasure to point to the map of Ireland with a long stick and hear them chant the places out.

'What are the main towns of County Cavan? All right. All together now. Cavan, Cootehill, Virginia . . .' all in a sing-song voice.

There were two cloakrooms, one for the girls and one for the boys. They smelled of Jeyes Fluid, as the master obviously poured it liberally in the evenings when the children had left.

It would have been a bleak little place had it not been for the huge copper beech which dwarfed it and looked as if it was holding the school under its protective arm. Like she felt safe in Barna Woods as a child, Maddy felt safe with this tree. It marked the seasons with its colouring and its leaves.

The days passed easily, each one very much like that which had gone before. Madeleine Ross made big cardboard charts to entertain the children. She had pictures of the flowers she collected in Barna Woods, and she sometimes pressed the flowers as well and wrote their names underneath. Every day the children in Shancarrig school sat in their little wooden desks and repeated the names of the ferns, and foxgloves, cowslips and primroses and ivies. Then they would look at the pictures of St Patrick and St Brigid and St Colmcille and chant their names too.

Maddy made sure that they remembered the saints as well as the flowers.

The saints were higher on Father Gunn's list of priorities. Father Gunn was a very nice curate. He had little whirly glasses, like looking through the bottom of a lemonade bottle. Now the school manager he was a frequent visitor – he had to guard the faith and morals of the future parishioners of Shancarrig. But Father Gunn liked flowers and trees too, and he was always kind and supportive to the Junior Assistant Mistress.

Maddy wondered how old he was. With priests, as with nuns, it was always so hard to know. One day he unexpectedly told her how old he was. He said he was born on the day the Treaty was signed in 1921.

'I'm as old as the State,' he said proudly. 'I hope we'll both live for ever.'

'It's good to hear you saying that, Father.' Maddy was arranging a nature display in the window. 'It shows you enjoy life. Mother is always saying that she can't get her wings soon enough.'

'Wings!' The priest was puzzled.

'It's her way of saying she'd like to be in heaven with God. She talks about it quite a lot.'

Father Gunn seemed at a loss for words. 'It's wholly admirable, of course, to see this world only as a shadow of the heavenly bliss Our Father has prepared for us but ...'

'But Mother's only just gone fifty. It's a bit soon to be thinking about it already, isn't it?' Maddy helped him out.

He nodded gratefully, 'Of course, I'm getting on myself. Maybe I'll start thinking the same way.' His voice was jokey. 'But I have so much to do I don't feel old.'

'You should have someone to help you.' Maddy said only what everyone else in Shancarrig said. The old priest was doddery now. Father Gunn did everything. They definitely needed a new curate.

And it wasn't as if the priests' housekeeper was any help. Mrs Kennedy had a face like a long drink of water. She was dressed in black most of the time, mourning for a husband who had died so long ago hardly anyone in Shancarrig could remember him. A good priests' housekeeper should surely be kind and supportive, fill the role of mother, old family retainer and friend.

It had to be said that Mrs Kennedy played none of these roles. She seemed to smoulder in resentment that she herself had not been given charge of the parish. She snorted derisively when anyone offered to help out in the parish work. It was a tribute to Father Gunn's own niceness that so many people stepped in to help with the problems caused by Monsignor O'Toole being almost out of the picture, and Mrs Kennedy being almost too much in it.

Then the news came that there was indeed a new priest on the way to Shancarrig. Someone knew someone in Dublin who had been told definitely. He was meant to be a very nice man altogether.

About six months later, in the spring of 1952, the new curate arrived. He was a pale young man called Father Barry. He had long delicate white hands, light fair hair and dark, startling blue eyes. He moved gracefully around Shancarrig, his soutane swishing gently from side to side. He had none of the bustle of Father Gunn, who always seemed uneasily belted into his priestly garb and distinctly ill at ease in the vestments.

When Father Barry said mass a shaft of sunlight seemed to come in and touch his pale face, making him look more saintly than ever. The people of Shancarrig loved Father Barry and in her heart Maddy Ross often felt a little sorry for Father Gunn, who had somehow been overshadowed.

24

It wasn't *his* fault that he looked burly and solid. He was just as good and attentive to the old and the feeble, just as understanding in Confession, just as involved in the school. And yet she had to admit that Father Barry brought with him some new sense of exhilaration that the first priest didn't have.

When Father Barry came to her classroom and spoke he didn't talk vaguely about the missions and the need to save stamps and silver paper for mission stations, he talked of hill villages in Peru where the people ached to hear of Our Lord, where there was only one small river and that dried up during the dry seasons, leaving the villagers to walk for miles over the hot dry land to get water for the old and for their babies.

As they sat in the damp little schoolhouse in Shancarrig, Maddy and Mixed Infants were transported miles away to another continent. The Brennans had broken shoes and torn clothes, they even bore the marks of a drunken father's fist, but they felt rich beyond the dreams of kings compared to the people in Vieja Piedra, thousands of miles away.

The very name of this village was the same as their own. It meant Old Rock. The people in this village were crying out to them across the world for help.

Father Barry fired the children with an enthusiasm never before known in that school. And it wasn't only in Maddy Ross's class. Even under the sterner eye of Mrs Kelly, who might have been expected to say that we should look after our own first before going abroad to give help, the collections increased. And in Mr Kelly's class the fierce master echoed the words of the young priest, but in his own way.

'Come out of that, Jeremiah O'Connor. You'll want your arse kicked from here to Barna and back if you can't go out and raise a shilling for the poor people of Vieja Piedra.'

When he gave the Sunday sermon Father Barry often closed his disturbing blue eyes and spoke of how fortunate his congregation were to live in the green fertile lands around Shancarrig. The church might be full of people sneezing and coughing, wearing coats wet from the trek across three miles of road and field to get there, but Father Barry made their place sound like a paradise compared to its namesake in Peru.

Some of them began to wonder why a loving God had been so unjust to the good Spanish-speaking people in that part of the world, who would have done anything to have a church and priests in their midst.

Father Barry had an answer for that whenever the matter was raised. He said it was God's plan to test men's love and goodness for each other. It was easy to love God, Father Barry assured everyone. Nobody had any problem in loving Our Heavenly Father. The problem was to love people in a small lonely village miles away and treat them as brothers and sisters.

Maddy and her mother often talked about Father Barry and his saintliness. It was something they both agreed on, which meant they talked about him more than ever. There were so many subjects which divided them.

Maddy wondered would there be the chance for them to go out to Rhodesia to Joseph's wedding. Her brother was marrying a girl from a Scottish family in Bulawayo. There would be nobody from the Ross side of the family. He had sent the money, and the wedding was during the school holidays, but Mrs Ross said she wasn't up to the journey. Dr Jims had said that Maddy's mother was fit as a fiddle and well able to make the trip. In fact, the sea journey would do nothing except improve her health.

Father Gunn had said that family solidarity would be a great thing at a time like this and that truly she should make the effort. Major and Mrs Murphy who lived in The Glen, the big house with the iron railings and the wonderful glasshouses, said that it was a chance of a lifetime. Mr Hayes the solicitor said that if it was his choice he'd go.

But Mother remained adamant. It was a waste, she said, to spend the money on a trip for such an old person as she was. She would soon be getting her wings. She would see enough and know enough then.

Maddy was becoming increasingly impatient with this attitude of her mother's. The wings theory seemed to apply to everything. If Maddy wanted a new coat, or a trip to Dublin, or a perm for her light straight hair, her mother would sigh and say there would be plenty of time for that and money to spend on it after Mother had gone.

Mother was in her fifties and as strong as anyone in Shancarrig, but giving the aura of frailty. Maddy did the housework, because until Mother had got her wings there would be no money to spend on luxuries like having a maid. Maddy's own wages as a Junior Assistant Mistress were so small as to be insignificant.

She was twenty-three and very restless.

The only person in the whole of Shancarrig who understood was Father Barry. He was thirty-three and equally restless. He had been called to order for preaching too much about Vieja Piedra, by no less an authority than the Bishop. He burned with the injustice of it. Monsignor O'Toole was doting, and knew nothing of what was being preached or what was not. Father Gunn must have gone behind his back and complained about him. Father Gunn was only a fellow curate, he had no authority over him.

Father Brian Barry roamed the woods of Barna, swishing angrily against the bushes that got in his way. What right had men, the pettiest and most jealous of men, to try to halt God's work for dying people, for brothers and sisters who were calling out to them?

If Brian Barry's own health had been better he would have been a missionary priest. He would have been amongst the people of Vieja Piedra, like his friend from the seminary, Cormac Flynn, was. Cormac it was who wrote and told him at first hand of the work that had to be done.

In the Church of the Holy Redeemer there was a window dedicated to the memory of the Hayes family relations who had gone to their eternal reward. There had been many priests in that family. On the window the words were written *The Harvest is Great but the Labourers are Few*. There it was, written in stained glass, in their own church, and the mad parish priest and the selfish complacent Father Gunn were so blind they couldn't see it.

In one of these angry walks Father Barry came across Miss Ross from the school, sitting on a tree trunk and puzzling over a letter. He calmed himself for a minute before he spoke. She was a gentle girl and he didn't want to let her know the depth of his rage and resentment in the battle for people's souls, and all the obstacles that were being put in his way.

She looked up startled when she saw him, but made room on the log for him to sit down.

'Isn't it beautiful here? You can often find a solution in this place, I think.'

He reached through the slit in his cassock to take cigarettes out of his pocket and sat beside her without speaking.

Somehow, she seemed to understand the need for silence. She sat, hugging her knees and looking out ahead of her, as the summer

27

afternoon light came in patches between the rowan trees and beeches that made up Barna Woods. A squirrel came and gazed at them, inquisitively looking from one to the other before he hopped away.

They laughed. The tension and the silence broken, they could talk to each other easily.

'When I was young I'd never seen a squirrel,' Father Barry said. 'Only in picture books, and there was a giraffe on the same page so I always thought they were the same size. I was terrified of meeting one.'

'When did you?'

'Not until I was in the seminary . . . someone said there was a squirrel over there and I urged everyone to take cover . . . they thought I was mad.'

'Well, that's nothing,' she encouraged him. 'I thought guerrilla warfare was sending gorillas out to fight each other instead of people.'

'You're saying that to make me feel good,' he teased her.

'Not a bit of it. Did they all laugh or didn't any of them understand?'

'I had a friend, Cormac. He understood. He understood everything.'

'That's Father Cormac out in Peru?'

'Yes. He understood everything. But how can I tell him what's happening now?'

As the shadows got longer they sat in Barna Woods and talked. Brian Barry told of his anguish over the work that had to be done and the burden of guilt he felt about the people of this place that seemed to call to him, but what did he do about Obedience to superiors? Maddy Ross told of her brother Joseph who had sent money and expected his mother and sister to come and be there for the happiest day of his life.

'How can I find the words to tell him?' Maddy asked.

'How can I find the words to tell Cormac there'll be no more support from Shancarrig?' asked Father Barry.

That was the day that began their dependence on each other – the knowledge that only the other understood the pressures, the pain and the indecision. The very thought that somebody else understood gave each of them courage.

Maddy Ross found herself able to write to her brother Joseph and say that she would love to come to his wedding, but that Mother did not consider herself strong enough to travel. It meant a lot of silences and sulks at home, but Maddy weathered it. She assembled a simple wardrobe and made her bookings.

Eventually her mother relented and began to show some enthusiasm for the trip. She didn't take this enthusiasm to the point of going with her daughter, but at least the stony silences ended and the atmosphere had cleared.

Father Barry too showed courage. He spoke directly to Father Gunn, and said that he accepted the ruling of the diocese that there was not to be exceptional emphasis on the missions in general or on one mission field in particular. He agreed that other themes such as tolerance and charity on the home front and devotion to Our Blessed Lady, Queen of Ireland, be brought to the forefront.

He also said that in his spare time, if he could run sales of work, he could set up charitable projects in aid of Vieja Piedra. He felt sure that there could be no objection. To this Father Gunn, with a sigh of pure relief, said that there would no objection.

In the summer of 1955 Maddy Ross and Brian Barry wished each other well, she on her journey to Africa, he on his fund-raising efforts so that Cormac Flynn would not be let down. When they met again in the autumn they would tell each other everything.

'We'll meet in the woods with the giant squirrels,' said Father Barry.

'Watching out for the military gorillas,' laughed Maddy Ross.

They were both looking forward to the meeting even as they were saying goodbye.

They were very much changed when they met again. They knew this just from the briefest meeting in the church porch after ten o'clock mass. Father Barry was rearranging the pamphlets that the Catholic Truth Society published, which were in racks for sale, but were always mixed up whenever he passed them by. The problem was that everyone wanted to read 'The Devil at Dances' and 'Keeping Company', but nobody wanted to buy them. Copies of these booklets were always well thumbed and returned to some position or other.

He saw Madeleine come out with her mother. Mrs Ross spent a lengthy time at the holy water font, blessing herself as if she were giving the *Urbi et Orbi* blessing from the papal Balcony in Rome.

'Welcome back, stranger. Was it wonderful?' He smiled at her.

'No. It couldn't have gone more differently than was planned.'

They looked at each other, both surprised by the intense way the other had spoken. Father Barry looked over at Mrs Ross, still far enough away not to hear.

'Barna Woods,' he said, his eyes dark and huge.

'At four o'clock,' Maddy said.

She hadn't felt like this since gym class back at school, where they did the wall bars and all the blood ran to her head, making her feel dizzy and faint.

When she found herself deliberating over which blouse to wear she pulled herself up sharply. He's a priest, she said. But she still wore the striped one which gave her more colour and didn't make her look wishy-washy.

When her mother asked her where she was going, she said she wanted to pick the great fronds of beech leaves in Barna Woods. They could put them in glycerine later and preserve them to decorate the house for the winter.

'I'll look for some really good ones that have turned,' she explained. 'I might be some time.'

She found him sitting on their log with his head in his hands. He told of a summer where everything he had done for Vieja Piedra had been thwarted, not just by Father Gunn, who had turned up dutifully at the bring and buy sale, at the whist drive and the general knowledge quiz, but because the interest simply wasn't there. And since he could no longer use the parish pulpit to preach of the plight of these poor people he didn't have the ear and the heart of the congregation any more. His face was troubled. Maddy felt there was more he wasn't telling. She didn't push him. He would tell what he wanted to tell. Now he asked about her: had her brother Joseph been delighted to see her?

'Yes, and no.' Her brother's fiancée was of the Presbyterian faith and had only agreed to be married in a Catholic Church to please Joseph. Now that his mother wasn't coming to the wedding Joseph had decided that he shouldn't put Caitriona through all this since, really and truly as long as it was Christian, one service was the same as another in the eyes of God.

So Maddy had gone the whole way to Africa to see her brother commit a mortal sin. There had been endless arguments, discussions and tears on both their parts. Joseph said that since they hardly knew each other their tie as brother and sister was not like a real family. Maddy had asked why then had he paid for her to come out to see him.

'To show people that I am not alone in the world,' he had said.

Oh yes, she had attended the ceremony, and smiled, and been pleasant to all the guests. She had told her mother nothing of this. In fact, she was worn out remembering to call the priest Father McPherson rather than Mr McPherson, which was the name of the Presbyterian minister who had married the young couple, in a stiflingly hot church under a cloudless sky – a church with no tabernacle, and no proper God in it at all.

They walked together to find the kind of sprays she wanted. She explained that she had made a sort of excuse to her mother for going to the woods. Then she wished she hadn't said that – it might appear to him as if she needed an excuse for something so perfectly innocent as a meeting with a friend.

But, oddly, it struck a chord with him.

'I made an excuse too, to Father Gunn and Mrs Kennedy, of course. I told him that I wanted to make a couple of parish calls, the Dunnes and the Brennans. Both of them are sure to be out, or at any rate unlikely to invite me in.'

They looked at each other and looked away. A lot had been admitted.

Speaking too quickly she told him about how you preserved flowers and leaves, and how the trick was to put very few in a vase with a narrow opening.

Speaking equally quickly he nodded agreement and perfect understanding of the process, and said that parish calls were an imposition on the priest and the people, everyone dreaded them, and how much better it would be to spend our life in a place where people really needed you rather than worrying had they a clean tablecloth and a slice of cake to give you. His face looked very bitter and sad as he spoke and she felt such huge sympathy for him that she touched him lightly on the arm.

'You *do* a great deal of good here. If you knew how much you touch all our lives.'

To her shock his eyes filled with tears.

'Oh, Madeleine,' he cried. 'Oh God, I'm so lonely. I've no one to talk to, I've no friends. No one will listen.'

'Shush, shush.' She spoke as to a child. 'I'm your friend. I'll listen.'

He put his arms around her and laid his head on her shoulder. She felt arms around her waist and his body close to hers as he shook with sobs.

'I'm so sorry. I'm so foolish,' he wept.

31

'No. No, you're not. You're good. You care. You wouldn't be you unless you were so caring,' she soothed him. She stroked his head and the back of his neck. She could feel his tears wet against her face as he raised his head to try to apologise.

'Shush, shush,' she said again. She held him until the sobs died down. Then she took out her handkerchief, a small white one with a blue flower in the corner, and handed it to him.

They walked wordlessly to their tree trunk. He blew his nose very hard.

'I feel such a fool. I should be strong and courageous for you, Madeleine, tell you things that will console you about your brother's situation, not cry like a baby.'

'No, you *do* make me feel courageous and strong, really, Father Barry ...'

He interrupted her sharply. 'Now, listen here. If I'm going to cry in your arms, the least you can do is call me Brian.'

She accepted it immediately. 'Yes, but Brian, you must believe that you have helped me. I didn't think I was any use to anyone, a disappointment to my mother, no support to my brother ...'

'You must have friends. You of all people, so generous and giving. You're not locked up in rigid rules and practices like I am.'

'I have no friends,' Madeleine Ross said simply.

That afternoon there wasn't time to tell each other all the millions of things there were still to tell – like how Brian had a letter from his great friend Cormac Flynn in Peru saying for heaven's sake not to be so intense about Vieja Piedra, it was just one place on the globe – Father Brian Barry hadn't been born into the world thousands of miles away with a direct instruction to save the place single-handed.

Father Brian Barry had been more hurt than he could ever express by that letter. But when he told Maddy and she tumbled out her own information about Kathleen White and how she had begged Maddy, her friend, not to write to her so intensely, they saw it as one further common bond between them.

She learned about his childhood – his mother who had always wanted a son as a priest, but who had died a month before his ordination and never received his blessing.

He heard of life with a mother who was becoming increasingly irrational – of a life lived more and more in fantasy – in a world where her cousins were people of great wealth and high breeding – where all kinds of niceties were important, the wearing of gloves, the owning of a coach and horses in the old days, the calling with visiting cards. None of it had any basis in reality, Maddy said, but Dr Jims said it was harmless. Lots of middle-aged women had notions and delusions of grandeur, and those harboured by Mrs Ross were no worse than a lot of people's, and better than most.

Their meetings had to be more and more conspiratorial. Maddy would stay late in the school, decorating her window displays. Father Barry would call with some information for the Kellys and happen to see her in the classroom. The door would be left open. He would sit on the teacher's desk, swinging his legs. If Mrs Kelly were to look in, and her anxious face seemed to look everywhere, then she would see nothing untoward.

But when they walked together in Barna Woods away from the eyes of the town they walked close together. Sometimes they would stop by chance at exactly the same time and she would lay her head companionably on his shoulder, and lean against him as they peeled the bark from a tree or looked at a bird's nest hidden in the branches.

Night after night Maddy lay alone in her narrow bed remembering that day he had cried and she had held him in the woods. She could remember the way his body shook and how she could feel his heart beat against her. She could bring back the smell of him, the smell of winegums and Gold Flake tobacco, of Knight's Castile soap. She could remember the way his hair had tickled her neck and how his tears had wet her cheeks. It was like seeing the same scene of a film over and over.

She wondered did he ever think of it, but supposed that would be foolishly romantic. And for Father Barry ... for Brian ... it might even be a sin.

Because of this new centre to her life Maddy Ross was able to do more than ever before. She could scarcely remember the days when the time had seemed long and hung heavily around her. Now there weren't enough hours in the week for all that had to be done. She had long back hired young Maura Brennan from the cottages, a solemn poor child who loved stroking the furniture, to do her ironing and that worked out very well. Now on a different day she got young Eddie Barton to come and do her garden for her.

Eddie was a funny little fellow of about fourteen, interested in plants and nature. He would often want to talk to her about the various things that grew in her garden.

'What do you spend the money on?' she asked him one day. He reddened. 'It doesn't matter. It's yours to spend any way you like.'

'Stamps,' he said eventually.

'That's nice. Have you a big collection?'

'No. To put on letters. Father Barry said we should have a pen-friend overseas,' he said.

It was wonderful to think how much good Father Barry was doing. Imagine a boy with wiry sticky-up hair like Eddie, a boy who would normally be kicking a ball up against a house wall, or writing messages on it, now had a Catholic pen-friend overseas. She gave him extra money that day.

'Tell him about Shancarrig, what a great place it is.'

'I do,' Eddie said simply. 'I write all about it.'

When Eddie got flu and his mother wouldn't let him out, Foxy Dunne offered to do the chore.

'I believe you're a great payer, Miss Ross,' he said cheerfully.

'You won't get as much as Eddie – you don't know which are flowers and which are weeds.' She was spirited and cheerful herself.

'Ah but you're a teacher, Miss Ross. It'd only take you a minute to show me.'

'Only till Eddie comes back,' she agreed.

By the time Eddie was better and came back to fume over the desecration he claimed Foxy had done in the garden, Foxy had got himself several odd jobs, mending doors, fixing locks on an outhouse. Her mother didn't like having one of the Dunnes around the place in case he was sizing it up for a job for himself or one of his brothers.

'Oh Mother! They shouldn't all be tarred with the same brush,' Maddy cried.

'You're nearly as unworldly as Father Barry himself,' said her mother.

There had once been a Dramatic Society in Shancarrig but it had fallen into inactivity. There was some vague story behind this, as there was behind everything. It had to do with the previous teacher having become very inebriated at a performance and some kind of unpleasantness was meant to have taken place. Nellie Dunne always said she could tell you a thing or two about the play-acting that went on in this town. It was play-acting in every sense of the word, she might say. But though she threatened she never in fact did tell anybody a thing or two about what had gone on; and whatever it was had gone on long before Father Gunn had come to Shancarrig. And Monsignor O'Toole wasn't likely to remember it.

Maddy thought that very possibly the members of whatever it had been were sufficiently cooled to start again. She was surprised and pleased at the enthusiasm – Eddie Barton's mother said she'd help with the wardrobe; you always needed a professional to stop the thing looking like children playing charades. Biddy, the maid up at The Glen, said that if there was any call for a step dance she would be glad to oblige. It was a skill which her position didn't give her much chance to use, and she didn't want to get too rusty. Both Brian and Liam Dunne from the hardware store said they would join, and Carrie who looked after Dr Jims' little boy said she'd love to try out for a small part, but nothing with too many lines. Sergeant Keane and his wife both said it was the one thing they had been waiting for and the Sergeant pumped Maddy's hand up and down in gratitude.

So Maddy started the Shancarrig Dramatic Society and they were always very grateful for the kind interest that Father Barry took in their productions. Nobody thought it a bit odd that the saintly young priest with the sad face should throw himself whole-heartedly into anything that was for the parish good. And of course the proceeds went to the charity of the missions in South America. And it was just as well to have Father Barry, everyone agreed, laughing a little behind Father Gunn's back, because poor Father Gunn, in spite of his many other great qualities, didn't know one side of the stage from the other, while Father Barry could turn his hand to anything. He could design a set, arrange the lighting, and best of all, direct performances. He coaxed the townspeople of Shancarrig to play everything from *Pygmalion* to *Drama at Inish*, and the Christmas concerts were a legend.

Only Maddy knew how his heart wasn't in any of it.

Only she knew the real man, who hid his unhappiness. Soon she found she was thinking of him all the time, and imagining his reaction to the smallest and most inconsequential things she did. If she was telling the story of the Flight into Egypt to the Mixed Infants at school she imagined him leaning against the door smiling at her approvingly. Sometimes she smiled back as if he were really there. The children would look around to see if someone had come in.

Then at home, when she was preparing her mother's supper, she would decorate the plate with a garnish of finely sliced tomato, or chopped hard-boiled egg and fresh parsley. Her mother barely noticed, but she could see how Brian Barry would respond. She would put words of praise in his mouth and say them to herself.

She spent her time in what she considered was a much more satisfactory relationship than anyone else around her. Mr and Mrs Kelly were locked in a routine marriage if ever she saw one. Poor Maura Brennan of the cottages, who married a flash harry of a barman, was left alone with her Down's syndrome child to rear. Major Murphy in The Glen had a marriage that defied description. They never went anywhere outside their four walls. In any other land they would have been called recluses, but here, because The Glen was the big house, they were admired for their sense of isolation.

There was nobody that Madeleine Ross envied. Nobody she knew had as dear and pure a love as she had known, a man who depended on her utterly and who would have been lost to his vocation if it had not been for her.

And then one night all of a sudden, when she least expected it, came a strange thought. It was one of those sleepless nights when the moon seemed unnaturally bright and visible even through the curtains, so it was easier to leave them open.

Maddy saw a figure walking past going to the woods. She thought first that it was Brian, and she was about to slip into some clothes and follow him. But then she saw at the last moment that it was Major Murphy, on goodness knew what kind of outing. It was easy to mistake them, tall men in dark clothes. But Brian was asleep in the presbytery, or possibly not asleep, maybe looking at the same moon and feeling the same restlessness.

That was when it came to Maddy Ross that Father Barry should leave Shancarrig.

He could no longer be wasted passing plates of sandwiches, rigging up old curtains, praising a tuneless choir, welcoming yet another bishop or visiting churchmen. There was only one life to be lived. He must go on and live it as best he could, serving the people of Vieja Piedra. The whole notion of there being only one life to live buzzed around in her head all night. There was no more sleep now. She sat hugging a mug of tea, remembering how her brother Joseph had said those very words to her, all that while ago when she had gone to Rhodesia for his wedding, about there being only one chance to live your life.

And Joseph, who had been given the same kind of education as she had had, and who came from the same parents, had been able to seize at the life he wanted. Joseph and Caitriona Ross had children out in

36

Africa. Sometimes they sent pictures of them outside their big white house with the pillars at the front door. Maddy had never told her mother that these little children weren't Catholics and might not even have been properly baptised. She and Brian had agreed that it was better not to trouble an already troubled mind with such information.

If Joseph Ross had only one life so had Maddy Ross and so had Brian Barry. Why couldn't Father Brian leave and go to South America? After a decent interval Maddy could leave too and be with him.

For part of the night as she paced the house she told herself that things need not change between them. They would be as they were here, true friends doing the work they felt was calling across the land and sea to them. And Brian could remain a priest. Once a priest always a priest. He wouldn't have to leave, just change the nature and scope of his vocation.

And then as dawn came up over Barna Woods Maddy Ross admitted to herself what she had been hiding. She acknowledged that she wanted Brian Barry to be her love, her husband. She wanted him to leave the priesthood. If he could get released from his vows by Rome so much the better. But even if he could not Maddy wanted him anyway. She would take him on any terms.

It was a curious freedom realising this.

She felt almost light-headed and at the same time she stopped playing games. She took her mother breakfast on a tray without fantasising what Brian would say if he had been standing beside them looking on. It was as if she had come out of the shadows, she thought, and into the real world.

She could barely wait to meet Brian. No day had ever seemed longer. Mrs Kelly had never been sharper or more inquisitive about everything Maddy was doing.

Why was she putting greetings on the blackboard in different languages? Spanish. And French, no less. Wasn't it enough for these boneheaded children to try and learn Irish and English like the Department laid down without filling their heads with how to say good day and goodbye in tongues they'd never need to use?

Maddy looked at her levelly. Normally, she would have seen Brian in her mind's eye standing by the blackboard, congratulating her on her patience and forbearance, and then the two of them wandering together in Barna Woods crying 'Buenos dias Vieja Piedra, we are coming to help you.'

But today she saw no shadowy figure. She saw only the small

quivering Mrs Kelly, who was wearing a brown and yellow striped dress and looked for all the world like a wasp.

Maddy Ross was a different person today.

'I'm putting some phrases in foreign languages on the blackboard, Mrs Kelly, because, despite what you and the Department of Education think, these children may well go to lands where they use them. And I shall put them on the blackboard every day until they feel a little bit of confidence about themselves instead of being humble and content to remain in Shancarrig pulling their caps and saying *good morning* in Irish and English until they are old men and women.'

Mrs Kelly went red and white in rapid succession.

'You'll do nothing of the sort, Miss Ross. Not in the timetable that is laid down for you.'

'I had no intention of doing it in school time, Mrs Kelly.' Maddy smiled a falsely sweet smile. 'I am in the fortunate position of being able to hold the children's interest *outside* school hours as well as when the bell rings. They will learn it before or after school. That will be clearly understood.'

She felt twenty feet tall. She felt as if she were elevated above the small stone schoolhouse and the town. She could hardly bear the slow noise of the clock ticking until she could go to Brian and tell him of her new courage, her hope and her belief that they had only one chance at life.

She met him at rehearsal under the eyes of the nosey people in town.

'How is your mother these days, Miss Ross?' he asked. It was part of their code. They had never practised it; it just came naturally to them, as so much else would now.

'She's fine, Father, always asking for you, of course.'

'I might drop in and see her later tonight, if you think she'd like that.'

'She'd love it, Father. I'll just let her know. I'm going out myself, but she'd be delighted to see you, like everyone.'

Her eyes danced with mischief as she said the words. She thought she saw the hint of a frown on Brian Barry's face, but it passed.

Miss Ross left the rehearsal and she imagined people thinking that she was a dutiful daughter, and very good also to the priest, to go home and prepare a little tray for her mother to offer him. As Maddy walked home, her cheeks burning, she thought that she had been a bloody good daughter for all her life, nearly thirty years of life in this small place. And come to think of it she had been good to the priest too. Good for him and a good friend.

Nobody could blame her for wanting her chance at life.

She sat in the wood and waited on their log. He came gently through the leafy paths. His smile was tired. Something had crossed him during the day; she knew him so very well, every little change, every flicker in his face.

'I'm late. I had to go into your mother's,' he said.

'What on earth for? You know I didn't mean ...'

'I know, but Father Gunn said to me, this very morning, that he thought I should see less of you.'

'What!'

Brian Barry was nervous and edgy. 'Oh, he said it very nicely of course, not an accusation, nothing you could take offence at ...'

'I most certainly do take offence at it,' Maddy blazed. 'How dare he insinuate that there has been anything improper between us. How *dare* he!'

'No, he didn't. He was very anxious that I should know he wasn't suggesting that.' He walked up and down as he talked, agitated, and anxious to get over the mildness of the message, the lack of blame and the motive behind it. It was just that Father Gunn wanted to protect them both from evil minds and idle wagging tongues. In a place this size when people had little real news to speculate about they made up their own. It would be better for Father Barry not to be seen so obviously sharing the same interests as Miss Ross, for both of them to make other friends.

'And what did you say, Brian?' Her pale eyes had flecks of light in them tonight.

'I said that he had a very poor opinion of people if he thought they would give such low motives to what was an obvious and proper friendship.'

But it was clear that Brian Barry had not found his own answer satisfactory. He looked confused and bewildered. She had never loved him more. 'I am sorry, Maddy, I couldn't think of what else to say.' He had never called her Maddy before, always Madeleine like her mother did.

She moved over to him and closed her arms around his neck. He smelled still of cigarette smoke, but his soap was Imperial Leather now, and he hadn't been eating the winegums. It was the chocolate cake given to him, Maddy realised, by her mother.

'It was perfect,' she whispered.

He looked very startled and moved as if to get away.

'What was perfect?' he asked, his eyes large and alarmed.

'What you said. It is a proper friendship and a proper love ...'

'Yes ... well ...' He hadn't raised his arms to hold her.

She moved nearer to him and pressed herself towards him. 'Brian, hold me. Please hold me.'

'I can't, Maddy. I can't. I'm a priest.'

'I held you years ago when you had no friend. Hold me now; now that I have no friend and they are trying to take you away.' Her eyes filled with tears.

'No, no, no.' He soothed her as she had stroked him all that time ago. He held her head to his shoulder and comforted her. 'No, it's not a question of being taken away ... it's just ... well, you know what it is.'

She snuggled closer to him. Again she could hear his heart beat in the way she had remembered so often from that first time. He was about to release her so she allowed sobs to shake her body again. He was so clumsy, and tender at the same time. Maddy knew that this was her man, and her one chance to take what life was presenting.

'I love you so much, Brian,' she whispered.

The answering words were not there. She changed direction slightly.

'You are the only person who understands me, who knows what I want to do in the world, and I think I'm the only person who knows what is best for you.' She gulped as she spoke so that he wouldn't think the storm was over, the need for consolation at an end. In the seven years since they had first held each other in these woods times had changed; when he offered her a handkerchief now it was a paper tissue, when he sat down beside her on their log to smoke it wasn't the flaky old Gold Flake, it was a tipped cigarette.

'You've been better to me than anyone in the world. I mean that.' His voice was sincere. He *did* mean it. She could see his brain clicking through all the people who had been good to him, his mother, some kind superior in the seminary possibly. She was the best of this pathetic little list. That was all. Why was she not his great love? She would have to walk very warily.

'I have wanted the best for you since the day I met you,' she said simply.

'And I for you. Truly.'

This was probably true, Maddy thought. Like he wanted the best for the people of Vieja Piedra, wanted it in his heart but wasn't able to do anything real and lasting about it.

'You must go there,' she said.

'Go where?'

'To Peru. To Father Cormac.'

He looked at her as if she was suggesting he fly to the moon. 'How can I go, Maddy? They'll never let me.'

'Don't ask them. Just go. You've often said that God isn't worried about some pecking order and lines of obedience. Our Lord didn't ask permission when he wanted to heal people.'

He still looked doubtful. Maddy got up and paced up and down beside him. With all the powers of persuasion she could gather she told him why he must go. She played back to him all his own thoughts and phrases about the small village where people had died waiting for someone to come and help them, where they looked up to the mountain pass each day hoping that a man of God would come, not just to visit but to stay amongst them and give them the sacraments. She could see the light coming to his eye: the magic was working.

'How would I get the fare to go there?' he asked.

'You can take it from the collection.' To her it was simple.

'I couldn't do that. It's for Vieja Piedra.'

'But isn't that exactly where you would be going? Isn't that why we're raising this money, so that they'd have someone to help them?'

'No, I don't believe that would be right. I've never been sure about the end justifying the means ... remember we often discussed that.' They had, here in this wood, sitting in her classroom, having coffee after the rehearsals for the plays.

She looked at him, flushed and eager in the middle of yet another moral dilemma, but not moved by the fact that he had held her close to him and felt her heart beat, her hair against his face, her eyelashes on his cheek. Was he an ordinary man or had he managed to quell that side of himself so satisfactorily that it didn't respond any more? She had to know.

'And when you go you can write and tell me about it ... until I come there too.'

His eyes were dark circles of amazement now. 'You come out there, Maddy? You couldn't. You couldn't come all that far and you can't be with me. I'm a priest.'

'We have only one life.' She spoke calmly.

'And I chose mine as a priest. You know I can't change that. Nothing will change that.'

'You can change it if you want to. Just like you can change the place

41

you live.' There was something in the direct simple way she spoke that seemed to alarm him. This was not the over-excitable intense Maddy Ross he had known, it was a serious young woman going after what she wanted.

'Sit down, Maddy.' He too was calm. He squatted in front of her, holding both her hands in his. 'If I ever gave you the impression that I might leave the priesthood then I must spend the rest of my days making up for such a terrible misunderstanding ...' His face was troubled as he sought some response in hers. 'Maddy, I am a priest for ever. It's the one thing that means anything to me. I've been selfish and impatient and critical of those around me, I don't have the understanding and generosity of a Father Gunn, but I do have this belief that God chose me and called me.'

'You also have the belief that the people of Vieja Piedra are calling you.'

'Yes, I do. If there was a way to go there I *would* go. You have given me that courage. I won't take the money that the people of Shancarrig raised. They didn't raise it for their priest to run away with.'

The moon came up as they talked. They saw a badger quite nearby, but it wasn't important enough for either of them to comment on. Brian Barry told Madeleine Ross that he would never leave his ministry. He had a few certainties in life. This was one of them. In vain did Maddy tell him that clerical celibacy was only something introduced long after Our Lord's time, it was more or less a Civil Service ruling, not part of the Constitution. The first apostles had wives and children.

'Children.' She stroked his hand as she said the word.

He pulled both hands away from her and stood up. This was something he was never going to think about. It was the sacrifice he had made for God, the one thing God wanted from his priests: to give up the happiness and love of a wife and family. Not that it had been hard to give up because he had never known it, and now he was heading for forty years of age so it wasn't something he would be thinking of, even if he weren't a priest.

'A lot of men marry around forty,' Maddy said.

'Not priests.'

'You can do anything. Anything.'

'I won't do this.'

'But you love me, Brian. You're not going to be frightened into some kind of cringing life for the rest of your days by a silly warning from Father Gunn, by Mrs Kennedy spying, by a promise made when

42

you were a child . . . when you didn't know what love was . . . or anything about it.'

'I still don't really know.'

'You know.'

He shook his head and Maddy could bear it no more. She reached out for him and kissed him directly on the lips. She moved herself into his arms and opened her mouth to his. She felt his arms tighten around her . . . He stroked her back and then because she pulled away from his clasp a little he stroked the outline of her breasts. She peeped through her closed eyes and saw that his eyes were closed too.

They stood locked like this for a time. Eventually he pulled away.

They looked at each other for moments before he spoke. 'You've given me everything, Maddy Ross,' he said.

'I haven't begun to give you anything,' she said.

'No but you have, believe me. You've given me such bravery, such faith. Without you I'd be nothing. You've given me the courage to go. Now you must give me one more thing . . . the freedom.'

She looked at him with disbelief. 'You could hold me like that and ask me never to be in your arms again?'

'That is what I'm begging you. *Begging* you, Maddy. It was my only sure centre. The only thing I knew . . . that I was to be a priest of God. Don't take that away from me or all the other things you have given will totter like a house of cards.'

This man had been her best friend, her soul mate. Now he was asking her permission and her encouragement to leave her life entirely, to step out of it and away from Shancarrig to the village that they had both dreamed about and prayed for and saved for all these years.

Such monstrous selfishness couldn't be part of God's plan. It couldn't be part of any dream of taking your chance in life. Maddy looked at him, confused. It was all going wrong, very very wrong.

He saw her shock, he didn't run away from it. He spoke very gently. 'Since I came to Shancarrig and even before it I've known that women are stronger than men. We could list them in this town. And I know more than you because I hear them in the Confessional. I'm there at their deathbeds when they worry not about their own pain but about how a husband will manage or whether a son will go to the bad. I've been there when their babies have died at birth, when they bury a man who was not only a husband but their means of living. Women are very strong. Can you be strong and let me go with your blessing?'

She looked at him dumbly. The words would not come, the torrent of words welling up inside her. She must be able to explain that he could not be bound by these tired old rules, these empty vows made at another time by another person. Brian Barry was different now, he had come into his kingdom, he was a man who could love and give. But she said none of these things. Which was just as well because he looked at her and the dark blue of his eyes was hard.

'You see, I want to go with your blessing, because I'm *going* to go anyway.'

They didn't meet again in Shancarrig without other people being present.

There were no more walks in the woods, no visits to the classroom. The rehearsals had to do without the kind help of Father Barry, Shancarrig Dramatic Society was told. He had been advised to take it easy. Somehow that was the hardest place, the place she missed him most. They had started these plays together; she didn't know how she would have the heart to continue. In fact, she feared the whole organisation would fall apart without him.

The Shancarrig Dramatic Society continued to thrive without Father Barry. In many ways his leaving gave them greater scope. They were able to do more comedies. They had never liked to suggest anything too light-hearted when Father Barry was there, he was so soulful and good it seemed like being too flippant in his presence.

In the weeks that seemed endless to Maddy the society decided to enter the All Ireland contest for the humorous one-act play.

'Poor Father Barry. He'd have loved this,' said Biddy from The Glen, who was going to play a dancing washroom woman in the piece.

'Go on out of that,' said Sergeant Keane's wife, 'we'd be doing a tragedy if poor Father Barry was here. Not that I wish the man any harm, and I hope whatever's bothering him gets better.'

The rumour was that he had a spot on his lung. Heads nodded. Yes, it was true he did have that colour, the very pale complexion with occasional spots of high colour that could spell out TB. Still, the sanatorium was wonderful and anyway it hadn't been confirmed yet.

He didn't avoid her eye, Maddy realised. He was totally at peace with himself, and grateful to her that she had nodded her head that night in Barna Woods and left without trusting herself to speak a word.

He thought she had seen his way was the only way.

The days were endless as she waited to hear that he had gone. It was three whole months before she heard what she had been waiting for. Father Gunn, visiting the school in his usual way, had asked her pleasantly if she could drop in at the presbytery that evening. Nothing in his face had given a hint of what was to be said.

When she arrived she was startled to see Brian sitting in one of the chairs. Father Gunn motioned her to the other.

'Maddy, you know that Father Barry is going to Peru?'

'I knew he wanted to.' She spoke carefully, but smiled at Brian. His face was alive and happy. 'You mean, it's settled? You're going to be able to go, officially?'

'I'm going with everyone's blessing,' Brian said. His face was full of love, love and gratitude.

'The Bishop is very understanding and when he saw such missionary zeal he said it would be hard not to encourage it,' said Father Gunn.

It had always been impossible to see Father Gunn's eyes through those glasses, but they seemed more opaque than ever. Maddy wondered had Father Gunn told the Bishop that Vieja Piedra alone and on Church business was infinitely preferable to another alternative.

'I hope it's every bit as rewarding for you as you and I have always believed it would be.' Her voice choked slightly.

'I wanted to thank you, Maddy, for all your help and encouragement. Father Gunn has been so wise and understanding about everything. When I told him that I wanted you to be the first to know he insisted that we invite you here, to tell you that it has all finally gone through.'

Maddy looked at Father Gunn. She knew exactly why she had been invited to the presbytery, so that there could be no tearful farewells, implorings and highly charged emotion in Barna Woods, or anywhere on their own.

'That's very kind of you, Father,' she said to the small square priest, in a very cold tone.

'No, no, and I must just get some papers. I'll leave the two of you for a few minutes.' He fussed out of the room.

Brian didn't move from his chair. 'I owe it all to you, Maddy,' he said.

'Will you write?' she asked, her voice dull.

'To everyone, a general letter in response to whatever marvellous fund-raising you do for me . . .' He smiled at her winningly as he had smiled at so many people. As he would smile at the poor Peruvians in the dry valley, who had been calling out for him. She said nothing.

And for the first time in seven years they sat in silence. They willed the time to pass when Father Gunn would have found his letters and returned to the sitting room of the presbytery. The sitting-room door had been left open.

The farewells were endless. Father Barry wanted no present, he insisted. He didn't need any goodbye gift to remind him of Shancarrig, its great people and the wonderful years he had spent here. He said he would try to describe what the place was like, their namesake on the other side of the world.

He cried when they came to see him off at the station. Maddy was in the back of the crowd. She wanted to be sure he was actually going. She wanted to see it with her own eyes. He waved with one hand and dabbed his eyes with the other. Maddy heard Dr Jims saying to Mr Hayes that he was always a very emotional and intense young man. He hoped he would fare all right in that hot climate over there.

And the time went by, but it was like a summer garden when the sun has gone, and although there's daylight there's no point in sitting out in it. More children came and went in Mixed Infants. They left Miss Ross and went up to Mrs Kelly. They still learned how to say *bonjour* and *buenos dias* in their own time. Maddy Ross had won that victory hard from Mrs Kelly – she was not going to give it up.

The fund-raising continued, but Ireland was changing in the sixties. There was television for one thing ... people heard about other parts of the world where there was famine and disaster. Suddenly Vieja Piedra was not the only place that called to them. Sometimes the collections were small that went in the money order to the Reverend Brian Barry at his post office in a hill town some sixty-seven miles from Vieja Piedra.

Yet his letters were always grateful and warm, and there were stories of the church being built, a small building. It looked like a shed with a cross on top, but Father Barry was desperately proud of it. Pictures were sent of it, badly focused snapshots taken from different angles.

And then there was the wonderful help of Viatores Christi, some lay Christians who were coming out to help. They were invaluable, as committed in every way as were the clergy.

Maddy heard the letters read aloud, and wondered why could Brian Barry not have become a lay missionary. Then there would have been the same dream and the same hope but no terrible promise about celibacy.

But she cheered herself up. If he had not been ordained as a priest he would never have come to Shancarrig, she would never have known him, never had her chance in life.

There had been five years of walking alone in Barna Woods, five plays in Shancarrig Dramatic Society, five Christmas concerts, there had been five sales of work, whist drives, beetle drives, treasure hunts. There had been five years of raffles, bingo, house to house collections. And then, one day, Brian Barry telephoned Maddy Ross.

'I thought you'd be home from school by now.' He sounded as if he were down the road. He couldn't be telephoning her from Peru!

'I'm in Dublin,' he said.

Her heart gave an uncomfortable lurch. Something was happening. Why had the communication not been through Father Gunn?

'I want to see you. Nobody knows I'm home.'

'Brian.' Her voice was only a whisper.

'Don't tell anyone at all. Just come tomorrow.'

'But why? What's happened?'

'I'll tell you tomorrow.'

'Tomorrow? All the way to Dublin, just like that?'

'I've come all the way from Peru.'

'Is anything wrong? Is there any trouble?'

'No no. Oh Maddy, it's good to talk to you.'

'I haven't talked to you for five years, Brian. You have to tell me why are you home? Are you going to leave the priesthood?'

'Please, Maddy. Trust me. I want to tell you personally. That's why I came the whole way back. Just get the early train, will you? I'll meet you.'

'Brian?'

'I'll be on the platform.' He hung up.

She had to cash a cheque at the hotel. Mrs Ryan was interested as usual in everything. Maddy gave her no information. Her mind was too confused. She knew there would be no sleep tonight.

For five years she had slept seven hours a night.

But tonight she would not close her eyes. No matter how tired and old she might look next morning Maddy knew that there was no point in lying in that same bed where she had lain for years, seeking sleep.

Instead she examined everything in her wardrobe.

She chose a cream blouse and a blue skirt. She wore a soft blue woollen scarf around her neck. It wasn't girlish but it was youthful. It didn't look like the ageing school teacher grown old in her love for the faraway priest.

Maddy smiled. At least she had kept her sense of humour. Whatever he was going to tell her he would like that.

He didn't seem to have got a day older. He was boyish, even at forty-five. His coat collar was up so she couldn't see whether he still wore his roman collar, but she had told herself not to read anything into that. Out in the missions priests wore no clerical garb and yet they were as firmly priests as ever they had been.

He saw her and ran to her. They hugged like a long-separated brother and sister, like old friends parted unwillingly, which is probably what they were. She pulled away from him to see his face, but still he hugged her. You can't kiss someone who is hugging the life out of you.

The crowd had thinned on the platform. Some caution seemed to seep back into him.

'There was no one from home on the train, was there?'

'Where's home?' She laughed at him. 'In all your letters you say Vieja Piedra is home.'

'And so it is.' He seemed satisfied that they weren't under surveillance. He tucked her arm into his and they walked to a nearby hotel. The lounge was small and dark, the coffee strong and scalding. Maddy Ross would remember for ever the way it stuck to the roof of her mouth when Brian Barry told her that he was going to leave the priesthood and marry Deirdre, one of the volunteers. It was like a patch of red-hot tar in her mouth. It wouldn't go away as she nodded and listened and forced her face to smile through tales of growth, and understanding and love and the emptiness of vows taken at an early age before a boy was a man, and about a loving God not holding people to meaningless promises.

And she heard how there was still a lot to be decided. Deirdre and he had realised that laicisation took such a long time, and brought so much grief, destroying the relationships of those who waited.

But in South America the clergy had understood the core values. They had gone straight to the heart of things. They knew that a blessing could be given to a union of which God would patently approve. What was the expression that Maddy herself had used so many years ago? Something about thinking in terms of the Constitution rather than in petty Civil Service bye-laws.

And he owed it all to Maddy. So often he had told that to Deirdre, who wanted to send her gratitude. If Maddy hadn't proven to him that he could be courageous and open up his heart to the world and to love, this might never have happened.

'Did you ever love me?' Maddy asked him.

'Of course I love you. I love you with all my heart. Nothing will destroy our love, not my marrying Deirdre or you marrying whoever you will. Maybe you have someone in mind?' He was roguish now, playful even. She wanted to knock him down.

'No. No plans as yet.'

'Well you should, Maddy.' Gone was the light-hearted banter, now he was being serious and caring. 'A woman should get married, and have children. That's what a woman should do.'

'And have you and Deirdre decided to have children?' She tried to put the smile back in her voice. It was so easy to let a sneer creep in instead, to let him know how she could sense that Deirdre was already pregnant.

'Eventually,' he told her, which meant imminently.

He was going to leave Vieja Piedra, and they were going to a place further down the coast of Peru. He would teach in a town, there was just as much work needed there, but they had found a native born priest, a real Peruvian, to look after the valley of Vieja Piedra. He talked on. Nothing would be said to Father Gunn. The fund-raising would take a different style. Nothing would be said to anyone really. In today's world you didn't need to explain or to be intense. It was a matter of seizing what good there was and creating more good. It was taking your chance when it was offered.

The only person who *had* to be told face to face was Maddy. That's why he had taken Deirdre's savings to come back and tell her, to thank her in the way that a letter could never do for having put him on this road to happiness.

'And did Deirdre not feel afraid that once you saw your old love you might never return to her?' Maddy's tone was light, her question deadly serious.

But Brian hastened to put her anxieties at rest. 'Lord no. Deirdre knew that what *we* had wasn't love. It was childlike fumblings, it was heavy meaning-of-life conversation, it was part of growth, and for me a very important part.' He wanted to reassure her about that.

The train back to Shancarrig left in fifteen minutes. Maddy said she thought she should take it.

'But you can't go *now*. You've only been here an hour.' His dismay was enormous.

'But you've told me everything.'

'No, I haven't told you anything really. I have only skimmed the surface.'

'I have to go back, Brian. I would have, anyway, no matter what you told me. My mother hasn't been well.'

'I didn't know that.'

'Of course you didn't. You didn't know a great many things, like Mrs Murphy in The Glen died, and that Maura Brennan brings her poor son around with her and he sits in every house in Shancarrig while she cleans floors and does washing. There are many things you don't know.'

'Well, they don't tell me. *You* don't tell me. You don't write at all.'

'I was ordered not to. Don't you remember?'

'Not ordered, just advised.'

'To you it was the same once.'

'If you'd wanted to write to me enough you would have,' he said, head on one side, roguish again.

She closed her mind to his disbelief that she would return on the next train. He had thought she would spend the whole day, if not the weekend, in Dublin with him. What was he to do now? No relations were meant to know he was back.

'Did I do the wrong thing coming back to tell you?' He was a child again, confused, uncertain.

She was gentle. She could afford to be. She had a lifetime ahead of her with little to contemplate except why her one stab at living life had failed. She reached out and held his hand.

'No, you did the right thing,' she lied straight into his face. 'Tell Deirdre that I wish you well, all of you. Tell her I went back to Shancarrig on the train with my heart brimming over.'

It was the only wedding present she could give him.

And she held the tears until the train had turned the bend and until she could no longer see his eager hand waving her goodbye.

MAURA

W hen the time came for Maura to go to school any small enthusiasm that there had ever been in the Brennan family for education had died down. Maura's mother was worn out with all the demands that were made on her to dress them up for this May Procession and that visit from the Bishop. Not to mention communion and confirmations. Mrs Brennan had been heard to say that the Shancarrig school had notions about itself being some kind of private college for the sons and daughters of the land-owning gentry rather than the National School it was, and that nature had always intended it to be.

And the young Maura didn't get much encouragement from her father either. Paudie Brennan believed that schools and all that were women's work and not things a man got involved with. And since Paudie Brennan was not a man ever continuously in work he couldn't be expected to take an interest financially and every other way in each and every one of his nine living children, and Maura came near the end of the trail. Paudie Brennan had too much on his mind what with a leaking roof missing a dozen slates, and a very different and worrying kind of slate altogether above in Johnny Finn Noted for Best Drinks, so what time was there to be wondering about young Maura and her book learning?

Maura had never expected there to be an interest. School was for books, home was for fights. The older brothers and sisters had gone to England – the really grown-up ones. They went as soon as they were seventeen or eighteen. They came home for holidays and it was great at first, but after a day it would wear off, the niceness, and there would be shouting again as if the returned sister or brother was an ordinary part of the family, not a visitor.

One day, Maura knew, she would be the eldest one at home – just herself and Geraldine left. But Maura wasn't going to England to work in a shoe factory like Margaret, or a fish shop like Deirdre. No, she was going to stay here in Shancarrig. She wouldn't get married but she would live like Miss Ross, who was very old and could do what she liked and stay up all night without anyone giving out or groaning at her. Of course, Miss Ross was a school teacher and must earn pots of money, but Maura would save whenever she started to work, and keep the money in the post office until she could have a house and freedom to go to bed at two in the morning if the notion took her.

Maura Brennan often stayed on late at school to talk to Miss Ross, to try to find out more about this magnificent lifestyle in the small house with the lilac bushes and the tall hollyhocks, where Miss Ross lived. She would ask endless questions about the dog or the cat. She knew their names and ages, which nobody else at school did. She would hope that one day Miss Ross might drop another hint or two about her life. Miss Ross seemed puzzled by her interest. The child was in no way bright. Even taking into account her loutish father and timid uneducated mother, young Maura must still be called one of the slower learners in the school. Even the youngest of that Brennan string of children, Geraldine, with the permanent cold and her hair in her eyes, was quicker. But Maura was the one who hung about, who found excuses to have meaningless little conversations.

One day Miss Ross let slip that she hated ironing.

'I love ironing,' Maura said. 'I love it, I'd do it all day but the one we have is broke, and my da won't pay to have it mended.'

'What do you like about it?' Miss Ross seemed genuinely interested.

'The way your hand goes on and on ... it's like music almost ... and the clothes get lovely and smooth, and it all smells nice and clean,' Maura said.

'You make it sound great. I wish you'd come and do mine.'

'Of course I will,' said Maura.

She was eleven then, a square girl with her hair clipped back by a brown slide, a high forehead and clear eyes. In a different family in another place she might have had a better chance, a start that would have brought her further along some kind of road.

'No, Maura, you can't, child. I don't want the other children to see you rating yourself as only fit to do my ironing. I don't want you making little of yourself before you have to.'

'How could that be making little of myself?' The question was without guile. Maura Brennan saw no lack of dignity in coming to the teacher's house to do household chores.

'The others ... they don't have to know, Miss Ross.'

'But they do, they will. You know this place.'

'They don't know lots of things, like that my sister Margaret had a baby in Northampton. Geraldine and I are aunts, Miss Ross. Imagine!' Maura had told the family secret easily, as if she knew that there was no danger that Miss Ross would pass on this titbit. There was the same simplicity as when she had spoken of ironing.

'Once a week, and I'll pay you properly,' Miss Ross had said.

'Thank you, Miss Ross, I'll put it in the post office.' It was the beginning for Maura Brennan. She warned young Geraldine not to tell anyone. It would be their secret.

'Why has it to be a secret?' Geraldine wanted to know.

'I don't know.' Maura was truthful. 'But it has.'

So if ever Mrs Brennan asked what was keeping Maura above at the school, Geraldine said she didn't know. It seemed daft to her, all this sucking up to Miss Ross. It wasn't as if Maura ever got anywhere at her books. She was slow and was always asking people to help her, Leo Murphy or Nessa Ryan, girls from important families, big houses. Geraldine would know better than to talk to them or their like. Maura was half daft a lot of the time.

When Maura started doing the ironing Miss Ross gave her a doll as well as the money. She said she had seen Maura admiring it and even taking off its crushed pink dress and giving it a good press. Anyone who thought that much of a doll should have it. Maura always told Geraldine that it was on loan. Miss Ross had lent it to her until the time Miss Ross married someone and had children of her own.

'Sure Miss Ross is a hundred. She'll never marry and have children,' Geraldine cried.

'People have them at all ages. Look at Mammy, look at St Elizabeth.'

Geraldine wasn't so sure about her ground on St Elizabeth, but she knew all about their mother. 'Mammy started having them and she couldn't stop. I heard her telling Mrs Barton. But after me she stopped all of a sudden.' Geraldine was nine and she knew everything.

Maura wished she had those kind of certainties.

The doll sat on a shelf in their bedroom. It had a china face and little china hands. When Geraldine wasn't there to laugh at her Maura would hug it and speak reassuring words, saying the doll was very much loved. Sometimes Miss Ross gave Maura things to wear, a nice coloured belt once, a scarf with a tassel.

'I never wore them in the school, Maura, no one will know they're mine.'

'But what would I mind if they knew?' Again the question was so honest and without guile that Miss Ross seemed taken aback.

'I wish I could help you with your lessons, Maura. I wish I could, but you don't really have the will to concentrate.'

Maura was eager to reassure her. 'I'll be fine, Miss Ross. There's no point in trying to put things into my head that won't go in, and what would I need with all those sums and knowing poems off by heart? It wouldn't be any use to me at all.'

'What's to become of you, though ... off to England like Deirdre and Margaret with no qualifications ... ?'

'No, I'm staying here. I'm going to get a house like this one, and have it the way you do, lovely and shiny and clean, and coloured china on a dresser and a smell of lavender polish everywhere.'

'It'll be some lucky man if you are going to do all that for him.'

'I won't be getting married, Miss Ross.' It was one of the few things she had ever said with conviction.

Her sister Geraldine believed her too, over this.

'Why don't you go the whole hog and be a nun?' Geraldine wanted to know. 'If you're so sure you're not going to get a fellow, hadn't you better be in a convent, singing hymns and getting three meals a day?'

'I can still pray in a house of my own. I'll have a Sacred Heart lamp on a small wooden shelf, and I'll have a picture of Our Lady, Queen of May on a small round table with a blue table cloth and a vase of flowers in front of it.'

She didn't say that she was going to buy a chair for the doll too.

Geraldine shrugged. She was twelve now, and much more grown up than her sister of fourteen, who would be leaving school this year. Geraldine's confirmation was coming up and between wheedling and complaining she and her mother had managed to get Paudie Brennan to put up money for a lovely confirmation dress. This was the first item of clothing that had ever been bought new to celebrate the confirmation of any of his nine children. The dress hung on the back of the bedroom door and had been tried on a dozen times. Maura had managed to persuade Geraldine to keep the hair from hanging over her eyes.

Geraldine was going to look gorgeous on her confirmation day. She had written to her sisters and brothers in England telling them of this event and, getting the hint, they had sent a pound note or a ten-shilling note in an envelope with a couple of lines scrawled to wish her well. Maura hadn't done that and she looked with envy at the riches coming in. It took a lot of ironing in Miss Ross's house to make anything like that amount of money.

Three days before confirmation Paudie Brennan, on a serious drinking bout, found himself short of ready cash and, deciding that the Lord couldn't possibly be concerned what clothes young Christians decked themselves in for confirmation ceremonies, managed to take the new dress to a pawnbroker in the big town and raise the sum of two pounds on it.

The consternation was terrible. In the middle of the shouting, tears and accusations being hurled backwards and forwards, Maura realised that this was all that would happen. Bluster and hurt, disappointment and recriminations. There was no question of anyone getting the dress back for Geraldine. That kind of money could not appear by magic. Credit had been arranged in the first place to buy it. There was no possibility of more funds being made available.

'I'll get it for you,' Maura said simply to a red-eyed, near hysterical Geraldine who lay on her bed railing at the unfairness of life and the meanness of her father.

'How can you get it? Don't be stupid.'

'I have that saved. Just get the ticket from him. We'll go on the bus, but you must never tell them, never never.'

'Where will they think we got the money? They might say we stole it.' Geraldine didn't care to believe that there was a way out.

'Da's not going to be able to say much one way or the other after what he did,' said Maura.

On the day, Paudie Brennan was dressed and shaved and his neck squeezed into a proper shirt and collar for the visit of the Bishop. It was a sunlit day, and the children from Shancarrig looked a credit to their school, people said, as they gathered for the group photograph outside the cathedral in the big town. Geraldine Brennan, resplendent with her shiny blonde hair and her frilly white dress, caught the eye of a lot of people.

'You have dressed her up like a picture. She's a credit to you,' said Mrs Ryan, of Ryan's Hotel. Her own daughter Catherine looked far less resplendent. It was easy to see that she was mystified and even put out that the young Brennan girl, daughter of a known layabout and drunk, should look so well.

'Ah, sure, you have to do your best, Mrs Ryan, Ma'am,' Maura's mother said. Maura felt her heart harden. If her mam had been the one in charge Geraldine would have stood there in some limp handout dress that had been begged from a family who might not have used all its castoffs. There had been no word of apology from her father, no question of any promised repayment from Geraldine. No questions, no interest.

Any more than anyone had asked what Maura would do when she left school in a few short weeks' time. She wouldn't be going to the convent in the town like Leo Murphy and Nessa Ryan. There were no plans for her to go into the technical school. She wasn't smart enough to be taken on as a trainee in one of the shops, or the hairdressing salon.

Maura was going to work as a maid, the only question was where – and this, she realised, was something she would have to work out for herself as well as everything else. Maura would really have liked a job where she could live in. In a lovely big house, with beautiful furniture in it. Somewhere like The Glen, where Leo Murphy lived.

She would call and ask them had they a place. It wasn't fair to ask Leo at school and embarrass her in case the answer was no. Or she could possibly get a place in the kitchens of Ryan's Commercial Hotel, or as a chambermaid. She wouldn't like that as much. There was nothing beautiful to touch and polish.

'Are you thinking about your own confirmation, Maura?' Father Gunn from Shancarrig was standing beside her.

'Not really, I'm afraid, Father. I was thinking about where I'd go to work.'

'Is it time for you to leave school already?' He was a kindly man with very thick glasses that made him look vaguer and more confused than he was. It seemed impossible for him to believe that another of Paudie Brennan's brood was ready for the emigrant ship.

'It is. I'll be fifteen soon,' Maura said proudly. Father Gunn looked at her. She was a pleasant open-faced child. Not a pretty face like the one being confirmed today, but still easy enough on the eye. He hoped she wouldn't fall for a child the way the elder sister had in Northampton. There were few secrets kept from a priest in a small community.

'You'll be needing a reference I suppose,' he sighed, thinking of the numbers of young people that he had written about, praising their honesty and integrity to anonymous English employers.

'I suppose they'll all know me in Shancarrig,' she said. 'I'll be looking for a job as a maid, Father. If you hear of anyone, I'm great at cleaning altogether.'

'I will, Maura, I'll keep my eyes open for you.' He turned away, feeling unexpectedly sad.

Maura went first to the back door of The Glen and waited patiently as the dogs raced around her, barking the news of her arrival, but nobody came to see what was her business. She had seen two figures

58

sitting in the front room. Surely they must have heard. After a lot of thought she went around to the front and Leo, tall and confident, came running down the stairs.

'Maura, what on earth are you doing?' she asked.

'I came wondering do your parents want anyone to work for them in the house, Leo,' she said to the girl who had been sitting beside her in school for eight years.

'Work?' Leo seemed startled.

'Yes, like I have to have a job working somewhere, and this is a big house. I wondered ... ?'

'No, Maura.'

'But, I know how to turn out a room ...'

'There's Biddy here already.'

'I meant as well as Biddy, under her of course.'

Leo had always been nice at school. Maura couldn't understand why she spoke so brusquely. 'It wouldn't work. You couldn't come here and clear up after me.'

'I have to clear up after someone. Wouldn't your family be as nice as anyone else's? Let me ask them, Leo.' She didn't say the place could do with a clean. She didn't plead. She had always been quick to recognise when something was impossible. And a look at Leo Murphy's face told her that this was now the case.

'Right then,' she said cheerfully. 'I had to ask.'

She knew Leo was standing at the door with the dogs as she walked down the avenue. Maura thought that she should have been allowed to talk to the people of the house, rather than being sent off by her own schoolfriend. Still, Leo had the air of being the one who made the decisions in that house. They mightn't have hired her if they knew Leo disapproved.

Imagine being able to make the decisions at nearly fifteen. But then Maura told herself that that's what she was doing herself. There were very few decisions made in Brennans' by anyone except herself.

Maura went then to Mrs Hayes. Mr Hayes was a solicitor so the Hayes family were very wealthy. They had a big house covered with virginia creeper, and a lovely piano in the drawing room. Maura knew this because Niall Hayes went to the same school. He was very nice. He told her one day how much he hated the piano lessons that his mother arranged for him twice a week, and Maura told him how much she hated going to the pub to tell her father his dinner was ready on Saturday and Sunday lunchtimes. It was a kind of bond between them.

But Mrs Hayes didn't want a young girl, she told Maura. She'd need someone older, someone trained.

She went to Mrs Barton, Eddie Barton's mother, who ran a dress-making business, but Mrs Barton said it was hard enough to put food on the table for herself and Eddie, without trying to find another few shillings for a child to be playing at pushing a brush around the floor. She had said it kindly, but the facts were the facts.

And Dr Jims said that he had not only Carrie to look after his son but there were many good years left in Maisie as well. So, everything now depended on going to the Ryans in the hotel. Maura had left that till last because she thought Mrs Ryan was very strong willed. She was a woman whom it might be easy to annoy.

She got the job, chambermaid. Mrs Ryan said she hoped Maura would be happy but there were three things they should get straight from the start – Maura was not to speak to Nessa just because they knew each other at school – Maura was to live on the premises, they didn't really want her going back to the cottages every night – and lastly, if there was a question of flirting or making free with any of the customers there would be words with Father Gunn about it and Maura would leave Shancarrig without a backward glance.

It suited Maura not to live at home. Her father was increasingly difficult these days. Geraldine had her friends in and out of the place, giggling in the bedroom. It would be nice to have a place of her own, a small room certainly, like a nun's cell, but all to herself.

Maura began work at once, and in her time off she did the ironing still for Miss Ross and she polished silver for Mrs Hayes, sitting quietly in the kitchen on her afternoon off from the hotel. She never spoke to Niall when he came home on holidays from his boarding school. Nobody would ever have known they had been schoolfriends and even companions in a kind of way too. If Niall ever saw her there he didn't seem to take any notice.

Not even as the years passed and Maura Brennan developed a small waist and began to look altogether more attractive. If you were born square and dull-looking in appearance you didn't ever think that things would change. Maura knew that her sister Geraldine was pretty but she didn't feel jealous. It was good that Geraldine had got a job up in the sawmills; they liked someone nice with a bright smile around the office. Maura never thought that it was bad luck to be square and making beds behind the scenes in a hotel.

In fact, she was so used to being square and dull-looking she was quite unaware that she had changed and had begun to look very attractive indeed.

The men who came to stay in Ryan's Commercial Hotel noticed, though. Maura had many an occasion to raise her voice sharply and speak in clear firm tones when men asked for an extra blanket, or complained of some imaginary fault in their rooms, just in order to give her a squeeze.

By the time she was eighteen years old, Mrs Ryan suggested to her husband that they put her behind the bar. She'd be able to attract custom. To their surprise, Maura refused. She'd prefer to continue the work she was doing, she had no head for figures. She would need a lot of smart clothes if she was to be in the public eye. She would be happier making beds and helping in the kitchen.

'At least, wait on the tables,' Mrs Ryan asked. But no, if her work was satisfactory she would prefer to keep in the background.

Breda Ryan shrugged. They had tried to better her, a girl from the cottages, poor Paudie Brennan's child, and yet she wouldn't seize the opportunity. Mrs Ryan had always thought that if the whole wealth of the world was taken back and divided out equally, giving the same amount to each person, you'd find in five years that the same people would end up having money and power and the same people would end up shiftless and hopeless. In a changing world, she found this view very comforting.

Maura didn't want to change because her life suited her just the way it was. She had three square meals a day. She could even choose what she wanted to eat in a hotel, which she mightn't have been able to do in a private house. She had the excuse which she could give her mother and father that the hotel needed her night and day. As a barmaid or waitress she might be expected to live out. And she wanted nothing to interfere with her savings and her plans.

Whenever she took the children she minded for walks she would always go the same way, past the places that she would buy when she had the money. There was the little gate lodge to The Glen. It was totally disused. People had lived there once, but now the ivy grew in the windows. That would be her first choice. Then there was the little house near where Miss Ross lived. It was painted a wishy-washy grey, but if Maura had it she would paint it pink and have window boxes full of red geraniums on each side of the hall door.

*

There wasn't much time for talking to friends these days. Not if you had to save as hard as Maura did. And she didn't go dancing – dances cost money, lots of money. First you had to buy something to wear, then the price of the bus fare to the town, and the admission to the dance hall, and the minerals. It would run away with your savings.

Maura had never been to a dance by the time her young sister Geraldine was ready to leave Shancarrig and join their sisters in England.

'Come on, just as my goodbye,' Geraldine had urged.

'I've nothing to wear.'

The sisters had remained friendly over the years as Maura had worked on in the hotel and Geraldine had worked in the office in the sawmills.

'I've plenty,' Geraldine said.

And indeed she had, Maura discovered. The bedroom they had once shared would never have held a second bed these days, with all the clothes strewn around it. Maura looked in wonder. 'You must have spent everything you earned on these,' she said.

'Don't be mean, Maura. There's nothing worse than a mean woman,' Geraldine said.

Was she mean? Maura wondered. It would indeed be terrible to be a mean woman. Yet, she didn't think she was mean. She gave a pound a week out of her wages to her mother and she always brought a cake or a half pound of ham when she came home to tea. She seemed to be giving Geraldine the price of the cinema for as long as she remembered. All she had been careful about was not spending on herself.

But perhaps that too was mean.

She fingered the dresses. A taffeta dress with shot silk in green and yellow colours, a red corduroy skirt, a black satin with little bits of diamanté at the shoulders. It was like Aladdin's cave.

'Do all your friends have clothes like this?' she asked.

'Well, Catherine Ryan from the place you work, she'd have different things. You know, well-cut, awful-looking garments you wouldn't be seen dead in. Some people have a ton of stuff. We swap a bit. What'll you wear?'

Maura Brennan wore the black satin with the diamanté decorations and set out for the dance in the big town. She looked at herself in the mirror of the ladies' cloakroom. She thought she looked all right. It was hard to tell what fellows would like, but she thought she'd get asked up to dance and not be left a fool by the side of the wall.

The first man who came over was Gerry O'Sullivan, the new barman in Ryan's Hotel.

'Well, don't tell me you're the same girl that I see in the kitchen in the back of beyond where we work,' he said, stretching out his arms to her.

And then the night flew by. They danced everything, sambas and tangos, and rock and roll, and old-time waltzes. She couldn't believe that it was time for the National Anthem.

'I have to find my sister and her friends,' she said.

'Aw, don't give me that. I've the loan of a car,' he said.

He was very handsome, Gerry O'Sullivan, small and dark with black hair and an easy laugh. But there was no question of it. They had all given five shillings to get their lift there and back in a big van.

'I'll see you tomorrow in the hotel,' she said, thinking that might cheer him up. She was wrong.

'Tomorrow you won't be looking like this, you'll be dressed like a streel and emptying chamber pots,' he grumbled, and went off.

Maura said very little on the way home. Geraldine's friends passed around a bottle of cider, but she shook her head. She supposed he was right: that was the way she dressed and that was what she did for a living.

'I'll write from England,' Geraldine said. Maura knew she wouldn't, any more than the others had.

A few days later Gerry O'Sullivan found her alone.

'I only said that because I was so mad wanting to be with you. I had a very bad mouth and I'm sorry.' He was so handsome and so upset. Maura's face lit up.

'I didn't mind a bit,' she said.

'You should have minded. Listen, will you come to the dance again, on Friday? I'll bring you there and back. Please?' She looked doubtful, because this time she literally didn't have anything to wear. Geraldine had taken her wardrobe across the sea to England. 'I'll be very nicely mannered all night long,' he said with a grin. 'And it's Mick Delahunty's Show Band and he won't be back this way for a good bit.'

She decided she could take the cost of one party dress from her savings. And the following week she took another, and the price of shoes and a nice bag. She'd never have her house at this rate, Maura told herself. But she found herself saying that you only live once.

Gerry O'Sullivan told her that she was the loveliest girl in the dance hall.

'Don't be making a jeer of me,' she said.

'I'll show you I'm not making a jeer of you.' Gerry was indignant. 'I'll not dance with you and see how you'll be swept away...' Before she could say anything he picked a girl from the waiting line and began to dance.

Red-cheeked and unsure Maura was about to step aside but from three directions arms were stretched out and faces offered a dance. She laughed, confused, and picked the nearest one. He had been right. She *was* the kind of girl men danced with.

'What did I tell you,' he murmured in the back of the car that night. He seemed excited by the thought of other men wanting Maura and not being able to have her. His own intention of having her had now become a near reality. No protestations were going to be any use, and in honesty Maura didn't want to protest any further.

'Not in the car, please,' she whispered.

'You're right.' He seemed cheerful. Too cheerful, in fact. From his pocket he took out one of the hotel keys.

'Room Eleven,' he said triumphantly. 'There'll be no one there. We'll be fine as long as we keep the light off.' Maura looked at him trustingly.

'Will it be all right?' she asked in a whisper.

'I'll not let you down,' Gerry O'Sullivan said.

She knew he spoke the truth. She knew it again five months later, after many happy visits to Room Eleven and even Room Two, when she told him she was pregnant.

'We'll get married,' he said.

Father Gunn agreed that it should be as speedily as possible. His face seemed to say that it would be no better or worse than a lot of marriages he was asked to officiate at with speed. And at least in this case they seemed to have a deposit for a house, which was more than you might have hoped for in some cases. Father Gunn talked about it to Miss Ross.

'It could be a lot worse, I suppose,' he said.

'She'll never settle in a poor house. She wanted to be well away from those cottages. She had her eyes on great things,' the teacher said.

'Well, faith and she should have her eyes on being grateful the fellow married her and putting her mind to raising the child and being glad they have a roof over their heads.' Father Gunn knew he sounded like a stern old parish priest from thirty years ago, but somehow the whole thing had him annoyed and he didn't want to hear any fairy stories about people having their eyes set on great things.

Maura decided to work until the day before the wedding. She looked Mrs Ryan straight in the eye and refused to accept any hints about the work being tiring in her condition. She said she needed every penny she could earn.

Mrs Ryan was cross to be losing a hard-working maid, and at the same time having an attractive barman marry beneath him because of activities obviously carried out under her own roof. She began to look more sternly at her own daughters, Nessa and Catherine, lest anything untoward should happen in their lives.

Nessa, the same age as Maura, had been all through Shancarrig school with her. 'What should I give her as a present?' she said to her mother.

'Best present is to ignore it and the reason for it,' Mrs Ryan snapped.

This reaction ensured, of course, that Nessa would go to great trouble to find a nice present. She rang Leo Murphy up in The Glen. Maura, putting away mops and buckets in the room at the end of the corridor, heard Nessa on the phone.

'Leo, she *was* in our class. We have to do something. Of course it's shotgun. What else could it be? You choose something, anything at all. Poor Maura, she expects so little.'

That's not true, Maura thought as she put away the cleaning equipment. She didn't expect so little, she expected a lot and mainly she got it. She had wanted to stay in Shancarrig rather than emigrating like the rest of her brothers and sisters, and here she had stayed. She had wanted the one handsome man that she ever fancied in her life, and he had wanted her. He was standing by her now and marrying her.

She had got more than she expected. She certainly hadn't thought that she would be having a baby and yet there was one on the way. The very thought of it made her pleased and excited. It took away the ache of sorrow about the place they would be living in.

With Gerry and a baby it wouldn't matter anyway.

Leo Murphy and Nessa Ryan gave her a little glass-fronted cabinet.

She couldn't have liked it more. She stroked it over and over and said how lovely it would look on a wall when she got her own treasures to put in it.

'Have you any treasures yet?' Nessa asked.

'Only a doll. A doll with a china face and china hands,' Maura said.

'That'll be nice for the baby...' Leo gulped. 'If you ever have one, I mean,' she said hastily.

'Oh, I'm sure I will,' Maura said. 'But the baby won't be let play with this doll. It's a treasure, for the lovely cabinet.'

She could see that the girls thought their money had been well spent, and she was touched by how much they must have given for it. As part of her continuing fantasy about a house, Maura used to look at furniture and price it. She knew well that this cabinet was not inexpensive.

Maura hoped that Geraldine would come home from England. She even offered her the fare, but there was no reply. It would have been nice to have had her standing as a bridesmaid, but instead she had Eileen Dunne, who said she loved weddings and she'd be anyone's bridesmaid for them. And with a great nudge that nearly knocked Maura over she said she'd do godmother as well, and laughed a lot.

Gerry's brother came to do the best man bit. His parents were old and didn't travel, he said.

Maura saw nothing sad or shabby about her wedding day.

When she turned around in the church she saw Nessa Ryan, Leo Murphy, Niall Hayes and Eddie Barton sitting smiling at her. She was the first of their class to get married. They seemed to think this was like winning some kind of race rather than having been caught in a teenage pregnancy. When they went to Johnny Finn's for drinks Mr Ryan from the hotel came running in with a fistful of money to buy them all a drink. He said he came to wish them well from everyone in Ryan's Commercial Hotel.

There was no word of the haste or the disgrace or anything. Maura's father behaved in a way that, for Paudie Brennan, could be called respectable. This week he happened to be friendly with Foxy Dunne's father, so the two of them had their arms around each other as they sang tunelessly together in a corner. If it had been one of the weeks when they were fighting, things would have been terrible – insults hurling across Johnny Finn's all afternoon.

And Father Gunn and Father Barry were there smiling and talking to people as if it were a real wedding.

Maura didn't see anything less than the kind of wedding day she had dreamed about when she was at school, or when reading the women's magazines. All she saw was Gerry O'Sullivan beside her, smiling and saying everything would be grand.

And everything *was* grand for a while.

Maura left her job in the hotel. Mrs Ryan seemed to want it that way. Possibly there would be social differences now that Maura was the wife of the popular barman, instead of just the girl from the cottages cleaning the floors and washing potatoes. But Maura found plenty of work, hours here and hours there. When it was obvious that she was expecting a child many of her employers said they would be lost without her. Mrs Hayes, who hadn't wanted her in the start, was particularly keen to keep her.

'Maybe your mother could look after the child, and you'd still want to go out and work?' she said hopefully.

Maura had no intention of letting any child grow up in the same house as she had herself, with the lack of interest and love. But she had learned to be very circumspect in her life. 'Maybe indeed,' she said to Mrs Hayes and the others. 'We'll have to wait and see.'

It seemed a long time to wait for the baby, all those evenings on her own in the little cottage, sometimes hearing her father going home drunk, as she had when she was a child. She polished the little cabinet, took out the doll and patted the bump of her stomach.

'Soon you'll be admiring this,' she said to the unborn baby.

It was Dr Jims Blake who told her about the baby boy. The child had Down's syndrome. The boy, who was what was called a mongol, would still be healthy and loving and live a full and happy life.

It was Father Gunn who told her about Gerry, and how he had come from the cottage to the church and told the priest he was going. He took the wages owing to him from the hotel, saying his father had died and he needed time off for the funeral. But he told Father Gunn that he was getting the boat to England.

No entreaties would make him stay.

Maura remembered always the way that Father Gunn's thick round glasses seemed to sparkle as he was telling her. She didn't know if there were tears behind them, or if it was only a trick of the light.

People were kind, very kind. Maura often told herself that she had been lucky to have stayed in Shancarrig. Suppose all this had happened to her in some big city in England where she had known nobody. Here she had a friendly face everywhere she turned.

And of course she had Michael.

Nobody had told her how much she would love him because nobody could have known. She had never known a child as loving. She watched him grow with a heart that nearly burst with pride. Everything he learned, every new skill – like being able to do up his buttons – was a huge hurdle for the child, and soon everyone in Shancarrig got used to seeing them hand in hand walking around.

'Who's this?' people would ask affectionately, even though they knew well.

'This is Michael O'Sullivan,' Maura would say proudly.

'I'm Michael O'Sullivan,' he would say and, as often as not, hug the person who had asked.

If you wanted Maura to come and clean your house you took Michael as well. And as they walked from job to job each day Maura used to point out the houses that she loved to her son – the little gate lodge, ever more covered with ivy and choked with nettles, that stood at the end of the long avenue up to The Glen, and there was the one near Miss Ross which she was going to paint pink if she ever bought it.

At night she would take the doll with the china hands and face out from its cabinet and the two cups and saucers she had been given by Mrs Ryan. There was a little silver plate, which had EPNS on the back, that Eileen Dunne had given when she stood as godmother to Michael. She said that this meant it wasn't real silver, but since the S stood for silver Maura thought it deserved a place in the cabinet. There was a watch too, one that belonged to Gerry. A watch that didn't go, but might go one day if it were seen to, and would hang on a chain. When Michael got to be a man he could call it his father's watch.

Most people forgot that Michael ever had a father; the memory of Gerry O'Sullivan faded. And for Maura the memory began to fade too. Days passed when she didn't think of the handsome fellow with the dark eyes who had cared enough to marry her, but hadn't got the strength to stay when he knew his child was handicapped. She had never hated him, sometimes she even pitied him that he didn't know the great hugs and devotion of Michael his son, who grew in size but not greatly in achievement.

Maura had got glances and serious invitations out from other men in the town, but she had always told them simply that she wasn't free to accept any invitation. She had a husband living in England and really there could be no question of anything else.

Her dream remained constant. A proper little home, not the broken-down cottage where only the hopeless and the helpless lived, where she had grown up and wanted to escape.

Then the Darcys came to Shancarrig. They bought a small grocery shop like the one Nellie Dunne ran, and they put in all kinds of new-fangled things. The world was changing, even in places like Shancarrig. Mike and Gloria Darcy were new people who livened the place up. No one had ever met anyone called Gloria before and she lived up to her name. Lots of black curly hair like a gypsy, and she must have known this because she often wore a red scarf knotted around her neck and a full coloured skirt, as if she was going to break into a gypsy dance any moment.

Mike Darcy was easy-going and got on with everyone. Even old Nellie Dunne who looked on them as rivals liked Mike Darcy. He had a laugh and a word for anyone he met on the road. Mrs Ryan in the Commercial Hotel felt they were a bit brash for the town, but when Mike said he'd buy for her at the market as well as for himself she began to change her tune.

It was good to see such energy about the place, she said, and it wasn't long before she had the front of the hotel painted to make it the equal of the new shopfront in Darcy's. Mike's brother, Jimmy Darcy, had come with them. He was a great house-painter and Mrs Ryan claimed that even the dozy fellows from down in the cottages, who used to paint a bit when the humour took them, seemed to think Jimmy did a good job. Mike and Gloria had children, two tough dark little boys who used to get up to all kinds of devilment in the school.

Maura didn't wait to see whether the town liked the Darcys or not; she presented herself on the doorstep the moment they arrived.

'You'll be needing someone to work for you,' she said to Gloria.

Gloria glanced at the round eager face of Michael, who stood holding his mother's hand. 'Will you be able to make yourself free?' she asked.

'Michael would come with me. He's the greatest help you could imagine,' she said, and Michael beamed at the praise.

'I'm not sure if we really *do* need anyone...' Gloria was polite but unsure.

'You do need someone, but take your time. Ask around a bit about me. Maura O'Sullivan is the name, Mrs Maura O'Sullivan.'

'Well, yes, Mrs O'Sullivan...'

'No, I just wanted you to know, because you're new. Michael's daddy had to go and live in England. You'd call me Maura if you had me in the house.'

'And you'd call me Michael,' the boy said, putting both his arms around Gloria's small waist.

'I don't need to ask around. When will you start?'

The Darcys were better payers than anyone else in the town. They seemed to have no end of money. The children's clothes were all good quality, their shoes were new, not mended. The furniture they had was expensive, not lovely old wood which Maura would have enjoyed polishing, but dear modern furniture. She knew the prices of all these things from her trips to the big town, and her dreams of furnishing the house that she'd buy.

Back in the cottage she had hardly anything worth speaking of. The small slow savings were being kept for the day she moved into the place she wanted. Only the glass-fronted cabinet with its small trove of treasures showed any sign of the gracious living that Maura yearned for. Otherwise it was converted boxes and broken second-hand furniture.

The Darcys had been in lots of places. Maura marvelled at how quickly the children could adapt.

They were warm-hearted too. They didn't like to come across Michael cleaning their shoes. 'He doesn't have to do that, Missus,' said Kevin Darcy, who was nine.

'I'm doing them great,' Michael protested.

'Don't worry, Kevin, that's Michael's and my job. All we ask you to do is not to leave everything on the floor of your bedroom so as we have to bend and pick it up.'

It worked. Gloria Darcy said that Maura and her son had managed to put manners on her children, something no one in any house had ever done before.

'Don't you find it hard, Mam, all the moving from place to place?'

Gloria looked at her. 'No, it's interesting. You meet new people, and in each place we better ourselves. We sell the place at a profit and then move on.'

'And will you be moving on from here too, do you think?' Maura was disappointed. She wouldn't ever get the kind of hours and payments that the Darcys gave her from anyone else. Gloria Darcy said not for a while. She thought they would stay in Shancarrig until the children got a bit of an education before uprooting them.

And their business prospered. They built on a whole new section to the original building they had bought and they expanded their range of goods. Soon people didn't need to go into the big town for their shopping trips. You could buy nearly everything you needed in Darcy's.

'I don't know where they get the money,' Mrs Hayes said one day to Maura. 'They can't be doing that much business, nothing that would warrant the kind of showing off they're doing.'

Maura said nothing. She thought that Mrs Hayes was the kind of wife who might well disapprove of Gloria's low-cut blouses and winning ways with the men of Shancarrig.

It was around this time that Maura became aware of financial problems in the Darcy household. There were bills that were being presented over and over to them. She could hear Mike Darcy's voice raised on the phone. But at the same time he had bought Gloria some marvellous jewellery that was the talk of Shancarrig.

'She has me broke,' he'd say to anyone who came into the shop. 'Go on Gloria, show them that emerald.'

And laughing, Gloria would wave the emerald on the chain. It had been bought in the big town in the jeweller's. She had always wanted one. And it was the same with the little diamond earrings. They were so small they were only specks really, but the thought that they were real diamonds made her shiver with excitement.

Shancarrig looked on with admiration. And the Darcys weren't blowing or boasting either. Nessa Ryan had been in the big town and checked. They were the real thing. The Darcys were new rich, courageous and not afraid to spend. With varying degrees of envy the people of Shancarrig wished them good luck.

The tinkers came every year on the way to the Galway races. They didn't stay in Shancarrig. They stayed nearby. Maura was struck with how Gloria looked like the Hollywood version of a gypsy, not the real thing. The real women of the travelling people looked tired and weather-beaten, not the flashing eyes and colourful garb of Gloria Darcy, and certainly not the real diamonds in the ears and the real emerald around her neck.

But this particular year people said some tinker woman must be wearing the jewels because, at the very time they were encamped outside Shancarrig, Gloria Darcy's jewellery case was stolen.

All hell broke loose. It could only be the tinkers.

Sergeant Keane was in charge of the search, and the ill will created was enormous. Nothing was found. No one was charged. Everyone was upset. Even Michael was interrogated and asked about what he had seen and what he had touched in his visits to the Darcy house. It was a frightening time in Shancarrig; there had never been a robbery like this before.

There had never been anything like this to steal before.

A lot of tut-tutting and head-shaking went on. It was vulgar of the Darcys to have displayed that jewellery; it made people envious. It put temptation in the way of others. But then, how had the gypsies known about it? They had only just come to camp. They hadn't been given dazzling displays of the glinting emerald on the chain around Gloria's throat.

'I'm sorry if the guards frightened Michael,' Gloria said to Maura.

'I don't mind about that. Sergeant Keane has known Michael since he was in a pram, he wouldn't frighten him,' Maura said. 'But I'm sorry for you, Mrs Darcy. You put a lot of store by those jewels. It won't be the same without them.'

'No, but there will be the insurance money ... eventually,' Gloria said. She said they weren't going to buy emeralds and diamonds again. Maybe put the money into paying off the extension and getting the place rewired and better stocked.

Maura remembered some of the conversations she had heard about the need to pay builders' bills. She went back over those financial difficulties she thought she had been aware of. Possibly the insurance money was exactly what the Darcys needed at this stage.

Indeed, it could be said to come at exactly the right time.

Maura had been used to keeping her own counsel for as long as she could remember. She had seen what the wild indiscretions of her own family had brought on themselves and everyone else around – her father's blustering revelations of any bit of gossip he knew, her mother's trying to play one member of the family off against the other.

Maura said very little.

She had sometimes suspected over the years that the envelope Father Gunn gave her each Christmas, saying that it was from Gerry O'Sullivan from no fixed address in England, actually came from the priest himself. But she never let Father Gunn know of her suspicions. She thanked him for acting as postman.

She sometimes wondered why she had become so secretive and close. When she was a youngster she had been open and would talk to everyone. Maybe it was just the whole business of Gerry and having to be protective of Michael. And because there had never been a real friend to talk to.

The robbery of the jewels had been a nine-day wonder. Soon people stopped talking about it. There were other things to occupy their minds.

There was always something happening in Shancarrig. Maura never knew why people called it sleepy or a backwater. Only people who didn't know the place would have used words like that. Maura and Michael helped at the Dramatic Society and there was a drama a week there from the time that Biddy who worked at The Glen started to dance and went on like something wound up until no one could drag her from the stage. And there was all the business about Father Barry not being well, and then going off to the missions.

There was Richard, that handsome cousin of Niall Hayes, who had come to The Terrace and broken a few hearts – Nessa's maybe – and Maura thought there might be a bit of electricity between him and Mrs Darcy, not that she would ever mention a word of it. Yet Nellie Dunne hinted of it too so that rumour might well be going around the place. Eddie Barton had opened all their eyes with his unexpected romance, and the news of Foxy Dunne from London was always worth people pausing to discuss.

There was plenty to distract the minds of Shancarrig from the missing emerald and diamonds.

Maura O'Sullivan and her son Michael went from house to house – the ironing for Miss Ross, who had lines set in her face now, and had begun to look like a waxwork image of her old mother – there was the silver polishing for Mrs Hayes – the two hours on a Saturday for Mrs Barton – but mainly, the Darcys.

There was a lot to be done in a house where there were two boys and where the parents were hardly ever out of the shop. Maura didn't wait to be asked to do things. She had her own routine.

She was doing the master bedroom, as Gloria called it, when she found the jewellery. It was on top of the wardrobe in a big round hat box. Maura had been dusting the top of the wardrobe with sheets of newspapers spread below to catch the falling dirt. She saw a neater way to stack the suitcases, but it involved lifting them down. Michael stood willingly to take them from her. And it was only because the hat box rattled that she opened it. It was as if there was a big stone in it. She didn't want whatever it was to fall out.

It was a red silk scarf with two small black velvet bags wrapped up in it.

Michael saw her stop and hold the wardrobe top for support.

'Are you going to fall down?' he asked anxiously.

'No, love.' Maura climbed down and sat on the bed. Her heart was racing dangerously.

There was no way that she could have accidentally discovered the lost and much-mourned jewellery. There would be no cries of delight if the gems were recovered and the insurance claim had to be cancelled.

She also knew that they had not got into the hat box by accident. The description had been given over and over. The emerald on its chain had been in a box on the desk downstairs, and the little earrings in their black velvet bag beside them. The room they were in, the sitting room, had a pair of glass doors opening on to the small back garden. A light-fingered, light-footed tinker boy could have been in and out without anyone noticing.

That was how the story went.

In all her time cleaning in this house Maura had never known the valuables kept in this hat box. It was not a place someone would have put them and forgotten about them.

'Why aren't you speaking?' Michael wanted to know.

'I'm trying to think about something,' she said. She put her arm around his shoulder and drew him close.

She seemed to sit there for a long time, yellow duster in hand, her feet squarely on the spread newspaper, her son enclosed in her arm.

That evening Maura put the two little black velvet bags in her cabinet of treasures. She had to think it out very cleverly. She mustn't do the wrong thing and end up the worse for this great discovery.

Weeks went by before she brought up the subject of the lost jewels. She waited until she had Gloria in the house on her own. She had left Michael playing with the chickens outside.

'I was thinking, Mam, Mrs Darcy ... what would happen if someone found your emerald chain say ... thrown in a hedge by the tinkers?'

'What do you mean?' Gloria's voice was sharp.

'Well, now that you've done all the renovations here ... and got used to not having it and wearing it round your neck ... wouldn't it be bad for you if it turned up?'

'It won't turn up. That lot have it well sold by now, you can be sure.'

74

'But where would they sell it? If they brought it into a jeweller's shop, Mrs Darcy, wouldn't people know it was the one that was stolen from you? They'd call the guards, not give them the money.'

'That crowd travel far and wide. They could take it to a shop miles from here.'

There was a silence.

Then Gloria said, 'Anyway, it hasn't been found.'

'My head is full of dreams, Mrs Darcy. I go walking by the hedges. I often find things ... what would happen if I were to find it?'

'I don't know what you mean.'

'Well, suppose I did find it, would I take it to Sergeant Keane and say where I came across it, or would I give it to you ...?'

Gloria's eyes were very narrow.

Maura saw her glance towards the stairs as if she were about to run up and check the hat box.

'This is fancy talk,' she said eventually. 'But I suppose the best would be, if you *were* to find it, to give it to me quietly. As you say, the insurance money was really more use to us than the jewellery itself at this stage.'

'What about a reward?' Maura looked confused and eager.

'We'd have to see.'

Maura went out to the chickens to find Michael, but she paused before she closed the door behind her and heard the light sound of Gloria Darcy's feet running up the stairs, and the sound of the suitcases being thrown from the high wardrobe to the floor.

Nothing was said.

It wasn't as hard for Maura as it might have been for others, because after a life of keeping her thoughts and opinions to herself it was relatively easy to work on in the house where Gloria and Mike Darcy obviously walked on a knife edge of anxiety around her.

They offered her cups of tea in the middle of her cleaning. They found things for Michael in the shop as gifts, but Maura said he mustn't be allowed to think of the shop as a wonderland where he could stroll and take whatever bar of chocolate he wanted. It would be very bad for him, and she had spent so much time trying to make him see what was his and what wasn't.

When she said this Maura O'Sullivan looked Mike and Gloria straight in the eye. She could see that she had them totally perplexed.

It was Gloria who broke eventually.

'Remember you were saying that you were a great one for finding things, Maura?'

'Yes indeed. I prayed to St Anthony for that good Parker pen of Mr Darcy's to turn up and didn't it roll out from behind where we keep the trays stacked in the kitchen.' Maura was proud and pleased with the results of her prayers.

'I was thinking about what you said ... and in our business, well ... we get to know a lot of people. Now, suppose you were to find the stuff that the tinkers took somewhere ... ?'

'Yes, Mrs Darcy?'

'Do you know what the very best thing to do with it would be ... ?'

'I do not. And I've been wondering and wondering.'

'You see, the insurance money has been paid and spent improving the shop, providing work for people, even for you in the house.' Maura held her head on one side, waiting. 'So, if it did turn up and you were able to give it to me I could get it sold for you, and give you some of it ...' Her voice trailed away.

'Ah, but if I knew the right place to sell it myself, then I could get plenty of money. Because, as you say yourself, you got the insurance money out of it already. You wouldn't want to be getting things twice over ... it wouldn't be fair.'

'But why would it be fair for *you* to get it all?'

'If I found it in a hedge, or wherever I found it, it's finders keepers, isn't it?'

'But no use of course if you didn't know where to sell it.'

This was the deal. They both knew it.

'I'll be going to the big town next week, Mrs Darcy.'

'Yes, for your Christmas shopping. Of course.'

'I get this envelope from Michael's father, through Father Gunn. I'll be spending whatever there is ...'

'I know.'

'And I was thinking, suppose I found the lost jewels by then, I'd be able to sell the emerald on the chain and I could give you back the diamonds, on account of you taking me straight to the right place, and that way ...' She let the sentence hang there.

'That way would be better, I suppose, than any other way.' Gloria's face was grim.

Niall Hayes was surprised when he heard that a Mrs O'Sullivan wanted to see him particularly. People usually wanted to see his father, Mr

Hayes Senior, the real solicitor as he had heard him described.

He was more surprised when he discovered that it was Maura Brennan from the cottages. He welcomed the two of them into his office – hardly anyone in Shancarrig had ever seen them apart.

'How have you been keeping, Maura?' he said, always a kind open fellow, despite his sharp snobby mother.

'I couldn't be better, Niall,' she said. 'We've had a bit of good luck. Michael's father always sends a bit to help out at Christmas time, and this year he was able to send a lot more.'

'Well, that's good, very good.' Niall couldn't see where the conversation was leading.

'And I'll tell you what we'd love, Niall ... You know the cottage at the gate of The Glen?'

'I do, indeed. And they're putting it up for sale.'

'I'd like to buy it for Michael and myself. Would you act for us?'

Niall paused. How could Maura have enough to buy and renovate a place like that?

'I'll talk to Leo,' he said.

'No, talk to me. Tell me what's fair to offer her. Fair to her, fair to me.'

That was the way Niall Hayes liked to do business. There wasn't enough of it around. People were changing, attitudes were different. They wanted sharp dealings here and there.

He patted Maura's hand. It would be done.

Maura told Father Gunn that Michael's father had given them a great deal of money this year, much more than other times. If the priest was surprised he didn't show it.

'I think that's the last payment, Father.' She looked into the priest's eyes behind the thick round glasses. 'I don't think you'll be getting any more envelopes to give out at Christmas.'

He looked after them as they went down the road – Maura and Michael, soon to be householders, soon to go into a place of dreams, and paint it and tidy it and fill it with treasures.

He knew that the longer he lived in this parish the less he would understand.

EDDIE

Eddie Barton only had a birthday once every four years, which was highly unusual. In fact, he thought he was the only person in the world in this situation. It came as a shock to him that other children had been born on this day. He was ten before he accepted it properly. Up to that he had thought he was unique.

Miss Ross, who was so nice at school, had told them all about Leap Year. Mr Kelly had frightened the wits out of him by saying that if a woman proposed to you on February twenty-ninth you had to say yes, even if she was the most terrifyingly awful person in the world. Mr Kelly had laughed as he said it but Eddie wasn't sure if it was a real laugh or not. Mr Kelly often looked sad.

'Did Mrs Kelly propose to you on my birthday?' Eddie asked fearfully. If the answer was yes then this indeed was another bad aspect of growing up.

But Mr Kelly had put his finger on his lips in a jokey sort of way and said, 'Nonsense and don't let Mrs Kelly hear a whisper of this or there'd be trouble.' It was to be a secret between them.

'I thought you said it was a well-known fact?' Eddie was confused.

'I did,' the teacher sighed. 'I did but I keep forgetting, even after all my years in a classroom, how dangerous it is to say anything, anything at all, to children.'

When Eddie's tenth birthday was coming up, his mother said he could be ten on the day before or the day after.

'I'd better wait until the day after,' he told Leo Murphy, who walked home after school with him because she lived in the big house, The Glen, up the hill, and Eddie lived in the small pink house halfway up the road. Leo had said that Eddie's house reminded her of a child's drawing of a house. It had windows that looked as if they were painted on. Eddie didn't know whether this was praise or not.

'What's wrong with that?' he had asked ferociously.

'Nothing. It's nice. It looks safe and normal, not like a jungle,' Leo had replied.

That meant she liked it. He was pleased.

Eddie liked Leo Murphy. If *she* were to ask him to marry her when he had a real birthday he wouldn't say no. The Glen would be a great place to live, orchards and an old tennis court. Fantastic.

Leo took things seriously.

'Why wait until March first?' she asked Eddie about his birthday. 'Suppose you died on the night of the twenty-eighth then you'd have missed your birthday altogether.'

It was unanswerable.

Eddie's mother said she didn't mind which day he had it just so long as he knew there'd be a cake and an apple tart and no more. He could have ten people or he could have two.

Eddie measured the cake plate carefully. He'd have three and himself. That way they'd have lots. He invited Leo Murphy and Nessa Ryan and Maura Brennan. They were the people he sat beside at class and liked.

'No boys at all?' Eddie's mother was a dressmaker. She was rarely seen without pins in her mouth or a frown of concentration on her face.

'I don't sit near any boys,' Eddie said.

His mother seemed to accept this. Una Barton was a small dark woman with worried eyes. She always walked very quickly, as if she feared people might stop her and detain her in conversation. She had a kind heart and a good eye for colour and dress fabrics in the clothes she made for the women of Shancarrig and the farmers' wives from out the country. They said that Una Barton lived for her son Eddie and for him alone.

Eddie had hair that grew upwards from his head. Foxy Dunne had said he looked like a lavatory brush. Eddie didn't know what a lavatory brush was. They didn't have one in their house, but when he saw one in Ryan's Hotel he was very annoyed. His hair wasn't as bad as that.

He liked doing things that the other boys didn't like doing at all. He liked going up to Barna Woods and collecting flowers. He sometimes pressed them and wrote their names underneath, and then stuck them on a card. His mother said that he was a real artist.

'Was my father artistic?' Eddie asked.

'The less said about your father's artistry the better.' His mother's face was in that sharp straight line again. There would be no more said.

He had to make a wish when he cut the cake. He closed his eyes and wished that his father would come back, like he had wished last year and the year before.

Maybe if you wished it three times it happened.

Ted Barton had left when his son was five. He had left in some spectacular manner, because Eddie had heard it mentioned several times when people didn't know he was listening. People would say about something, 'There was nearly as much noise as the night Ted Barton was thrown out.'

And once he heard the Dunnes in their shop say that if someone didn't mind himself it would be another case of Ted Barton, with the suitcase flung down the stairs after him. Eddie couldn't imagine his mother shouting or throwing a suitcase. But then again she must have.

She told him everything else he asked, but never told him about his father. 'Let's just agree that he didn't keep his part of the bargain. He didn't look after his wife and son. He doesn't deserve our interest.'

It was easy for her to say that but hard for Eddie to agree. Every boy wanted to know where his father was, even if it was a terrible father like the Brennans' or a fierce one like Leo Murphy's, with his moustache and being called a Major and everything.

Sometimes Eddie saw people getting off the bus and dreamed that maybe it was his father coming for him – coming to take him on a long holiday, just the two of them, walking all round Ireland, staying where they felt like. And then he'd imagine his father saying, with his head on one side, 'How about it, Eddie son, will I come home?' In the daydream Eddie's mother would always be smiling and welcoming and there would be less work to make her tired because his father would be looking after them now.

After tea they played games. They had to play on the floor of Eddie's bedroom, because Mrs Barton needed to bring her sewing machine back on to the table downstairs.

They said if only Eddie had a birthday in the summer they could all have gone up to Barna Woods. Eddie showed them some of the pressed flowers.

'They're beautiful,' Nessa Ryan said.

Nessa never said anything nice just to please you. If Nessa Ryan said they were good then they must be.

'You could even do that for a living,' she added.

At ten they usually didn't think as far ahead as that, but today there had been a talk on careers in school and an encouragement to think ahead and try to get trained for something rather than just gazing out the window and letting the time pass by.

'How could I get trained to press flowers?' Eddie was interested, but Nessa's momentary enthusiasm had passed.

'We'll have another go at blow football,' she said.

It had been Eddie's birthday present. His one gift. He hadn't really wanted it but his mother had heard from the Dunnes in the shop that it was what every child wanted this year and she had paid it off over five weeks. She was pleased the game was being used. Eddie secretly thought it was silly and tiring and that there was too much spit trying to blow a paper ball through paper tubes that got chewy and soggy.

When the party was over he stood at the door of the pink house in the moonlight and watched Leo skipping up the hill to her home. You could see the walls of The Glen from here. She waved when she reached the gate.

Nessa and Maura went downhill, Maura to the row of cottages where she lived. Eddie hoped that her father wouldn't be drunk tonight. Sometimes Paudie Brennan fell around the town shouting and insulting people.

Nessa Ryan had run on ahead. She lived in Ryan's Hotel. She could have anything she wanted to eat any time. She had told that to Eddie when he had explained about the cake and the apple tart. But there must have been something of an apology in his face because Nessa had said quickly that she didn't get as much *cake* as she liked. It was really only chips and sandwiches.

The moon was shining brightly, even though it was only seven o'clock. His mother's sewing machine was already whirring away. There she would sit surrounded by paper patterns and the big dummy which used to frighten him when he was a child, always draped with some nearly finished garment, as she listened to the radio. She would smile at him a lot, but when he came upon her alone he thought her face looked sad and tired. He wished she didn't have to work so hard. And it would keep whirring until he slept. It had been like that as long as he remembered. Eddie wondered was his father looking at the moon somewhere. Did he remember his son was ten-years-old today?

That night Eddie wrote a letter to his father.

He told him about the day and the pressed flowers that Nessa Ryan had admired so much. Then he wondered would his father think that bit was sissy so he crossed it out. He told his father that there was a big wedding in the next town and that his mother had been asked to do not only the bride's dress but the two bridesmaids and the mother and aunt of the bride as well. The whole church nearly would be dressed by Mrs Barton. And that his mother had said it came just in the nick of time because something needed to be done to the roof and there wasn't enough money to pay for it.

Then he read that last bit again and wondered would his father think it was a complaint. He didn't want to annoy him now that he had just found him.

With a jolt Eddie realised that he hadn't found his father, he was only making it up. Still, it was kind of comforting. He crossed out the bit about the roof costing money and left in the good news about the wedding dresses. He told his father about the careers lecture at school and about there being lots of jobs for hard-working young fellows over in England when he got old enough. He thought that maybe his father might be in England. Wouldn't it be marvellous if he met him by accident over there in a good job with prospects.

He wrote often that year. He told his father that Bernard Shaw had died, in case he might be somewhere where they didn't get that kind of news. Mr Kelly at school had said he was a great writer but he had been a bit against the church. Eddie asked his father why people would be against the church.

His father didn't answer, of course, because the letters were never sent. There was nowhere to send them to.

It wasn't that Eddie was all *that* lonely and friendless. He did have friends, of course he did. He often went up to The Glen to play with Leo Murphy. They used to hit the ball across the net to each other on the tennis court, and Leo had a great swing on a big oak tree. She hadn't known it was an oak tree until he told her and showed her the leaves and the acorns. It was extraordinary to have all those trees and still not know what they were.

Eddie often took oak leaves and traced around them. He loved the shape – there were so many more zig-zags than in the leaves of the plane trees, or the poplar. He liked the chestnut leaves too, and he never played the silly game that the others did at school – peeling away the green bits to see who could have the most perfect fillet, like a fish with no flesh, only bones. Eddie liked the texture of the leaves.

He didn't write any of this to his father, but he did tell him when de Valera got back again and Nessa Ryan had said there had been a terrible shouting match one night in the hotel and they had to send for the guards because some people didn't agree that it was great he was back. He went on writing and told a lot of fairly private things.

Still, he didn't mention that he was afraid of someone proposing to him on his birthday when he was twelve. It seemed such a stupid thing to be afraid of. But Eddie had great fears of Eileen Dunne at school, who had a terribly loud laugh and about five brothers who would deal with him if he refused her.

'You weren't thinking of asking me to marry you on Friday, were you?' he asked Leo hopefully. She had just raised her head from a book.

'No,' Leo said. 'I was thinking about the King of England being dead and my father being all upset about it.'

'Would you?' he asked.

'Would I what? Be all upset?'

'No. Ask me to marry you.'

'Why should I? You never asked *me* to marry you.'

'It's the day, you see. It's the day women can.'

'Men can every other day of the year.'

Eddie had worked that out. 'Suppose I asked you now, and we were engaged, then if anyone asked me on Friday I could say that I wasn't free.'

He looked very worried. Leo wasn't concentrating one bit. She was reading her book. She always had a book with her. This time it was *Good Wives*. It seemed a fine coincidence to Eddie.

'What *is* it, Eddie?'

'Just say yes. You don't have to.'

'Yes, then.'

Eddie was flooded with relief. He wasn't having a party for his twelfth birthday, he was too old. He was getting a bicycle, a second-hand bicycle. His mother had told him he could cycle to school on the day. He thought he'd keep it until next day, he said. His mother looked at him affectionately. He was such a funny little thing, quirky and complicated but never a moment's trouble to her, which was more than she could have hoped the day that bastard had left her doorstep.

People sometimes said it must be hard for her to bring a boy up all on her own. But Una Barton thought they had a reasonable life together. Her son told her long rambling tales, he was interested in helping her cook what they ate and would dry the dishes dutifully. She wished there was more money or time to take him to the seaside or to Dublin to the zoo. But that wasn't for their kind. That was for boys who had fathers that didn't run away.

Eddie didn't want to remind anyone it was his birthday, just in case Eileen Dunne might get it into her head, or Maura Brennan's young sister Geraldine. But nobody seemed to have realised the opportunity they had of proposing to Eddie, or to anyone. They were far more interested in Father Barry, who had come to give them a talk about the missions and to show them a Missionary magazine which had competitions in it and a Pen-Friends Corner. There were people in every part of the world who wanted to exchange ideas with young Irish people, he said. They could have a great time writing to youngsters in different lands.

Father Barry was very nice. He seemed kind of dreamy when he spoke and he sometimes closed his eyes as if the place he was talking about was somehow nearer than the place where he was. Eddie liked that. He often thought about being out with trees and flowers when he should have been thinking about the sums on the blackboard. Father Barry pinned up the page with names of the boys and girls who wanted pen-friends. They could all speak English. They lived in far lands. One of them said he liked botany, flowers and plants. His name was Chris and he lived in Glasgow, Scotland.

'That's not very far to be writing,' Niall Hayes said dismissively. He had picked a boy in Argentina.

'There's more chance he might write back if he's not too far away,' Eddie said.

'That's stupid,' said Niall.

In his heart Eddie agreed that it was. Maybe the boy in Scotland wanted someone more exotic, not from a small town in Ireland. But the real reason he had picked Chris Taylor was that Scotland wouldn't be too dear a stamp and because he had said he liked plant life. Eddie had always thought botany was a kind of wool. He checked with Miss Ross. He didn't want to get involved in writing about knitting or sheep or anything. Not that a boy would like knitting. Miss Ross said botany was plants and things that grew.

He wrote to Chris, a long letter. It was extraordinary to be writing one that would actually go into the post box. Other twelve-year-olds might have had to suck their pens and think of something more to say to use up another sheet of paper, but not Eddie Barton. He was well used to writing long letters about the state of the world in general and Shancarrig in particular.

The letter came back very quickly but it came addressed to Miss E. Barton. It had a Glasgow postmark on it. Eddie looked at it for a long time. It must be for him. His mother's name was Una. But why had Chris Taylor called him Miss? Burning with shame he opened the letter.

Dear Edith,

I wouldn't read your name properly and maybe yours is an Irish name, but I hope I'm right in guessing Edith.

The letter went on, a friendly interesting letter, lots about Scottish fir trees and pine cones, a request to send some pressed flowers, an inquiry about whether it might be good to learn the Latin names of things in case it was going to be easier to find them when you looked them up – Chris had gone to the library and spent two hours looking up a very ordinary maple and couldn't find it because he didn't know it was called *Acer*.

Eddie read on, delighted. It was nice of Chris to take so much trouble to write, especially since he obviously thought that Eddie was a girl, and a girl called Edith. Ugh. He even asked what kind of a convent was it if the teachers were called Miss Ross and Mrs Kelly and weren't nuns.

Then on the last page Eddie got an even worse shock. Chris was closing in hope that there would be a letter soon, and saying that he was delighted to find a kindred spirit on the other side of the sea, and then signed his name

Christine

Chris was a girl.

He went hot and cold thinking about the stupid mistake. She wouldn't write to him any more once she knew he didn't go to a convent school like she did, once she knew he was a twelve-year-old boy with baggy trousers and spiky hair. It was a great pity because that was just the sort of person he would have liked to write to. And it was her fault. Not his. She was the one who had the name that could have been anything. He had a perfectly normal male name, Eddie. He could imagine what they'd say at school if they knew he had got himself a *girl* in Scotland as a pen-friend when they were all finding fellows in India or South America.

Typical sissy Eddie Barton, they'd say.

He'd love to have sent Chris, whether it was a boy Chris or a girl Chris, some of the pressed flowers. All of a sudden Eddie realised that's what he'd do, he'd *pretend* to be a girl. Just get her not to put the Miss on the envelopes any more.

And for four years Eddie Barton and Christine Taylor wrote to each other, long long letters, pouring out their hearts in a way that neither of them could to anyone else.

Chris told how her mother had this dream of moving out of the city and into a house on an estate, a place with a garden and a garage, even though they didn't have a car. Chris hated the idea, she would be miles from the library and the art gallery and the places she went to when school was over. The girls at school didn't want to do anything except go to the sweet shop and talk about the fellows. Chris sent a picture of herself in school uniform and wanted Edith to send one too. In desperation Eddie sent one of Leo which he stole from The Glen when he was visiting there.

Chris wrote and said she hadn't thought of him as tall like that. She had a feeling from what he wrote that he was short and stocky and had hair that stood up. Eddie trembled when he read this as if she had found him out. He thanked the heavens that Scotland was so far away and that she would never visit. It would have been better still if she had been in Argentina, then the thought needn't have crossed his mind.

It was hard to keep up the fiction of school life when he had left Shancarrig school at the age of fourteen and now went to the Brothers in the big town every day on the bus. He told Chris that truly he wasn't happy at school and he preferred to talk about other things in his letters, like the rowan tree, like the fact that his mother was getting headaches from working too hard, like he wondered was there any way of finding out where his father was, so that he could just let him know what things were like.

He wrote about Father Barry and how he had been preaching about this village in Peru called Vieja Piedra and then had to stop, and people said the Bishop didn't like money going out of the diocese to foreign places instead of being spent at home. Chris seemed to understand. She asked him why didn't he help his mother with the sewing – it wasn't hard, they could share it.

Eddie burned with frustration over that. He realised he had made himself sound selfish and unhelpful while his only crime was that he was a boy. Everyone knew boys didn't do sewing.

He was getting on very badly at school, but he couldn't tell Chris. How could he tell of Brothers who were loud and rough with him, who often hit him with a belt when he least expected it, and one who even mocked his stutter?

Chris asked him for another picture when he was sixteen. He had none of Leo. He couldn't bear to ask her personally so he wrote her a note.

'For a long complicated reason which I'll explain to you some time, I need a photograph of you. I want you to know that it has nothing at all to do with that promise of marriage I once forced you to give. You are free from that vow, but could I have a picture next week?'

She didn't reply, but then just before his sixteenth birthday he met her unexpectedly in the middle of the town.

'Did you forget the picture?' he asked.

Leo looked distracted. She hadn't remembered.

'Please Leo, it is very important. You know I wouldn't ask you unless it were. Can I come to the house and see if you have one?'

It *was* important. Chris had sent him a picture of herself on *her* sixteenth birthday a month back. A dark girl with big eyes and a nice smile.

'*No.*' He had never known her so adamant.

'Well then, will you bring me one?'

She looked at him, as if deciding what would be the way that would cause less interference in her life.

'Oh God, I'll bring you one,' she said.

He looked hurt. 'I thought we were friends in a sort of a way,' he said.

'Yes, yes of course we are,' she relented.

'So, don't bite my head off. It's got nothing to do with being engaged.'

'What?'

Eddie decided that Leo Murphy never listened to anything anyone said. She wasn't like Chris Taylor who cared about everything.

Except of course that she thought Eddie was a girl, a fellow conspirator in life. Eddie had been forced to write and say that yes he had got his periods when he was eleven. He had managed to say that he fancied the film star Fernando Lamass and that he liked red tartan as a colour for a winter skirt.

But mainly Chris wrote about interesting things – she only descended into these female things every now and then. It always gave him a start.

He posted the photograph and waited.

He knew that she would write with a card for his birthday, usually flowers and bows and entirely unsuitable things he couldn't show to anyone. This year it was a small envelope.

'Do not open until Wednesday 29th,' it said.

Eddie took it away to read when he was on his own. He had explained to his mother that he had this pen-friend, a boy in Scotland.

'What does the Scots boy say?' his mother asked him from time to time.

'Not much. All about flowers and trees,' Eddie would say.

'Keeps you out of harm's way, I suppose,' Mrs Barton would say.

Eddie knew she sounded gruffer than she was.

In his bedroom he opened the letter from Chris and got such a shock that he had to sit down.

'I always told myself that when we were both sixteen I would tell you that I have known since the very beginning that you were a boy. I was afraid to tell you that I knew in case you'd stop writing. I *like* you being a boy. You're the nicest boy I ever met in my whole life. Happy birthday dear Eddie and thank you for your friendship.'

His first feeling was shame. How dare she have made a fool of him for four years? Then bewilderment. *How* did she know? He had agreed to having periods, being at a convent, wearing a red plaid skirt. Then came an entirely different feeling. A feeling of excitement. She knew he was a boy, and she liked him. She was afraid she'd lose him. He went to the drawer where her letters were. He read bits over and over.

'You are so easy to talk to. You really understand. You have a marvellous mind, people here are so ignorant.'

Eddie Barton was sixteen years old and in love. He went to Barna Woods. It was icy cold but he didn't care. He found an old log which he sat on, and thought about the new turn of events in his life. He must put a letter in the post to her before six o'clock. There was no question of going to school, there was far too much to think about.

Through the day he felt overwhelming regret about some of the things he had written, whole paragraphs that she must have known were lies. Then he was swept with an irritation. Why had she asked him to help his mother with the sewing when she knew he was a boy? But he mainly wanted his letter to her to be perfect and to say what he felt without frightening her off. He took the picture out again. Huge dark eyes, like an Italian. Then his heart lurched. She had no idea what he looked like. She thought he looked like Leo Murphy. Well, no she didn't, but she had no idea. Eddie wished he was tall and strong, that he looked like Niall Hayes' cousin, Richard, who had come to visit.

Everyone said he was so handsome. Eddie wished more than ever that he could find his father and ask his advice.

But his father didn't turn up on Eddie's sixteenth birthday any more than he had on any other anniversary, so he knew he would have to write it alone.

He decided to go to Miss Ross and her mother and ask if he could write the letter there. It would be warm and dry. There would be no fear of his mother asking him what he was doing, saying something that was bound to irritate him. He often did some work on the garden for Miss Ross, who wouldn't mind him coming in on a wild cold day like this.

She was just coming back from the school for her lunch when he arrived. She wore a belted raincoat which swished as she walked along. Eddie wondered if Chris wore a raincoat like that. He might ask her but somehow it seemed a bit personal, that swishy sound. Something he didn't want her to know about, and the feeling it gave him.

Miss Ross looked tired and pale. She said he was an answer to prayer. If he would just chop a few logs for her not only could he sit by the fire and write for the afternoon, she would give him a big bowl of soup as well.

'It's my birthday, Miss Ross. That's why,' he said.

She seemed to find the explanation perfectly satisfactory, and asked nothing about why he had absented himself from the Brothers without any permission. She couldn't imagine Brother O'Brien saying to a lad of sixteen that he should celebrate the day.

'What kind of a letter? Is it an application for a job?' Miss Ross asked.

'No. It's more a letter to a friend.' He was scarlet as he spoke.

'Yes, well if the friend's in a convent boarding school don't forget the nuns might read it.' Miss Ross was full of wisdom.

'No, the friend's not in a boarding school.' Eddie knew he sounded stiff.

'Well, you're all right then.' Eddie thought Miss Ross sounded as if she was trying to be cheerful for his sake. And maybe a little envious.

Eddie looked around the room before he began his letter. He had never noticed the house very much before, thinking of it as a place to take off his shoes before he came in from the garden. He remembered that Maura Brennan, who had been his friend at Shancarrig school, had always said she loved this house and that when she got old she would have one just like it, with lovely pieces of furniture that she would polish until they shone and china ornaments on shelves and thick rich velvet curtains. Eddie admired the colours; everything seemed to match with everything else, not like in his own home where the carpet was brown and the curtains were yellow and the table cloth was green; it looked as if everything was chosen to clash with everything else. He knew this was not the case, it was because they didn't have enough money to get things that would look nice. His mother had great taste in the clothes she made. She was always advising her customers what went well with their eyes or their complexion.

But still, that didn't help him to write to Chris Taylor.

He sat for a long time, the old grandfather clock ticking. Miss Ross had gone back to Shancarrig school; her mother was having her afternoon rest upstairs.

'Dearest Chris,' Eddie wrote. 'I can't tell you how good it is to be able to write as myself. I wanted to so often but once I had begun with the silly lie I had to keep it going in case you stopped writing. Your letters are the most important thing in my life. I couldn't bear them to stop.'

And then it was easy. Page after page. He tried to imagine himself sitting in this small house in Glasgow. She called it a two up two down, meaning the number of rooms. Her mother had never realised the dream of moving to an estate. Her father kept pigeons and hadn't much interest in anything else. Her two brothers were at sea and only came home for a very short visit now and then. She wanted to go to a school of art but she wasn't good enough. Her mother said to get a job in the florists and be grateful for it; most people had to do work they hated. At least Chris liked flowers so she'd be ahead of the game.

What would this girl like to read from Eddie, now revealed as a man? He knew one thing. There must be no more pretence.

'I'm small and square and have hair that sticks up. I don't think I ever told you properly about school and how much I hate it, because when I was meant to be a girl I couldn't tell you how rough they are there and how they think I'm as thick as the wall. I don't think I am, and your letters make me think I have something.'

There was no trouble finding the words. When he read it over he thought she would think it was a fair explanation for his years of deceit. Not too much apology, more setting the record straight.

He was surprised when Miss Ross came back from school.

'That's a letter and a half, Eddie,' she said approvingly.

'Would you have said I was thick, Miss Ross?'

'No, I wouldn't, and you're not,' she said.

He grinned at her and ran off. She looked out the door and saw him heading for the post office, skipping and jumping over puddles.

The letters came fast and thick. They wrote to each other about hopes and fears, about books and paintings, about colours and designs. They kept nothing back.

'If we ever meet I must show you the ferns of Barna Woods,' he wrote once.

'What do you mean "if we ever meet"? It's "when we meet"!' she wrote back, and his heart felt leaden because he knew he had made Shancarrig sound too beautiful, too exciting, too romantic for Christine Taylor.

'That boy must have nothing to do but write letters,' his mother said one day when the usual fat envelope arrived from Scotland.

'It's not a boy, it's a girl.' Eddie knew he'd have to explain some time.

'What do you mean? Did he turn into a girl all of a sudden?' Mrs Barton didn't like the sound of it being a girl.

'No, it's a different one.' Eddie didn't feel that any further explanation would help.

'Why Scotland?' his mother said.

'It's nice and far away,' he grinned. 'If I have to be writing to a girl, Ma, isn't it better that I write to one in a far off country?'

'At your age you shouldn't be writing to a girl at all. There'll be plenty of time for that later. Too much time if you're your father's son.'

There had been much mention over the years of Ted Barton's interest in women, always vague and generalised, never specific and detailed. Eddie had long given up the hope of getting any more information than the sketchy amount he already had. His father had been thrown out because of a known association with another woman. When he had left Shancarrig that night the woman had not gone with him. She might even be someone he knew. Someone he had spoken to. If only it was someone nice like Miss Ross then maybe she could have told him more about the man who had left their lives.

'Did my father ever like Miss Ross?' he asked his mother suddenly.

'Maddy Ross?' His mother looked at him in surprise.

'Yes. Could she have been his love?'

'Well, given that she was about twelve or thirteen when he left town it isn't entirely likely, but that doesn't say it should be ruled out either.' His mother had even managed a wry smile as she said this.

Eddie thought she was less bitter. He must remember to tell this to Chris when he wrote; they had no secrets. She told him about her father being laid off in the shipyard and her mother getting an extra shift in the factory. Chris was doing Saturdays in the local flower shop. It wasn't like she thought it would be, working with flowers. It was very mechanical, stiff little arrangements and awful cheaty ways of making flowers look alive when they were almost dead.

They wrote to each other when they should have been trying a last desperate effort at their books. Christine said that they were snobby in her convent and didn't like the girls whose mothers worked in factories. Eddie wrote that the Brothers had a down on anyone with a bit of soul at all and that they had him written off as a no-hoper. The results of the exams were a foregone conclusion to them both.

In the summer of 1957 they wrote and told each other of poor results, bad marks and limited futures.

'I had a word with Brother O'Brien. He doesn't think it worth trying to repeat the year,' Eddie's mother said glumly. She had taken the bus into the big town to buy materials, threads, zip fasteners and spare pieces for the sewing machine. She had used the opportunity to visit the school.

It hadn't been a happy encounter.

'I told him that other boys had fathers who could pay for this kind of thing, but that we weren't in the lucky position to know where your father is or has been for the last dozen years.' Her face had that old bitter look which Eddie hated.

'Ma, you threw him out. You asked him to go. You can't keep blaming him for everything after he went, only for what he did before he went.'

'And that was plenty for one lifetime, let me assure you.'

'You always *assure* me these things but you never explain them.'

'Oh, you've words at will, just like him.'

'And was Brother O'Brien sympathetic? I bet he wasn't. He couldn't care about anyone's father, or mother, or anyone at all.'

His mother gave him an odd look.

'He wasn't sympathetic. Neither to you nor to me. But I think he does care about people. He said there was no point in my lamenting the absence of a husband, that it was mainly women who did all the consulting whether their husbands were alive or around or whatever.'

'And what else?'

'He said that you had got it into your head you were too good for the school, above them and their plain ways. And that would have been fine if you were a real artist burning to paint or to write, but the way things were he didn't know what would become of you. He sounded sorry.'

To Eddie it had the ring of truth. That was exactly the way Brother O'Brien would speak, and there was some truth in it. He could see the big man with his red face regretting that he couldn't find a place for the boy. Brother O'Brien loved his boys to get into banks and insurance offices, the Civil Service, and the very odd time even into a university.

There would be nowhere for Eddie Barton.

If he hadn't had his lifeline of letters to hold him together as support and strength Eddie would have been very depressed that summer. But Chris wrote every day. She said they must get themselves out of this situation. She would not work in a factory like her mother, nor would she train to be a florist.

They had begun to talk of love now, they ended each letter with more and more yearning and wishes that they could meet. Eddie said that perhaps he had made Shancarrig sound too attractive. Maybe they could meet in some foreign land where there would be warm winds and palm trees. Chris said that nobody could love anybody if they met in the grey streets around her home. She was all for somewhere exotic too.

The world of fantasy became an important part of their letter-writing. It almost took over from the practical side. Chris Taylor went to work in a department store in Glasgow. She hated it, she said. It was very tiring. Her legs ached more than usual. Eddie wrote and asked did her legs usually ache, she had never mentioned it before. But she didn't mention it again so he thought it must have been just a phrase.

Eddie Barton went to work in Dunne's Hardware. He hated it. He wrote to Chris about the days talking to farmers who came in to buy chicken wire and plough parts. He said he was sick of harrows and rakes and if he had to talk about linseed oil or red oxide for painting a barn again he thought he might actually lie down and die. He wrote about how ignorant the Dunnes were. Their aunt, Nellie Dunne, ran a small grocery shop and she gave people credit which was the only reason why anyone shopped there. Eddie worked for old Mr Dunne and his sons Brian and Liam. Eileen, who was his own age, worked in Ryan's Hotel, but was always giving him the eye when she came in.

'I tell you this...' he wrote to Chris, 'not to make myself sound great or to make you jealous, but to remind myself how lucky I am that stupid girls like Eileen with her forward pushy ways form no part of my life now that I know what love is. Now that I have you.'

Sometimes she wrote about going to a dance, but she said she sat in a seat on the balcony most of the time and thought about what he had said in his last letter.

Sometimes Nessa Ryan and Leo Murphy came into the shop to talk to him. The Dunnes never minded him talking to them because they were as near to the Quality as Shancarrig possessed. If Maura Brennan came in, or anyone else from the cottages, it would be different. But old Mr Dunne seemed to take positive pleasure out of a visit from young Miss Ryan of the hotel and young Miss Murphy from The Glen.

'And how goes the good Major?' he would ask Leo about her father.

'Talking to himself as usual,' Leo muttered once and they all giggled.

Mr Dunne didn't like such disrespect.

'And how are they all in Ireland's leading hostelry?' he would ask Nessa Ryan about her family's hotel.

Nessa always said it was doing fine thank you.

Eddie wrote to Chris about how strained and worried Leo Murphy looked when she should have had no worries in the world. She had got six honours in her Leaving Certificate. She had all the money in the world; she could have gone to university in Cork or Galway or Dublin, yet she always seemed to be biting her lip.

Chris wrote back and said you never knew what worries people had. Perhaps Leo wasn't well, maybe it was her health. What did she look like? In shame Eddie wrote and said that Leo looked like him, or rather, the pictures he had sent of him when he was meant to be a girl were of Leo.

'She's very good-looking,' Chris wrote back anxiously.

'I never noticed it,' he wrote. 'Perhaps I should have stayed a girl.'

'No. You're lovely as you are,' she said in the next letter.

They knew that they must talk. Neither household had a phone but Chris could use the public phone and Eddie could be in Ryan's Hotel waiting for the call. They rehearsed it in letters for some weeks.

'We mightn't like each other's voices,' Chris wrote. 'But it's important to remember that we like each other so the voice doesn't matter.'

'What do you mean we *like* each other?' wrote Eddie. 'We love each other. That's what we must remember on Saturday night.'

They made it Saturday so that they could look forward to it all week.

He dressed himself up and put on a clean shirt.

'On the town again I suppose.' His mother hardly seemed to look up but she had taken in that he was smartly turned out.

'Aw, no, Mam. There's nowhere much to go on the town in Shancarrig.'

'Well, where are you going if I might ask?' Her tone wasn't as sharp as the words. She was aching to know.

'Just down to Ryan's Hotel, Mam, for a cup of coffee.'

'Eddie . . . ?'

'Yes, Mam.'

'Eddie, I know I'm nagging you but you won't . . .'

'Mam, I told you I don't drink. I didn't like the smell of it or the taste of it the once I tried.'

'I don't mean drink.' She looked him up and down, a boy setting out for a date, for romance.

'What do you mean?'

'You wouldn't get involved with that Eileen Dunne, now would you? They'd be bad people to get on the wrong side of . . .'

'Who are you telling! Don't I work for them?'

'But Eileen . . . ?'

He knelt beside his mother and looked up into her face.

'If she were the last woman in Ireland I wouldn't want her.'

Anyone would have known that he was speaking the truth. Eddie's mother waved him off with a lighter heart.

Chris was to ring at eight. Eddie positioned himself in the hall. The telephone would ring at the reception desk, then whoever was on duty would look around and say, 'Eddie Barton, I don't know . . . oh yes, *there* he is,' and she'd motion Eddie to go into the booth. Then he would speak to her. To the girl he loved.

Another good thing about it being a Saturday was that awful Eileen Dunne wouldn't be working at the desk. She was in the dining room on Saturdays, her dress tight across the bottom and the bosom, and a small white apron making no attempt to cover her at all.

Eddie's heart was beating so strongly it reminded him of the big clock in Shancarrig school and the thudding sounds it made as the seconds ticked on.

Soon, soon. Ten minutes. Nine.

He jumped a foot in the air when he heard the phone ring. He hadn't noticed that Eileen Dunne *was* working at Reception tonight. Please may she not make any remark, may she not say something stupid that Chris would hear all the way away in Scotland.

'Yes, he's here. Hold on. *Edd . . . ie?*'

He was at the desk.

'Yes?'

'There's someone on the phone for you. Will you take it here at the desk? God, you're looking like a dog's dinner tonight.'

'I'll go into the box,' he said, his face red with fury.

'Right. Hold on till I get this bloody thing through. There's more plugs and wires than a hedgehog's backside. Are you going in to town to the dance?'

He ran in to the dark phone booth, his hands trembling. Damn Eileen Dunne to hell. Please may Chris not have heard.

'Hello?' he said tentatively.

It must be the Scottish telephone operator on the line. He could hardly understand her. She was saying something about difficulty in getting through.

'Can you put me on to Chris, please?' He knew his voice was shaky but it had been a bit of luck that she hadn't come straight through. She wouldn't have heard that stupid stupid Eileen. Any moment she'd talk to him.

'This *is* Chris,' he managed to decipher from the strange speech. 'Do you mean you canna hear me?'

It wasn't Chris's voice. It was like someone imitating a Scottish comedian. Every word was canna and wouldna.

'That's never you, not you yourself, Chris?' he said. She must be playing a joke.

'Och, Eddie, stop putting on that Irish blarney bit. You're like the fellows they have at Christmas concerts in the church, with their afther doing this and afther doing that.'

There was silence. They realised that neither of them was putting on an act. This is the way they were. The silence was broken by their laughter.

'Oh God, Eddie . . . I forgot. I had you talking normally in my mind.'

His heart was full of love. This strange way she spoke didn't matter a bit. 'I thought you'd be like a real person too,' he said.

Then it was back to the way they were in letters. Until the three minutes ran out.

'I love you, Chris, more than ever.'

'And I love you too,' she said.

They lived for Saturdays, and yet as they wrote to each other the phone calls were never as good as they expected. Sometimes they literally didn't understand what the other was saying and they wasted precious time explaining.

They were desperate to meet. The time was very long.

'We'd better meet soon before we're too old to recognise each other,' she wrote.

'While we still remember what we wrote to each other.'

They each kept their letters in shoe boxes. It seemed a small thing but a bond ... another bond. Yet they hesitated each to ask the other to their town. Eddie couldn't bear the explanations, the doing up of the spare room, the questioning from his mother, the eyes of Shancarrig.

Chris said that if he had found it hard to understand her voice then her family and her neighbours in Glasgow would be incomprehensible.

She obviously yearned for Barna Woods and the hill with the big rock on it, the rock that gave its name to the town. She wanted to see Eddie's pink house and meet his mother.

He wanted her here and he didn't want her. He wanted to leave Shancarrig for ever, and yet he couldn't. One man had left his mother already, Eddie couldn't go.

Then at last he heard himself inviting her. He didn't really intend to, it just came out.

It had been a long hard day in Dunne's when nothing had gone right. Old Mr Dunne was like a devil, Liam had been scornful, Brian had been giving him orders, and to make matters worse their cousin Foxy who had been in Eddie's class at school had come back for a visit.

Foxy worked on the buildings in England. He was doing well by all accounts. He had started by making billycans of tea for Irishmen working on the lump, building the big roads over in Britain. He came home every year, eyes bright and darting around him as usual.

Normally Eddie was pleased to see Foxy, he had a quick wit and was always ready with a joke.

Today it hadn't been like that. 'Don't let him speak to you like that,' Foxy said to Eddie when Mr Dunne had called him an ignorant bosthoon.

'Fine words, Foxy. He's only an uncle to you, but he pays my week's wages.'

'Still and all, you're letting him walk over you. You'll be here for the rest of your life with a shop coat on you stuck behind a counter.'

'And what are you going to be?' Eddie had flared back.

'I've got the hell out of here. I wouldn't sit here listening to my uncle mumbling and bumbling, and my Aunt Nellie letting people run up bad debts because they're Quality. I'm in England and I'll make a pile of money. And then I'll come back and marry Leo Murphy.'

It was the longest speech that Foxy had ever made. Eddie had been surprised.

'And will Leo marry *you*?'

'Not now, she won't. Not the way I am. No one would marry either of us, Eddie. We're eejits. We have only one good suit each with an arse in the trousers of it. We have to *do* something with our lives instead of standing round here like fools. What class of a woman would want the likes of us?'

'I don't know. We might have a charm of our own.' Eddie was being light-hearted but he felt that Foxy was right.

Foxy turned away impatiently. 'I can see you in twenty years still saying that, Eddie. This place makes us all slow and stupid. It's like a muddy river dragging us down.'

Eddie had been thinking about it all day. He didn't dress up for the phone call that night. It was his turn to call the Glasgow phone box.

'Come over to Ireland. Come to Shancarrig,' he said when Chris answered the phone.

'When? When will I come?'

'As soon as you can. I'm sick of being without you,' he said. 'There's nothing at all else in my life except you.'

Their letters changed tone. It was confident now. It was 'when' not 'if'. It was definite. The love was there, the need, the surprise that one other person could feel exactly the same about everything as another.

There were the details.

Chris would take her two weeks holidays from the flower shop. Eddie could take his two weeks off from Dunne's. She would get the boat from Stranraer to Larne, and the train to Belfast maybe?

'Will I come to meet you there? I've never been to the North of Ireland. It'll be familiar to you, red buses, red pillar boxes. Like England.'

'Like Scotland,' she corrected him. She had never been to England in her life.

Or would she take a train to Wales, and get the boat from Holyhead? Maybe that would be a nicer way to go. She could see Dun Laoghaire and a bit of Dublin before taking the train to Shancarrig.

'I don't want you wandering around on your own, meeting Dublin fellows. I'll come and meet you off the boat,' he suggested.

Chris said no, she wanted to arrive in Shancarrig on the train herself. She knew about the station, and the flowers that now spelt out the word Shancarrig. He had written that long ago to her.

Eddie could be on the platform.

He prayed that it would be a fine fortnight, that the sun would shine into Barna Woods between the branches, that there would be a sparkle on the River Grane. He knew you shouldn't pray for something bad to happen to another human but he hoped that somehow Eileen Dunne would be in hospital when Chris arrived, and that Nessa Ryan wouldn't be superior towards him, and that he'd be free of Brian and Liam Dunne and their bad-tempered father because he was on holidays.

He hoped most of all that his mother would be nice to Chris. They had never had anyone to stay, and Eddie had distempered the walls, and painted the woodwork in the small stuffy room they had called a box room up to now. His mother had been curiously quiet.

'What kind of a girl is she?' was all she had asked.

'A girl I write to, I write to her a lot. I like her through the post and on the telephone. I've asked her to come over here so that ... well, so that I wouldn't be the one going off on you.'

His mother looked away so that he wouldn't see the look of gratitude in her face. But he saw all the same.

'I'll make curtains for the room,' she said.

Please let them like each other.

They had got ham for tea, cooked ham and tomatoes, and a Fullers chocolate cake with four chocolate buttons on the top.

His mother had cleared the sewing away so that the place would look like a normal house. There were blue curtains on the window of the box room, and a matching bedspread. On the makeshift dressing table there was a little blue cloth and Eddie had gathered a bunch of flowers.

It was nearly time. The train would be at three. Only four hours. Three. Two. It was time.

*

Liam Dunne was on the platform; there was a delivery coming down with the guard on the train.

'What are you doing?' Liam asked. 'Aren't you meant to be on your holidays? If you're doing nothing you could give me a hand ...?'

'I most definitely *am* on my holidays and I'm meeting a friend,' Eddie said firmly.

The train whistled and came around the corner. She got off. She carried a big suitcase, square with little firm bits over the corners like leather triangles to preserve it.

She had a red jacket and a navy skirt, a navy shoulder bag and a huge bright smile.

He had been afraid for a moment that she might think Liam Dunne was him. Liam was taller and good-looking in a rangy sort of way. Eddie felt like a barrel. He wished his spine would shoot up and make him willowy.

He started to walk towards her and saw her foot. Chris Taylor had a big built-up shoe. He willed his eyes away from it, and on to her smiling eager face.

Liam was busy with the guard, hauling things from the luggage van, and nobody was watching them.

Eddie had never kissed anyone in his life apart from fumbles at dances. He put his arms around Chris.

'Welcome to Shancarrig,' he said first, then he kissed her very gently. She clung to him.

'I didn't tell you about my foot,' she said, her face working anxiously.

'What about your foot?' He forced himself not to look at it again to see how bad it was. Could she walk? Did it drag? His head was whirling.

'I didn't want you to pity me,' she said.

'Me? Pity *you*? You must be mad,' he said.

'I can walk and everything, and I can keep up. I'll be able to see every bit of Barna Woods with you after tea.'

She looked very young and frightened. She must have been worried about this for ages, like he worried about the place not being as nice as he described.

'I don't know what you're going on about,' he tried to reassure her, but he knew it wasn't working.

'My leg, Eddie. I've got one shorter than the other, you see. I wear a special shoe.'

He could read how hard it was for her to say this. How often she must have rehearsed it. He urged himself to find the right words.

He looked down at her foot in its black shoe with the big thick raised sole and heel.

'Does it hurt?' he asked.

'No, of course not, but it's the way it looks.'

He took both her hands in his. 'Chris, are you mad?' he asked her. 'Are you off your head? It's me. It's Eddie, your best friend. Your love. Do you think for a moment that it's part of the bargain that our legs had to be the same length?'

It was, as it happened, exactly the right thing to say. Chris Taylor burst into tears and hugged Eddie to her as if she was never going to leave him go. 'I love you, Eddie.'

'I love you too. Come on, let's go home.' He carried her case and they walked to the gate of the station.

Chris was still wiping her eyes. Liam Dunne stood watching them.

'Don't mind him.' He nodded in Eddie's direction. 'That fellow's as thick as the wall. He's always upsetting people and making them cry. There's plenty of real men in Shancarrig.'

She gave him a bright smile.

'I bet there are. I've come all the way from Scotland to investigate them.' She tucked her arm into Eddie's and they went out the gate.

Eddie felt ten feet tall.

'Who was that?' she whispered.

'Liam Dunne. Desperate . . .'

'Don't tell me. I know all about him. The younger son, the one that'll take over if Brian goes to England and the old man dies.'

'You know it all,' he said in wonder.

'I feel like I'm coming home.'

As they walked up the road and he pointed out Ryan's Hotel where he had sat waiting for the phone calls, and the church where Father Gunn waved to him cheerfully, the pubs and Nellie Dunne's grocery, he knew that in many ways she had come home. He knew that he had been right, she was the centre of his life. It would be fine when he brought her home to his mother.

Afterwards nobody could ever tell you exactly how and why Chris Taylor came to live in Shancarrig. One day she had never been heard of and then the next there she was, as if she had been part of the place all her life.

If people asked Mrs Barton about her they were told that she was a marvellous girl altogether and a dab hand at the sewing. There was nothing she couldn't turn her hand to. Look at the way she had made them go into furnishings, for example. Chris Taylor had loved the curtains and bedspread in her little room the day she arrived. Her praise was unstinting. Mrs Barton was a genius.

Eddie never thought of his mother's dressmaking as anything except a way to make a living; he knew she didn't particularly like some of the women whose dresses she made. He hadn't realised that the work was artistic in itself.

Chris opened his eyes for him. 'Look at the way the ribbon falls, look at the colours she's put together... Eddie, it's easy to see where you got your artistic sense from...'

His mother reddened with pleasure. There were no derisory remarks about his father. In fact, Chris was able to introduce the first reasonable conversation about the long-departed Ted Barton that had ever been held in this house.

'I suppose he was a restless kind of a man. Better for him to be gone in a lot of ways.'

And to his surprise Eddie heard his mother agreeing. Things had really begun to change around here.

Chris was part of Shancarrig.

They knew her coming in and out of Dunnes to see Eddie or to give him a message, they knew her in the hotel where she became friendly with Nessa Ryan. No one ever spoke dismissively to Chris Taylor as people had been known to do to Eddie Barton. She talked furnishings and fabrics to Nessa's mother. There was going to be a grant for the hotel to make it smarter, the kind of a place where tourist visitors might stay as well as commercial travellers.

They couldn't stay in Ryan's the way it was. Chris seemed to know the way it should be – pelmets, nice wooden pelmets covered in fabric, she had seen it all in an American magazine, you stuck the fabric to the plywood, and then the curtains draped properly down below. And, of course, bed covers to match.

Nessa Ryan and her mother were very excited.

'How would we get it started? Would we need to call someone in from Dublin? Who'd do it?'

'We would,' Chris said simply.

'We?'

'Mrs Barton and I. Let us do one room as a sample and see.'

'Wooden pelmets...? You couldn't do that...?'

'Eddie could, he could get the plywood. Liam Dunne could help him . . .'

The room was a huge success. The whole hotel would be done the same way. They had chosen a fabric which would tone in with Eddie's pressed flowers, with his large bold designs, flowers from Barna Woods, a place in the locality, especially commissioned from a local artist.

'You can't call me a local artist,' Eddie had protested.

'You are local. You live here, don't you?' she said simply.

The plans were afoot. Chris and Eddie's mother would be able to do it between them, but they needed someone to organise it, someone who would go and choose the right fabrics, someone with an eye for colour, someone whose pictures were already on the wall.

Flushed and happy Chris told Eddie the plan.

'You can leave Dunne's. We'll have a business, all of us . . .'

'I can't leave . . . if we get married I have to support you.'

'What's this *if*? Are you changing your mind? I've come over here and lived with you, set myself up shamelessly in your house and you say "if"?'

'I want to ask you something properly.'

'Not here, Eddie. Let's go up to the woods.'

Eddie's mother stood by the window and watched the two of them walk together, the limping figure of this strange strong Scottish girl, the stocky figure of her own son, who had grown taller since Chris had arrived.

She knew nothing about the kind of family over in Scotland who let their daughter wander away to another land without seeming to care.

She cared little now about the past. Once she had lived in it and felt burdened by it, now she thought only about the future, the proposal that was going to be made in Barna Woods and accepted, the new life that was ahead of all of them.

DR JIMS

I n Shancarrig they only knew him as Dr Blake for about six weeks. Then they all started to call him Dr Jims. It had to do with Maisie, of course. Maisie who couldn't pronounce any name properly, not even one as ordinary as James. She had been asked to call Dr James to the telephone and in front of the whole waiting room she had said that Dr Jims was wanted. Somehow, the name had stuck. James Blake was too young a man to be given a full title, not while the great Dr Nolan held sway in Shancarrig.

Jims Blake got very accustomed to people asking for the real doctor when they came to The Terrace, and if a call came in the night which Dr Jims answered, the gravest doubts were expressed. He learned to say that he was only holding the fort for the real doctor, and Dr Nolan would be along at a more convenient hour to give his approval.

But it was a good partnership – the wise old man who knew all the secrets of Shancarrig and the thin eager young man, son of a small farmer out the country. The old man who drank more brandy at night than was good for him and the young man who stayed up late reading the journals and reports ... they lived together peaceably. They had Maisie doting on both of them and resenting the fact that people kept getting sick and needing to disturb the two men in her life, the great Dr Nolan and poor young Dr Jims.

Dr Nolan was always saying that Jims Blake should find a wife for himself and Maisie was always saying that there was plenty of time.

Matters came to a head in 1940 when Dr Nolan was seventy and Dr Jims was thirty. It had been a busy time. There was a baby to be delivered in almost every house around them. A little girl Leonora up at The Glen, a first daughter to the Ryans at the hotel, another Dunne to the cottages, a son for the wife of wild Ted Barton, another Brennan to add to Paudie's brood.

Dr Jims would come back tired to the big house in The Terrace – the tall house, one of a line facing the hotel. It formed the centre of the town in a triangle with the row of shops. The bus stopped nearby and the movement of Shancarrig could be charted from any of the windows. Dr Jims' work took him to the far outlying districts as well, but the centre of life remained this small area around the place where he lived.

Even though it was comfortable there were ways in which it was not a real life. Dr Nolan was able to put it into words. 'I'm not going to let you make the same mistake as I did,' the old man said. 'A doctor needs a wife, really and truly. I had my chances and my choices in the old days, like you do now. But I was both too set and too easy in my ways. I didn't want to disrupt everything by bringing a woman in. I didn't really need a woman, I thought.'

'And you didn't either,' Dr Jims encouraged him. 'Didn't you have a full life ... where was there room for a wife? I've seen too many doctors' wives neglected, left out ... maybe the medical profession should take a vow of celibacy, like the clerics. It might be something we could bring up at the Irish Medical Association.'

'Don't make a jeer out of it, Jims. I'm serious.'

'So am I. How could I marry? Where would I get the stake for a house? I still send a bit home to the farm. You know that. I have to be averting my eyes for a bit, in case I think I might want a wife.'

'And who are you averting them from?' The old man drank his brandy, looking deep into the glass and not at his partner.

'Not anybody in particular.'

'But Frances Fitzgerald, maybe?'

'Ah, come on out of that. What could I offer Frances Fitzgerald?'

But Jims Blake knew that the old man had seen through him. He most desperately wanted to advance things with Frances, to go further than the games of tennis with other people present, the card evenings at The Glen or in Ryan's Hotel.

He'd hoped it hadn't been as transparent to other people.

Yet again Dr Nolan seemed to read his mind.

'Nobody would know but myself,' he said reassuringly. 'And you could offer her half a house here.'

'It's your house.'

'I won't be here for ever. It's taking more of this stuff to ease the pain in my gut.' He raised his brandy glass to show what he was referring to.

'The pain in your gut would be less if you had less of that stuff.'

'So you say, with the arrogance of youth ... We'll get the top two floors done up for you. The Dunnes can come in on Monday and lean on their picks and shovels and we'll see what they can do. Frances will want her own kitchen ... she won't want Maisie traipsing around after her.'

'Charles, I can't ... we don't even know if Frances is interested ...'

'We do,' said Dr Nolan.

Jims Blake didn't even wait to let that sink in.

'But I can't afford ...' he began.

Charles Nolan's face winced with pain and anger. 'Stop being such a defeatist, such a sniveller… I can't this, I can't that… Is that how you made yourself a doctor…?'

His face was red now proving his point.

'Listen here to me, Jims Blake, why do you think I took you on here? Think about it. It wasn't for your great moneyed connections and class. No. I took you on because you were a fighter, and a dogged little fellow. I liked your thin white face and your determination. I liked the way you forced them to let you study, and took jobs to make up the extra money that they couldn't give you. That's what people need in a doctor – someone who won't quit.'

'I could pay you so much a month for it, I suppose. I could take on more of the work.'

'Boy, aren't you doing almost all the work already. I'm only giving you what's fair…'

And it was settled like that. Dr Jims was to have the upstairs part of the house. Everyone said it was very sensible. After all, Dr Nolan wasn't getting any younger. Wasn't it sensible that a bedroom be built for him on the ground floor?

Maisie sniffed a bit, especially since it became known that Dr Jims was now courting Miss Fitzgerald.

The Dunne brothers were in regularly, wondering should the kitchen be facing the front or the back of the house. It might be good to have it looking out on the town. There was a nice view of Shancarrig from upstairs in The Terrace. But then, traditionally a kitchen was at the back. They puzzled at it.

Before they came to any solution their work was rendered unnecessary. Dr Charles Nolan died of the liver complaint he had been ignoring for some years, and he willed his house to his partner Dr Blake.

Before he died he spoke of it to Jims. 'You're a good lad. You'll keep it all going fine here, if only you'd learn to…'

'You've got years yet. Stop making a farewell speech,' Jims Blake said to the dying man.

'What I was *going* to say, if only you'd learn that there are people, myself included, who are quite glad to be coming to the end of their lives, who don't *want* to be told that there are years of pain and confusion ahead of them…'

Jims held his partner's hand – it was a simple gesture of solidarity where no words would have worked.

'That's more like it,' said Dr Nolan. 'Now, will you promise me to have a family and a real life for yourself? Don't be forced to leave this place to some whippersnapper of a junior partner, like I am!'

'You can't leave it all to me ...' He was aghast.

'I was hoping to leave it to Frances as well. Tell me you've made some move in that direction ...'

'Yes. We were hoping to marry ...' His voice choked, realising that his benefactor wouldn't now be at the wedding.

'That's good, very good. I'm tired now. Get me into hospital tomorrow, Jims. I don't want to die in the house where she's coming as a bride.'

'It's your house. Die wherever you want to,' Jims blazed at him.

The old man smiled. 'I like to hear you talk that way. And where I would like to die is the hospital. Tell that young Father Gunn to come up there to me, not to be upsetting Maisie by coming here. And move that brandy bottle back to my reach.'

It didn't take Shancarrig long to recognise Dr Jims as the real doctor. Everything had changed. There was no old Dr Nolan any more to know their secrets so they told them to Dr Jims instead. He was a married man now, of course, and his wife a very gentle person – one of the Fitzgeralds who owned a big milling business.

It had been a good match – that's what outsiders thought. But they only knew the surface. They didn't know about passion and love and understanding. Frances, with her gentle solemn face transformed so often with a quick smile that lit up her whole being, was a wife that he never dreamed possible.

She would creep up behind him and lock her arms around his neck. She would feed him pieces of food from her plate when Maisie wasn't looking. When he was called out at night Frances sometimes left a note on his pillow saying, 'Wake me up. I want to welcome you home properly.' In every way she made him grow in confidence. Jims Blake walked with a lighter step and a smile in his eyes.

The fact that Dr Nolan had left him the house made Dr Jims even more respected in the community. If the old doctor had thought so much of him then this must be a good man. Sometimes Jims Blake felt unworthy of all the respect he got in Shancarrig.

When he visited his dour family on their small bleak farm and saw the lifestyle that he would have been condemned to had he not fought so hard to study medicine, he felt guilty. He was saddened that they had so little, and even the money he gave them was stored under a mattress, not used to buy his mother and father a better standard of life.

He had tried to explain this guilt to Frances but she calmed him down. He had done everything he could for the family. Surely that was as much as anyone was expected to do – he couldn't do any more.

Frances said that *they* were a family now she and Jims and the baby they were expecting. There was no tie that bound them to the bleak family of Blakes in the small wet farm, or the distant, undemonstrative Fitzgeralds wrapped up in their business affairs. They were a little unit in themselves.

And so it was for a while.

Jims often thought that the spirit of old Dr Nolan would have been pleased to hear the way that Number Three The Terrace rang with laughter. First Eileen was born, then Sheila. No son and heir yet, but as people said, God would send the boy in his own good time.

There were many attempts for the boy – all ending in miscarriage.

Frances Blake was a frail woman – the efforts to hold a child to full term were taking a great toll on her health.

Several times Jims asked himself what would the old doctor have advised if he had been involved in a family where this had been the situation. He could almost hear Dr Nolan's voice.

'This is a thing you could work out between the pair of you . . . Now the good God up in heaven doesn't have a book of rules saying you must do this or that, and so many times . . . The good God expects us to use our intelligence . . .'

And he might go on to explain some of the most elemental details of times of high fertility and low fertility, suggesting the latter as the wiser time to indulge in what he called the business of marriage.

But always he would urge the couple to talk to each other.

Jims Blake somehow found it hard to talk to his own wife.

The problem was all the greater because he loved her so much. He desired her *and* he wanted to protect her. A combination of that was hard to rationalise. He had worked out her ovulation as carefully as he could, they had tried to make love at the times she was least likely to conceive. He had held her face in his hands and assured her that his two little girls were plenty, they didn't need to try for a son. Let them live their lives without putting her to any additional strain, without placing her health in danger.

Sometimes she looked sad, he didn't know if it was because she feared that he didn't desire her as much as he once had. Perhaps it was because she really did yearn to give him a son. He found it impossible to believe that two people who loved each other so much could still have areas of misunderstanding. And yet, whenever he approached her she seemed so receptive and willing that he had to believe this was what she wanted too.

When Frances became pregnant again in 1946 the girls Eileen and Sheila were five and four — two cherubs sitting in their Viyella nightdresses and red flannel dressing gowns while he read them stories. This time he hoped for a son to join them.

In the coldest winter that Ireland had ever known Frances Blake gave birth to her son. And in the house with log fires burning in every room, with a midwife from the hospital in the big town in attendance, as well as her husband who had, even at the age of thirty-seven, delivered thousands of children into the world . . . she died.

They had never even discussed what to call the baby. They hadn't dared to hope it would live, nor had they dared to hope it would be a boy.

Father Gunn, arriving at the house to the news of the birth and death, enquired if the child was sickly, and whether there should be an emergency baptism.

'I think the child is healthy enough.' Jims Blake's voice was empty.

'Well, we'll leave it for a while then. It'll bring some cheer to the household to have a baptism.' Father Gunn was optimistic. He tried to see some light at the end of the seemingly endless dark tunnels of this particular winter. He had been burying far more than he baptised.

'Maybe you could get it over with, Father.' The young doctor looked white and strained.

'Not now, Jims. Wait a bit. Give the lad a start, find godparents for him. Think of a name. He has a life to live, Frances would want that for him.'

'He mightn't live, let's do it now.'

Something about the face of Jims Blake made Father Gunn know that this was not so. But he couldn't close the doors of heaven to a little soul.

He still had his stole on.

'Bill Hayes is downstairs, he could be the godfather. What about a godmother?'

'Maisie will stand for him . . .'

'But later, the boy might like to . . .'

'It doesn't matter what the boy might like later on. Will we do it or will we not?'

Father Gunn said the words of baptism while pouring the holy water on the head of Declan Blake. He had asked was there to be any other name – people usually had two.

'Declan will do,' said Jims Blake.

Maisie, her face red from crying, her voice almost inaudible from a heavy chest cold, made the vows together with Bill Hayes, the local solicitor – they would look after the spiritual welfare of this child.

Bill Hayes, the local solicitor in Shancarrig, had children the same age as Jims Blake's, including a newly born baby girl, safely delivered from a living wife not four weeks previously.

Never short of the right word in terms of the law, Bill Hayes found himself totally unable to give any meaningful sympathy at a time like this.

'If you were a drinking man I'd get you drunk, Jims,' he said.

'But you're not a drinking man either, Bill.'

'Still, I could become one if it would help you.'

The doctor shook his head.

He had seen too many people opting for this solution.

'Would I sit with you downstairs by the fire?'

Poor Bill Hayes was truly at a loss for the comforting small talk that came to him so easily in his office when consoling those who had been cut out of wills or who had lost a court case. Nothing seemed appropriate to say.

'No. Go home, Bill. I beg you. I'll sit by myself. There's a doctor coming in from the town. He'll be staying in the spare room tonight . . . in case I get a call-out. He'll do it for me tonight. I wouldn't be much good to anyone.'

'Did Frances know she had a son?' Bill Hayes asked. He knew his wife would want to know – it wasn't the kind of question he would normally ask.

'No. She knew nothing at all.'

'Well, well. He'll grow up a credit to you both. I know that.'

Jims tried to remember that he had a son, a boy who would grow in this house, as the girls had grown. A baby who would be fed with a bottle, and who would cry in the night. A baby who would smile and flail with little fists. A baby boy who would sit in a dressing gown and want to hear stories read aloud to him.

Suddenly it was all too much for him. He could see other pictures crowding in. A little boy with a school satchel, struggling along the road to Shancarrig school. A boy with a hurley going to a match. He almost felt dizzy with the responsibility of it all.

A wave of loneliness swept over him. There would be no Frances ever again. No Frances so proud of the girls in their little powder-blue coats, going up the church with them at mass. No Frances to talk to in the evening. She was lying ice-cold already. Tomorrow she would be taken to the church and then the whole of Shancarrig would process to the churchyard.

His father and mother would come, his sisters and his brother, rosary beads dangling from their hands, nudging each other, whispering. No help or support to anyone.

The Fitzgeralds would come, the women in hats looking down at the Blake women in headscarves. There would be stiff and stilted conversation in the house.

Not one of them knew how terrible it was that his wife had died, and that he felt responsible. If it hadn't been for that time ... the time they must have conceived the child ... Frances would be alive and well tonight.

He said goodbye to Bill Hayes, who left with some relief. And then Jims Blake sat down at his fire and tried to count his blessings, like he always urged his patients to do.

He listed a good marriage with Frances as a blessing. Nearly seven years of it. Great passion, great friendship, a happy time full of hope.

He listed his little girls, he listed the big house in The Terrace, left to him by his good, kind partner. And a big steady doctor's practice. He counted in having escaped from his own family as a blessing, and he added his own good health. He did not include his son, the baby not yet one day old.

Everyone said that it was the worst funeral they were ever at – the rain lashing against the church, the traces of old snow slippery on the ground, a freezing east wind as they walked to the cemetery.

Jims Blake insisted that the girls be taken home after the mass. In fact, as he stood shaking hands with the congregation of sympathisers, many of them with heavy colds and flu, he begged them not to come to the grave.

'Things are bad enough already, don't get pneumonia,' he urged them.

But in Shancarrig people felt it was only right and respectful to accompany a funeral to the final resting place. They stood, a wretched group, as the wind caught the coats of the grave diggers and blew the few flowers away from the top of the coffin, hurtling them in a macabre sort of dance around the gravestones.

Back in The Terrace they asked in hushed tones how he would manage. What was he going to do? The loss of Frances wasn't just that of a wife, it was the loss of the person who managed the home. Three little children. Every time they said three he got a shock.

He thought of Eileen and Sheila with their little faces. He had forgotten about the baby.

This wasn't at all healthy, he told himself. And as his relations and friends drank sherry and ate plates of sandwiches in the rooms downstairs he went up wearily to look at his son.

The child was sleeping as he went into the room.

Tiny and red as all children, he seemed swamped and smothered by the bedding, his tiny perfect little fists with their minuscule nails on the pillow. Was it his imagination or did the baby look more helpless and alone than any other child? As if he knew he was motherless from the moment he had come on earth.

'I'll do my best for you, Declan,' he promised aloud. It was curiously formal and he felt himself remote as he said it. It was like a contract or a bargain between strangers, not a father to his infant son.

He hadn't heard anyone come into the room they called the nursery, but turned to find Nora Kelly, the young schoolmistress married to the master.

'Can I pick him up?' she whispered softly, as if she were in a sickroom.

'Of course, Nora.'

He saw the woman who had been aching to have her own child lift the tiny baby and hold him to her breast.

She said nothing, just walked around the room.

Her stance was that of a woman who had always nursed a child. Her hold on the baby was sure, her love obvious. No one except Jims Blake would know the amount of examination she had undergone to try and discover why she could not conceive.

He watched, almost mesmerised, as she walked to and fro crooning a very soft sound to the baby boy.

He didn't know how long they were there – the strange tableau of the doctor, the teacher and child. But he felt this slow urge coming over him to give away his baby son. He wanted more than anything in the world to say to Nora Kelly: 'Take him home, you have none, you never will have any. I don't want this child that killed Frances … Bring him back home and rear him as your own.'

In a more civilised society that's what people would have done. Why would it be the scandal of Shancarrig, the talk of the county and, moreover, a crime against the law of the land, for someone to walk out of this room with the child they so desperately wanted, taking him from a home where he wasn't needed?

Then he pulled himself together.

'I'll go on down, Nora. Stay here a bit if you want to.'

'No, I'd better come down too, Doctor,' she said.

He knew that the same solution had crossed her mind, and she was banishing it, as he had.

It was on occasions like this that Mrs Kennedy, the mournful bleak-looking housekeeper to Father Gunn, came into her own. She slid almost invisibly into the house of the bereaved, suggesting, helping and organising. She would arrive with a supply of gleaming white table cloths to hand them, then in a trice sum up what the house would need in order to give hospitality to those who would come to sympathise. A quick word with the hotel across the road from The Terrace about extra cups, glasses and plates while Maisie listened to it all wringing her hands. Mrs Kennedy had the authority of the clergy because she had worked with them for so long.

She never interfered, she just guided.

Maisie wouldn't have known about the need for good hot soup to serve with the sandwiches, nor that a room should be cleared for people's coats and umbrellas. Mrs Kennedy managed to imply that she was the voice of order and sanity in sad circumstances like these. And in houses rich and poor all over Shancarrig people had gone along with her, feeling a sense of overpowering relief that someone was taking charge.

Jims Blake greeted people, accepted their condolences, poured them more drinks, inquired about their health, but he did so with only part of his brain. He was working out what arrangements he was going to make. He did so by elimination. He would not have either of his unmarried sisters to live in the house, and he must make that clear before any offer was made. He would not have anyone from the Fitzgerald side of the family either, though they were less likely to present themselves.

Maisie couldn't manage a baby. It would be too expensive to have a live-in nurse. What was he to do?

As he had done so often, he asked himself what old Charles Nolan would have done. Again the voice came to him, booming as it would have been. 'Isn't the countryside crawling with young girls dying to get out from under their parents? Any one of them will have brought up a rake of brothers and sisters. They'll be well able to look after one small baby.'

He felt better then, and was even able to smile at Foxy Dunne, one of the boldest of the entire Dunne clan from the cottages – a red-haired boy in raggy trousers who had come to the door to sympathise.

'I'm sorry for your trouble,' Foxy had said, standing confidently in the cold outside Number Three The Terrace.

'Thank you, Foxy. It was good of you to call.'

The boy was looking past him to the table where there was food and orange squash.

'Well then...' Foxy said.

'Would you like to come in and ... sympathise inside?'

'That's very good of you, Sir,' said Foxy, and was past him and at the table in two seconds.

Maisie looked disapproving and was on the point of ejecting him. Mrs Kennedy frowned heavily.

Dr Jims shook his head.

'Mr Dunne has come to sympathise, Maisie. Mrs Kennedy, can you please give him a slice of cake?'

The nurse was booked to stay for a month and Jims Blake began his search for the girl who would bring up his son. It didn't take long.

He found Carrie, a big-boned, dark-haired girl of twenty-four, living on the side of a hill, deeply discontented with a life that involved cooking for six unappreciative brothers. He had been to the house on several occasions, usually to deal with injuries from threshing machines or otherwise around the farm. He had never treated the girl, but when he was called to their place to stitch the father's head after yet another violent altercation with some farm machinery, it occurred to Jims Blake that Carrie might be glad of the offer of a place, and a better situation.

They walked to the farmyard gate and he told her what he had in mind.

'Why me, Doctor? I'd be a bit ignorant for the kind of house you run.'

'You'd be kind. You could manage a child. You managed all this lot.' He jerked his head back at the house where she had looked after brothers, older and younger than herself, since her own mother died.

'I'm not very smart,' she said.

'You're fine. But here's a few pounds anyway, in case you want to buy yourself some clothes to travel in.'

It was a nice way to put it. He knew the travelling which meant taking a few belongings on the next lift she could get to the town wasn't important, but it covered the fact that she hadn't an outfit to wear.

Maisie sniffed a bit at the news of the new arrival, but not too much. After all, the poor young doctor was still in mourning, and mustn't be upset. And it had been very clear from the outset that Carrie would help Maisie in the house. There would be no question of meals on a tray for a fancy nurse.

Declan Blake was only ten days old when Carrie took him in her arms.

'He's a bit like my own,' she said quietly to Dr Blake.

'You had one of your own?' The world was full of surprises. She had never consulted him about the pregnancy.

'Up in Dublin. He's given away, it was for the best. He's three now, somewhere.'

'As you say, it would have been hard to have reared him.' His voice held its usual gentle sympathetic tone, but it came from the heart. This gawky girl wouldn't think it was at all for the best that her three-year-old had been given away.

'I'll do a good job minding this little fellow, Dr Jims,' she said.

It reminded him of his own vow to the child. Everyone was promising this tiny baby some kind of care, as if the baby feared he wouldn't get any.

The summer eventually came that year, and Dr Jims took his little daughters by the hand up to Shancarrig school.

He walked around the three classrooms with them, and showed

them the globe and the map of the world. He pointed out the ink wells in the desks and told them that soon they'd be dipping their own pens in there and doing their exercises. Solemnly they all studied the charts showing the Irish lettering for the alphabet.

'You'll be able to speak Irish when you leave here,' he promised them.

'Who would we speak it to?' Eileen asked.

Mrs Kelly was standing at the door and gave one of her rare smiles.

'It's a good question,' she said ruefully.

Dr Jims had sent her to Dublin again for further tests, none of the results being remotely helpful. There was no reason that specialists could find why the Kellys were not conceiving a child. He remembered his strange urge to bundle the baby into her arms on that unreal day back at The Terrace. He knew how near he had been to saying something so unsettling that it could never have been unsaid.

Again, this time she seemed to be thinking along the same lines.

'How is Declan?' she asked the children. 'It won't be long now until you'll be bringing him along to school with you.'

'Oh, he'd be useless. He never says anything at all,' Eileen said.

'And he'd wet the floor,' Sheila added, in case there was any question of enrolling the baby.

'Not now. The child's only ten weeks old on Friday. You were the same at that age.' Mrs Kelly spoke in her stern teacher's voice. Eileen and Sheila drew back in awe.

Jims Blake noted that Nora Kelly remembered the exact age of the baby boy he had wanted to give her.

If he had been asked he couldn't have said without counting back to the April day when Frances had died.

'Come on now, girls. We mustn't delay Mrs Kelly.' He began to shepherd them home.

'I'm sure you're dying to be back to him,' she said.

'Yes. Yes, of course.' His voice sounded false and he knew it.

As they closed the school gate he wondered was he unnatural not to hurry home to see a sleeping infant? He didn't think so. When Eileen and Sheila were babies he didn't see them for hours on end, and then only when presented with them by Frances after bathtime. Surely that was the way most men felt?

He mustn't dwell on that one highly charged moment on the day of his wife's funeral. Rationally of course he had no intention of giving away the baby that she had died bringing into the world. It was foolish to keep harking back to it with guilt.

He had perfectly normal feelings towards this child, and the hiring of Carrie had been inspired. She had indeed a natural instinct of motherhood, and she seemed to know that they wanted as little sign of a baby about the house as possible.

The girls went to the nursery each evening to play with him and to hear stories of Carrie's wild brothers, and the desperate injuries they had endured. She told them nothing of the child born in Dublin and given away. She sat rocking the substitute baby Declan in her arms.

Jims Blake called in from time to time. Not every day.

He knew that Mrs Kelly at the school would find this unbelievable.

That evening he went into the nursery.

Carrie was sitting at a table with pen and ink and several sheets of screwed-up paper.

'I was never one for writing, Doctor,' she said.

'We're all good at different things. Aren't you marvellous with the child?'

'Anyone would love a baby.' She shrugged it off.

'Yes,' he said.

Something in his voice made her look up. 'Well, it's different in your case ... I mean, being a man and everything, and your poor wife dying giving birth to him.'

'I don't blame him for that.' It was true. Jims Blake blamed himself, not his son, for the death of Frances.

'You'll grow to love him. Wait till he starts to call you Daddy ... and clings to your legs. They're lovely at that age.'

She must have been thinking about her brothers, he realised. She didn't see her own child grow.

He changed the subject. 'Could I help you at all with the writing ... or is it private?' He saw Carrie look at him. In many ways he had the same status as Father Gunn, a man who knew secrets, a man who could be told things.

Carrie had a brother in gaol. None of the rest of the family wrote to him. She wanted him to feel that he wasn't forgotten, that there'd be a place for him when he got out. It was told trustingly and simply.

He sat down at the table and took out his pen.

He wrote a letter to the boy, whose head he had stitched some years back, as if the letter came from Carrie. He told of the changes in the farm, the new barn, the way they had let the lower field go to grass. He told how Jacky Noone had got a new truck, and how Cissy had married. He said that Shancarrig looked fine in the summer sunshine and would be waiting to greet him when he came home.

Haltingly Carrie read it aloud, and tears came to her eyes. 'You're such a good man, Doctor. You knew what I wanted to say, even though I didn't know myself.'

'Here. You can have my fountain pen as a present. You'll get into less of a mess with it than trying to dip that thing there.' The baby began to cry and the doctor stood up. He walked to the door without going to see the child. 'Copy that out, Carrie, yourself. It's no use sending the boy my letter. You copy it and next time I'll give you more ideas.'

She picked the child up and looked at him with a face confused. A man so kind as to spend time writing a letter to her gaol-bird brother, a man who would give her his own good pen, but wouldn't pick up his son who was ten weeks old.

When Declan Blake was three Carrie had a cake for him with three candles and there was a party in the nursery. Maisie made special drop scones for the occasion. The girls got him presents of sweets and they all sang 'Happy Birthday' before he blew the candles out.

Jims Blake looked at the small excited face of his son, the snub nose and the straight shiny hair washed especially for the day. He was wearing a new yellow jumper which Carrie must have bought in the town. He left money for the children's clothes with Carrie and for the food with Maisie. Together they ran his house very well for him.

He had a curious empty feeling when the birthday song was over, as if something were expected of him.

It was only ten years ago in this house that Charles Nolan had urged him to marry. Ten years of visiting people and hearing their troubles and learning their hopes, realistic or wildly beyond their reach. He didn't know what his own hopes were. He had never had time to work them out, he told himself.

The children were still looking at him.

In his mind he asked old Charles Nolan what to do and he heard himself saying . . .

'Why don't we sing "For He's a Jolly Good Fellow" . . . ?'

Their eyes lit up, Carrie's face softened, the girls shouted the chorus and Declan clapped his hands to be the centre of such attention. Jims Blake felt the moment frozen for a long time.

The day came sooner than he ever thought it would when Declan should be brought to school.

'A great day for you, Doctor, to see your son setting out with a satchel,' Carrie had said.

Jims Blake looked at the child. 'It's a great day all right. Isn't it, Declan?'

Declan looked up at him solemnly, as if he were a stranger. 'It is, yes.' He spoke shyly, and half hid himself behind Carrie, scuffing his new shoes a little on the ground, and seeming awkward.

Probably all children that age are awkward with their fathers, the doctor told himself. He watched from the window as his son went off to school on wobbly legs.

The doctor meant to ask how the day went, but he was out on calls when Declan came home, and the next morning there wasn't time to talk either. It was a week before he even knew that there was a problem about Carrie delivering Declan to the school.

'The other children call him a baby,' Carrie explained.

'He's too young at five to walk all that way by himself,' his father protested.

'Other children do. All the young Dunnes come up from the cottages on their own...'

'Those Dunnes aren't children at all, they're like monkeys. They were climbing trees barefoot when they were two years old.'

Jims Blake was indignant that there should be any comparison.

'But it's terrible to have him made a jeer of. Maybe he could go with the girls...?'

'The girls say they don't want him traipsing after them. They have their own friends...'

Carrie looked at him as if he had let her down. Jims Blake felt a wave of self-pity sweep over him. Why was he always made out to be in the wrong? He thought he was doing his best for all of them, not loading Eileen and Sheila down with dragging their baby brother, and now he was the worst in the world as a result.

None of his patients challenged what he said. They took their tablets, drank their medicine bottles, changed poultices and dressings, made journeys into hospitals for tests, without ever doubting him.

Only at home did his every action seem suspect.

Later, when he was helping Carrie with her letters, as he did every week, underlining a spelling mistake lightly in pencil, she looked at him, troubled.

'You're a very good man, Doctor.'

'Why do you say that?'

'You correct me without insulting me. I write "yez" meaning "you all" and you just say, "Wouldn't it be better to put you all, it might be clearer"... You don't say I'm pig ignorant!'

'But you're *not* pig ignorant.'

'Maybe you shouldn't be teaching me all the time. Maybe you should be doing pot hooks with Declan.'

'Pot hooks?'

'It's how they teach them to write.'

'I don't want to be cutting across Mrs Kelly and her ways.'

He did look at Declan's copy book though, and asked him knowledgeably, 'Are these pot hooks, then?'

'Yes, Daddy.'

'Very good. Very good, keep at them,' he said. There was the familiar feeling that it hadn't been the right thing to say.

Since he had organised them all to sing 'For He's a Jolly Good Fellow' when Declan was three, there had hardly been a time when he was sure that the right thing had been said.

Eileen and Sheila always asked about his patients, ever since they had been very young.

'Is Mrs Barton going to die?' They liked the quiet dressmaker who lived with her only son in the pink house on the hill.

'No, of course not. She's only got the flu.'

'Is Miss Ross going to have a baby?' They had seen her knitting and thought the two went together.

'Was there much blood in the car crash?'

He parried their questions, kept the secrecy and diffused the sense of drama, and always he was aware that his son never asked him questions.

As the years went by he was even more aware of it. The girls left Shancarrig school and went to be boarders at a good convent school fifty miles away. There was now only the doctor and Maisie and Declan left in the house.

Carrie had given her own notice when Declan made his first communion.

'He's seven now, Doctor. He's a grown lad. He can dress himself, keep his room tidy, do his homework and all. You don't need me.'

'And maybe you're thinking of getting married?' There was nothing Dr Jims didn't see or know.

'I'm not going to say much about it.'

'And is it the father of the little lad?'

'Yes, it is. Thanks to you, Doctor, I was able to write to him a bit, tell him things, speak my mind. You're a great man for getting people to say things out. There's far too many round here who bottle it all up.'

He was pleased at her praise. 'You'll have another child. I know you'll never forget the first one, but you'll be a family now.' He was full of happiness for this dark-haired angular girl, who had such a poor start in life.

'And you'll have a chance to get to know your son more, maybe, when I'm gone.'

'Ah, that will come, that will come. I was thinking of getting a desk up here for him to do his homework.'

'The girls always did it downstairs, you know, more in the hub of things.'

'But he'd like it here. More independent. Wouldn't he?'

'He might feel a bit shut away.' Her eyes were troubled.

'Not a bit of it, it would let him concentrate. Anyway, enough of such things. You'll come back and see us?'

'Of course I will. It was the best seven years of my life. I grew up properly in this house. I was very privileged.' He tried to brush it away. 'I mean it, Doctor Jims. I wouldn't even have been able to use a word like privileged when I came here. Isn't that living proof?'

When she was gone he made deliberate efforts to get involved in his son's world.

Always he seemed choked off.

Declan did his homework silently up in the room that used to be called the nursery, then he would come down and sit with Maisie in the kitchen while she prepared the supper. Dr Jims was out so often it seemed only sensible for the boy to eat with Maisie, after all he had eaten his meals with Carrie when she was there to look after him.

He tried to think of things to interest Declan. 'Are you on to fractions yet, lad?'

'I don't know.'

'You must know. Either you are or you aren't.' His voice was suddenly impatient.

'We might be. Sometimes you call things one thing and they call it another at school.'

'And how's your friend, Dinnie?'

'Vinnie.'

'Yes, Vinnie. How is he?'

'He's all right, I think, Dad.'

'Well, surely you know whether he's all right or not?' Again the impatience arising without control, the tone of his voice changing.

'I mean, I haven't seen him for ages.'

'Aren't you friends any more?'

'I don't know. We might be. He's living in the town, I'm here.'

Guilt then. Had he not listened? Had he ever been told? Surely other parents had this confusion about their children's friends.

And of course, girls were easier too, anyone knew that. There had never been any trouble about Eileen and Sheila. He knew who their friends were. They talked about them, they brought them to The Terrace. When they came home from boarding school they always sought out Nessa Ryan from the hotel, and Leo Murphy, the daughter of Major Murphy up at The Glen.

Boys were hard to fathom. They lived in a secretive world of their own, it seemed. Jims Blake looked back on his own childhood, on the small bleak farm with the dour uncommunicative father who had hardly ever thrown him a word. He was behaving so differently from that silent man, and still meeting rebuff, it seemed.

The girls talked to him very easily. Eileen came and sat on a footstool in his study, hugging her knees. 'Leo Murphy's got all odd and snooty this year,' she complained.

'Is that a fact?' Jims Blake had his own worries about the mental health of Miriam Murphy, the girl's mother.

'Yes. She wouldn't let me in when I went up to The Glen, just said she couldn't play today. *Play*, as if I was a child or she was a child.'

'I know, I know.' He was soothing.

'And Nessa Ryan says the same thing about her, snooty as anything. She won't let you into her house, as if anyone wanted to go.'

'Maybe Maisie could make you a nice tea here . . .'

'She doesn't want to go to anyone else's house either, Nessa says.'

'At least you have Nessa,' he said consolingly.

Eileen flounced. 'Yes, and who needs Leo Murphy and her big house? Ours is much smarter than theirs anyway.'

'Don't be boasting about our good fortune in having a nice house,' he said.

He had tried to tell them all about the good fortune in being given a house of such quality by the late Dr Nolan, but his loyal daughters dismissed it. They thought their father was worth it and more, they said.

Eileen was going to go to university if she got a lot of honours in her Leaving Certificate. She would be an architect. She would love that. The nuns said she had all the brains in the world and by the time she was qualified the world, and indeed Ireland, would be moving to the point where women architects would be quite acceptable. It would be the 1960s after all. Imagine.

And Sheila wanted to do nursing, so he was already sending out feelers for her to the better training hospitals in Dublin.

Declan would do medicine, of course, so the main thing was to get him into a good boarding school. He had spoken to the Jesuits, the Benedictines, the Vincentians and the Holy Ghost Fathers. There were advantages and drawbacks in all of them. He checked the records, the achievements, the teaching records and he chose the one that came out best overall. The bad side was that it was further away than any other school.

'You won't be able to go and see him much there,' Eileen said.

'He'll come home in the holidays.' Dr Jims knew he was being defensive. Again.

'But it's lovely to have visitors at school. We loved you coming on Sundays.'

He used to go every second week, a long, wet drive in winter. He had never taken Declan. At first he would have been too young and restless for the drive, and the girls would have hated him to be troublesome when he arrived in the parlour. Then later, it didn't seem the right thing to suggest.

A ten-year-old boy wouldn't *want* to be dragged off to a girls' school of a Sunday even if he had been invited. It would be a sissy sort of thing for a boy.

He intended to spend more time with the boy during the summer before Declan went to boarding school, but there was so much to do. There was the whole business of Maura Brennan's child for one thing.

He had always liked Maura, the only Brennan girl to stay in Shancarrig. The others had long gone to unsatisfactory posts in England.

Maura had a dreamy quality about her, an acceptance of what life had to offer. He remembered the day he had confirmed her pregnancy.

'He'll never marry me, Dr Jims,' she had said, big tears waiting to fall from her eyes.

'I wouldn't be sure of that. Aren't you a great catch for any man?' He had said it but his heart wasn't in the words. He had thought Gerry O'Sullivan would disappear but he had been wrong, Gerry stayed. There had been a wedding, he had gone in to Johnny Finn's to drink their health.

And then when he had delivered her child it was he who saw the epicanthic folds around the eyes. It was he who had to tell Maura O'Sullivan, as she so proudly called herself, that her son was a child with Down's syndrome.

He remembered how he had held the girl in his arms and told her it would all be all right. Even when Father Gunn had told him that Gerry O'Sullivan, father of the boy, had taken the train from Shancarrig station and was gone before the baptism, he remembered the sense of hearing his own voice mouth the words of comfort, telling Maura that everything would be fine.

And he had been right to say that she would always love young Michael with an overpowering love. That much had been true even if Gerry O'Sullivan was never seen in the streets of Shancarrig again.

There was a human story everywhere he turned ... in the small houses and in the big ones.

There was something seriously wrong up at The Glen and he didn't know how to cope with it. Frank Murphy, a quiet man who bore his war injuries bravely, had something much more serious on his mind than the bad leg he dragged after him so uncomplainingly.

Jims Blake thought it had to do with his wife. But Miriam Murphy was someone he had never examined. She assured him she was as strong as a horse. She was an attractive woman with a dismissive manner if crossed, and he had liked her red-gold hair and her effortless way of looking elegant while walking around the big gardens with a shallow basket, an old silk scarf draped over her shoulders.

People in Shancarrig had long grown accustomed to the fact that Mrs Murphy never came down to the shops. There were accounts in the shops and the delivery boys who called on bicycles always got a friendly wave from the mistress of The Glen. They would deal with Biddy the maid, or with the Major himself.

But this summer there was something different about Miriam. A vacancy in her eyes that was more than disturbing. And a cautious protective look in Frank's that hadn't been there before. Charles Nolan had told him often enough about families who guarded their secrets, who kept their unstable people hidden. Often it was better not to pry.

Jims Blake wondered what old Charles would have made of the situation in The Glen. Not only was the Major in a state of distress, but their daughter Leo, who had been such a close friend of his daughters, had also begun to show signs of strain. He met the girl when driving past Barna Woods.

'Do you want a lift back up to the house, Leo?'

'Are you going that way?'

'A car goes whatever way you point it.'

'Thanks, Doctor.'

'Have you lots of new friends for yourself this summer, Leo?'

She was surprised. No, it turned out she hadn't any. Why did he ask? Without putting his own children in the role of complainers he hinted that she hadn't been around.

'We went on a bit of a holiday, you see, to the seaside.'

That was true. He had heard Bill Hayes say that the Major had packed dogs and all into the car and driven off without warning.

'Ah, but you're back now, and still no one ever sees you. I thought you'd gone off with the gypsies.' They had just driven in the gate of The Glen as he said this. She looked at him, as white as a sheet. 'It's all right, Leo. I was only joking.'

'I hate jokes about the gypsies,' she said.

He wondered had they frightened her in the woods. Dark, suspicious and always on guard, they had given him a pheasant once, when he had delivered a child for them. Unsmiling and proud they had handed him the bird, wrapped in grass, to thank him for the skill they hadn't sought, but had used because he was passing near during a difficult birth.

The Major appeared at the door. 'I won't ask you in,' he said.

'No, no.' His reputation as a discreet man who could be told anything rested on ending conversations when others wanted to. He never probed a step further, but his face was always open and ready to hear when others wanted to tell.

His son Declan never wanted to tell anything.

'Will you like being at the school do you think, Declan?'

'I won't know, not really, until I get there.'

Had there ever been a boy so pedantic, so unwilling to talk?

*

Maisie wanted to know had he settled in? Was the bed aired? Were there any other boys from this part of the world there?

Dr Jims Blake could answer none of this. His only memory was his son's hand waving goodbye. He wasn't clinging, like one or two other lads were, loath to leave mothers go. Nor was he chatting and making friends as some of the more outgoing boys seemed to be doing.

They had to write letters home every Sunday. Declan wrote of saints' days, and walks, and doing a play, making a relief map. Jims Blake knew that these letters were supervised by the priests, that they were intended to give a good impression of the school and all its activities. Sometimes the letter lay unopened on the hall table along with the advertising literature from pharmaceutical companies that was sent to all doctors on a mailing list.

Declan didn't write to Eileen, now in a hostel in Dublin while she studied architecture in University College. He didn't write to Sheila, now nursing in one of Dublin's best hospitals. He sent a birthday card to Maisie, but they knew very little about his world at school.

The reports said that he was satisfactory, his marks were average, his place in the class was in the top end of the lower half.

His school holidays seemed long and formless. The doctor got the impression that he was dying to be back at school.

'Would you like to ask any of your friends to stay?'

'Here?' Declan had been surprised.

'Well, there's plenty of room. They might like it.'

'What would they do, Daddy?'

'I don't know. Whatever they do, whatever you do anywhere.' He was irritated now. It was this habit of answering one question with another that he found hard to take.

It never came to anything, that suggestion. Nor the invitation to go to Dublin.

'What would I do in Dublin for two days?'

'What does anyone do in Dublin? We could see your sisters, take them out to lunch. That would be nice, wouldn't it?' He realised he sounded as if he was talking to a five-year-old, not a boy of fifteen. A boy who had grown apart from Eileen, now nearly qualified as an architect, from Sheila, now almost a qualified nurse.

The visit never happened. Neither did the outing to the Galway races, which had been long spoken of as a reward when Declan's Leaving Certificate was over.

Jims Blake said he could put his hand on his heart and swear that he had made every move to try and get close to his son, and that at every turn he was repelled.

It wasn't a thing that he would normally talk to another man about, but he did mention it to Bill Hayes. 'Do you find it like ploughing a hard field trying to get a word out of your fellow, Niall, or does he talk to you?'

'Niall would talk to the birds in the trees if he thought they'd listen. He has a yarn for every moment of the day. Not much knack of dealing with clients, though.'

Bill Hayes shook his head gloomily. His son too seemed a slight disappointment to him. Although a qualified solicitor he showed no signs of being able to attract new business or, indeed, cope with the business that was already there.

'And does he talk to *you*?' Dr Jims persisted.

'When he can get me to listen, which isn't often. I don't want to hear rambling tales about the mountains and the lakes when he goes out to make some farmer's will for him. I want to hear that it's been done properly, the man's affairs are settled and everything's in order.'

Dr Jims sighed. 'With me it's just the opposite. I can't get him to talk about enrolling up at the university. He keeps making excuses.'

'Talk to him at a meal. Don't serve him until he answers your question . . . That'll get an answer out of him. Boys love their food.'

Jims Blake was ashamed to say why this wouldn't work, to admit that his son still ate meals in the kitchen with Maisie, out of habit, out of tradition. No point in laying up two places in the dining room. Who knew when the poor doctor would have to be called out?

But the summer of 1964 was moving on. Arrangements would have to be made, fees must be paid, places in the Medical School reserved, living quarters booked.

'Declan? No one would ever think we lived in the same house, lad . . .'

'I'm always here,' the boy said. It wasn't mutinous or defensive, it was said as a simple fact.

Jims Blake was annoyed by it.

'I'm always here too,' he said. 'Except when I'm out working, as you will be.'

'I'm not going to do medicine, Dad.'

Somehow, it came as no surprise. He must have been expecting it. 'When did you decide against it?' His voice was cold.

'I never decided *for* it, it was only in your mind. It wasn't in mine.'

They talked like strangers, polite but firm.

Declan would like to join an auctioneering firm. His friend Vinnie O'Neill's father would take him on. He'd like the life. It was the kind of thing that appealed to him, looking at places, showing them to customers. He was good at talking to people, telling them the good points of a place. There'd be a very good living in it for him. Vinnie was going off to be a priest. There was no other boy in the family, only girls. Mr O'Neill liked him, got on well with him.

Jims Blake listened bleakly to the story of a man he didn't know, a man called Gerry O'Neill, whose estate agent's signs he had seen around the place. A man who got on well with Declan Blake and regarded him as a kind of son now that his own was going to enter the priesthood. Silently he accepted the plans, plans that involved Declan going to live in the big town. He could have Vinnie's room, apparently. It would be easier to have him on the spot, and the sooner the better.

Vinnie was going to the seminary next week. Declan thought he'd move in at the weekend.

Jims Blake heard that Maisie wouldn't miss him because so much of her life was now centred around the church. And she had got used to him being away at school.

'And what about me?' Jims Blake said. 'What about my missing you?'

'Aw, Dad, you're your own person. You wouldn't miss me.'

It was said with total sincerity, and when the boy realised that there actually was loneliness in his father's face, he seemed distressed.

'But even if I were going to be doing medicine wouldn't I be away all the time?'

'You'd be coming back to help me in the practice, and take over. That's what I thought.'

There was a silence. A long silence.

'I'm sorry,' Declan said.

Later Jims wondered should he have put his arm around the boy's shoulder. Should he have made some gesture to apologise for the coldness and distance of eighteen years, to hope that the next years would be better. But he shrugged. 'You must do as you want to,' he said. And then he heard himself saying, 'It's what you've always done.'

He knew it was the most final goodbye he could ever have said.

Sometimes when he was in the town Jims Blake called in to O'Neill's. Like someone probing a sore tooth he was anxious to see the man and the home where Declan Blake felt he belonged. Gerry O'Neill, a florid man with a fund of anecdotes about people and places, regarded himself as a great raconteur. Jims Blake found him boring and opinionated. He sat and watched unbelievingly while the man's wife and daughters and Declan laughed and encouraged him in these tales.

The eldest girl was Ruth, a good-looking girl, her Daddy's pet. She was doing a commercial course in the local secretarial college so that she could help in the business. They talked of O'Neill's Auctioneers as if it was a long-established and widely respected family firm, instead of a Mickey Mouse operation set up by Gerry O'Neill himself on the basis of being a fast talker;.

'Invite Ruth to The Terrace some time, won't you?' Jims asked his son.

He could see that Declan was very attracted to the dark-eyed girl in his new family.

'I don't think so . . .'

'I'm not asking you to live there, I'm just asking you to bring the girl to Sunday lunch, for God's sake.' Again, the harsh ungracious words that he didn't mean to speak. His son looked taken aback.

'Yes, well. Of course . . . some time.'

Jims Blake contemplated getting an assistant. He realised now how the lonely old Charles Nolan must have relished him coming to stay in that house all those years ago. How he had felt able to will him the place, as well as the practice. Jims had thought the same thing would have happened with Declan. He had foreseen evenings like he had had with Charles, discussing articles in the *Lancet* and the *Irish Medical Times*, wondering about a new cure-all cream with apparently magical qualities that had come from one of the drug firms.

There was a phone call every week from Sheila in her Dublin hospital, and a letter every week from Eileen, now working in an architect's practice in England.

He had almost forgotten what Frances had looked like, or felt like in his arms. He should not have felt like an old man, after all he was only in his late fifties, yet he had the distinct feeling that his life, such as it was, was over.

Declan did bring Ruth to lunch eventually. And the girl chattered easily and eagerly, as she did in her own home. She asked questions, seemed interested in the answers. She asked Maisie about doing the flowers for the altar. Maisie said she was a girl of great breeding, and that Declan was very lucky to have met her and not some foolish fast girl, like he might well have met in the town.

On her third visit she took the initiative and leaned over to kiss him goodbye.

'Thank you, Dr Jims,' she said. She smelled of Knight's Castile soap, fresh and lovely. He was not surprised his son was so taken by her.

He was horrified when he saw Declan some weeks later. The boy arrived on a Thursday afternoon, Maisie's half day. He was ashen white, but the circles under his eyes were deep purple shadows.

He paced the house until the last patient left. 'Will there be any more?'

'I have to go out the country. One of Carrie's brothers. Do you remember Carrie?'

'Of course I do. Can I come with you?'

Somehow Jims Blake found the right silences and didn't choose the wrong words. He didn't ask what had the boy out on a working day, and looking so terrible. Instead he smiled and opened the hall door for him. They walked together to the car, father and son, down the steps of Number Three The Terrace, as he had always wanted to walk with a son.

They talked of nothing during the drive out to the farm where one of Carrie's brothers had impaled himself on yet another piece of rusting machinery. Declan watched wordlessly as his father cleaned the wound and stitched it.

The talk came on the way back.

They stopped under the shadow of the Old Rock, the big craggy monument from which Shancarrig took its name. They walked a little in the crisp afternoon with the shadows of the trees lengthening.

Jims Blake heard the story. The terrible tale of a boy invited into a good man's house. How Gerry O'Neill would lie down dead when he knew Ruth was pregnant. How her brother Vinnie, studying to be a priest, would never forgive such a betrayal.

The boy had not slept or eaten for a week, and presumably neither had the girl. It was the end of the road. Declan wanted them to run away, but Ruth wouldn't go, and in his saner moments he realised that she was right.

'You realise how bad things are, if I had to tell you,' he said to his father.

Jims Blake bit back the retort. At another time he might have made the remark that would drive the boy back into the shell from which he had painfully dragged himself. He didn't ask what Declan wanted of him. He knew that Declan himself barely knew. So instead he did what he had been intending to do all his life, he put his arm around his son's shoulder.

He pretended not to notice the flinching in surprise. 'I'll tell you what I think,' he said. His voice was calm, almost cheerful. He could feel his son's shoulders relaxing under his arm. 'I have this friend up in Dublin, we did our training together. He's in gynaecology and obstetrics. A specialist now. Quite a well-known man ... I'll recommend that young Ruth go to see him for a D and C... Oh, don't worry, these names are always very alarming. It's called a dilatation and curettage, just an examination under anaesthetic of the neck of the womb. Clears up any disorders. A lot of girls have them...'

Declan turned to look at him.

'Is that...? I mean is that the same as...?'

Jims Blake had decided how to play it. 'As I was saying to you, there's no knowing what names all these things go by, the main thing is that Ruth will go in there and be out in a day or two and it can all go through this house and this address without having to bother anyone else.'

They walked back to the car and drove to Shancarrig. The mood was not broken.

His son came in to Number Three The Terrace and sat with him as they lit a fire, because the evening was getting chilly. Declan had a small brandy and some of the colour had returned to his face.

Jims Blake remembered how old Dr Nolan had often said to him that the ways of world were stranger than anyone would ever believe. Dr Jims Blake agreed with him as he sat there and realised that the only companionable evening he had ever had with his son was the evening he had arranged to abort his own grandchild.

NORA KELLY

Nora and Jim Kelly had no pictures of their wedding. The cousin with the camera had been unreliable. There was something wrong with the film, he told them afterwards.

It didn't matter, they told him.

But to Nora it did. There was nothing to mark the day their marriage began. It hadn't been a very fancy wedding. During the Emergency of course people didn't go in for big flashy do's, not even people with more class and style than Nora and Jim. But theirs had been particularly quiet.

It took place in Lent, because they wanted to have a honeymoon in the Easter Holidays, the two young teachers starting out life together. Nora's mother had been tight-lipped. A Lenten wedding often meant one thing and one thing only, that the privileges of matrimony had been anticipated and that an unexpected pregnancy had resulted.

But this was not the case, Nora and Jim had anticipated nothing. And the pregnancy that her mother feared might disgrace the whole family did not result, even after many years of marriage.

Month after month Nora Kelly reported to her husband that there was no reason to hope for a conception this time either. They shrugged and said it would happen sooner or later. That was for the first three years. Then they consoled each other in a brittle way. Why should two school teachers who had the entire child population of Shancarrig to cope with want to bring any more children into the world?

Then they decided to ask for help.

It was not easy for Nora Kelly to approach Dr Jims. He was a courteous man and kind to everyone. She knew that he would not be coy, or too inquisitive. He would reach for his pad and write, as he nodded thoughtfully.

Nora Kelly was pale at the best of times and this was not the best of times. She was a slight young woman with flyaway fair hair. She did it in a braid, which she rolled loosely at the back of her neck.

Nobody in Shancarrig had seen her with hair loose and flowing. They thought her expression a little stern, but that was appropriate for the school mistress. Her big husband looked more like a local farmer than the master – it was good to have some authority written on the face of the family.

Someone who had known Nora before she married said she was one of three young girls always dashing about and riding precarious bicycles, in a town some sixty miles away. They were three young harum-scarums, it was said. But it didn't sound likely.

She had no relations there now, she had no identity or past. She was just the school mistress – a sensible woman, not given to fancy dressing or notions. Not too fancy a cook either, to judge by what she bought in the butcher's, but a perfectly qualified woman to be teaching their children. It was of course a terrible cross to bear that the Lord hadn't given her children, but who ever knew the full story in these cases?

As she had expected, Dr Jims was kindness itself. The examination was swift and impersonal, the advice gentle and practical – some very simple, maybe even folk, remedies. Dr Jims said that he never despised wisdom handed down through the generations. He had got a cure from the tinkers once, he told her. They knew a lot of things that modern medicine hadn't discovered yet. But they were a people who kept their ways to themselves.

The old wives' advice hadn't worked. There were tests in the hospital in the big town. Jim had to give samples of his sperm. It was wearying, embarrassing, and ultimately depressing. The Kellys were told that, as far as medical science could determine in 1946, there was no reason why they should not conceive. They must live in hope.

Nora Kelly knew that Dr Jims found it hard to deliver this news to her, in an autumn where his own wife was pregnant again. Their little girls were already up at the school, this was another family starting. She saw his sympathy and appreciated it all the more because he didn't speak it aloud. It wasn't easy to be a childless woman in a small town; she had been aware of the sideways glances for a long time. Nora knew that the ways of God were strange and past understanding by ordinary people, but it did seem hard to understand why he kept giving more and more children to the Brennans and the Dunnes in the cottages, families who couldn't feed or care for the children they already had, and passing her by.

Sometimes when she saw the little round faces coming in to start a new life at school the pain she felt in her heart was as real as if it had been a physical one. She watched their little wobbly legs and the way the poorest of them came in shoes that were too big and clothes that were too long. If she and Jim had a child of their own they would look after it so well. It seemed every other woman in the village only had to think about conception to become pregnant – women who claimed to have enough already, women who sighed and said, 'Here we go again.'

When the doctor's baby son was born, in the coldest winter that Shancarrig ever knew, the year that the River Grane had frozen solid for three long months, his wife died at the birth.

Nora Kelly held the infant child in her arms and wished that she could take the little boy home. She and Jim would rear him so well. They would take out the baby clothes, bought and made many years ago, now smelling of mothballs. He would grow up in their school. He would not be over-favoured in front of the others just because he was the teachers' son.

For a wild moment that day in the doctor's nursery, when she had come to sympathise at the funeral, she thought that the doctor was going to give her the baby. But of course it was fantasy.

Nora had heard that couples who didn't have children often grew very close to each other. It was as if the disappointment had united them and the shared lifestyle, without the distractions of a family, made it easier for them to establish an intimacy.

She wished it had happened in her case, but in honesty she couldn't say that it had.

Jim grew more aloof. His walks of an evening became longer and longer. She found herself sitting alone by the fire, or even returning to the schoolroom to draw maps for the next day.

By the time she was twenty-eight years old her husband reached towards her to make love very rarely.

'Sure what's the point?' he said to her one night as she snuggled up to him. And after that she kept very much to her own side of the bed.

They had agreed not to say it was anyone's fault, but Nora looked to her side of the family. Her own two sisters had given birth to small families; one had only two, the other had an only child, while the sisters and sisters-in-law of Jim Kelly seemed to breed like rabbits.

Her sister Kay, who lived in Dublin, had two little boys. Sometimes they came to stay. Nora would feel her heart lurch when she saw how eagerly Jim reached for them and how happily he took them on walks. It was different entirely to the way he taught the children in the school. In the classroom he was patient and fair, but he was formal; there was no happy wildness like with her nephews. He used to take the small boys by the hand, and let them wade through the shallows of the River Grane and bring them to pick mushrooms up near the Old Rock, or to prowl through Barna Woods looking for bears and tigers.

Nora's sister never failed to say: 'He's a born father, isn't he?' Nora's teeth never failed to be set on edge.

She had more contact with her twin sister Helen, even though Helen lived on the other side of the world in Chicago.

She had sent grainy photographs of the baby, little Maria. Helen had gone to Chicago when Nora went to the training college. She didn't have the brains, she said, and she wanted no more studying. She wanted to see the world and make sure she didn't end up in some one-horse town like the one they'd come from.

In fact, Shancarrig was a much smaller one-horse town than their native place. Nora was sure that Helen must pity her. What had she got with all her brains? Marriage, to the increasingly silent Jim, school mistress in a tiny backwater, and no children.

Helen's life had been much more exciting. She had worked as a waitress in Stouffers. It was a coffee house – one of the many coffee houses of that name – and they had restaurants as well. She met Lexi when he was delivering the meat from the yards.

Big, blond, handsome Lexi, Polish Catholic, silent, whose dark blue eyes followed her everywhere she went. Helen had written about how he asked her out, how she had been taken to meet his family. They spoke Polish in the home, but in broken English told Helen she was welcome.

When they married in one of the big Polish churches in Chicago no one of Helen's family was there to give her courage. Who could afford a journey halfway across the world in 1942, when that world was at war?

And then Maria was born in 1944, baptised by a Polish priest. There were potato cakes served at the christening party, except they called them latkes, and there was a terrible soup called polewka, which they all drank at the drop of a hat.

Maria was beautiful. Helen wrote this over and over. Nora knew from experience that there wasn't much point in believing old wives' tales – they certainly hadn't been much use in her predicament – but she did believe that twins sort of knew about each other, even when they were almost five thousand miles apart.

She read and reread Helen's letters for some hint of what was troubling her, because Nora Kelly knew that life on Chicago's Southside was not as it was described in the very frequent letters.

On an impulse she wrote to her one spring day in 1948.

'I know it sounds like a tall order, but why don't you bring Maria over to see us in the summer? When the school closes Jim and I have all the time in the world and there's nothing that would please us more.'

Nora wrote warmly inviting Lexi too, but the implication was that he would not be able to take the time. Helen, working only part time in the restaurant now, could arrange leave.

Nora described the flowers and the hedges around Shancarrig. She made the river sound full of sparkle and the woods as if they were on the lid of a box of chocolates.

Helen replied by return of post. Lexi wouldn't be able to make the trip, but she and Maria would come to Shancarrig.

Nora could hardly wait. Their elder sister Kay said that Helen must have money to burn if she could just leap on a plane and fly off to Dublin on the spur of the moment. But Nora felt that it might well have taken a lot of explanations and excuses, as well as unimaginable scrimping and saving. She kept quiet about this. She would hear everything when Helen came home.

It was a relief to the twins when, after the big reunion in Dublin, they were able to leave Kay and travel together on the train to Shancarrig. They held hands and talked to each other, words tumbling and falling, finishing each other's sentences and beginning new ones ... and mainly they said that the camera had not done the little girl justice.

Maria was beautiful.

She was four and a half, with a smile that went all the way around her face. She sang and hummed to herself, and was happy with the piece of cardboard and colouring pencils which Nora had brought to greet her.

'Aren't you great!' Helen exclaimed. 'Everyone else gives her these ridiculous ornaments or lacy things that she breaks or tears up.'

'Everyone else?'

'The Poles,' confessed Helen, and they giggled like the children they had been when they said goodbye so many years ago.

The sun shone as the train pulled into Shancarrig. There on the platform stood the master, Jim Kelly, waiting to meet his sister-in-law and little niece.

Maria took to him straight away. She reached up with her small chubby hand and he held it firmly while carrying the heavy suitcase in the other.

'Oh Nora.' Helen's eyes were full of tears. 'Oh Nora, you're so lucky.'

As they left the station and walked down to the row of shops where of late she had felt that she had been an object of pity, the childless school teacher Nora *did* feel lucky.

Nellie Dunne looked out of her door.

'Aren't you looking well today, Mrs Kelly!' she said.

'This is my sister, Miss Dunne.'

'And you have a little girl, do you?' Nellie Dunne asked. She wanted to have all the news for whoever came in next.

'That's my Maria,' said Helen proudly.

When Nellie was out of hearing Nora said, 'It'll be a nine days wonder in the place that someone belonging to me produced a child.'

Helen laid her hand on her twin sister's arm.

'Shush now. We'll have weeks on end to talk about all that.'

They walked companionably through Shancarrig, and home to make the tea.

But Nora Kelly did not have weeks on end to talk to her twin sister about life in Chicago and life in Shancarrig. Five days after she arrived Helen was killed when a runaway horse and cart went across the path of the bus which, swerving to avoid them, hit Helen, killing her outright.

Nora Kelly was in Nellie Dunne's with Maria when it happened. The child was trying to decide between a red and a green lollipop, holding them up against her yellow Viyella dress with the smocking on it, as if somehow one would look better with the outfit than the other.

The sounds were never to leave Nora's mind. She could hear them over and over, each one separate, the wheels of the cart, the whinnying of the horse, the irregular sound of the bus scraping the wrong way, and the long scream. Then silence, before the cries and shouts and everyone running to see what could be done.

Afterwards people said there was no scream, that Helen made no sound.

But Nora heard it.

They took her into Ryan's Hotel. She was given brandy, people's arms were around her, everywhere there were running footsteps. Someone had been sent up to the schoolhouse for Jim. There was Major Murphy from The Glen, a military man trying to organise things on some kind of military lines.

There was Father Gunn with his stole around his neck. He had run from the church to say the Act of Contrition into the lifeless ear of the dead woman.

'She's in heaven now,' Father Gunn told Nora. 'She's there, praying for us all.'

A great sense of the unfairness of it all rose in Nora. Helen didn't want to be in heaven praying for them all, she wanted to be here in Shancarrig telling the long complicated tale of a strange marriage to a silent man who drank, not like the Irish people drink, but differently. She wanted to arrange that her daughter came to Ireland regularly rather than grow up speaking Polish, hardly noticed amid the great crowds of other children in the family. Lexi's brothers and sisters had produced great numbers of new Chicagoans, apparently. Helen had begun to fear that Maria might get lost and never know a life of her own, be a personality and character in her own right like all the children in Shancarrig were. Nora had told her about the children who filled the classrooms during term time, each one with a history and a future.

Nora could not take it in. It couldn't have happened. Every minute seemed like half an hour as she sat in the lounge and a procession advanced and retired.

The voice of Sergeant Keane seemed a hundred miles away when he spoke of the telegram to Chicago, or the possibility of a phone call.

'We can't wire that man and say Helen is dead.' She heard her own voice as if it was someone else's. The words sounded unreal. The Sergeant explained that they could send a telegram asking him to phone Ryan's Hotel and someone would be here to give the message.

'I'll stay,' said Nora Kelly.

No one could dissuade her. It was not three o'clock in the afternoon in Chicago, it was early morning. Lexi was on his meat delivery rounds. It might be many hours before he got the telegram. She would be in the hotel, whatever time he phoned. Mrs Ryan organised a bed to be brought to the commercial lounge; the commercial travellers would understand that this was an emergency, that Mrs Kelly had to be near the phone, day or night.

She drank tea and they brought jelly for Maria. Red jelly, with the top of the milk. Every spoonful seemed to be in slow motion.

Then, at ten o'clock at night, she heard them coming to tell her that the call had been put through. She spoke to the man with the broken English. She had lain on the bed with the curtains pulled to keep out the evening sunlight of Shancarrig. And now it was almost dark. She

145

spoke as she had drilled herself to speak, without tears, trying to give him all the information as calmly as possible.

'Why do you not weep for your sister?' He had a broken English accent, like a foreigner in a film.

'Because my sister would want me to be strong for you,' she said simply.

She asked did he want to speak to Maria, but he said no. She told him that Helen's body would be brought to Shancarrig church the next night, and the funeral would be on the following day, and that Mr Hayes had found out about flights. He had been on the phone to Shannon Airport all day . . .

She was cut short. Lexi would not come to the funeral.

Nora was literally unable to speak.

The slow voice spoke on. It would not be possible, they were not people who had unlimited money. Who would he know to walk with him behind his wife's coffin? There would be prayers said for her in his own parish, in his church. He returned again to the accident and how it had happened. Who was at fault? What part of Helen had been hurt to kill her?

The nightmare continued for what Nora Kelly thought was an endless time. It was only when the operator said six minutes that she realised how little time had actually passed.

'Will you ring again tomorrow?' she said.

'To say what?'

'To talk.'

'There is nothing to talk about,' he said.

'And Maria . . . ?'

'Will you look after her until we can come for her?'

'Of course . . . but if you are going to come for her, could you not come for Helen's funeral?'

'It will be later.'

The days of the funeral passed without Nora being really aware of what was going on. Always she saw Jim, his big hand stretched out to little Maria, whose crying for her mama grew less and less. They told her Mama was with the angels in heaven, and showed her the holy pictures on the wall and in the church to identify where her mother had gone.

And as the days passed Nora went through her sister's possessions, while Jim took little Maria up to Barna Woods to pick flowers.

146

Nora sat on her bed and looked at her sister's passport and official-looking cards for work and insurance. She could find no return air ticket. Was it possible that Helen had intended to stay here and not to return? There were letters from a solicitor 'regarding the matter we spoke of'. Could this solicitor have been arranging an American divorce? Did the strange tone of voice mean that Lexi was too upset to talk? Or that all love and feeling had gone from his marriage with Helen? Her head was whirling. Why had they not talked at once, she and Helen? It had been part of the slow getting back to knowing each other, the delighted realisation that each had only to begin a thought and the other could finish it.

What a cruel God to have taken this away from them five days after they had found it.

Kay the eldest sister was as usual practical.

'Don't grow too fond of the child,' she warned Nora. 'That unfeeling lout will be back for her the day it suits him.'

What did people mean ... don't grow too fond of? How could anyone put a limit to the love she felt for this little girl with the big dark blue eyes, the head of curls and the endearing habit of stroking her cheek?

After a week Nora found herself saying to Jim, 'Is the child asleep yet?' and realised she was certainly coming to regard Maria as her child.

His reply was tender. 'I read her a story but she wants another from No, she says No has better stories.'

He was smiling at her affectionately, like before. He didn't turn away from her in bed any more, he reached for her like before. It was as if Maria had made their life complete.

'I suppose Kay's right about not getting too fond of her,' Nora said one summer evening, as they sat watching Maria play with the three baby chickens that Mrs Barton, the dressmaker, had brought along in a box as something to entertain the little girl.

'I keep hoping he won't want her back,' Jim said. It was the first time in four weeks it had been mentioned.

'We shouldn't get up our hopes ... any man would want his only child.'

'Any man would have come to his wife's funeral,' Jim said.

Nora wrote letters regularly. She described the funeral, the flowers, the sermon. She told about the grave under a tree in the churchyard, and how on Sundays she went there with Maria to lay flowers on it.

In a year a stone would be put up, Lexi must let her know what he would like written on the tombstone.

She told him about the bus driver who would never be the same again after the accident; the man who walked alone up to Shancarrig Rock. Everyone had told him that it had not been his fault. No one could have faulted him, it was an Act of God that the horse had shied at that very time. But he said that he would never drive again, and had come with flowers to the grave when he thought no one was looking.

She wrote that Maria said God Bless Daddy and a lot of other names every night, so she assumed that these were grandparents or relations. She didn't want him to think that that side of the family had been forgotten. She said that when the term started in September Maria would join the Mixed Infants. She was almost five – five was the age the children began coming to school.

She wrote and told him about the place, the huge big copper beech tree in the playground, and the maps on the schoolroom walls. She stopped saying 'until you come for her' and 'for the present time'. Instead she just wrote as if it was all agreed that Maria would stay here for an unspecified amount of time.

The children accepted her totally. They never thought it odd that she called Mrs Kelly 'No'. They thought it was just because she was babyish and younger than they were. Geraldine Brennan from the cottages decided to be her protector. Nora Kelly had to watch carefully in case part of the protecting might also mean eating Maria's little sandwich lunch.

The communications from Lexi were minimal. He wrote to say that he was grateful for her letters. His hand was not educated, and his grasp of grammar poor. He told her little or nothing about his intentions. He asked many times about the accident, what court case had resulted and whether the compensation had arrived. Once he inquired whether Helen had any valuables with her that needed to be looked after.

In Shancarrig too, people began to think of Maria as belonging to Jim and Nora. She was even called by their name.

'Hey, Maria Kelly, come over here and see the tadpoles!' Nora heard one day during dinner hour, when they played in the yard. Her heart soared with pleasure.

By accident she did have a child, a child of her own.

A child who had a fifth birthday party with a cake and candles. A child who had her first Christmas in Shancarrig and sang carols by the crib in the church.

'Do you remember the church back in Chicago at Christmas?' Nora asked, as she wrapped the child up in a warm scarf before taking her back up the road home from the church.

Maria shook her curly head. 'I can't think,' she said, and Nora smiled in the dark. The less Maria thought, the greater seemed the likelihood of her remaining with them.

Mr Hayes, father of Niall, an easy-going boy often put upon by the others, came to see her.

'My wife says he's being bullied by the other boys. Your husband will probably say it'll make a man of him. I wonder would you and I be better able to reach some kind of consensus?' he asked.

Nora Kelly smiled at him. It was typical of the way he did things, seeing was there a gentle way around things before you went in guns blazing.

'I think he needs to make a friend of Foxy Dunne,' she said after some thought.

'Foxy? That little divil from the cottages?'

'He's as smart as paint, that Foxy. He'll get himself out of that place, and away from the mess he's growing up in.'

'How should he make a friend of this fellow, so? Ethel would be afraid he'd lift the silver.' Bill Hayes looked rueful.

'He won't. He'd be a good ally for Niall. Niall's gentle. He doesn't need another gentle friend like Eddie, he needs a fighter in his court.'

'You can solve it all, Mrs Kelly.'

'I wish I could. I wish I knew how to keep my sister's child. I wish I believed that possession is nine tenths of the law.'

'You're too honourable for that.'

'I think my sister was going to leave her husband. I have letters from a solicitor... They don't say much, though.'

'They never do,' Bill Hayes admitted ruefully.

She sighed. He was telling her what Father Gunn and Dr Jims were telling her. Do nothing. Live in hope. If the man hadn't come over in six months it was a good sign.

When a year had passed it was even better.

When the time came for the Holy Year ceremonies at the school and the big dedication ceremony, Maria Kelly was part of their family and part of Shancarrig. She called Jim Daddy and she called Nora Mama No.

'It sounds like something from Japan, or from *Madam Butterfly*!' Jim said to Nora. He was always good-natured these days.

'She can't call me Mother, she remembers her mother,' Nora said.

'She seems to have forgotten her father though.' Jim spoke in a whisper.

At night Maria's prayers included a litany of friends at school, and the chickens – now hens – that Mrs Barton had given her. She prayed for all kinds of unlikely people, like little Declan Blake, who was pushed in his pram by that strange, abstracted maid, Carrie. Maria loved Carrie and Declan, and often asked Mama No if they could have a baby like Declan to play with. She prayed for Leo Murphy's dog, Jessica, which had broken its paw, and she prayed that Foxy Dunne would give her one of his worms in a jam jar. But the Polish names and her father's name had gone from the list.

It didn't take her long to realise she was in a privileged position being the daughter of the school.

'What would happen if you didn't know your tables?' Geraldine Brennan asked with great interest. 'Would you get your hand slapped like the rest of us?'

'No, she wouldn't.' Catherine Ryan from the hotel knew everything. 'She can grow up knowing nothing if she likes.'

'That's very unfair,' Geraldine Brennan complained. 'Just because my mam and dad aren't teachers I can get belted to bits, but you can do what you like.'

Marie Kelly didn't like Dad and Mama No being criticised. She worked harder than ever.

'Go to bed, child. You'll hurt your eyes,' Jim Kelly said, as Maria was learning her poem by the light of the oil lamp.

'I have to know it, I *have* to. It's much worse on me than any of the others. If I'm not word perfect I *must* be beaten, or else they'll be giving out about you and Mama No.'

Jim and Nora Kelly spoke in whispers that night. No child of their own could have brought them greater pleasure and happiness. It was as if she had been given to them as a gift from God in 1948, five long years ago.

*

Mattie, the postman, had delivered good and bad news to every house in Shancarrig. He knew when the emigrants' remittances arrived, he knew when a letter was unwelcome. He always hesitated slightly before handing Mrs Kelly any letter with a Chicago postmark.

When he was delivering an envelope with American stamps that was bigger and bulkier than usual, and looked more serious than the short scrappy-looking ones which had come before, Mattie asked if he could come in for a drop of water. Mrs Kelly poured him a cup of tea.

'I don't want to be in the way or anything ... it's just in case it was bad news. I know that you're on your own today. Hasn't the master taken the children up to the Old Rock?'

It was true. Early in each summer term Jim organised an outing. The whole school would go – all fifty-six children. Father Gunn used to go too, and bring the elderly Monsignor O'Toole when he felt able. The old Monsignor liked to know that the children didn't think of the Old Rock as some kind of pagan place. That was the trouble with ancient monuments that dated back to before St Patrick ... people didn't relate them to God.

Nora Kelly had decided not to go today, and here, as ill luck would have it, was the news from Chicago. Could they be legal papers? Her hand trembled. She opened it. There were newspaper cuttings, a description of how Maria's father Lexi, had opened his own shop, his own butcher's place, a beautiful meat shop. He wanted his daughter to know this, to be proud of him.

Would Nora please show them to Maria? And perhaps she might write. 'She is a big girl now, it is strange that she does not write.' Nora Kelly put her head in her hands and wept at her kitchen table.

Mattie, who bitterly regretted not dropping the letter on the table as he would have done ordinarily, reached out and patted her heaving shoulders.

'It'll be all right, Mrs Kelly. You were meant to have her,' he kept saying, over and over.

Nora Kelly pulled herself together, washed her face and combed her hair. She put on her summer hat, a black straw one, and set off down the road to The Terrace, the row of houses in Shancarrig where Dr Jim Blake and Mr Bill Hayes, the solicitor, lived.

Nellie Dunne, looking out her open door over her counter, saw the school mistress walking briskly, cheeks flushed, face determined. Maybe she was heading for the doctor's? She might have news for him. They often said when you stopped worrying about having a child of your own that was the very time you conceived.

But Nora Kelly went up the steps to the Hayes household. Her business was legal, not medical.

Mr Hayes seemed to notice a change in her, a determination to have the compensation settled and done with.

'Has anything happened, Mrs Kelly?' he asked gently. 'It's just that up to now you were the one to put it on the long finger, saying that money couldn't bring your sister back and that the child lacked for nothing.' He was polite but questioning.

'I know,' Nora Kelly agreed. 'That's what I did think. But now I think my only hope is to get the compensation, whatever it is, and give it to him.'

'Him?'

'Her father. He's not interested in anything else, believe me.'

'But the compensation is for Maria as well as for him.'

'We'll give it all to him if he'll let us keep the child.'

'Ah Nora, Nora . . .' Normally Niall Hayes' father didn't call her by her first name. He seemed upset.

'What are you trying to say to me, Mr Hayes?'

'I suppose I'm saying that you can't buy the child.'

'And I'm saying that that's exactly what I'm going to do,' she said, face flushed and eyes bright, much too bright.

Wearily Bill Hayes took out the file and together they went through the letters from CIE – the transport company – the solicitors for the insurance, and copies of his own to them. There was a sum. It would be agreed eventually. At most it would be £2,000, at the least £1,200. If they agreed to take something nearer the lower figure it would be sooner rather than later. But perhaps, after all this time, they should hold out for more.

'Take whatever you can get, Mr Hayes.'

'Forgive me, but should your husband perhaps . . . ?'

'Jim is as desperate to keep her as I am. More so, if that's possible.'

'There is absolutely no guarantee . . .'

'I know, but I have to have *something* to offer him. He's written to say he owns a shop. He's as proud as punch of it. Now he's started wanting her to write to him . . .' Her lip was trembling.

'Perhaps this is the first time he feels able to. You know Americans, they set a lot of store on having their own business . . .'

'Please don't stand up for him. I could have borne it if he had come over and taken her away at once. Not now. Not all those years of ignoring and neglect and now...'

'She might come for holidays...'

Nora Kelly's mouth was a thin line. 'You mean very well, Mr Hayes, but it's not a help.'

'Fine, Mrs Kelly. I'll get it moving, inasmuch as anything ever moves in the law.' Bill Hayes waved his hand around shelves filled with envelopes and documents tied up in pale pink tape.

'Will you write a little note to your father?' Nora asked Maria that night.

'What for? To thank him for the day up at the Old Rock?' She looked surprised.

Nora swallowed, and could hardly speak. Maria thought of Jim as her father. The man who was so proud of the new shop selling best meats in Chicago didn't even exist for her.

A few days later she brought it up again.

'We've had a letter from your Papa Lexi in Chicago. He wanted you to see the pictures of his new meat shop.'

Maria took the newspaper cutting.

'Ugh! Look at the dead animals hanging there,' she said, handing it back.

'That's his job. Like Jimmy Morrissey's father.' Nora wished she could leave it, but she knew that she dare not. 'Anyway Maria, it would be good to write him a letter and say the shop looks very nice.'

'It doesn't!' Maria said, giggling her infectious laugh.

Her hair, long now but still curly, was tied with a coloured ribbon. She always had her head in a book – the early years of long bedtime story sessions had paid off. She was tall and suntanned and strong. She was nearly ten years old, a girl that anyone would love to claim as a daughter.

'But he'd like to hear,' Nora insisted.

'It would only be pretending.' She pulled the newspaper cutting towards her again and looked, as Nora knew she must, at the picture of the tall, handsome man standing beside his shop.

'Is this him?' she asked.

'Yes.'

She looked uneasy, her dark blue eyes seeming troubled.

'What will I say?'

'Oh. Whatever you think. Whatever comes into your mind to say. I can't be dictating it for you.'

'But, nothing comes into my mind to say. I don't know. I don't feel safe when I think about ... all this.'

Nora Kelly put her arms around Maria. 'We'll make you safe, pet. Believe me, we will.'

Maria wriggled away. It was too emotional.

'Yes. Fine. Okay, I'll say something. Will I say "you look fine and rich"?'

'*No*, Maria. Whatever else you say, I beg you not to say that.'

'Ah Mama No, I don't know what to say. I think you are going to have to dictate it to me.'

'I think I am,' agreed Nora.

They kept the letters respectful and distant, telling little about life in Shancarrig, mentioning nothing of the Kellys who were her real parents, but giving vague sentiments of goodwill to a stranger in Chicago.

Nora noticed with delight how briefly and casually Maria read the stilted letters which came back, each one beginning 'My dear daughter Maria'.

The man had little to say, and said it badly.

'He's not much at spelling, is Papa Lexi,' Maria said.

'Now, now!' Jim corrected her.

'Is he a secret? Do people know about him?'

'Of course he's not a secret, love. Why do you think that?'

'Because we don't talk about him. And nobody else has another papa miles away.'

'We do talk about him, and you write to him. Of course he's not a secret.' Nora was very anxious to take any glamour or mystery away.

'Do you write to him, Mama No?'

'I do, love. But about business.'

'The meat business?' She was genuinely puzzled.

'No. Legal things, you know, after your mother's accident...'

'Why do you have to write about that?'

'Oh, you know. Red Tape. Formalities. All that.' Nora was vague.

Maria lost interest. Instead she wanted to tell Mama No about Miss Ross.

'I saw her climbing the tree this morning,' she said, giggling at the thought of the elegant Miss Ross actually getting her leg up on the lower branch and hauling herself up into the higher parts of the tree.

'Nonsense! You imagined it.'

'No, I didn't. I was looking out my window at six o'clock this morning, and she came into the school yard. I swear she did.'

'What on earth could she have been doing at that hour?'

'Well, I saw her. She'd been up all night. She was coming back from Barna Woods.'

'I think you've been reading too many stories – you can't tell what's true from what's made up.'

Nora shook her head. The very idea of Miss Ross climbing the beech tree. Really.

'Miss Ross?'

'Yes, Maria.'

'Miss Ross, did you climb the beech tree yesterday morning?'

Miss Ross's face was red. 'Did I what, child?'

'It's just … it's just, I told Mama No, and she said "nonsense".'

'That's what it is too, Maria. Nonsense.'

Miss Ross turned and walked away.

Nora heard the conversation. There was something about the way the young teacher spoke that didn't ring true.

'I was wrong about Miss Ross,' Maria said.

'Maybe it was the light. It's full of odd shadows at that time of morning.' Nora spoke kindly.

They exchanged a glance and somehow Maria seemed to know that Nora knew it wasn't something that had been made up. That it was something which might indeed have happened.

'I never thanked you properly for putting us right about that young divil, Foxy Dunne,' Mr Hayes said to Nora Kelly when she called to see him next time. 'It was absolutely the right thing for young Niall. Foxy taught him to catch rabbits – we have six of them out in the back. All male. Foxy taught him how to work that out too.'

Nora laughed. 'There's not much that fellow doesn't know.'

Bill Hayes looked out his window at the back garden. 'Look at that. He showed Niall how to build a proper little house for them, and put up a wire run from the hutch. It's very professional, and he's only a child.'

'He'll go far,' Nora said. She knew too that visiting The Terrace had a civilising effect on Foxy Dunne. He combed his hair and washed his hands without being asked to. He ate slowly, like his hosts. He was a fast learner.

Nora liked talking to Bill Hayes. He was a quiet man and people who didn't know him well might think he was a little too precise and fussy. But nobody's life was easy. Nora Kelly knew it was not a bed of roses living with the gloomy Ethel Hayes, who hadn't smiled for a long time. She knew that everyone's business was safe and secret in Number Five The Terrace. And that she would get the best advice that she could be given.

'Well now, you didn't come to talk to me about rabbits and hutches. I'm being very remiss.' He moved back to his desk and picked up some papers. 'We do have an offer now ... they're delighted to be able to close the file after five and a half years.'

'How much?'

'Thirteen hundred. Now we could get ...'

'That's fine, and here's a note from Jim saying he agrees too, in case you think I'm doing all this on my own.'

'No, no ...' But he took the note.

'I'll write tonight. When would we have the money?'

'Oh, in a week or two.'

'And would there be a certain percentage legally for him and for Maria?'

'I'd advise that half be for her, to be invested ...'

'You do know what we are going to do with her portion, don't you?'

'Yes, and I must say again how very unwise it is from every point of view. Suppose the child does stay with you, will she thank you for handing away what is her legal inheritance?'

Nora Kelly wasn't listening ... she would write tonight.

She went to the post office to get a stamp, and Katty Morrissey looked up from behind the grille.

'Well, isn't that the coincidence! There was a telegram for you half an hour ago. I was going to get Mattie to go out with it.'

Nora felt cold. Her hand trembled as she opened the envelope, and in full view of Katty Morrissey and Nellie Dunne, who had materialised as usual when any drama was about to unfold, she read that Lexi was arriving in Shannon Airport on Friday morning and would be with them on Friday afternoon.

'Would you like a glass of water, Mrs Kelly?'

'No, Miss Dunne, thank you very much. I would like nothing of the sort.' Nora Kelly gathered every ounce of strength and walked out of the post office, leaving Nellie and Katty to say to each other, before they said it to the rest of Shancarrig, that the school teachers' time was up. The real father was on his way from the United States to take his child home.

'You don't look well, Mrs Kelly.' Maddy Ross had come up behind her as she crossed the bridge on the way back up home.

'Neither do you, Miss Ross,' Nora countered. There would be no sympathy from this young teacher who had her life before her – a life with marriage and children in it.

'I'm fine. A little tired. I don't sleep at night. I walk a lot in the woods – it clears my head.' She had a strange, almost wild, look about her.

Jim had said, over and over, that it was essential for Shancarrig school to keep Miss Ross. Her salary was small, as the Department would only pay the minimum. And only Maddy Ross, who had a house, and a mother with private means of a sort, would be able to live on what went into her envelope every month.

But sometimes Nora thought that Miss Ross had a giddiness and light-headedness that none of their silliest fourteen-year-old girls had ever managed to reach. And more than once she thought, God forgive her, that Miss Ross was almost flirting with young Father Barry. Nora kept her own counsel about this, not even confiding to Jim.

'Do you sometimes feel the world is bursting with happiness?' Maddy Ross asked her as they walked together up the road.

Nora Kelly, who could well have done without this feverish conversation, replied tersely that she didn't think that at all, and particularly not today. So if Miss Ross would excuse her she would like to be left to her own thoughts.

She saw Maddy Ross shrink away like an animal that has received a blow.

Still, there was no time to think about that now, the young teacher's nonsense could be dealt with later. Right now she had to cope with the event that she had dreaded since the week after her sister died – the arrival of her brother-in-law in Shancarrig to take his daughter home.

She walked like a woman in a dream. Not since the time of Helen's death had Nora felt this sensation of being outside her body, as if she was watching another being going through the motions – of filling a kettle, of setting a table.

When Jim came in she was sitting motionless at the table. He saw the telegram and needed to ask very little.

'When is he coming?' he said.

'Friday.'

'Nora. Oh Nora, my love. What are we going to do?'

He put his hands over his face and wept like a baby.

She sat there stroking his arm, listing the possibilities. Could they leave Shancarrig and hide somewhere? No, that was ridiculous, he would get the guards. Could they pretend that Maria was too sick to travel? Could they get Mr Hayes to brief a barrister in Dublin who would fight a case against her being taken away from them? Each solution was more unlikely than the one which had gone before.

They could ask Maria to beg him. No. They must never do that.

Perhaps for the child it *was* the best. A comfortable living in the New World. A whole lot of cousins, a ready-made family, a welcome home as if the five years since she left Chicago airport in 1948 were just a pause in her real life.

Nora and Jim Kelly realised that this was one occasion when they could do absolutely nothing. They would have to wait for Friday and all it would bring.

By the time they showed Maria the telegram they had calmed each other sufficiently to speak without letting their emotions show.

'Is he going to take me away from here?' Maria asked.

'Well, we don't know what he plans, do we? After all, he just says "arriving to visit you". He doesn't say anything about ... anything after that.'

'I don't want to go.'

'Now, that's not the way to start,' Jim Kelly said.

'Well, what *is* the way to start ... ?' Maria was flushed. They hadn't realised how independent she had become, how strong in her own views. 'This is my home. You are my parents. I don't want to go away with someone I don't remember, someone who didn't come for me when my real mother died.'

'He couldn't. And you mustn't begin by making him an enemy.'

'He *is* an enemy. I don't want to meet him, I'll run away.'

'No, Maria, please. Please, that would be the worst thing.'

'What would be the best thing?'

'I suppose it would be to reason with him, tell him how much you think of Shancarrig as your home, and of us as your ... well, your people.'

'My parents,' Maria said stubbornly.

'He won't want to hear that,' Nora said.

'I don't care what he wants to hear. Why should I have to beg him to let me stay in my own home?'

'Because life isn't fair, and you're only ten years of age.'

Maria ran out the door through the yard, and across the fields towards Barna Woods.

When she came home later that night, she was very silent. And pale. Nora, who knew every heart-beat of this child, knew that it was something else, something not to do with what was going to happen on Friday.

'Did something happen to frighten you?'

'You know everything, Mama No.'

'Was it something you saw?'

'Yes.' She hung her head.

Nora's cheeks burned. How could life be so cruel, that someone must have exposed himself to the little girl on this of all days?

'You can tell me,' she said.

'Not really. It's really very bad. You won't believe me.'

'I will. I always do.'

'I saw Miss Ross and Father Barry kissing each other.' She blurted it out.

Immediately Nora knew she was telling the truth. Without a shadow of a doubt she realised that this was indeed what had been going on under her eyes.

A priest of God and their Junior Assistant Mistress.

But even the scandal, and the need to tell Father Gunn tactfully, and the whole attendant list of complications, faded away compared to the shock that it had all given to Maria.

'Do you remember when you told me Miss Ross had climbed the tree? I didn't really believe you, but I did later. And I most certainly believe you now. But Maria, we have so much to worry about, you and I. Let us put this to the very back of our minds, right back behind everything, and later we'll talk about it. Just you and I. It's best to tell nobody, nobody at all. These things have explanations.'

'Don't send me to Papa Lexi.'

'You'll be strong and good when he comes. I'll help you every step of the way. We'll ask him can you share your time between us. Hey, wouldn't that be great? Two countries. Two continents. And we all want you. Not everyone has that.'

'Will it work?'

'Yes,' said Nora Kelly, knowing that she had never spoken such an untruth in her whole life.

They survived the four days to Friday.

People were very kind, which they expected, but also very tactful which they hadn't expected. They did practical things.

Mrs Ryan in the hotel looked up the time of the flight, and since it would be arriving in the early hours of the morning, worked out what time he could be expected in Shancarrig. Maybe lunchtime. If it would be easier they could have lunch at Ryan's Commercial Hotel, she suggested, a private room.

Mr Hayes, the solicitor, offered to take him through the steps of the settlement one by one, pointing out how it had been the best thing to do.

Dr Jims dropped by with sleeping tablets in case they were finding the nights long.

Leo Murphy, daughter of the Major up at The Glen, said that Maria could come up and hit a ball around on the tennis court if she liked. Even though she was four years younger it would be all right, because of things being difficult.

Young Father Barry said, with eyes of glazing sincerity, that God was a God of Love above all, and that he would open this man's heart to see the love the Kellys had for Maria.

Nora Kelly preferred not to think too deeply about the God of Love that Father Barry interpreted, but she thanked him all the same.

Father Gunn said that Polish Catholics were very devoted to Our Lady, and that Mrs Kelly should show him the plaque on the wall, where the school had been dedicated to the Blessed Virgin.

Foxy Dunne said he had heard there was a bit of a problem, and he knew some very tough people, or his brothers did, if reinforcements were called for. Jim Kelly put on his sternest face when refusing this offer, but gripped Foxy by the arm and told him he was a great fellow for all that.

Eddie Barton told his mother that the gypsies were coming again –

wouldn't it be great if they were to kidnap Maria and then for her to be found and brought back after the man had gone back to Chicago.

Mrs Barton was altering Nora Kelly's best dress for her, with a trim of lace down the front, and on the collar and cuffs. She wanted to look the equal of anyone in Chicago for the visit. 'I only tell you what Eddie said, just in case. It might work,' she said, mouth full of pins.

'God bless you both,' Nora Kelly said, looking at her pale reflection in the mirror.

In many ways it was like a Western where they are all waiting for the gunmen to come to town. Down by the station Mattie the postman happened to be waiting with his bicycle, just waiting, looking into the middle distance as it were. Sergeant Keane was sitting on a window sill by the bus stop, throwing the odd word to Nellie Dunne who had come out from behind her counter to stand at her doorway.

The Morrisseys in the butcher's shop were making frequent sorties out on to the street, and Mrs Breda Ryan from the hotel seemed to find a lot of activity that took her to the entrance porch of their premises.

Although none of them would have admitted it, and no one pretended to see the curtains of the presbytery move as Mrs Kennedy watched from one window and Father Gunn from another ... they were all waiting.

Someone would let the Kellys know the moment the man came into the town. They never thought he would arrive by car, and because it was an ordinary car, not a big American Cadillac, nobody knew it was Lexi when he drove into Shancarrig and looked around him to see where the schoolhouse was.

Not seeing it in the centre or near the church he took the road over the Grane and arrived at a huge copper beech tree, where the one-storey building had the notice Shancarrig National School.

Behind was the small stone house of Jim and Nora Kelly. They were sitting waiting for the message that would tell them by which route he had arrived. They certainly had not expected the man himself.

He was big and handsome, fair curly hair around his ears, eyes dark blue. He must be thirty-six or thirty-seven. He looked years younger – he looked like a film star.

Nora and Jim stood in their doorway, their sides touching for strength. She longed to hold her husband's hand, but it would look too girlish. It wasn't in their manner to do a thing like that; hip to hip was enough.

'I am Alexis,' he said. 'You are Nora and Jim?'

'You're very welcome to Shancarrig,' Nora said, the untruthfulness of the words hidden, she hoped, by the smile she had nailed on her face.

'My daughter Maria?' he said.

'We thought it best that she go to a friend's house. We will take you to her whenever you like.' Jim spoke loudly to try and hide the shake in his voice.

'This house of her friend?' he asked.

'It's ten minutes' walk, maybe two or three minutes in your car. Don't worry. She's there, she knows you're coming,' Jim said. He thought he could sense suspicion in Lexi's voice.

'We felt it would be more fair on you not to have to tell her in her own home … what she thinks of as her own home.' Nora looked around the kitchen of the small house where she had spent all her married life.

'Tell her?'

'Well, talk to her. Meet her, get to know her. Whatever it is you want to do.' Jim knew his voice was trailing lamely. These monosyllables from Lexi were hard to cope with. Somehow he had expected something totally different.

'It is good that she is not here for the moment. May I sit down?'

They rushed to get him a chair, and offer him tea, or whiskey.

'Do you have poitín?' he asked.

Nora's warning bells sounded. She remembered her sister Helen telling of this morose drinking, this silent swallowing of neat alcohol.

'No. The local teacher has to set a good example, I'm afraid. But I *do* have a bottle of Irish whiskey that I bought in a bar, if that would do.'

He smiled. Lexi, the man who had come to take their daughter, smiled as if he was a friend. 'I need a drink for what I am to tell you.'

Their hearts were like lead as they poured the three little glasses, lest he think them aloof. They proposed no toast.

'I am going to marry again,' Lexi told them. 'I am to marry a girl, Karina, who is also Polish. Her father owns a butcher's shop too, and we are going to combine the two. She is much more young than I am, Karina. She is twenty-two years of age.'

'Yes, yes.' Nora was holding her breath to know what would come next.

'I tell you the truth. It would be much more easy for our marriage if Karina and I were to start our own family ... to begin like any other couple. To get to know each other, to make our own children ...'

Nora felt the breath hissing between her teeth. She gripped her small glass so hard she feared it might shatter in her hands. 'And you were wondering ...?' she said.

'And I thought that perhaps, if my daughter Maria is happy here ... then perhaps this is where she might like to be ... But, you see, it is not fair that I leave her with you ... you have your life. You have been so good to her for so long ...'

The tears were running down Nora's face. She didn't even try to wipe them away.

Lexi continued, 'I have made many inquiries about the finances because I want you to have the money to do so. But always when I talk of the money you do not reply. I fear there may be no money. I fear to give you money in case you think I am trying to give you a bribe ...'

Jim Kelly was on his feet. 'Oh Lexi, sir, we'd *love* to keep her here. She'll always be your daughter. Whenever you want her she'll go on a holiday to you ... but it's our hearts' desire that she stay with us.'

Nora spoke very calmly. 'And maybe she would see you as Uncle Lexi more than Papa Lexi, don't you think?' She didn't know where she found the strength to say the words that Lexi wanted to hear. She didn't dare to believe that she had got them right until she saw his face light up.

'Yes, yes. This would be much better for Karina, that she think of her as a niece, not a daughter. Because, in many ways now, that is what she is.'

Nora saw, out of the corner of her eyes, a shadow move on the beech tree in the school yard. It was Foxy Dunne, hovering. He had seen the car and guessed the driver.

'Foxy!' she called. He came swaggering in. This man was an enemy, he wouldn't be civil to him. 'Foxy, could you do us a favour? Maria is over at The Glen with Leo Murphy. Would you go over and tell her to come home, and tell her everything's fine.'

'It's a long journey over to The Glen,' Foxy said unexpectedly.

'It's ten minutes, you little pup,' said Jim Kelly.

'It'd be easier if you let me drive over for her.' He looked at the car keys on the table.

'Hey, how old are you?' Lexi asked.

'I've driven everything. That's dead easy.'

'He's thirteen and a half,' said Nora.

'That's a grown man,' said Lexi. 'But don't you put a scratch on it. I have to take it back to Shannon airport tonight.' He threw him the keys.

Tonight. The man was going back to his new life tonight. Without Maria.

The sunlight streamed into the kitchen as they talked, as they sat as friends and spoke of the past and the future, until Maria arrived, white-faced from the journey. Foxy had driven her three times round Shancarrig to get value from the drive, and then spotted Sergeant Keane so had put his foot down to get her back to the schoolhouse.

Nora put her arms around the girl.

'We've had a great chat, my love,' she said. 'This is Lexi, maybe even Uncle Lexi. He'll be going back to America tonight, and he wants to meet you and get to know you a little bit before he goes.'

Maria's eyes were wide trying to take it in.

'Before he goes off and leaves you here with us. Which is what we all agreed is where you want to be,' said Nora Kelly, who had told her daughter Maria that everything would be all right, and had now delivered on her promise.

NESSA

It was Mrs Ryan who wore the trousers in Ryan's Commercial Hotel. Everyone knew that. And just as well, because if Conor Ryan had married a mouse the place would have gone to the wall years ago.

Conor Ryan certainly hadn't married a mouse when he wed Breda O'Connor. A small, thin girl with restless eyes and straight black shiny hair, she was a distant cousin of the Ryans. They met at a family wedding. Conor Ryan told her that he was thinking of going off to England and joining the British army. Anything to get out from under his parents' feet – they ran this hole-in-the-wall hotel in a real backward town.

'What do you want going into the army? There might be a war and you'd get killed,' she said.

Conor Ryan implied that it mightn't be a huge choice between that and staying put with his parents.

'They can't be *that* bad,' Breda said.

'They are. The place is like the ark. No, the ark was safe and dry and people wanted to get into it. This is like a morgue.'

'Why don't you improve it?'

'I'm only twenty-three, they'd never let me,' he said.

Breda O'Connor decided there and then that she would marry him. By the time Britain declared war on Germany they were already engaged.

'*Now*, aren't you glad I didn't let you join the army?' Breda said.

'You haven't lived with my father and mother yet,' he said, with a look of defeat and resignation that she was determined to take out of him.

'Nor will I,' she said with spirit. 'We'll build a place of our own.'

Conor Ryan's father said that he had picked a wastrel, a girl who thought they were made of money, when the outhouse was converted into a small dwelling for the newlyweds.

Conor Ryan's mother said there would be no interfering from a fancy young one who thought she was the divil and all because she had a domestic science diploma. Conor reported none of these views to the bride-to-be. Breda would find out soon enough what they were like. She had assured him that she had been given fair warning.

As it happened she never really found out how much they had resented her coming to their house, and marrying their only son while he was still a child.

Breda never heard how his parents prophesied that when she had a few children out in that cement hut she was getting built for herself in the yard it would soften her cough.

The Ryan parents fell victim to a bad flu that swept the countryside in the winter of 1939.

Two weeks after the winter wedding of Conor and Breda the same congregation stood in the church for the double funeral of the groom's parents.

There was a lot of head-shaking. How hard it was for a young girl to step in like that. It would be too much for her. She was only a little bit of a thing. And you'd need to light a bonfire under Conor Ryan to get any kind of action out of him. It was the end of Ryan's Commercial Hotel for Shancarrig.

Never were people so wrong.

Breda Ryan took control at once. Even on the very day of the funeral. She assured the mourners that they would be very welcome to come back to the hotel bar for drinks rather than going up to Johnny Finn's pub, as they thought they should do out of some kind of respect.

'The best respect that you could give my parents-in-law is to come to their hotel,' Breda Ryan said.

Within a week she made it known that she didn't like to be referred to as the *young* Mrs Ryan.

'My husband's mother has gone to her reward, and the Lord have mercy on her she is no longer here to need her name. I am Mrs Ryan now,' she said.

And so she was. Mrs Ryan of Shancarrig's only hotel, a part of the triangle that people called the heart of the town – one side The Terrace where the rich people like the doctor and Mr Hayes the solicitor lived, one side the row of shops – Nellie Dunne's the grocery, Mr Connors the chemist, the other Dunnes who ran the hardware business, the butcher, the draper – the few small places that got a meagre living from Shancarrig and its outlying farms. The third side of the triangle was Ryan's Hotel.

Not very prepossessing, dark brown throughout, floors covered in linoleum. The rooms all had heavy oak fireplaces, the pictures on the walls were in dark heavy frames. Most of them were of unlikely romantic scenes with men in frock coats, never seen in Shancarrig or even in the county, offering their arms to ladies in outfits similarly unknown.

There were some religious pictures in the hall ... the one of the Sacred Heart had a small red lamp burning in front of it. The sideboards in the hall and dining room were stuffed with glass never used on the table, and Belleek china.

Mrs Ryan had plans to change and improve it all but first she must see that people came to it as it was.

She made sure that the smell of cooking didn't meet guests at the hall door by putting heavy curtains outside the kitchen doors. She installed a glass-fronted noticeboard near the reception desk and put up details of concerts, hunt balls or other high-class events in neighbouring towns.

She intended to make the hotel the very centre of Shancarrig, the place where people would come to look for information. The bus and train times were there too for all to see, in the hopes that it would encourage travellers to come and have a drink or a coffee as they waited.

Her plans had only just begun when she realised she was pregnant.

Her first child was born in 1940, a little girl, delivered by young Dr Jims because the baby arrived in the middle of the night and Dr Nolan was getting too old to come out at all hours.

'A lovely daughter,' he said. 'Is that what you wanted?'

'Indeed it's not. I wanted a strong son to run the hotel for me.' She was laughing as she held the baby.

'Well, maybe she'll run it till she gets a brother.' Dr Jims had a warm way with him.

'It's no life for a woman. We'll find a better job for Vanessa.' She held the child close.

'Vanessa! Now there's a name.'

'Oh, think big, Doctor. That's what I always believed.'

Conor Ryan poured a brandy for the doctor, and the two men sat companionably in the bar at 4.30 a.m. to drink to the new life in Shancarrig.

'May Vanessa live to see the year two thousand,' said Dr Jims.

'Won't Nessa only be a young one of sixty then! Why are you wishing her a short life?' said the new father.

She was Nessa from the start. Even her strong-willed mother was not able to impose her will on the people of Shancarrig on this point. And when her sister was born the baby was Catherine, and the third girl Nuala. There were no strong sons to run the hotel. But by the time they realised there never would be, the women were so well established in Ryan's that the absence of a boy wasn't even noticed.

Nessa always thought she had got the worst possible combination of looks from her parents.

She had her mother's dead-straight hair. No amount of pipe cleaners would put even the hint of a wave or a kink in it. And she inherited her father's broad shoulders and big feet. Why could she not have got his curly hair and her mother's tiny proportions? Life was very unfair. Everyone admired people with curly hair.

Like Leo's hair.

Since Nessa could remember she had been best friends with Leo Murphy. Leo was the girl who lived up at The Glen. She was almost an only child. Lucky thing. Not a real only child like Eddie Barton, the son of the dressmaker, but Leo's two brothers were very old and didn't live at home.

Nessa had even known Leo before the day they both started at Shancarrig school. Leo had been invited to come and play with her. Mrs Ryan had said she wanted Vanessa to have a proper friend before she started in there and had to consort with the Dunnes and the Brennans.

'What's consorting?' Nessa asked her mother.

'Never mind, but you won't be doing it anyway.'

'That's why you're off to school, to learn things like that,' said Conor Ryan, folding back the paper at the race card to see could he pick a likely winner in the afternoon races.

The first day at school Nessa Ryan sat beside Maura Brennan. Together they learned to do pot hooks.

'Why are they called pot hooks?' Nessa asked, as the two girls slowly traced the S shapes in their headline copy books.

'They look a bit like the hooks that hang over the fire. You know . . . to hold the pots,' Maura explained.

Nessa told this information proudly to her mother.

'What! Have they got you sitting next to one of the Brennans from the cottages?' she said crossly.

'Don't be putting notions into her head. Isn't the poor Brennan child entitled to sit beside someone? Isn't she a human being?' Nessa's father was defending Maura Brennan for something. Her mother was still in a bad temper about it, whatever it was.

'That's not what you say when her father comes in here breaking all before him, and swearing like a soldier.'

'He takes his trade to Johnny Finn's after what you said to him that time...'

'You sound as if you're sorry, as if you miss that good-for-nothing drunk. It was a fine day for this house when I shifted him out. You agreed yourself.'

'I did, I did.'

'So what are you going on about?'

'I don't know, Breda...' He shook his head. Nessa realised whatever it was ... her Daddy really didn't know. He didn't know about things like her mother did. About running a hotel, and being in charge.

'Will I not sit beside her?' Nessa asked.

Her mother's face softened. 'Don't mind me, your father is right. The child's not to be blamed.'

'We don't have pot hooks, do we?'

'No. We have a range, like any normal person would. The Brennans cook over an open fire, I expect. Did you not see Leo Murphy at school today?'

'She was sitting beside Eddie. They got told off for talking.'

'What else happened? Tell me all about it.'

'We played a game around the tree, you know, like a big ring o' roses.'

'I did that myself,' said her father.

She saw her mother going over and putting her arm around his shoulder. They were smiling. She felt safe. Maybe her mother *did* love her father even if he didn't know how to run a hotel. When anyone came to the hotel they asked for Mrs Ryan, not for Mr, that's if they knew the place. Otherwise it was a delay while Mr Ryan sent for his wife.

Nessa grew up knowing that she should get her mother, not her father, in any crisis. At the start she thought this was the same in all families.

But she learned it wasn't always the case. She discovered that Leo Murphy's mother didn't know where anything was, that Major Murphy and Biddy the maid ran The Glen between them. Leo never had to consult her mother about anything. It was a huge freedom.

She learned that Maura Brennan's mother had to go out begging because Mr Brennan drank whatever money he got. When Nessa wondered why Mrs Brennan didn't stop him with a word or a glance as her mother would have, Maura shrugged. Women weren't like that, she said.

Niall Hayes said that his mother didn't have any say in the house. His father paid all the bills, and dealt with things that happened. Foxy Dunne said that his mother hadn't been known to open her mouth on any subject, but of course his father had never been known to close his, so that made up a pair of them.

Only Eddie, whose father was dead or had gone away or something, said that his mother was in charge. But she didn't like being in charge, he said. She kept thinking there should be a man around the place.

Sometimes they even made jokes about Nessa's mother, about how different she was from the other women in Shancarrig. Nessa didn't like that very much but in her heart she had to admit it was true. Her mother was rather too interested in her for her liking. She wanted to know everything that happened.

'Why do you want to know so much?' Nessa asked her once.

'I want to make sure you don't make the same mistakes that I made. I want to try and help your childhood.' Her mother had seemed very simple and direct in that answer, as if she was talking to someone her own age, not talking down.

'Leave the child alone,' her father said, as he said so often. 'Aren't they only children for a very short time? Let them enjoy it.'

'I don't know about the very short time,' Nessa's mother said. 'There are quite a few people around here who never grew up.'

When people stopped to admire young Nessa Ryan on the street they often asked, 'And whose pet are you?' It was only a greeting, not a question, but Nessa took it seriously.

'Nobody's,' she would say firmly. 'There's so much work in a hotel there's no time to have pets.' People laughed at the solemn way the child spoke, in the parrot fashion she must have heard at home.

Her mother didn't approve. 'You're the most petted child in the country. Stop telling people that there's no one spoiling you,' she said.

But Nessa didn't think this was so. She wondered was she a foundling. Had the dark gypsies, the families who came through every year, left her on the hotel doorstep? Had she been found up at the Old Rock, left there by a wonderful kind noblewoman with long hair – someone who was in great secret trouble and left her baby while she escaped?

Nessa didn't know exactly what she wanted but she knew very definitely that it was something different from what she had got. She would never be able to please her mother, no matter what she did, and her father was too soft and easy-going for his views to count.

Sometimes when she was feeling particularly religious and near to God she used to ask him to make her popular and loved.

'I'm not asking to be pretty, God, I know we're not meant to pray for good looks. But I am asking to be liked more. People that are popular are very very happy. They can go around doing good all the time. Honestly God, even children. I'd be a great child and a great grown-up. Just try it and see.'

The years of Nessa Ryan's childhood saw a great change in Ryan's Commercial Hotel.

After endless rationing and petrol shortages brought about by the war in Europe, suddenly cars appeared on the road again. Instead of the hotel's visitors arriving at Shancarrig railway station and walking across to where Ryan's stood taking up one side of the three-cornered green that formed the centre and heart of the place, they now drew up outside the door. Most people were loath to leave their cars in the street, even though this was the best part of Shancarrig. Visitors didn't know that The Terrace where Dr Nolan and then Dr Jims lived in Number Three and where the Hayes family lived in Number Five was about the best address in the county. They wanted safe parking for their cars.

The hotel was no longer dark brown. The dark colours had been replaced by cream and what Breda called a lovely restful *eau de nil*. She had toured other smarter hotels and discovered that this pale greenish shade was high fashion.

The more sober of the heavy-framed pictures had been relegated to the master bedroom, out of view of any visitors.

More bathrooms had been installed, chamber pots were hidden discreetly in bedside cupboards rather than being placed expectantly under beds.

The women who served in the dining room of Ryan's Commercial Hotel wore smart green dresses now, with their white aprons and little white half caps. The days of black outfits were over. There were comfortable chairs in the entrance hall encouraging guests to think of it as it used to be.

When Nessa and her sisters, Catherine and Nuala, were young they were kept well out of sight of the hotel visitors, but were trained to say good morning or good evening to anyone they encountered, even scarlet-faced drunks who might not be able to reply.

Nessa's mother had cleared up the hotel yard. Old and broken machinery was removed, outhouses were painted. No longer was the place used as a dumping ground. Guests were told that ample parking facilities existed.

And the visitors changed too.

A trickle of American servicemen who had got to know Europe during the days of war, returned again in peacetime bringing their wives, particularly if there was any Irish heritage in the family tree. They would stay in hotels around the country and try to find it out. They became a familiar sight, sometimes still in uniform, and looking very dashing as they would book into Ryan's Commercial Hotel.

Father Gunn said he was worn out tracing roots from old church records.

There were the commercial travellers too. The same people coming regularly, once a month – once a fortnight sometimes. Usually two or three rooms would be booked by the various representatives coming to take orders in Shancarrig and outlying areas.

Nessa's mother treated them with great respect. They would be the backbone of their business, she told her husband. Conor Ryan shrugged. He often thought them a dull crowd, abstemious too, no bar profit from them. Pale, tired men, anxious about their sales, restless, uneasy.

It was Nessa's mother who insisted on the commercial room, and lighting a fire there. There were a few tables strewn around, they could fill their order books and smoke there. They could bring in a cup of tea or coffee.

Conor Ryan thought it a waste. Why couldn't they sit in the bar like any other person? He had noted that few of them followed either horses or dogs, there was little conversation with them at the best of times.

At school everyone was always interested in the hotel and its goings on. They always asked about what the farmers ate for breakfast on the fair days once a month, and whether any of the beasts had ever backed into the windows and broken them, as happened once down in Nellie Dunne's grocery when she forgot to put up the barriers.

Nessa told of the huge breakfasts served all morning, and of how fathers and sons would take turns, one to mind the animals while the other would eat bacon and eggs heaped high on plates.

'Who was your best friend when you were young?' Nessa asked her mother when Breda Ryan was brushing the dark shiny hair which she persisted in admiring so much despite all Nessa's complaints.

'We didn't have time for best friends then. Stay still, Vanessa.'

'Why do you call me Vanessa? Nobody else does.'

'It's your name. There, that looks great.'

'I look like the witch in the school play.'

'Why are you always saying such awful things about yourself, child? If you think these stupid things, other people will too.'

'That's funny. That's what Leo said too.'

'She's got her head screwed on her shoulders, that one,' Mrs Ryan said approvingly.

'We'll be going into the convent together next year, every day on the bus. Maybe she'll be more my friend then.'

In a rare moment of affection Nessa's mother held her eldest daughter close.

'You'll have plenty of friends. Wait and see!' she said.

'It had better start soon. I'm nearly fourteen,' Nessa said glumly.

In magazine stories Nessa had read of girls whose mothers were like friends. She wished she had a mother like that, not one so brisk and so sure of everything. Nessa had never known an occasion when her mother had been wrong, or at a loss for a word. Her father now, that was different, he was always scratching his head and saying he hadn't a clue about things. But Nessa felt her mother was born knowing all the answers.

On their last day at Shancarrig school Nessa Ryan stood between Niall Hayes and Foxy Dunne during the school photograph. Mrs Kelly always liked to have a picture taken on that day, and they were urged to dress themselves up well so that future generations could see how respectable had been the classes that had gone through these schoolrooms.

It had become a tradition now. The formal photograph taken under the tree outside the schoolhouse door. The very last moment of the year, organised to calm them down after the other tradition of name carving and the boisterous racing around the classroom collecting the books and pencils while singing:

> *No more Irish, no more French*
> *No more sitting on a hard school bench*
> *Kick up tables, kick up chairs*
> *Kick the master and the mistress down the stairs.*

That there had been no French ever learned in Shancarrig and that there were no stairs in the schoolhouse were details that didn't concern them. All over the world children sang that song on the last day.

Those who were only thirteen, and would have to return to school after the summer, looked on enviously. This was the day when they wrote their names on the tree. The boys had brought penknives. Everyone was busy digging at the wood of the old beech tree.

Nessa wished she could enjoy this like the others did. They all seemed very intense. Maura Brennan had been planning for weeks where she would put her name. Eddie Barton said he was going to carve his in a drawing of a flower so that it would look special in years to come. Foxy was saying nothing, but looked knowing all the same.

Nessa took the extra knife from Master Kelly and wrote Vanessa Ryan, June 1954. She felt there was more to say, but she didn't know what it was.

The sun was in their eyes as they squinted at Mrs Kelly's camera.

'Stand up straight! Stop fidgeting there!' She spoke knowing these were the last commands she would ever give them.

Foxy Dunne stroked Nessa's hair, which hung loose on her shoulders. 'Very nice,' he said.

'Take your hands off me, Foxy Dunne,' she snapped.

'Just admiring, Miss Bossy Boots. Admiring, that's all.' He didn't look the slightest bit put out.

Imagine Foxy, from that desperate house of Dunnes, daring to touch her hair.

'It is very nice, your hair,' Niall Hayes said. Square, dependable, dull Niall, who had never had an original thought. He said it as if he were trying to curry favour with Foxy and excuse him for his views.

'Well,' she said, at a loss for words. To her surprise she felt her face and neck redden at the praise. Nessa Ryan hadn't known a compliment from a boy before. She put her hand up to her face so that they wouldn't see her flush.

'Smile, everyone. Nessa, take your hand away from your face at once. Leo, if I see you put your tongue out once more there's going to be trouble. Great trouble.'

Everyone laughed, and it was a happy picture for the schoolhouse wall.

As they walked together for the last time from Shancarrig school, Nessa and Leo were arm in arm and Maura Brennan walked with them. Maura would get a job as a maid or in a factory, she had said she didn't want to go to England like her sisters. Nessa felt a flash of sympathy for the girl who hadn't the same chances as she had. Nessa's father had said about the Brennans and the Dunnes from the cottages that they had a poor hand dealt to them, very few aces there.

'Don't describe everything in terms of cards,' Mrs Ryan corrected him.

'Right. Then I'd say that the bookie's odds against the Brennans and Dunnes were fixed,' he said, grinning.

But Maura Brennan never complained.

She was always very agreeable and quiet, as if she had accepted long ago that her father was a disgrace and her mother was always asking for handouts. Foxy Dunne was different, he behaved as if his family were dukes and earls instead of drunks and layabouts. You'd never know from looking at Foxy that his father and brothers were barred from almost every establishment in the town. They weren't even allowed into their Uncle Jimmy's the hardware shop.

Foxy neither apologised for them nor defended them. It was as if he regarded them as separate people.

Nessa wished she could be like that sometimes. It hurt her when her mother was sharp to her easy-going father. It annoyed her when her father just shrugged and took none of the responsibility.

'There's a gypsy telling fortunes. They say she's terrific,' Maura said.

'Will we get our fortunes told?' Leo's eyes were sparkling.

Nessa knew that her mother would be very cross indeed if they went anywhere near the tinkers' camp. So would Leo's mother, but Leo didn't care. It would be wonderful to be as free as that.

'She'd only tell you back what you'd tell her,' Foxy said. 'That's what they do. They ask you what you want to be and then they tell you two minutes later that this is what's going to happen to you.'

'But that's dishonest,' Niall Hayes objected.

'That's life, Niall.' Foxy spoke as if he knew much more of the world from his broken-down cottage than did Niall Hayes, the lawyer's son who lived in The Terrace.

'So? Will we go?' Leo was on for any excitement.

'We could read palms to know what's going to happen to us,' Eddie said suddenly.

That seemed much safer to Nessa. Her mother need never know of this. 'How could we do it?' she asked.

'It's easy. There's a life line and a love line, and a whole lot of ridges for children.' Eddie sounded very confident.

'Where did you learn all this?' Foxy asked.

'I got interested in it through a friend,' he said.

'Is that your pen-friend?' Leo asked. He nodded.

A wave of jealousy flooded over Nessa. How did Leo know everything about everyone else and hardly anything about Nessa, who was meant to be her best friend?

'If we're going to do it, let's do it.' Nessa spoke sharply.

They walked up through Barna Woods, up towards the Old Rock. No one needed to lead the way or decide where they were going. Once anything of importance had to be done, it was always at the Old Rock.

Eddie showed them their life lines. Everyone seemed to have a long one.

'How many years to the inch, do you think?' Foxy asked.

'I don't know,' Eddie admitted.

'Lots, I'd say.' Maura wanted to believe the best.

'Now. This is the heart line.' These varied. Nessa's seemed to have a break in hers.

'That means you'll have two loves,' Eddie explained.

'Or maybe love the same person twice. You know. Get your heart broken in the middle and then he'd come back to you,' Maura suggested.

'I might break *his* heart, whoever he is.' Nessa tossed her head.

'Yeah, sure. It doesn't say. Back to the lines.' Eddie moved away from troubled waters.

Foxy's heart line was faint.

So was Leo's. 'Is that good or bad?' Leo asked.

'It's good.' Foxy was firm. 'It means that neither of us will have much romance until it's time for us to marry each other.'

They all laughed.

Eddie moved to children. You'd know how many you were going to have by the number of tiny lines that went sideways at the base of your little finger. Maura was going to have six. She giggled. She'd be like her mother, she said, not knowing when to stop. Leo was going to have two. So was Foxy. He nodded approvingly. Eddie and Niall didn't look as if they were going to have any. They kept searching their hands and uttering great mock wails of despair.

Nessa had three little lines.

'That's three fine little Ryans to bring into the hotel with you,' Foxy said approvingly. He had already pointed out to Leo that they each had a matching score of two on their hands.

'Not Ryans,' Nessa corrected him sharply. 'They'll be my husband's name.'

'Yeah, but if you're anything like your ma they'll be thought of as Ryans,' Foxy said.

Nessa wouldn't let him see how annoyed she was. She fought back the tears of rage at his mockery.

'Don't let him upset you,' Leo said. 'Let it roll off.'

'It's all right for you. You don't care about your family,' Nessa snapped.

The others were still counting their future children. Leo and Nessa sat apart.

Although Nessa's eyes were bright, she would not allow herself to cry. She felt she had to keep talking, it might stop her starting to weep. 'If anyone says anything about your mother or father, Leo Murphy, you just laugh.'

'It wouldn't matter *what* they say, Nessa you eejit. It's only important if it upsets you, otherwise it's just words floating around in the air.'

Leo had lost interest as usual.

She went off to join the others, who had discovered the line in your hand that meant money. It looked as if the only one who would have any wealth to speak of was Maura Brennan from the cottages, the least likely one of them all.

Nessa didn't wait around to hear how her own future was mapped out in terms of wealth. Maybe Foxy would make some joke about her father's love of horses and greyhounds. It was so unfair, she raged. You couldn't answer back. You couldn't say that Foxy Dunne's father was even barred from Johnny Finn's, which meant he must have done something spectacular in terms of drunkenness.

Nor could you say that Foxy had one brother in gaol, and one who had got on the boat to England an hour ahead of the posse before *he* was in gaol too. It seemed that by being so really desperate Foxy's family had put themselves above being spoken badly of.

And yet she got annoyed at home when her mother would say those very things about the Dunnes. She found herself defending her friends in her home and defending her family when she was with her friends.

She couldn't bear it when Maura Brennan wiped her nose on her sleeve, because she knew her mother would sigh and shake her head.

But it was just as bad and even worse if Eddie and Niall were around when her mother would speak sharply to Dad, and tell him to clear the papers away, put on his jacket and make some pretence of running a hotel. She had seen them exchange glances once or twice at her mother's sharpness of tongue.

She longed to explain that it was needed, that Dad would sit there for ever telling long pedigrees of dogs and horses in far-away race tracks, while people waited to be served. She wished they knew that her father didn't take offence like other men might.

Nessa wanted her friends to be interested in tales she told about what her parents discussed over supper at home, but no one could care less. She wanted her mother and father to listen to stories about Foxy being mad enough to fancy Leo, without sniffing and saying something dismissive about both of them.

Up to now, she had felt safe in her family. It was one of the many bad things about growing up that you began to feel it wasn't as safe as it used to be.

A few days after the end of term the convent where Nessa would go to school sent a message saying that they would like to see the new pupils in advance.

'We'll dress you up smartly. It's important to make a good impression,' her mother said.

'But they're not going to refuse me, are they?'

'Will you ever learn? You want them to treat you as someone important, then *look* like someone important.'

'They're nuns, Mam. They don't look at things in that snobby way.'

'They don't, my foot.' Her mother was adamant.

They had a good outing. Leo went in her ordinary clothes, she hadn't dressed up at all.

'She doesn't need to,' Nessa's mother had said when they saw Leo arriving in her ordinary pink cotton frock, with its faded flower pattern and frayed collar.

'Why?'

'Because she is who she is.'

It was a mystery.

Leo was in great form that day, she and Nessa laughed and giggled at everything. They laughed all the more because they had to keep such solemn faces in the convent.

The corridors were long and smelled of floor polish. Little red lights burned in front of statues and pictures of the Sacred Heart, little blue lights in front of Our Lady.

Mother Dorothy, the Principal, spoke to them very earnestly about the need to behave well in school uniform. She told them that it would all be very very different from Shancarrig. She made Shancarrig sound as if it were on the back of the moon.

'Are you two great friends?' Mother Dorothy asked.

'Everyone's friends in our school,' Leo shrugged.

The nun's bright eyes seemed to take it all in.

Leo was all for exploring the town.

'We'd better go back,' Nessa said. 'They'll be wondering where we are.'

Leo looked at her in surprise. 'We're nearly fifteen, we've gone to see the convent where we are going to be imprisoned for the next three years. What can they be worried about?' she asked.

'They'll find something,' Nessa said.

'You're a scream.' Leo was affectionate.

And then, about three weeks later, Leo became almost a different person as far as Nessa was concerned. She was never around, and seemed unwilling to stir from The Glen at all. She'd gone off mysteriously for a holiday with her mother and father and the two great stupid dogs without even telling anyone where she was going.

The summer was endless. There was nobody to play with. Maura Brennan had gone around asking everyone could she be a maid in their house, and eventually Nessa's mother had given her a job, as a chambermaid in the hotel. Maura slept in, which was stupid because it was only ten minutes' walk to the cottages. But then again, Mother had said would Maura want to sleep in that place, and would you want to have her sleeping there?

Eddie Barton was lost in his old pressed flowers, and writing letters. Niall Hayes was complaining all the time about the school he was going to start in next September. He seemed to want reassurance that it was going to be all right.

Nessa wished that Leo was more like Niall, dependent on her, asking for advice. She thought Niall should be more like that tough little girl up in The Glen, able to survive on her own, fight her own battles.

Her mother noticed, like she always did.

'I've told you a dozen times, lead and they'll follow.'

'I could lead a thousand miles and Leo would never follow.' Nessa wished she hadn't admitted it, but it was out before she knew it. Breda Ryan sighed, she looked disappointed. 'I'm sorry, Mam, but it's different for you. You were always a born leader. Some people just have it in them.'

Her mother looked at her thoughtfully.

'I've been thinking about your hair,' she said unexpectedly.

'Well, don't think about it,' Nessa cried. 'Don't always think about how everyone else could do things better if only they did them like you.'

'Nessa!' Her mother was shocked at the outburst.

'I mean it. I'm fifteen. In some countries I could be married and have my own family. *You* always know best. *You* know Dad can't talk about greyhounds. *You* know that we can't call anyone a fella because you think it's vulgar, we have to say boy or man or something that no one else says.'

'I try to give you some manners. Style, that's all.'

'No. That's not all. You don't let us be normal. Maura is below us for some reason. Leo Murphy's family is above us because they live in a big house. You're *so* sure of everything, you just *know* you're right.' Nessa's face was red and angry.

'What brought this on, may I ask?'

'My hair. I was having an ordinary conversation with you and suddenly you said you wanted to talk to me about my hair. I don't care *what* you want, I won't do it. I won't do it. I'll go and tell Dad you want me to cut it or dye it or put it in an awful bun like yours. Whatever you want I won't do it.'

'Fine, fine … if that's the way you feel.' Her mother stood up to leave the sitting room.

Nessa was still in a temper. 'That's right. You'll go down now to Daddy and frighten him. You'll tell him I'm being so difficult you don't know how to handle me, and then poor Dad will come and plead with me, and ask me to apologise.'

'Is that what you think I'm going to do?' Her mother looked distant and surprised.

'It's what you've done for years.' She was in so far now it didn't matter what she said.

'As it happens I was *going* to tell you about your hair. That it never looked better, that you should get a good cut. I was going to suggest that we went to Dublin together and I took you to a good place that

I asked about.'

'I don't believe you!'

'Well, believe what you like. The address is here on a piece of paper. I was going to say we could go on the cheap excursion on Wednesday. But go on your own.'

'How can I go on my own? I've no money.'

'I was going to ask your father to give you the money.'

'But you're not now. I see. You mean I lost it all by being badly behaved.' Nessa gave a mirthless laugh to show she knew the ways of adults.

'Ask him yourself, Nessa. You're too tiresome to talk to any more.'

Nessa didn't ask her father, so he mentioned it on Tuesday night. Why didn't she take the day trip up to Dublin and have a nice hair cut. She said she didn't want to go, she said her mother hated her, she said her mother was only making her feel guilty, she said her hair was horrible, that it was like a horse's tail.

She said she wouldn't go to Dublin on her own.

'Take Leo. I'll stand you both,' he said.

'You can't, Dad.'

'Yes, I can. I make some of the decisions around here.'

'No, you don't.'

'I do, Nessa. I make the ones I want to.' There was something about his voice. She believed him utterly.

Leo went to Dublin with her.

The hairdresser spent ages cutting and styling. 'You should come back every three months.'

'What about in five years?' Nessa said.

'Don't mind her,' Leo interrupted. 'She looks so great now they'll have her up every week.'

'Do I really?' Nessa asked.

'Do you really what?'

'Look great? Were you just saying it to be polite to her?'

'But you're terrific-looking. You *must* know that. You're like Jean Simmons or someone.' Leo said this as if it was as obvious as that it was day rather than night.

'How would I know? No one ever told me.'

'I'm telling you.'

'You're just my friend. You could be telling me just to keep me quiet,' Nessa complained.

'Ah God, Nessa. You can be very tiresome sometimes,' Leo said.

It was the same word as her mother had used. She had better watch it.

It was an up and down relationship with her mother all the years that Nessa Ryan went to school every day in the big town.

It was no use talking to Leo because Leo didn't seem to consider her own mother as any part of her life. If Nessa couldn't go to the pictures it was because her mother wanted her to clean the silver. If Leo couldn't go to the pictures it was only because Lance and Jessica – the dogs – needed to go for a run, or because her father wanted help with something.

Mrs Murphy was never mentioned.

Nessa heard that Mrs Murphy of The Glen was not a strong woman and possibly suffered from her nerves, but this wasn't talked about much in front of children. Leo seemed very distracted, as if there was something wrong at home, but even in the cosiest of chats she couldn't be persuaded to talk about it.

And there were so few other people to talk to.

She wasn't encouraged to talk to Maura Brennan who worked as a chambermaid in the hotel. Every time she stopped in a corridor to speak to Maura, Maura looked around nervously.

'No, Nessa. Your mother wouldn't like us to be chatting.'

'That's bull, Maura. Anyway, I don't care what she wants.'

'I do. It's my bread and butter.'

And there was no answer to that.

Sometimes Mrs Ryan was terrific, like when she got them all dancing lessons – Leo, Nessa and her young sisters Catherine and Nuala, the two Blake girls. It had been the greatest of fun.

Sometimes Mother was horrible – when she had asked Father to leave the bar the night he won eighty-five pounds on a greyhound. 'I just didn't want to lose *two hundred* and eighty-five pounds, Nessa,' she had explained afterwards. 'He was going out in to the streets looking for greyhounds, or anything that approached them in shape, to buy them drinks.'

Nessa had fumed over it. Her father should have been allowed his dignity. He should have had his night of celebration.

Her mother had been wonderful about the record player, and Nessa built up her own collection – 'Three Coins in the Fountain', 'Rock Around the Clock', 'Whatever Will Be Will Be'. But by the time she bought Tab Hunter's 'Young Love' her mother had become horrible again, saying that Nessa was now leaving school with a very poor Leaving Certificate.

There was no question of university, no plan for a career, nothing except the usual refuge of those who couldn't think what to do – the secretarial course in the town.

Nessa became very mulish that summer. Several times her father asked her for the sake of peace to try and ensure they had a happy house.

'You're so weak, Daddy,' she snapped at him one day. She was sorry instantly. It was so like something she felt her mother would have said.

'No, I'm not weak actually. I just like a quiet life without the people I love fighting like tinkers, that's all.' He spoke mildly.

'Why do you nag me so much?' she asked her mother. 'I mean, it's not going to make either of us happier, and it's upsetting Daddy.'

'I don't think of it as nagging. I think of it as giving you courage and strength to live your own life. To be full of courage. Honestly.' She believed her mother too when she said that.

'Did you always have courage?'

'No I did not. I learned it when I came to this house. When I had to cope with the pair on the wall.'

'The what?'

'Your sainted grandparents,' her mother said crisply.

Nessa looked up in shock at the elderly Ryans who had always been spoken of with such admiration and respect in this house.

'Why did it need courage to cope with them?' she asked.

'They would have liked your father to have lived in a glass case and they could have thrown sugar at him,' Mrs Ryan said.

When she said things like this she seemed very normal, like someone you could talk to, but she didn't say them often enough.

So, the summer she was eighteen Nessa began her course in shorthand and typewriting with a very bad grace.

Leo Murphy wouldn't come with her, a series of vague and unsatisfactory excuses about being needed up at The Glen. It was a confused time in Shancarrig.

Eddie Barton was so depressed working in Dunne's that he could hardly raise his eyes when you went in to talk to him. Niall Hayes was in Dublin setting up his plans to study law. Foxy was in England on the building sites. The Blake girls were studying in Dublin. She wasn't meant to talk to Maura. Her mother asked so many questions about who she went to the pictures with in the big town it sometimes seemed hardly worth the whole business of going.

She was ready for something exciting to happen the weekend Richard Hayes came to town.

He was very handsome, not square like Niall. He was tall and slim and very grown up, seven or eight years older than Nessa – twenty-five or twenty-six. He had been sent away from Dublin because of some disgrace with a girl.

Everyone knew that.

He had been banished to Shancarrig. Where apparently there would be no girls. Or no girls worth looking at.

Nessa dressed herself very very carefully until she caught his eye.

'Things *are* looking up,' he said. 'I'm Richard Hayes.'

'Hello, Richard,' Nessa said in a voice she had been practising for weeks.

His smile was warm but it made her nervous. She longed to run away and ask someone for advice, and as it happened at that very moment her mother called for her.

'Now I know your name,' he said.

'Only my mother calls me Vanessa,' she said.

But she was glad to escape.

Her mother had seen it all. 'What a handsome young man,' she said.

'Yes.' Nessa bit her lip.

'You have absolutely no competition,' her mother assured her. 'That's a man who likes pretty girls, and you are the prettiest girl in Shancarrig.'

The next time he met her he suggested that she take him for a walk.

'I'd love to do that but I'm practising my awful grammalogues,' said Nessa.

'Shorthand is going out of fashion, it'll all be machines soon,' he said.

'You may very well be right, but not before I do my Certificate exams. So maybe I'll see you later in the evening,' she said. She could see by his eyes that she had done the right thing. He was more interested than ever before.

'Absolutely, Vanessa,' he said with a mock bow.

She took him for long walks around her country.

She brought him up to the Old Rock and told him all its legends. She brought him to the school and showed him the tree where they had carved their names. She took him to the graveyard and pointed out the oldest tombstones to him. She showed him the children fishing in the river, and explained how you caught little fish with your hands if you could trap them in the stones.

She told him about Mattie the postman, who didn't go to mass but could deliver any letter to anyone if it just had their name and Shancarrig on it. She brought him to meet Father Gunn and Father Barry, saying that she was being a guide. Mrs Kennedy, the priests' housekeeper, looked very disapproving so Nessa just laughed and sat up on her table, saying that she had brought Richard Hayes here especially to taste one of Mrs Kennedy's scones. They were legendary.

Privately she told Richard they were legendary because they were as heavy as stones.

Nessa took Richard Hayes to visit Miss Ross in her house, she brought him to Nellie Dunne's shop, she took him to every nook and cranny in about three days.

'It's your introduction,' she said to him cheerfully. 'So that you'll never say you weren't shown the place properly.' She could sense that he was delighted with her, that he thought her a confident, bright young woman.

And indeed, that is what she was.

She was proud of her dark thick hair, her clear skin, her bright yellow and red blouses, and most proud of all that she wasn't silly and giggling like so many others were with him. Her mother had given her this gift, this belief that she was the equal of any Adonis who came to Shancarrig.

But Nessa would not settle for a weaker man like her mother had done. She wouldn't take second best, which was obviously how her mother must regard her father. There would be no dull, plodding, average fellow for Nessa. Not now. Not now that she had seen the admiring glance of a man like Richard.

He was the kind of man who came through a town like this once every fifty years. She was lucky to have caught his eye, she must be absolutely certain not to lose it again. This was the kind of man you could dream about night and day, someone who would occupy all your thoughts. But for some reason she didn't really allow herself to think about what she felt for him, this charming attentive Richard Hayes, who seemed to want to spend every free minute he had in her company. Yes of course she wanted to think that he really liked her, but some warning voice made her think that she could only keep his attention if she didn't seem to care.

It was an act.

Life shouldn't be an act. Yet she felt that they were unequal somehow. She must play this one very carefully.

Of course she heard a lot of stories about why he had come to help his Uncle Bill in the office. Some people said that Mr Hayes was getting too busy to manage on his own and that he had little hopes of his son Niall ever learning enough about the business. Niall was off to University in Dublin where he would serve his time in a solicitor's office as well. It would be four or five years before he'd qualify – old Bill Hayes was quite right to take this bright young man into his firm.

There were others who said that Richard had been sent to Shancarrig to cool his heels – there had been talk of an incident in Dublin, an incident involving a judge's daughter. There was another story about a broken engagement and a breach of promise action settled at the last moment.

In the stories Richard Hayes, cousin of the solid Niall, was always shown as a playboy.

The feeling was that Shancarrig would be very small potatoes indeed for someone who had seen and done as much as this handsome young man of twenty-five or so who had taken the place by storm.

'Isn't he fantastic?' Leo had said when she saw him for the first time.

'He's very easy to talk to.' Nessa was quick to let her best friend know just how far she was ahead in the race which every woman in Shancarrig seemed to have joined.

'I wish he'd come into the bar more,' Nessa's mother said. 'He's such an attractive kind of fellow he'd be a great draw.'

'I'd say that boyo has been asked to leave more bars than a few,' Conor Ryan said with the voice of a man who has seen it all and knew it all.

Unexpectedly Gerry O'Sullivan, their personable young barman, agreed.

'Real lady killer,' he said. 'The kind they'd go for each other's throats over.'

'That's what we don't need,' Mrs Ryan said firmly. 'Maybe it's just as well he's not in here every night.'

'Who is there in Shancarrig that would cut anyone's throat over a fellow? There's not that kind of passion and spark around the place at all.' Conor Ryan was back reading the forecasts for race meetings in towns he would never visit, on courses he would never walk.

Breda Ryan looked thoughtfully out at the front desk where Nessa was painstakingly practising her typing. They were meant to do an hour a day homework, and she had covered up the keys of the hotel machine with Elastoplast so that she couldn't see the letters.

Nessa's hair was shiny, her eyes were bright, her neckline low. They didn't have to look far for any passion and spark as far as Richard Hayes was concerned.

Nessa fought off three attempts by her mother to talk about sex.

'I *know* all that, didn't you tell me that years ago when I got my periods first.'

'It's different kind of telling now, there are other things to be taken into consideration ... please, Nessa.'

'There are no other things, I don't want to talk about it.' She wriggled away.

She didn't want to hear her mother say anything coarse or frightening. She was terrified enough already. These were problems that no mother could solve.

Richard Hayes told Nessa that she was beautiful. He called into the hotel and sat up on the reception desk to talk to her. It was the middle of the afternoon, a time when hotel business was slack and when Richard very probably should have been in his uncle's office.

He told Nessa that she had wonderful dark looks and she reminded him of Diana the mistress.

'Was she good or bad?'

'She was beautiful. Don't you know about her?'

'No, the nuns sort of dwelt more on the New Testament. She was the one that was extremely chaste, wasn't she?'

'That's her story and she's sticking to it,' he laughed, and she reddened. It seemed to her that he was eyeing her as if he was thinking along those lines himself.

He stroked her cheek thoughtfully.

'What happens if a girl is less than extremely chaste here?' he asked.

'They go to their grannies or to England.' She hoped that her cheeks didn't still look so red. It was just that he was looking at her breasts

189

and appreciating her in a way that a man might if he wanted to make love.

Or maybe she was just fancying it. Nessa didn't know these days if anything was real or whether she was imagining a whole series of looks and gestures and feelings that didn't exist at all.

'I'd be very careful if we were ... to do anything that might cause a trip to your Granny's,' he said. 'You know, really careful. There would be no danger at all.'

From somewhere she found a confident answer.

'Ah but there wouldn't be any question of that, Richard,' she said.

He was more interested than ever.

'Are you afraid?'

'No. There could be other reasons why people might say no to you.'

'But you do like me, that I know.' He was playful.

'But do I *love* you, and do you love *me*? That's what you'd have to ask yourself before going wherever people go.'

'Like up to the Old Rock?'

He had only been in Shancarrig ten days and already he knew where the lovers went. To the little hollow in Barna Woods where the road to the Old Rock began.

'If only we knew what love is, Vanessa Mary Ryan, then we could rule the world.' He sighed a heavy mock sigh.

'And would we rule it well, Richard Aloysius Hayes?' she laughed.

'How did you know that?'

'I asked Niall what the RAH stood for on your tennis bag.'

'And he told you? The swine!'

They were fencing now, and laughing. He caught her by the wrist.

'I'm not joking, you're the loveliest girl for miles around.'

'You haven't seen any others.'

'Excuse me but I have. I went on a tour of inspection, brought my tennis bag up to The Glen, got no game, and no great joy out of your so-called best friend, little bag of nerves with a frizzy head, she is.'

'Don't speak like that about Leo.'

'And I studied Madeleine Ross.'

'She's ancient.'

'She's three years older than I am. And let me see who else. Pretty little Maura Brennan who works in Ryan's Ritz, but I think she's been to the Old Rock with a young Mr O'Sullivan. We'll have wedding bells there if I'm not greatly mistaken.'

'Maura? Pregnant! I don't believe it.'

He held up his hands defensively.

'I could be wrong,' he said.

'She's a fool. Gerry O'Sullivan will never marry her...' Nessa had let it slip out.

'Aha ... so it's not just a question of loving each other. It's a question of the chap marrying the girl, is it?'

Nessa had lost that one. 'I must be off,' she said.

She barely made it upstairs on shaking legs and went into her room. There she found her sisters Catherine and Nuala starting up guiltily from the dressing table where they had been reading her diary.

'I thought you were meant to be at the reception desk,' Catherine said, flying immediately to the attack.

'We hadn't read anything private really,' begged Nuala, who was younger and more frightened.

Frightened she had reason to be.

Nessa Ryan, eighteen and desired by the most handsome man in Ireland, drew herself up to her full height.

'You can explain all that later,' she said, taking the key out of the inside of the door. 'I'm locking you in until I find Mother.'

'Don't tell Mam,' roared Nuala.

'Mam won't like what you've been up to,' Catherine threatened.

But Nessa had the upper hand. She had written nothing in her diary, it was all in the back of her shorthand notebook which never left her side.

She had been coming up to write more, to tell herself of the passion in his voice, the tingles she had felt when he held her wrist, how he had said that he could love her.

She ignored the pleas and lamentations from her room and set off to find her mother.

In the corridor she met Maura Brennan carrying sheets.

'Is everything all right, Maura?' she asked.

'Why do you ask?'

'Well, I don't know. You look different.'

'I *am* different. I'm getting married next week to Gerry. I haven't told everyone else. It was only just arranged.'

'Married?'

'I know. Isn't it great!'

Nessa was dumbfounded. Perhaps there was a different set of rules, perhaps fellows *did* marry you if you went to the Old Rock with them.

Maybe her mother and the nuns and Catholic Truth Society pamphlets had it all wrong. She pulled herself together.

'That's great, Maura,' she said. 'Congratulations.'

Nessa found her mother, and told her of the two criminals locked in the bedroom.

'Give them a very bad punishment,' she ordered.

'Did they find anything to read, anything they shouldn't have?' Her mother's eyes were anxious.

'If I have to say to you once more that there is nothing to find, nothing to discuss, I will go *mad*.' The words were almost shouted.

To her surprise her mother looked at her admiringly.

'You know, I think Richard may be good for you after all. You're getting to be confident at last. You'll be a leader yet.'

It was true. She did feel more in control. She was delighted to find that her mother took such a strong stand with Catherine and Nuala. And so, unexpectedly, did her father.

'A person must be allowed to have their private life and their dreams,' he told the two sulking girls, who were allowed no outings for a week. 'It's a monstrous thing to invade someone's life of dreams.'

'There was nothing there,' Catherine said.

'To say that is making it worse still.'

The two girls were startled.

There was Nessa, usually the one in trouble, Nessa who had been making calf's eyes at Niall Hayes's cousin, and all she was getting was praise for doing something as dangerous as locking them in a bedroom.

'Suppose there had been a fire?' Catherine even suggested as a possibility.

She got little support.

'Then you would have burned to death,' said their mother.

Eddie Barton came in sometimes for a chat.

'Are you doing a line with Richard Hayes?' he asked Nessa.

'What's a line?'

'I don't know, I often wondered. But are you?'

'No I'm not. He comes in and out. He's very handsome, probably too handsome for me.'

'I know what you mean,' Eddie said unflatteringly.

'Thanks a lot, friend.'

'No, I didn't mean that. You're fine-looking and you've got much better-looking than when we were all young, honestly...' Eddie was flustered now and he saw he was making gestures to show how much better-looking Nessa had got. Gestures that indicated a bosom and a small waist. But she didn't seem offended. 'Looks are important, aren't they?' He seemed anxious.

'I suppose so, though people keep saying they're not.'

Eddie was running his hand through his spiky hair. 'I wish fellows improved, all fellows, like all girls seem to.'

'Aren't you a grand-looking fellow, Eddie?' Her voice was encouraging and light, she thought.

'Don't make fun of me.' His face was red.

'I'm not.'

'Yes you are. I've hair like God knows what, I'm pushing a brush around bloody Dunne's all day. Who'd look at me?'

He banged out of the hotel, leaving Nessa mystified. As far as she knew Eddie had never asked any girl in Shancarrig out, and had shown no interest at all in any of the females around the place. He did come in from time to time to make mysterious phone calls to Scotland. It was too hard to understand, and anyway she had far more important things on her mind.

Richard took Nessa to the pictures in the town in his uncle's car.

'He lets you drive this?'

'He doesn't go out at night.'

'Niall never drove it.'

'Niall never asked.'

Niall Hayes was staying with a schoolfriend of his. Together they were going to a three-week course in book-keeping. They hated it. Niall had sent several letters and postcards to Nessa saying how dreary it was. He hoped university would be better.

'I think Niall fancies you desperately,' Richard said as he kissed Nessa in his uncle's car.

She drew away.

'I don't think so,' she said, cool, ungiggly. Her mother was right. She had grown up a lot since Richard had come to Shancarrig.

'Oh I think he does. Doesn't he take you to the pictures? Doesn't Niall plan journeys to the Old Rock with you like I do?' He repeated his own words about his younger cousin.

'Niall never asked,' said Nessa.

'Niall will be back tomorrow, Ethel was telling me,' Mrs Ryan said to Nessa.

'That should shake the town to its foundations,' Nessa said.

'You and he were always good friends.' Her mother's voice was mild so Nessa became contrite.

'That's true, we were. He's got very mopey though, Mam. Not easy to talk to.'

'Everyone doesn't have the charm of his cousin Richard.'

'Richard's normal. He's nice to people, he's pleasant. He's not always grousing and groaning about things the way Niall is.'

'Maybe Niall has something to grouse and groan about.'

'What? What any more than the rest of us?'

'Well, his best girl is starry-eyed about his cousin, his place in the firm isn't nearly as secure as it used to be ... *and* he doesn't have a wonderful understanding mother like you do. He has dreary old Ethel.'

They laughed as they sometimes could nowadays like sisters, like friends.

'What would *you* do for Niall if you were his friend?' Nessa asked. She thought she saw her mother watching her very carefully, but she couldn't be sure.

'I'd encourage him to fight for his place over there. He's Bill's son. It's *his* business. I'd tell him that there are only a few chances and you should take them. Oh, I suppose I'd go on a bit about letting grass grow under your feet.'

'He mightn't listen to me.'

'No. People often don't listen when others are out for their good.'

'Did Dad listen to you?'

'Ah, yes. But that was different, I loved your father. Still do.'

'I don't *love* Niall, but I am very fond of him.'

'Then don't let him get walked on,' said Breda Ryan.

Nessa invited Niall to come over to the hotel and have a drink with her. It felt very grown up.

'You look great,' he said.

'Thanks, Niall. You look fine too.'

'I meant *pretty* like ...' he said.

'What work are you doing in the office?' She changed the subject.

'Filing! Taking things out of torn envelopes and putting them into non-torn envelopes. God, Dinny Dunne could do that on one of his good days.'

Niall was full of misery and Nessa was full of impatience. Why hadn't he the fire to get up and go, the sheer charm of his cousin?

They were the sons of brothers, after all. Richard's father must have been the one with the spirit.

Richard had told his uncle that a younger man should go around on home visits, which meant that he had the use of the car and could be out all day. Who knew how long it took to make a will or to get the details in a right-of-way claim? Who could measure how many hours it might involve talking to a publican about the extinguishing of a licence or to a woman about a marriage settlement involving a farm?

Richard was sunny and cheerful to everyone.

If he had been asked to do the files he would have made it into the most prestigious job in the office. Why could Niall not see this? Why did he hunch his shoulders and look defeated? Why didn't he throw back his head and laugh?

'Did you see much of Richard while I was away?' Niall asked, cutting across her thoughts.

'He's been around, he's been very lively.'

'He's not reliable, of course,' Niall said.

'Don't be such a tell-tale, Niall.' Her lightness of voice hid her annoyance. She wanted to hear nothing that would puncture her idea of Richard Hayes, no silly family story of shame or disgrace.

'It's just that you should know.'

'Oh, I know all about him,' she said airily.

'You do?' Niall seemed relieved.

'A girl in every town. We even had that Elaine down from Dublin last week. No, there are no secrets.'

'Elaine was here? After all that happened!'

'Right in front of your house. Dropped him off from a real posh car.'

'There'll be hell to pay if anyone knows that. She was the one.'

'The one?'

'The one that had the ... the one who got into ... the one.'

'Oh yes, I supposed she was.' Nessa's heart was leaden. Niall didn't have to finish any of his sentences. The stories had gone before, the judge's daughter who was reported to have been pregnant.

Imagine her coming down to Shancarrig, pursuing Richard after all that.

She must be pretty desperate.

'So that's all right.' Niall looked at Nessa protectively, as if he was relieved that he didn't have to rescue her from a quagmire of misunderstanding.

'We're all fine here, it was a lovely summer. *You* sound as if you had a terrible time.' She led him into a further catalogue of his woes so that she could follow her own line of thought. Surely Richard couldn't still be involved with this girl. Then of course it was known that this girl, unlike Nessa, would go to bed with him. And had.

Is this all he wanted? Surely he wanted other things – fun and chat, and kissing, and a girl who was seven years younger than him who looked like Diana the mistress?

If only there was someone to ask. But there was no one.

On Maura Brennan's wedding day Leo suggested they go to the church.

'Maura won't like it. She doesn't want to mix because of working in the hotel.'

'That's pure rubbish,' Leo said. 'It's just your mother who doesn't want her to mix. Let's go.'

As they sat waiting for the sad little ceremony to begin Nessa was pleased to see Niall Hayes and Eddie Barton come in as well.

'I got an hour off from the desperate Dunnes,' Eddie whispered – he worked for the more respectable branch of the family in Foxy's uncle's hardware shop. He seemed very miserable about it.

'I'm allowed out from sticking labels on envelopes,' Niall said.

'I'm meant to be at the typing course but I told my mother we had a day off. I'm watched like a hawk,' Nessa complained.

'We weren't the most successful class ever to come out of Shancarrig school, were we?' asked Leo with a little laugh.

'Well, at least the rest of us . . .' Nessa stopped. She had remembered before that Leo had looked very upset when she had been referred to as a lady of leisure.

Leo flashed her a smile of gratitude. They sat in supportive silence, the four of them, as they watched their schoolfriend Maura, pregnant and happy, marry Gerry O'Sullivan, small, handsome, with one best man but no other friend or family in the church.

'He doesn't look very reliable,' whispered Niall.

'Jesus, Mary and Holy Saint Joseph, who do you think *is* reliable these days?' Nessa hissed.

'*I* am, for what it's worth.' He looked at her and suddenly she saw that he did like her, much more than in the sort of hang-dog dependent way she had thought. Niall Hayes was keen on her. It didn't give her the kind of boost that she had thought it might. In the days when nobody fancied her she would love to have had a few notches on her gun, affections to play with, hearts to break.

But Niall was too much of a friend for that.

'Thank you,' she said very simply in a whisper.

Maura was delighted with the present they bought her, a little glass-fronted cabinet. Leo had remembered Maura saying that she would love to collect treasures and display them in a cabinet. There were tears of joy in her eyes when they delivered it to the cottage where she would be living – only a stone's throw from where her father still fell home drunk every night.

'You're great friends,' she said, her voice choked.

Nessa felt a blanket of guilt almost suffocate her. For years Maura had been working in Ryan's Hotel and hardly a sentence exchanged between them. If only she had the courage of a Leo Murphy she would have taken no heed of offending her mother, of crossing boundaries of familiarity between staff and owners.

But she *did* have courage these days and she would show it, use it. When she got back to the hotel her mother asked where the festivities were going to be held.

'You know that it will be a few drinks in Johnny Finn's and whatever bit of cold chicken poor Maura managed to put out on plates for those that will drag themselves back to her cottage for it.'

'Well, she should have thought of all that...' her mother began.

'No she shouldn't, she should be having a reception here by right. She was my schoolfriend, she and Gerry both work here. Anyone with a bit of decency would have given them that at least.'

Breda Ryan was taken aback.

'You don't understand...'

'I don't like what I do understand. It's so snobby, so ludicrous. Does it make us better people to be seen to be superior to Maura Brennan from the cottages? Is this what you always wanted, a place on some kind of ladder?'

'No. That's not what I always wanted.' Her mother was calm and didn't show the expected anger at being shouted at in the front hall of the hotel.

'Well, what did you want then?'

'I'll tell you if you take that puss off your face ... and stop shouting like a fishwife. Come on.' Her mother was talking to her like an equal. They walked into the bar.

'Conor, why don't you take a fiver from the till and go up to Johnny

Finn's to buy a few drinks for Gerry and Maura?'

Nessa's father looked up, pleased.

'Didn't I only suggest...?'

'And you were right. Go on now while they're still sober enough to know you're treating them. Nessa and I'll look after the bar.'

They watched as Conor Ryan moved eagerly across to the festivities, hardly daring to believe his good luck. Nessa sat still and waited to be told. Mrs Ryan poured two small glasses of cream sherry, something that had never happened before. Nessa decided to make no comment; she raised the glass to her lips as if she and her mother had been knocking back drinks for years.

'People want things at different times. I wanted a man called Teddy Burke. I wanted him from the moment I saw him when I was sixteen until I was twenty-one. Five long years.' Nessa looked at this stranger sipping the sherry; she was afraid to speak. 'Teddy Burke had a word for everyone, but that's all it was ... a word ... I thought it was more. I thought I was special. I built a life of dreams on it. I couldn't eat. I lost my health and my looks, such as they were. They sent me away to do a domestic economy course.

'Do you know, I can't really remember those years. I suppose I must have followed the course – I got my exams and certificates – but I only thought of Teddy Burke.' She paused for such a long time that Nessa felt able to speak.

She spoke as a friend, as an equal. 'And did he know, did he have any idea...?'

'I don't think so, truly. He was so used to everyone admiring, I was just one more.' Her mother's eyes were far away as she sat there in the empty hotel bar, her dark hair back in a loose coil with a mother-of-pearl clasp on it. Her pale pink blouse had its neat collar out over her dark pink cardigan – she looked every inch the successful businesswoman. This story of a thin frightened girl loving a man for five years – a man who didn't know she existed – was hard to believe.

'So anyway, one day I was told that Teddy Burke was going to marry Annie Lynch, the plainest girl for three parishes, with a bad temper and a cast in her eye. Everything changed. He was marrying her for her land, for her great acres running down to the lakes and over green valleys, for the fishing rights, for the stock. A man as handsome and loving as Teddy Burke could trade everything for land.

'It made me wonder what I really wanted.

'And I went to a cousin's wedding and met your father and I decided that I wanted to go far from where I lived, where I would remember Teddy Burke's laugh and his way with people. I decided that I wanted to make your father strong and confident like Teddy was when he got the land, like Annie Lynch always was because she had the land ... I put my mind to it.'

There was a long silence. Nessa was taking it in.

'Were you ever sorry?'

'Not a day, not once I decided. And hasn't it turned out well? The hotel has survived, the pair out in the pictures in the hall would have let it run into the ground, and they'd have let your father go off to the British army.'

'Why are you telling me this now?'

'Because you thought that all I wanted was to put ourselves above other people. I may have done that by accident but it wasn't what I set out to do.'

'Does Dad know about Teddy Burke?'

'There was nothing for him to know but a young girl's silliness and dreams.'

Mattie came in, his sack of letters delivered.

'This town is going to hell, Mrs Ryan,' he said. 'A wedding party bawling "Bless this House" above in Johnny Finn's and the women of the house sipping sherry in Ryan's.'

'And no one to pour a pint for the postman,' laughed Nessa's mother.

The moment was over, it might never come again.

Nessa began to look at other people in a new light after this. Perhaps everyone had a huge love in their life, or something they thought was a huge love. Maybe Mr Kelly up at the school had fancied a night-club singer before he settled for Mrs Kelly. Maybe Nellie Dunne had once been head over heels in love with some travelling salesman who had come many years ago to Ryan's Commercial Hotel, but who had married someone else. Maybe one of those old men in the commercial room had been Nellie's heart's desire.

It wasn't so impossible.

Look at Eddie Barton, falling in love with someone in Scotland. It had never been exactly clear how he had got in touch with her in the first place, but apparently he had been writing to Christine Taylor for ages, and phoning her from the hotel.

And then she had arrived over and was living with his mother.

Nessa was amazed at the change in Eddie. He was speaking to the Dunnes, cousins of Foxy, as if he was their equal. He was in the hotel with Christine discussing improvements and ways to decorate the bedrooms.

Love did extraordinary things to people.

Eileen Blake from The Terrace said that she was stopping for a coffee in Portlaoise on her way back from Dublin and who was there but Richard Hayes and a girl, and they were booking in. As man and wife.

Young Maria Kelly from Shancarrig schoolhouse was reported to have been at a dance with him in the big town, but her parents didn't know because she had climbed in and out her window through the branches of the old copper beech tree that grew in the yard.

Nessa Ryan heard all these facts in the space of three days. She came across them accidentally, they were not brought in as deliberate bad news to her door.

She felt, not as she had feared she might – no sense of cold betrayal, no rage that a man should tell her she was special and he wanted her to be his girl, and yet behave the same way with half the country. Very clearly and deliberately she felt her infatuation with him end. Perhaps she *was* her mother's daughter much more than she had ever believed. She was not ready to give him up but she would have him in her life under different terms.

Richard came into the commercial room of the hotel. There were no travellers staying and so Nessa was using the room to do her shorthand homework.

'I have to go into town tomorrow. I could pick you up outside your college,' he offered.

She could imagine the eyes of her classmates when Richard Hayes leant across to open the door of the car for her.

'And where would we go then?' she asked.

'I'm sure we'd find somewhere,' he said.

Nessa looked back into the bar where her mother and father were standing, well out of earshot.

'They're not listening.' Richard was impatient. But that wasn't what concerned Nessa. She looked at them and saw her mother stroke Dad's face gently, lovingly.

She saw that it really never mattered who talked to the men from the brewery, the biscuit salesmen, who hired or fired the barmen. It wasn't important that Sergeant Keane dealt with her mother over the licensing laws, not her father. Mother had forgotten Teddy whatever he was, he'd have been no good to her. She had found what she really wanted, someone she could share her own strength with. Nessa saw for the first time that her mother had got what she wanted. It wasn't a case of settling for second best.

And with a shock of recognition she felt that she was going to follow exactly the same path. It wouldn't be a question of aiming high and searching for fireworks. There might be an entirely different way to live your life. Unbidden, Niall's worried face came to mind. She longed to calm him and tell him it would all be all right.

She looked straight at Richard, right into his eyes.

'No thanks,' she said. 'No to everything. Thank you all the same.'

It wasn't at all easy to do.

But she would not live in fear of him and how he would react. Nothing was worth that.

'Well, well, well.' He looked around the room scornfully. 'So *this* is all you are ever going to amount to. A second-rate shabby hotel ... a grown woman still a prisoner to her mother.' He looked very angry and put out. People didn't usually speak to Richard Hayes like this. Girls certainly didn't.

Nessa was furious.

'It is *not* a shabby hotel. It's my home. *My* home. I live here and I choose to live here. You can't even live where you want to because they run you out of town. Don't come down here and start criticising us. It doesn't sit well on you. And answer me one thing: how would I amount to any more if I were to go off to the glen with you and roll around for five minutes on the ground?'

'It would be longer than five minutes,' he said mischievously. She hadn't lost him. He fancied her all the more because she was refusing him.

What a wonderful power.

It was the making of Nessa Ryan.

She didn't flirt with him like every other woman within a hundred-mile radius seemed to. She did not want to be known as his girl.

It was as if she had turned around the relationship, made it businesslike, affectionate but in no way exclusive. She teased him about his latest conquests, real and supposed, she knew that her very lack of jealousy was driving him wild. She was happy in the knowledge that he desired her. When she met him it was always with other people.

She finished her course at the college and went to work full time for her mother and father.

It was she who decided to lift the hotel on to a higher level. She contacted the tourist board about grants, and organised that they got money advanced to improve their facilities. She asked visiting Americans to write letters to their local papers praising Ryan's so as to get them further custom.

She told her mother to drop the word Commercial from the title.

'Ryan's makes it sound like a pub,' her mother complained.

'Call it Ryan's Shancarrig Hotel,' said Nessa.

A few eyebrows were raised. Nellie Dunne presided over several conversations about the Ryans having notions.

'That young one is the cut of her mother,' said Nellie. 'I remember when Breda O'Connor came in and took the whole establishment from Conor's mother and father. That Nessa will do the same.'

But Nessa Ryan showed no signs of friction with her mother and father. She would laugh with her mother about the Sainted Grandparents who glared from the picture on the wall. She told her father that he looked handsome in a jacket and begged him to have nice framed pictures of racehorses on the wall, so that they might attract a few of the horsey set and give some legitimacy to her father's constant topic of conversation.

Catherine and Nuala were mystified by her. The most handsome man around seemed to be waiting on their sister Nessa and she barely gave him the time of day. They watched uncomprehending as Nessa became more and more attractive-looking, her dark shiny hair always loose and cut with a fringe. A style that owed nothing to the hairdresser but a lot to a picture in a children's book she had seen, a picture of Diana the mistress.

Nessa got on well with her mother. The two of them often drove to Dublin to look for fittings and fabrics. At an early age she seemed to have their trust, and to be allowed a lot of freedom that was later denied to the more spirited Catherine and Nuala.

'Why can't we go to Galway on our own? Nessa did,' Catherine complained.

'Because you're both so unreliable and untrustworthy you'd probably go under a hedge with the first pair of tinker boys you met,' Nessa said cheerfully to them. They felt it a great betrayal, there should be *some* solidarity between sisters. Imagine mentioning going under hedges in front of their mother, putting ideas in her mind.

'I have no solidarity with you,' Nessa said. 'You steal my make-up, you wear my nylons, you spray yourself with *my* perfume. You don't wash the bath, you do nothing to help in the hotel, you can't wait to get away from here. *Why* should I help you?'

Put like that it was hard to know why.

'Flesh and blood,' Catherine suggested.

'Overrated,' Nessa told her.

'Would you try for hotel management, do you think?' her mother suggested. 'It would teach you so much. There's a great course in Dublin.'

'I'm happy here,' Nessa said.

'I don't ask you about Richard...' her mother began.

'I know, Mother. It's one of the things I love about you.' Nessa headed her off before she could start.

She wondered how long would be his exile in Shancarrig, and on Niall's behalf she worried lest he had made too permanent and important a niche for himself with his Uncle Bill.

Mr Hayes came in to drink in Ryan's Shancarrig Bar with Major Murphy, Leo's father, sometimes. Nessa served behind the bar from time to time. She said it helped her to know what the customers wanted. Mr Hayes dropped no hint of how long his nephew would stay, but to Nessa's distress he showed little enthusiasm about his son's return.

'Hard to know what he learned up there, you couldn't get a word out of him,' she heard him say to Dr Jims Blake one evening. She didn't want to join in the conversation but later she brought up the subject.

'Niall seems to be enjoying university and studying hard,' she said.

'Divil a bit of a sign he gives of either.'

'Oh now. All fathers are the same. Still, business is good. There'll be plenty for Niall to take on when he comes back.'

'Oh, I don't know. What with Richard...' He let his voice trail away.

'But Richard won't be here for ever?' Her voice was clear and without guile.

Bill Hayes looked at her directly. 'There's something keeping him here. I had a notion it might be yourself?' he said.

'No, Mr Hayes, I'm not the girl for Richard.' There was no play-acting, nothing wistful – she seemed to be stating a fact.

'Well, something's keeping him here, Nessa. It's not the pay, and it's not the social life.'

'I expect he'll move on one day, like he moved in.' Her voice was bland, expressionless.

'I expect so.' He sounded troubled.

Niall was home the following week.

'I hear they're giving you a car for your twenty-first birthday,' he said to Nessa.

'It's meant to be a surprise, shut up about it,' she hissed.

'I didn't know it was a secret. Isn't it great though? A car of your own.'

'You could have one too.'

'How, might I ask? I'm not the doted-on daughter of the house.'

'No, but you're the eldest son of the house, and you never show the slightest interest in your father's business.'

'I'm only qualifying as a bloody solicitor, that's all.' Niall was offended.

'But what kind of a solicitor? You don't even ask him what's going on. You don't know about the competition.'

'Richard, I suppose.'

'No, you fool. He's the family, he's on your team. The competition. You know Gerry O'Neill the auctioneer in the town? Well, he has a brother who's taking a lot of the conveyancing, even out this way. You have to fight back.'

'I didn't know that.'

'You don't ask.'

'When I do ask can I help I'm told to tear up files and put labels on envelopes.'

'That was three years ago, silly.' She put her arm around his shoulder. 'Bring your father in here for a pint, treat him as an equal.'

'He wouldn't like that.'

'I used to be like that, I spent my whole childhood thinking my mother wouldn't like this or that. I was wrong. They want us to have minds of our own.'

'No. They want us to be reliable,' Niall insisted.

'Yes, well. You and I *are* reliable, so they've got that much. Now they want us to have views, opinions, be out for the common good.'

He looked at her with great admiration.

'Have you . . . ?' he began.

She knew he wanted to say something about Richard.

'Yes?' Her voice stopped him asking.

'Nothing,' Niall said.

'See you and your father tonight.'

When Nessa Ryan got her car for her twenty-first birthday she first took her mother and father for a drive around Shancarrig, waving to everyone they passed. She caught her mother's eye in the driving mirror more than once and they smiled. Friends. People who understood each other. She was doing the right thing. Thanking them publicly, showing Shancarrig that Breda O'Connor had come here twenty-two years ago and made a triumph of her life.

It was six o'clock and the angelus was ringing as she headed back home. People would be coming in to Ryan's Shancarrig now for a drink. There would be autumn tourists to check in – the coach buses arrived in the evening.

As they passed Eddie Barton's house Eddie and his Scottish Christine were in the garden. Nessa screeched to a halt.

'I'll come back for you later. I'll pick up Leo, Niall and Maura and take you all for a spin,' she called.

'Just Eddie,' Christine said. 'So it will be like old times.'

'You too.'

'No. Thanks, but no.'

'She knows what she's doing,' Nessa's mother said approvingly.

'Like all women, it seems to me,' Conor Ryan said. His sigh was happy, not resigned. Nessa knew this now. Once she thought he was yearning to be free, now she believed that her father had the life he wanted.

Maura wouldn't come, Nessa knew that, but she would love to be asked. She would be so pleased for the car to pull up at her cottage and for a group of the nobs, as Mrs Brennan would call them, to get out and beg her to join them.

But she would stay and mind Michael – her little boy, two-and-a-half-years old, a loving child, a child who never knew his father. Gerry O'Sullivan the handsome barman had been reliable enough to marry Nessa, but not reliable enough to stay when the child had been born handicapped.

Nessa ran up the steps of Number Five The Terrace. The door was never locked.

'Hello, Mr Hayes. I've come to take your right-hand man out for a drive in my new car,' she said.

'Congratulations, Nessa. I heard of the birthday and the car. Richard should be with you in a minute,' he said.

'I meant Niall,' she answered.

'Oh yes,' he said.

'I don't know *why* you're not out playing golf yourself, Mr Hayes, with all the help you have in here.' She was playful, confident, she knew he liked her. Three years ago she wouldn't have raised her glance to him, let alone her voice.

'Oh, my wife wouldn't like that,' he said.

Nessa thought of Niall's mother, a solid glum-looking woman, dressed always in browns or olive green. No spark, no life. Mr Hayes would have been better with a woman like Nessa's mother, or Nessa herself.

Niall had heard her voice. 'Did the car arrive?'

'It did. And I've come to drive you off in it.' She linked her arm in his and appeared not to notice as Richard arrived out of the other door, straightening his tie and assuming that all the fuss in the hall meant someone had called for him.

Richard Hayes was standing at the top of the steps as Nessa ushered Niall into the front seat.

'Didn't you want . . . ?' Niall began.

'Yeah. I wanted you but I waited till after six not to annoy your father. Let's pick up Eddie.'

If Niall had been going to say anything about Richard he didn't now. He settled back happily in the front seat. Eddie came, on his own. Chris had things to discuss with his mother. They drove up the long drive of The Glen. Leo was at the door waiting to meet them.

'Will I show the car to your parents?' Nessa asked.

'No. No, I'd rather not,' Leo said.

Possibly Leo's mother and father might not have been able to afford a car for her. Or maybe her mother wasn't well. Nobody had seen Mrs Murphy in ages, and Leo's brothers, Harry and James, never came home from wherever they were. Biddy their maid was as silent as the grave, as if she were defending the family. Perhaps they had their secrets. Nessa didn't mind.

Not nowadays.

And she was right about Maura. Maura wouldn't come out with them, but she had a cake and they ate it together companionably in her cottage. The glass-fronted cabinet had a few items in it – a spoon in a purple velvet box, a piece of Connemara marble, and one of Eddie's pressed flowers that he had done under glass as a christening present for the baby Michael.

There was a picture of Gerry O'Sullivan in a small frame on the mantelpiece.

'Isn't it great how we all stuck together,' said Maura. And they nodded, unable to speak. 'All we need is Foxy to come home and we'd be complete.'

'He's doing very well,' Leo said unexpectedly. 'He'll be able to buy the town the way things are going.'

'Does he want to buy the town?' Niall asked.

'Well, he'd like to be a person of importance here, that's for certain,' Leo said.

'Wouldn't we all?' Niall said.

'You *are*, Niall. You're a solicitor. If ever I have any business I'll bring it to you,' Maura said.

They laughed good-naturedly, Maura most of all.

'But remember when we did our fortunes *you* were going to be the one who was going to be wealthy, not Foxy. Maybe you *will* have business,' Eddie Barton said. They all remembered the day they left Shancarrig school. It was seven years ago – it seemed a lifetime.

Nessa drove them up to the base of the Old Rock. They left the car and scampered up as they had done so often before.

It was hard to read their faces, but Nessa thought that Eddie's future seemed certain, bound up with the Scottish Chris who had come in some unexplained way into his life.

She knew that Maura would never consider herself unlucky. She would like a better house, maybe she was saving for one – there was no sign of her hard-earned wages in the cottage they had visited.

Leo would always be unfathomable but it was Niall, good dependable Niall, that Nessa was thinking about today. Leo and Eddie wandered off to stand on the stone where you were meant to be able to view four counties. Sometimes it was easier in this evening light. You could see a steeple that was in one county, a mountain that was in another.

Niall sat beside her, his jacket too small for him, his shirt crumpled. His hair was the same soft brown-black as his cousin Richard's, but jagged and not lying right. His eyes were troubled as he looked at her.

'We'll be very happy, Niall,' she said to him, patting his hand.

'I hope you will.' His voice was gruff with generosity and wishing her well, and loneliness. She could hear it, as her mother must have heard the eagerness in Conor Ryan's voice all those years ago, and coped with it.

'You and I,' Nessa said. 'We will get married, won't we? You will ask me eventually?'

'Don't make fun of me, Nessa.'

'I was never more serious in my life.'

'But Richard?'

'What about him?'

'Don't you . . . ?'

'No.'

'Well, didn't you . . . ?'

'No.'

'I thought that you didn't even *see* me,' he said.

'I've always seen you. Since the day you told me my hair was nice, the day we left Shancarrig school.'

'I wrote your name on the tree,' he said.

'You what?'

'I wrote JNH loves VR, very low down near a root. I did then, and I do now.'

'John Niall Hayes, Vanessa Ryan. You never did!'

'Will we go and see it?' he said. 'As proof.'

They had their first kiss in the sunset on her twenty-first birthday, on the hill that looked down over the town. Nessa knew that there would be a lot of work ahead. She would have to fight the apathy of his glum mother, the refusal to relinquish power by his father. She would have to decide where they would live and how they would live. Richard would move on sooner or later. Possibly sooner, now that this had all been planned.

Over the years she would reassure Niall Hayes that there had never been anything to fear from Richard, he was not a lover, nor even a love. He was someone who came in when she needed it and gave her the surge of confidence that her mother had never been given.

And yet, the reason that she felt so sure had a lot to do with being her mother's daughter.

RICHARD

R ichard hated the sight of the Old Rock. It meant that they were back in Shancarrig for their miserable summer holiday. Back in Uncle Bill and Aunt Ethel's dark gloomy house, with the solicitor's office on the ground floor and the living quarters upstairs. Bedrooms with heavy furniture, nothing to see, nothing to do. A one-horse town and a pretty poor horse at that.

For as long as he could remember they had come here for a week in July. All through the war years, or the Emergency as it was called, they had travelled down from Dublin on a train fuelled by turf. If the weather was anyway bad the turf was bad and the journey was endless.

Richard's father would walk every night for miles with Uncle Bill. They both carried blackthorn sticks and pointed happily to places they had played when they were children – the gravelly shallows of the River Grane where they had caught their fish, the great Barna Woods which had got so small since they were young, the huge ugly heap of stones they called the Old Rock.

They would stand outside Shancarrig school and marvel at the old copper beech where they had carved their initials in 1914, twin boys aged fourteen, KH and WH – Kevin and William. It made Richard sick to see them so full of happy memories over nothing.

He was a handsome boy and a restless one. He thought this week of enforced idleness in his father's old village a waste of time. Even when he was very young he had asked if they really needed to go.

'Yes of course, we need to go. It's only one week out of fifty-two,' his mother had said.

It gave him hope that she didn't like it either. But she wasn't the soft touch on this as she was on other things. She was adamant.

'Your father doesn't ask much from us. Just this one week. We will do it and do it with a good grace.'

'But it's so boring, and Aunt Ethel is so awful.'

'She's not awful, she's just quiet. Bring something to entertain yourself – books, games.'

He noted his mother brought knitting. She usually managed to get two jumpers finished in their week in Shancarrig.

'You're a powerful knitter,' Aunt Ethel had said once.

'I love it. It's so restful,' his mother had murmured. Richard noticed that she didn't say that she hardly produced the needles and wool at all when she was in Dublin. She regarded Shancarrig as her knitting time – her purgatory on earth.

Uncle Bill's children were all very young; the eldest boy Niall was a whole seven years younger than Richard, a child of five when Richard was twelve and looking for company.

By the year 1950 Richard was seventeen. It would be his last holiday in this terrible place.

As he stood at an endless school dedication with bishop and priest and self-important people from around he vowed he would never come back. It made him feel claustrophobic, as if he was being choked.

Richard Hayes was leaving his Jesuit boarding school that year. He would get his Leaving Certificate and Matriculation and go to university to study, not medicine like his father, but law. Next summer he could legitimately be away on some study course or be abroad.

They would never drag him to this village again. Let his sisters come, they seemed perfectly happy to play with the village children and run free. Richard Hayes had done his stint.

There was only one good-looking girl at the ceremony, in a blue and white dress, and a straw hat with the same material around the brim. She was shading her eyes from the sun and listening intently to the speeches. She was slim with a tiny waist and a pretty if pale face.

'Who's that, Uncle Bill?' he asked.

'Madeleine Ross. Nice girl, a bit under her mother's thumb though, and will probably go on that way.'

'She's going to stay here all her life?' Richard was horrified.

'Some of us do that willingly.' His uncle sounded huffy.

'Oh I know, Uncle Bill, I meant she seems so young.'

'I was young when I decided to come back here to live, all those years ago. If old Dr Nolan had wanted someone in the practice at that time then your father would have come back too. It's home, you see.'

Richard shuddered at the very thought.

The Dublin Hayeses lived in Waterloo Road, which was ideal for anyone with children at university. Richard was within walking distance of his lectures and, even more useful, within walking distance of all the night-time activities that went with being a student. The pubs in Leeson Street were literally on his way home, the student dances nearby, the parties in Baggot Street where fellows had flats only a stone's throw away.

Richard Hayes offered to do up the disused basement of his parents' house so that he could live there. To study, he said. To be out of the way.

His father and mother never heard or saw any sign of anything untoward. They were pleased with their son who was unfailingly charming as he came to sit at their table for supper at six and for weekend lunches. He was always smiling politely as he passed his bag of laundry to Lizzie to wash, and managed to make his own part of the house off limits.

'You've enough to do up here, honestly. I'll keep my own place tidy below,' he had said with his boyish smile. So without anyone realising it he had got his own little self-contained flat down in the basement. At eighteen years of age he had a freedom undreamed of by other undergraduates.

His parents had no idea that their son brought a series of girlfriends home and that not all of them left before morning. He had posters on his walls, chianti bottles that had been turned into lamps, coloured Indian bedspreads over chairs and sofas and his own bed.

There were very noisy studenty parties with loud songs and crashers. The kind of parties that Richard Hayes gave were usually for two people, and sometimes for four. There were two rooms in his little basement flat, and all you had to do was to leave confidently and authoritatively, as if you had every right to be there.

'Don't slink in and out,' Richard warned one girl. 'Walk out of the gate as if you had been delivering a note in my door. They wouldn't in their wildest dreams believe anything else.'

And he was totally correct in his belief that his parents knew nothing of his private life. They told their friends, and Richard's Uncle Bill down in Shancarrig, that the law studies seemed to be going very well, and that unlike a lot of young tearaways their son seemed to be a homebird, which was all they could have wanted for him and more.

So it came as a complete shock when shortly before Richard's finals there was the unpleasant business of Olive Kennedy and her parents.

It appeared that Olive was pregnant and that Richard Hayes was to blame.

Richard felt that the scene was like a play, a film of a court case. Nobody seemed to be speaking the truth.

Not Olive, who was crying and saying that she had thought it would be all right because Richard loved her and they were getting married. Not the Kennedy parents who said their daughter had been ruined. Not his own parents who kept protesting that their son could never have done anything like this. He lived at home for heaven's sake, he was under their watchful eye.

Olive made no mention of the many nights she had spent in the basement in Waterloo Road – perhaps she didn't want her family to know that. The location of the conception was not discussed, only the responsibility for it. And what was to be done now. Richard spoke clearly. He was very very sorry. He denied nothing, but he said that he and Olive were far too young to consider marriage. They had never committed themselves to it. He seemed to think that this was all that was needed.

His manner, respectful and firm, won the day. It now became a matter of negotiation: Olive was to go to England and have the child; she would return having given the baby for adoption and resume her studies. Some financial contribution should be expected for this. It was agreed between the fathers.

'Olive, I wouldn't have had this happen for the world,' Richard said as they left.

'Thank you, Richard.' She lowered her eyes, pleased that he still respected her and loved her even if they were too young to marry.

That was when Richard Hayes, as he let his breath out slowly in relief, began to realise that he must be by some kind of accident a bit of a lady-killer.

Richard kept his head down and studied hard for months after this event. He invited his parents down to his flat on several occasions so that they could see every sign of a blameless life and a hard-working son.

Bit by bit, without his having to tell any story, they began to see this Olive as a scheming wanton girl who had set out to get their Richard. They began to think he had behaved decently in the face of such temptation.

They watched proudly as he received his parchment, was admitted to practise as a solicitor and got a job in a first-rate office in Dublin. Even before his first month's salary they gave him money for clothes – he went to a tailor and his real good looks were obvious to everyone he met.

Particularly Elaine, one of the apprentices in the office. She was a niece of the senior partner, and the daughter of a judge. She wore the most expensive of twin-sets, her pearls were real ones, her handbags and silk scarves came from Paris. They looked a very elegant couple when they were seen together.

But they were rarely seen together because Richard said he wasn't a suitable escort for her. A penniless young solicitor starting off ...

'You're not penniless, my uncle pays you a fortune ...' She used to cling to his arm as if she never wanted him out of her sight.

'But we're too young, you and I ...' he begged, knowing that she found him all the more irresistible the more he protested.

'We could grow up,' she said, looking at him directly.

So Richard Hayes saw a lot of Elaine the judge's daughter, but always in his flat where nobody else saw them.

For three years they lived a hidden life, behaving perfectly correctly to each other in the office, wrapped around each other passionately all night. It amazed him how easily she was able to tell her parents that she was staying with girlfriends.

As she stood in the sunlight barebottomed, wearing only the top of his pyjamas and frying eggs for their breakfast, he marvelled at his luck, that such a beautiful and clever girl should make him her choice in this way.

'Do you love me at all, Richard?' she asked as she turned the eggs on the pan.

He lay back on his bed, luxuriating and waiting for the breakfast that would be brought to him on a tray before they got up and dressed and made their separate ways to the office. He loved the very clandestine nature of it all, the fact that nobody in the office knew.

'What an extraordinary question! Why do you ask?' he said.

'It's always dangerous when people answer questions with another question.' She laughed, pretty Elaine with the golden hair and the expensive clothes thrown on the floor of his flat.

'No seriously, we loved each other twice last night and once this morning ... and you ask me an odd thing like that?' He seemed puzzled.

'No, I meant real love.'

'That's real love. It seemed pretty real to me.'

'I'm pregnant,' she said.

'Oh shit,' he said.

'I see where we stand.' Elaine threw the plate of fried eggs into the sink and picked up her clothes.

'Elaine wait ... I didn't mean ...'

From the bathroom he heard over the running water her voice call back.

'You're so bloody right, you didn't mean it. You didn't mean any bloody word you said.'

She was out of the bathroom, dressed and furious. He came towards her.

'Don't touch me. You've said what you wanted to say.'

'I've said nothing. We have to talk.'

'You've talked. You said "shit". That's what you said.'

It was awkward in the office. She wouldn't catch his eye or agree to meet. Then she went missing for four days.

At home alone Richard didn't dare to let his thoughts follow the train they were heading down. Was it possible that she could have gone to have an abortion?

In the Dublin of 1958 such things were not unknown. There had been stories, none of them pleasant, of a nurse ... He headed away from that thought. Elaine wouldn't have done that on her own.

But then, had he not shown how he didn't want to be involved? He telephoned her house; when he gave his name to the maid he was told that Elaine didn't want to speak to him.

This time there was no carpeting, no council of war as there had been in the case of Olive Kennedy. This time he was told by the senior partner that his position with the firm was now being terminated.

'But why?' Richard cried.

'I think you know.' The older man, Elaine's uncle, stood up and turned away.

It was the coldest gesture that Richard had ever seen. Now to explain to his parents.

He wanted to try to get another job first: to tell his parents that he had decided to change offices. This way it might not appear so bald. He had reckoned without the power of the senior partner, brother of the judge, and the smallness of Dublin legal circles. The word was out about him. He didn't know which word it was but it must have had something to do with being unreliable, a seducer of young women, someone unwilling to pay for his pleasure.

There were no jobs for Richard Hayes, whose record in the law was not so staggering that it would override the other considerations.

He told his parents.

It was not an easy conversation. There were very few solutions, and to his horror he realised that the only one which seemed possible was Shancarrig.

In July of 1958 he installed himself in Number Five The Terrace. He wandered disconsolately around the village, looking without interest at the church with its notices of upcoming events, like whist drives in aid of some villagers in South America who apparently needed a church ... just like this one.

He walked hands in pockets across the River Grane and up towards the school where he remembered going to some tedious ceremony years ago. The place hadn't changed at all. Nor had the ill-kept river bank with its row of shabby dwellings, nor the clumps of trees they so proudly called Barna Woods. He couldn't bear to make the climb he had done so often as a child to the Old Rock. He came home shoulders hunched wearily and crossed the bridge back into the town.

A group of youngsters were playing on the bridge and turned to look at him as he passed. He realised that whatever he did in this village would be under the scrutiny of hundreds of eyes. It was an appalling thought.

Everything about Shancarrig depressed him.

The small fat beady-eyed priest welcoming him, and saying it would be a pleasure to have him in the congregation – what could he mean? And the wraith-like priests' housekeeper with a face like the Queen of Spades – a sour woman called Mrs Kennedy who looked straight through him and seemed to read his inner soul. She nodded dryly on being introduced, as if to say she knew his type and didn't like it.

His uncle's home offered little joy to him. Although Uncle Bill was a pleasant enough man and an efficient solicitor he had managed to encumber himself with such a mournful wife. Aunt Ethel saw little to celebrate in the world. And the children were not going to rate high on any ladder of companionship.

Niall was now about eighteen and at an age when he should have been full of the joys of spring, but he appeared disconsolate and without any fire. It didn't occur to Richard that his cousin Niall might merely be lacking in self-confidence; Richard had never known that state. He wondered why the boy didn't ask to borrow his father's Ford which was parked outside The Terrace. That way he could have toured the countryside and found wider horizons. There must be *some* social life for a boy in this place, but Niall had seemingly never found it; he stayed around the house, moving between The Terrace and Ryan's Hotel.

Richard looked at the bedroom he had been given – a huge heavy dark mahogany wardrobe which despite its great size found it difficult to hold the suits and coats of the young solicitor down from the city.

His Aunt Ethel had proudly shown him the hot and cold running water; he had the only room with a hand-basin. The bed would never welcome a companion. To manoeuvre a girl up those stairs past offices, kitchens, sitting rooms and bedrooms would be a feat that few would undertake. It would be celibacy, or else find someone else with a place of their own, which didn't look at all likely in Shancarrig.

There were, of course, pretty children.

Like Nessa from the hotel. He saw the huge interest in her eyes, the eagerness and shyness, the trying to please, the fear she was boring him.

He was not arrogant, he was realistic about this kind of response. If you were nice to girls, if you smiled at them and listened to them, just *liked* them, they opened up like flowers.

He supposed it helped being reasonably good-looking, but he truly thought it was a matter of liking them. Many a man in Dublin who had envied Richard's success had been so anxious for the conquest that he forgot to enjoy the chase. That must be where the secret, if there were a secret, lay.

He spent a lot of time wooing Vanessa Ryan. She was the best in town. He had been on an exploratory mission.

There was Madeleine Ross the school teacher, very intense and spiritual, deeply caught up in this attempt to convert some Spanish-named place that apparently meant Shancarrig in Peruvian or whatever. He suspected that she might harbour longings for the rather fey-looking priest, but he was very sure that neither of them had done anything about this hothouse passion if it existed.

There was a tough little girl who came from a falling-down Georgian mansion called The Glen, frizzy hair, good legs, strong face. There was some secret there too. Money, maybe, or a mad relative. He had called and been discouraged from calling again.

There were a few others, unsatisfactory.

Nessa with her clear eyes and dark good looks was the only one. To his surprise he didn't wear her down. He must be losing his touch, he thought. His winning Dublin ways didn't work here.

He threatened her that they wouldn't see each other any more ... gentle loving threats of course, but she got the message ... She said no.

And continued to say no.

It was a constant irritant to see her across the road in her parents' hotel, growing more attractive and confident by the week. Her dark hair shining as it hung framing her face, she wore clear yellows and reds that set off her colouring. She laughed and joked with the customers; he had even seen American men look at her approvingly.

The years passed slowly.

They were not as bad as he feared his years of exile would be, but still he yearned to be back in Dublin.

Elaine came to visit him.

'I'm getting married,' she told him.

'Do you love him?' he asked.

'You'd never have asked that question a few years ago. You didn't think love existed.'

'I know it exists. I haven't come across it, that's all.'

'You will.' She was gentle.

'About the baby ... ?'

'There never was a baby,' she said.

'*What?*'

'There never was. I made it up.'

The colour drained from his face.

'You sent me here, you got me drummed out of Dublin on a lie.'

'There *could* have been a child, and your response would have been exactly the same. "Oh shit." That's all you would have said if we created a child between us.'

'But *you* ... why did you let yourself be seen in that light by everyone ... tell your father and your uncle ... and let people think ... ?'

'It seemed worth it at the time. It's a long time ago.'

'And why are you telling me *now*? Is the interdict lifted? Is the barring order called off? Can I crawl back to Dublin and they'll give me a job?'

'No, it's much more selfish. I wanted to tell you so that you'd know there never had been a child, no child born, no child aborted. I wanted you to know that in case ...'

'In case what?'

'In case ...' She seemed lost for words. He thought she was going to tell him that she worried lest he was thinking about this child, in case he felt ashamed. He had never thought of it as a child, real or imaginary as it now proved to be.

'In case Gerald ever heard. In case you might ever say ...'

He realised she was more frightened of Gerald knowing about her past than anything to do with him.

'Tell Gerald you're white as the driven snow,' he said. He had been so right not to marry this devious lady.

It was around this time that his young cousin Niall asked him for advice.

'You sort of know everything, Richard.'

'Oh yeah?'

'Well, I know you're good-looking and everything but you know how to be nice to people and make them like you. Is there a trick?'

Richard looked at him, his hair unkempt, the jacket expensive but out of fashion, the trousers baggy. Mainly the boy's stance was what held him back: his shoulders were rounded, he looked down and not at the people he was talking to; it came from a natural diffidence but it made him look feeble and untrustworthy.

At another time and in another place Richard might have given the boy some brotherly advice; after all Niall *had* asked, which could not have been easy.

But this was the wrong time.

The business with Elaine had ruffled him. He began to doubt his own success with women, and there was also the fact that that little madam, Nessa Ryan across the road in the hotel, had become altogether too pert and self-confident. Richard Hayes didn't feel in the mood to give out advice.

'There's no trick,' he said gruffly. 'People either like you or they don't. That's the way it goes through life.' He looked away from the naked disappointment on the boy's face.

'You mean people can't get better, more popular, or successful?'

Richard shrugged. 'I never saw anyone change, did you?'

Niall had said nothing.

He looked increasingly mopey at meals in The Terrace. Richard wondered what work they would find for the lad to do when he came back to Shancarrig full time, as he undoubtedly would. It might make more sense for him to cut his teeth in a solicitor's office somewhere else. But this was his father's firm. He should come back and claim his inheritance lest Richard take it over from him. Not that Richard was going to stay here for ever. After Elaine's revelations he thought that it might well be time for him to go back to Dublin.

But that was when he got to know Gloria Darcy.

The Darcys were newcomers. This meant they hadn't been born and raised here for three generations like everyone else. They had been considered fly-by-nights when they came first, but that was before their small grocery shop became a larger grocery shop, and before they started selling light bulbs, saucepans and cutlery and began to bite into the profits of Dunne's Hardware. Mike and Gloria Darcy always smiled cheerfully in the face of any muttering.

'Isn't there plenty for everyone?' Mike would say with his big broad smile.

'This place is only starting out, it'll be a boom town in the middle sixties,' Gloria would say with a toss of her long dark curly hair and her gypsy smile.

She often wore a handkerchief tied around her neck so that she looked like a picture of a gypsy girl – not like the tall silent tinker girls who came into Shancarrig when they camped each year at Barna Woods, more like an illustration from a child's story book.

Bit by bit they were accepted.

Gloria was flashy, the women all agreed this. Richard heard his Aunt Ethel tut-tutting about her to Nellie Dunne and to Mrs Ryan, but there was nothing they could put their finger on. Her neckline wasn't so low as to raise a comment nor were her skirts too short. It was just that she walked with a swish and a certainty. Her eyes roamed around and lit up when they caught other eyes. There was nothing demure about Mrs Gloria Darcy.

Richard met her first when he bought a packet of razor blades. He didn't like the fussy Mr Connors the chemist – a small man with bad breath who was inclined to keep you half the day. When he saw packets of razor blades in the window of Darcy's he regarded it as a merciful escape.

'Anything else?' Gloria asked him, her smile wide and generous, her tongue moving slightly over her lower lip.

If it weren't for the fact that her husband stood not a foot away Richard would have thought she was flirting, being suggestive.

'Not for the moment,' he said in exactly the same tone, and their eyes met.

He warned himself not to be stupid as he walked back to The Terrace. This would be the silliest thing that a human could do.

What he must do now was sort out a new job in Dublin, and leave this town without having committed any major misdemeanour. He had been saving his salary quite methodically over the three years of his exile in the sticks. There was no point in buying finery to be paraded here, there were no places for meals, no going to the races. He had learned a lot about the rural practice, for all the use it would be to him in the future. But human nature was the same everywhere: perhaps his stay here might have been a better apprenticeship than he had ever thought possible.

It was early closing, the day his Uncle Bill usually walked up to The Glen and went for a stroll with the old Major Murphy. What the two of them talked about it would be hard to know. But today Bill Hayes was still in his office.

'I'm in a quandary,' he said to Richard.

'Tell me about it.' Richard sat down, legs stretched, face enthusiastic and receptive. He knew his uncle was pleased to be able to talk.

There was no one else in the house, not dour Aunt Ethel nor sulky Niall.

'It's up at The Glen. Miriam Murphy keeps telephoning me, saying she wants to set her affairs in order.'

'Well?'

'Well, Frank says not to take any notice of her – she's rambling.'

'She is a bit daft, isn't she?' Richard encouraged his uncle to speak.

'I suppose so, I mean it's not the kind of thing you'd ask a man. Not something that you'd talk about to a friend.' Bill Hayes looked troubled.

Richard thought that it should be the most important thing you might talk to a friend about, whether your wife was going off her head or not, but the more he heard of marriage the less likely anyone seemed to do anything normal within its bonds.

'So what do you think you should do?' he asked, expert as always in finding out what the other man wanted before giving his own view.

'You see, I think she has something pressing on her mind, some crime, even ... imaginary, of course.'

'Well, if it's imaginary ...'

'But suppose it's not, suppose it's something she wants to make restitution for?'

'You're not Father Gunn, Uncle Bill. You're not Sergeant Keane. All you have to do is make her will, or not be free to make it if that's what you'd prefer for Major Frank's sake.'

'It's worrying me.'

'Why don't I go and see her? Then you won't have failed either of them.'

'Would you, Richard?'

'I'll go today while you and Major Murphy take your constitutional.'
His smile was bright.

'I don't know what I'd do without you, Richard.'

'You'll have a son of your own to help you in no time. You won't need me, I'll head off to Dublin soon.'

'Not too soon.'

'All right, not too soon, but soonish.' He stood up and clapped his uncle on the shoulder.

What was one more mad old bat of a woman confessing to the Lord knew what!

He had his lunch in the dark dining room of The Terrace; they talked of other things and he waited until his uncle and the Major would be well clear before he went to The Glen.

He didn't even have to go into the house to find her. Mrs Miriam Murphy half lay, half sat across the rockery. She was wearing a long white dress, possibly a nightgown; her hair streaked with grey was loose on her shoulders.

She was crying.

There was some garden furniture strewn about. Richard Hayes pulled up a chair for himself.

'I'm from Bill Hayes's office, I'm his nephew. He says you're anxious for us to sort something out for you.'

'You're too young,' she said.

'Ah no, Mrs Murphy, I'm older than I look. I'm twenty-eight, well on my way to thirty.' His smile would have broken down the reserve of any woman in Ireland, but Miriam Murphy's mind was miles away.

'That's what he was, twenty-eight, if you could believe him,' she said.

Richard was nonplussed. 'Well, what do you think we should do?' he said.

He knew his uncle wanted the woman to say that she had changed her mind, that she wanted no will made, no affairs sorted out. He must try to lead her in that direction.

'It's too late to do anything. It was done,' she said. He nodded uncomprehendingly.

There was a long silence between them. She seemed quite at ease lounging, half lying over the rock plants and the jagged edges of the stones that made up the rockery. He didn't suggest that she sit somewhere more comfortable – he knew that this was irrelevant.

'So perhaps we should leave things as they are?' He looked at her, pouring out reassurance.

'Is that enough?' she asked.

'I think it is.'

'You don't think we should leave them the place, The Glen, for themselves whenever they come this way?'

'Leave it to who exactly?'

'The gypsies.'

'No, no. Definitely not. People are always trying to leave them places. They want to be free,' he said.

'Free?'

'Yes, that's what they like best.' He stood up, anxious to be away from the mad staring eyes. It wasn't healthy for that girl Leo to stay here all the time. Why didn't she get a training, a job?

'If you think so.' Mrs Miriam Murphy didn't look relieved, she looked only resigned.

He walked down the long drive and was about to head down the hill to Shancarrig. God, the sooner he was out of a place like this the better. Walking along the road towards him was Gloria Darcy.

'Well, well, well. You have had a shave, I see.' She looked directly at his face.

'What do you mean?'

'I sold you razor blades this morning, don't tell me you've forgotten me already?' She was most definitely leading him on. Her laugh was unaffected, she could see the impression that she was making on him.

'No, Mrs Darcy, I imagine that very few people forget you,' he said. He was being equally gallant and flattering, giving as good as he got.

'And were you going to walk straight home down the hill or go the better way through the woods?'

He knew he stood at a crossroads. He could have said that he was needed back at the office, that he had work to catch up with, that he had to make a phone call to Dublin. He might have said anything.

But he said, 'I was hoping to find some attractive company to walk me through Barna Woods, and now I have.'

They laughed as they walked. She teased him about his city suit, he said she was dressing deliberately like a pantomime gypsy. She asked what he had been doing at The Glen, he said that there was a secrecy like the seal of Confession about matters between lawyer and client. He asked if the Darcy's had a proper title to their shop, they hadn't bought it through his uncle's firm . . . She said the same seal of

Confession applied to business deals.

By the time they came out into the sunshine again, and walked by the cottages to the bridge, they were well aware of each other. Much more than attractive faces and winning ways. They were people who could talk and play. They were a match for each other.

So when he went to buy things there he went knowing that it was a move, a degree of courtship. He bought more razor blades.

'My, what a strong beard we must have,' she said. Again within her husband's hearing.

When he bought a pound of tomatoes she asked him was he going on a picnic in the woods. Mike Darcy was serving another customer.

'No, my aunt wants some more, that's all.'

'No, she was in this morning and bought plenty,' said Gloria, eyes dancing and full of mischief.

The teasing visits and banter went on for some days.

'It's lovely of you to come and see me so often,' she said, pressing her body towards the counter. She wore a chain around her neck, the pendant was between her breasts, the eye followed it down as it was intended to.

'Yes, it's lovely of me, you never come to call on me,' Richard said.

'Ah, but I can't make excuses about civil bills and statements of claim,' she said. 'You can invent all the tomatoes and razor blades in the world.'

'So we'll have to meet on neutral ground,' he suggested.

They met two days later at the church when they both attended the funeral of Mrs Miriam Murphy.

It was pneumonia, Dr Jims Blake had said. Brought on by exposure, someone else had said, Mrs Murphy had taken to sleeping out on the rockery of their garden. It was a sure fact that money and position didn't bring you happiness.

Richard Hayes looked at the small wiry Leo as she walked down the church supporting her father. Two strange men, the brothers from abroad, had come for the funeral. They looked military, they knew hardly anyone.

There was a gathering in Ryan's Hotel. Young Nessa had done up one of the downstairs rooms as a special function room. It was exactly what was needed for this occasion. Coffee and sandwiches and some drinks. Those who wished to adjourn to the bar could do so. It had never been done before in Shancarrig; you either went back to someone's house or you went to the pub. This was a new respectability.

'Very clever of you to have thought this up, Nessa,' he said admiringly. Genuinely so.

'Leo is my friend. It's not easy for her to have people at the house.' Nessa hadn't time to talk to him – these days she was great with young Niall, and already the boy was beginning to look the better for it. His hair was smarter, he had got a new jacket. Somehow he even seemed to walk taller.

Gloria and Mike Darcy were in the gathering though somehow Richard wondered had they been invited in the strict sense of the word.

As people moved around offering sympathy and trying to place Harry and James who had long left Shancarrig, Gloria found herself next to Richard.

'So now we're on neutral ground,' she said.

'Yes, but very crowded neutral ground,' he said, shaking his head in exaggerated sorrow.

'Have you any suggestions for somewhere that's not crowded?' She couldn't have been more direct. Had she asked him to make love to her she could not have said it more clearly.

'Well, since your place, my place and this hotel are out of the question, let's think of somewhere that might be deserted at this moment.' He wasn't serious. There was nowhere they could go in Shancarrig, literally nowhere.

'There's The Glen,' she said. She saw the look of revulsion on his face. They were sympathising over the death of the woman who had lived all her life in The Glen; Gloria could not possibly be considering going there to use the empty house. 'Not the house, the gate lodge,' she said.

'How would we get in?' Already he had bypassed any moral objections to a place in the grounds. That was different.

'The back window is open, I checked.'

'Twenty minutes?' he asked. It would take him ten to say his goodbyes, two to go back to his room for condoms.

'Fifteen,' she said, and again she ran her tongue along her lower lip. His goodbyes were courteous and very swift.

There was a crotchety old farmer who lived out that direction. If he was asked he could say he got a message to visit him but then he had turned out not to be there. But why was he taking these kind of precautions? No one would ask him. Nobody would dream he was about to do what he was about to do.

She was there before him, lying on a divan covered with a rug. The place smelled musty but not of damp.

'Did you bring anything?'

'Yes, that's what delayed me. I had to go back to my room for them. I don't carry them always just in case,' he laughed, patting his pocket.

'Now don't be so unromantic. I meant champagne, something like that.'

'No, I'm afraid not.' He looked crestfallen.

'Never mind, I did.' Her white teeth flashed as she bit the foil from the top of the bottle, there were cups on the dresser. They laughed as they drank it too quickly so that the fizzy liquid went up their noses. And they kissed.

'Did you go back to the shop for this?' He marvelled at her speed.

'No. I had it with me in my big shoulder bag.' She laughed at her own wickedness and the confidence that it would have needed.

'Let me take off these dark respectable clothes. They don't suit you,' he said.

'Well, it was a funeral. I couldn't wear my red skirt but ...' She was wearing a red petticoat, trimmed with white lace, she wore no brassiere, just a gold chain around her throat. She looked so abandoned and wild as she lay there laughing up at him he could scarcely bear the moments of waiting.

'I've longed for you, Richard Hayes,' she said. And he sank into her as if he had known her all his life.

After that it was always urgent and never easy. If only the Murphys lived a more regular life, Richard groaned to himself. If he could know they would stay in the big house, or stay out of it, then the gate lodge would have been the ideal place for his meetings with Gloria. But they could never be sure; they would have no excuse if they were seen going in and out of the window.

It took them weeks to work out some kind of a pattern to the curious ways of Leo and her father.

Leo eventually started a secretarial course which involved going to the town on the bus. This gave her day a shape. The Major, who walked the long avenue with his old dogs, that he kept calling Lance and Jessie, was less predictable. Richard tried to find out more of his movements by asking his uncle, but it seemed that a friendship of twenty-five years was based on Bill Hayes knowing nothing whatsoever about Frank Murphy. It was hard to believe, but that was the way it was.

And there was the time that Hayes and Son, Solicitors, were asked to see to a property. Richard and Gloria had many happy meetings there in the guise of showing it to clients.

Gloria could get away so easily it was almost frightening.

'Does Mike never ask where you're going?'

'Lord no. Why should he?'

'Well, if I had a beautiful wife like you I wouldn't let her wander off … to do the devil knows what …' He squeezed her and held her to him again.

'Then you wouldn't be a husband, you'd be a gaoler,' she laughed. He thought about it.

There was some truth in what she said. If you married someone just to guard her like a possession it was like an imprisonment. But look at it the other way, if Mike was more careful and caring about his wife then surely Gloria wouldn't wander free as she was.

Sometimes he spoke about her children, her little boys, Kevin and Sean.

'What is there to say?'

'Aren't you afraid they'll find out, that they'd hate you for this?'

'Darling Richard, you are riddled with guilt. I think we should make a regular thing of visiting Father Gunn together after we meet.'

'Don't tease me. I only say these things because I love you.'

'No, you don't.'

'I do. I never said it to anyone before.'

'We say it at the moment we make love, because at that moment everyone loves. But you don't love me in an everyday sort of way.'

'I could.'

'No, Richard.' She put her fingers on his lips and then into his mouth, and then she kissed him and soon the words were forgotten.

She was the ideal lover. He could never have dreamed of anyone so passionate and responsive, a beautiful woman who found him desirable and wasn't afraid to say so. A witty, flowing, secret love whose dark eyes flashed at him when they met in Ryan's Hotel, in the shops or at the church.

After years of girls wanting more from Richard here was someone who wanted no more at all. Not public recognition, not a commitment, and obviously because of the heavy band she already wore on her finger, not an engagement ring. For quite a time it was the perfect romance.

And then he began to notice small changes in his own attitude. He couldn't say that Gloria had changed, she had always been light-hearted in their daring and the fear of discovery ... and enthusiastic about the pleasure they gave each other.

No. It was Richard who changed.

He couldn't bear to see her holding her little boys by the hand. He thought back to his own mother and father, the respectable Dublin doctor and his busy bridge-playing wife. Theirs had been a house of stability as he grew up in Waterloo Road. His mother had always been there for them. Suppose she had been someone who sneaked out to the arms of a lover while his father worked? He dismissed the thought as some kind of guilty fantasy.

There had been no way in which he had compared his life with that of his parents before, why was he holding up their staid and plodding existence as some kind of example now? Gloria was a wonderful mother to Kevin and Sean. What she had with Richard was something totally different, something separate entirely.

Then Richard found himself uneasy about Mike, big handsome Mike Darcy with his teeth as white and even as his wife's, who stood long hours in the grocery shop they were so busy building up together. Mike, who would go to endless trouble to find something Richard ordered, furrowing his brow to think where they might get that particular chamois leather Richard wanted. He didn't like the man being so generous with his time and help for him. Mike's innocent face was a reproach to Richard Hayes.

Gloria only laughed when he mentioned it. 'What Mike and I have is different to what you and I have ... Let's keep them separate,' she said.

'But I know about him, he doesn't know about me.'

'Why do men have to think everything's a game, with rules?' she laughed.

And then there were times when he wondered if he *did* know about Mike and Gloria and what they had together. He would see the way they leant towards each other in the shop when they thought no one was looking. He saw the way Mike Darcy sometimes stroked his wife's body.

A very unfamiliar feeling of raging jealousy came over him when he saw them touch.

'You don't do this with Mike, do you?' he begged her one afternoon in their gate lodge.

'Nobody could do what you and I do. This is ours.'

'But does he want to ... ? I mean do you and he ... ?'

'You're so handsome when you look worried, Richard,' she said.

'I must know.'

Suddenly she sat up, eyes flashing. 'No, you must not know. There is no must about it. We are not master and slave ... you have no right to know anything that I do not wish to tell you. Do I ask you any such questions ... ?'

'But there's nothing to know about me.' He was wretched.

'That's because this is the way I choose to see things. I am not curious, suspicious, asking where I should ask nothing.' Her voice held an ultimatum.

Accept things as they were or there would be no more to accept. He longed to know if she had known other men since her marriage to Mike, if they failed at this test and had been sent away.

He would have killed any man, any traveller who walked into Ryan's Hotel, if he had said he shared a bed with Gloria Darcy. Yes, he would have taken this man by the throat and shaken him to squeeze out his life, uncaring about what onlookers or the law would say or do. Why then was Mike able to stand and fill bags with sugar and other bags with potatoes and not wonder where his beautiful wife went to in the afternoons?

It was becoming more difficult too for Richard to be free in the afternoons since young Niall had joined the firm. The boy had definitely gained a new confidence, which Richard suspected was due to the blossoming of a friendship and even courtship with the glossy young Nessa Ryan from the hotel.

Gone were the days when Niall Hayes was happy with the menial jobs, the work of a glorified clerk. Now he wanted to learn, to share, to study Richard's ways with clients. 'Can I come with you to the place that there's all the fuss about the title?' he would ask.

This was one of Richard's mythical excuses for being out of the office. He had described a difficult old farmer set in his ways who had to be cajoled and flattered into revealing his documents.

'No, Niall. It wouldn't work out ... this fellow is as mad as a wasps' nest. You wouldn't know what he'd do if I brought anyone else. I've only got as far as I have because I go on my own and put in endless bloody hours with him.'

'Well, can I see the file on him?' Niall asked.

'Why? What do you want to bother yourself with that old fart for, there's plenty of other work to do ...'

'But won't we need to know when ... ?'

The words remained unfinished, the sentence hung in the air – when ... Richard went back to Dublin – something they all knew would happen. There wasn't room for two partnerships in the firm. The business simply wasn't there; even two salaries was beginning to strain Bill Hayes. Niall was the son of the family.

Surely Richard would be going back any day now.

Only Richard knew that he could never leave Shancarrig and the woman he loved.

'I *do* love you,' he said defensively to Gloria, as they sat smoking a cigarette by their little oil stove one cold evening in the gate lodge.

'I know.' She sat hugging her knees.

'No, you don't know. You said we shouldn't talk of love, that I only felt it at the moment of taking you. That's what you said.'

'Stop sounding like a schoolboy, Richard.' She looked beautiful as she sat there in the flickering light.

'What are you thinking about?' he asked.

'About you and how good you make me feel.'

'What are we going to do, Gloria?'

'Well, get dressed and go home, I imagine.'

'About everything?'

'We can't solve everything, we can only solve things like not letting the light be seen through the windows and not getting our death of cold in all the rain.'

'What will you say ... about where you've been?'

'That's not your concern.'

'But it is, you are my concern.'

'Then let me handle it.' Again he saw the warning in her eyes, and he felt frightened.

They had met in late summer and continued through autumn and a cold wet winter; soon it would be spring. Surely some solution would have to be found.

But for Gloria spring meant that she could wear fresh yellow and white flowery dresses, and white sandals and take her lover to hidden parts of Barna Woods, to dells with bluebells and soft springy grass. Again an ache came over him. How did she know where to find such places? She hadn't grown up in this place – had other men taken her here? Not only could he never ask, he must never think about it. He hated that the shop was doing so well, he wanted to be her provider and give her things but she would never take them.

'What would I say, Richard? I mean I could hardly say that the handsome young solicitor who drops in to buy an inordinate amount of razor blades bought me a silver bracelet, now could I?'

But with increased prosperity Mike Darcy bought his wife jewellery. There was an emerald pendant, there were diamonds. Nobody in Shancarrig had ever known such extravagance. Quite unsuitable, Richard's Aunt Ethel had said, shaking her head about it.

Richard agreed from the bottom of his heart but was careful not to express this.

To his surprise young Niall had the opposite view.

'What do people work for if it isn't to get themselves what they want?' he asked.

'I hope you wouldn't throw your money away on emeralds for Gloria Darcy and her like,' his father said in ritual dismissive vein to his son.

These days Niall Hayes answered back. 'I'm not sure what you mean "her like", but if I loved someone and I earned my money lawfully I would feel very justified in spending it on presents for her,' he said.

Suddenly the room was silent and drab. Aunt Ethel looked at her son in some surprise. On her cardigan there was no jewellery; there never had been any except the engagement ring, wedding ring and good watch. Perhaps life might have been better if Bill Hayes had visited a shop and looked at jewels.

'Let's celebrate our anniversary,' Richard said to Gloria.

'Like what? Dinner for two in Ryan's Shancarrig Hotel, a bottle of wine?'

'No, but let's do something festive.'

'I find what we do is fairly festive already.' She laughed at him.

'You must want more, you must want more than creeping around.'

She sighed. It was the weary sigh of a mother who can't explain to a toddler how to tie his shoe laces. 'No, I don't want any more,' she said resignedly. 'But you do, so we'll do whatever you like for the anniversary.'

It was hard to think what they could do. The mystery was that they had spent a year as lovers without being discovered. In a place of this size and curiosity it was a miracle.

Perhaps they could go to Dublin. He would find an excuse and she would surely be able to think of some reason to go away as well.

Before he suggested it he would plan what they would do, otherwise she would shrug and say that they might as well stay here. He wanted to take her into Dublin bars, restaurants, he wanted people to admire her and be attracted by her beautiful face and sparkling laugh. He wanted to see her against some other background, not just the grey shapeless forms of Shancarrig. In all his years there Richard had never been able to like the place, it was lit up only by Gloria and he wanted to take her away from it.

He planned the visit to Dublin, how he would meet her off the train in Kingsbridge in his car – he would have gone up the day before so that there would be even less suspicion – how he would show her the sights – she didn't know Dublin well, she had told him. He would be her guide.

They would check into one of the better hotels. He would check out the room first, make sure it was perfect ... they would walk arm in arm down Grafton Street. If they met anyone from Shancarrig they would all laugh excitedly and say wasn't it great coming to Dublin how you ran into everyone from home.

The more he thought about it the more Richard realised that he did not want Gloria in Dublin just for one night, he wanted her there always. He didn't want them in a furtive hotel room, he wanted them in a home of their own. Together always.

There were the most enormous difficulties in the way. The biggest, most handsome and innocent was Mike Darcy, smiling and welcoming with no idea that his wife loved another.

There were the children. Richard loved the look of them, dark boys with enormous eyes like Gloria. They had their father's slow, lopsided grin too, but it was silly to work out characteristics and assign them to one parent or the other.

He wished he could get to know the children, but it had been impossible. If he could get to know them then they would find it easier to come as a little family to Dublin to live with him. Richard realised suddenly that he was no longer planning an illicit trip to celebrate an anniversary, he was planning a new life. He must take it more slowly.

He must not rush things and risk losing her.

*

The anniversary was all that he could have wanted and more.

The hotel welcomed them as Mr and Mrs Hayes with no difficulty. Gloria's large rings did not look as if they had been put on for the occasion, they had a right to sit on her hand.

They had champagne in their room, they walked the city. He showed her places that he had loved when he was a boy, the canal bank from Baggot Street to Leeson Street. It thrilled him to be so near Waterloo Road. It was quite possible that his father could walk by on his way to the bookshop on Baggot Street Bridge, or his mother going to the butcher's shop to say that last Sunday's joint had not been as tender as they would have expected and the Doctor had been very disappointed.

He didn't see his parents but he did see Elaine pregnant and contented-looking, getting out of her mother's car. She hadn't seen him, and under normal circumstances he would have let her go on without stopping her. But these were not normal times. He wanted to show her Gloria, he wanted her to see the magnificent woman on his arm.

He called and she waddled over.

'Oh, Mummy will be sorry to have missed you,' she said. He had waited carefully until her mother had driven off. He didn't think his name was held in any favour in that family.

'I'd like you to meet Gloria Darcy.' The pride in his voice was overpowering.

They talked easily. Gloria asked her was it the first baby. Looking Richard straight in the eye Elaine said yes it was, she was very excited.

Gloria said she had two little boys of her own, and that you wished they'd never grow up and yet you were so proud of every little thing they did. She was saying all the things that Elaine wanted to hear. She also told her that the old wives' tales about labour were greatly exaggerated – it was probably to put people off having children before they were married.

'Oh, very few of us would be foolish enough to do that,' Elaine said, looking again at Richard.

He realised with a shock that he had been a monster of selfishness. Suddenly he was glad that Elaine had lied to him, that she had never carried his baby. But Olive Kennedy had. She had gone to England and given birth to their child. Where was this child now? A boy or girl in an orphanage, in a foster family, adopted.

How could he have not cared before? He felt his eyes water.

They had drinks in the Shelbourne Bar, and lunch in a small

restaurant near Grafton Street that he had heard was very good.

He managed to meet three people he knew slightly. That wasn't bad for a man four years in exile from the capital city. He had chosen the place well.

'Did you love that girl Elaine a lot?' Gloria asked.

'No, I have never loved anyone except you,' he said simply.

'I thought you looked sad when you left, your eyes were full of tears ... but it's not my business. I'd be very cross with you for asking prying questions,' she said, squeezing his hand warmly.

He could barely speak.

'I'll die if I can't be with you always, Gloria,' he said.

'Shush now.' She put her finger in the little glass of Irish Mist that she was drinking and offered it to him to suck. Soon the familiar desire returned, banishing for the moment the sense of loss and anxiety about returning her to real life in Shancarrig. They went back to their hotel and celebrated their anniversary well and truly.

He never asked what excuse she had made to Mike, whether it was shopping, or a visit to a hospital, or seeing an old friend. He knew she didn't want him to be a party to her lies. It could not have been hard to lie to Mike, his enthusiasm and simplicity wouldn't take into account the deviousness of the world around him, a wife who would betray him, a casual friend Richard Hayes walking in and out of his shop not for the errands he pretended but to feast his eyes on Gloria, to remind himself of the last time and look forward to the next time.

Kevin Darcy was at Shancarrig school. Sometimes Richard stopped him on the road just for the excuse to talk to him.

'How's your mammy and daddy?' he'd say.

'They're all right.' Kevin hadn't much interest.

'What did you learn at school?' he might ask.

'Not much,' Kevin would say.

One day Richard saw him with a cut head. He fell off the tree, Christy Dunne explained. Richard went to the shop to sympathise. Mike was out in the yard supervising the building of the new extension. Darcy's was now almost three times the size it was when they had bought it first.

'Oh, for God's sake, Richard, it's only a scrape. Don't be such a clucking hen,' Gloria said.

'He was bleeding a lot, I was worried.'

'Well, don't worry, he's fine. I put a big plaster on him, and gave him two Crunchies, one for him and one for Christy. There wasn't a bother out of him.' He looked at her with admiration. How was she so calm, so good and wise a mother as well as everything else?

He was still more admiring when the burglars came the following week and stole all the jewellery that Mike Darcy had bought for his wife.

Sergeant Keane was in and out of the place, inquiries were made everywhere, tinkers had been in Johnny Finn's pub, you couldn't watch the place all the time.

Gloria was philosophical. It was terrible, particularly the little emerald, she loved the way it glowed. But then what was the alternative? You watched them day and night, you made the place into something like Fort Knox. It would be like living in a prison; she shivered. Richard remembered how she had once said that to be married to a suspicious husband who checked up on her would be like living with a gaoler. She needed to be free.

Maura O'Sullivan, who minded the Darcy children and cleaned the house for them, also worked in his aunt's house. He tried to find out more about the household, but Maura, unlike the rest of Shancarrig, was not inclined to gossip.

'What was it exactly you wanted to know?' she would say in a way that ended all inquiries.

'I was just wondering how the family were getting over the loss,' he said lamely.

Maura nodded, satisfied. She always brought her son with her, an affectionate boy called Michael who had Down's syndrome. Richard liked him and the way he would run towards whoever came into the room.

'Daddy?' he said hopefully to Richard.

The first time he had said this Maura explained that the child's father had had to go to England, and that consequently he thought everyone he met was his father.

'Daddy, my daddy?' he asked Richard again and again.

'Sort of, we're all daddys and mammys to other people,' Richard said to him.

Niall had heard him.

'You're very kind, Richard. It comes naturally to you. I mean it, you're terribly nice to people, that's why you're so successful.' Richard was surprised, the boy had never made a speech like this.

'No I'm not. I'm quite selfish really. I'm surprised it doesn't show.'

'I never saw it. I was jealous of you of course with women, but I didn't think you were selfish.'

'Not jealous of me any more?'

'Well, I only like one person and she assures me that she's not under your spell ... so ...' Niall Hayes looked happy.

'She never was. I thought she was lovely like anyone would, but it was admiration from afar, I assure you.'

'That's what she says.' Niall sounded smug and content.

'I'm not cramping your style in work here, am I?' Richard wanted to have it out. This seemed a good time.

'No. No of course not, it's just that I suppose we expected ... everyone thought that sooner or later ...'

'Yes, and one day I will but ... not just yet.'

'You're saving, I know.' Niall was understanding.

'How do you know?'

'Well, you never go anywhere, you only have a shabby car. You don't buy jazzy suits.'

'That's right,' Richard admitted. 'I'm saving.' This was his cover, he realised. He was putting together a stake to buy a practice in Dublin.

The months went on. Gloria bought him a silk tie.

'You said no presents.' He fingered the cream and gold tie lovingly.

'I said you weren't to buy *me* any, that's all.'

'I want to buy you a piece of jewellery. Not an emerald, a ruby – a very small ruby. Let me,' he begged.

'No, Richard. Seriously, when could I wear it? Be sensible.'

He bought it anyway. He gave it to her in the gate lodge.

Their Wednesday afternoons there were totally secure. Major Murphy walked with his uncle rain or shine, and Leo had got a job working in the office of one of the building contractors' firms in the town. It seemed an unlikely job, but Gloria told him that she heard Leo was still in touch with that mad Foxy Dunne, who was going from strength to strength on the building sites in England. The word was that he would come back and set up his own firm. The word was that he and Leo had an understanding.

'Foxy Dunne, son of Dinny Dunne?'

'Oh, Foxy Dunne is like the papal nuncio in terms of respectability compared to his father. You know him falling out of Johnny Finn's most nights.'

'Well, well, well.' He realised he was getting a small-town mentality;

he was finding serious difficulty in believing that Major Murphy of The Glen would let his daughter contemplate one of the Dunnes from the cottages. He was glad however that it meant Leo worked far away. It left the coast much more clear.

Gloria looked at the ruby for a long time.

'You're not angry?'

'How could I be angry that you spent so much on me? I'm touched, but I'll never wear it.'

'Couldn't you say ... ?'

'We both know there's nothing I could say.'

'You could wear it here with me.'

'Yes, I will.'

She took the ruby away and had it made into a tie pin, then she gave it back to him. 'I'll put on a chain to wear it when I am with you, but for the rest of the time you keep it. Wear it on the tie that I gave you, then you'll think of me.'

'I think of you always,' he said.

Too much perhaps.

It was the beginning of the withdrawal. He saw it and blinded himself to it. He feared that someone else had come to town, but he knew there could be no one. She didn't dream up schemes to meet him for five minutes any more, and although she lay and took his loving she didn't implore him to love her as she once had, begging, encouraging and exciting him to performances that he had thought impossible.

He felt it was the place, it was getting too much for them. There had been endless complications about builders' suppliers, and the building of the extension, and the hostility of the Dunnes who said that they weren't anxious to build the place that was going to be direct competition with them. There had been delays over the insurance money for the jewellery. There was a problem about the newspaper delivery they planned, Nellie Dunne had created difficulties.

In his uncle's office Niall was restless and urging that he be involved in more cases, have consultations with clients and barristers, and in general learn his trade. Richard felt he was putting him off at every turn.

It was time to take Gloria away.

He began to explain it and for once he wouldn't listen when she tried to stop him. 'No, I've shushed enough. We have to think. It's been nearly two years. We must have our own home, our own life together. I don't wish Mike any harm but he has to know, he has to be told. He's a decent man, he'll agree to whatever we suggest. Whatever's for the best ... he can come to Dublin to see the boys, we'll never hide from them who their real father is ... he'd prefer to be taken into our confidence from the start ... well, not exactly from the start but from now ...' His voice trailed away as he looked at her face.

They sat in the gate lodge. They hadn't undressed. Their cigarettes and the little tin they used as an ashtray and cleaned after each visit sat between them on the table. It was an odd place to be talking about their future. It was an odd expression on her face as she listened. It showed utter bewilderment and shock.

He thought first it was the enormity of what they were about to do ... coupled with the disruption for the children. He must reassure her. 'I've been looking at houses in Dublin, a little out of the city so that we could have privacy and so that Kevin and Sean would have a local-type school, not somewhere huge like the big Christian Brothers in the city ...' He stopped. He had not read her look right.

She didn't want reassurance, she wanted him to stop talking straight away. 'None of this is going to happen, you must know this. Richard, you *must* know.'

'But you love me ...'

'Not like this, not to run away with you ...'

'Why have we been doing all this ... ?' He waved his hand wildly around the room where they had made love so often.

'It had nothing whatsoever to do with my leaving here. That was never promised, never on the cards.'

He was the one bewildered now, and confused. 'What was it all about?' he asked, begging to be told.

She stood up and walked around the room as she spoke. She had never looked more beautiful. She spoke of a happy time with Richard, how he had made her feel wonderful and needed, how she had given him no undertaking, no looking ahead.

She said that her future was here in Shancarrig or very possibly another small town. They might sell up to the Dunnes and move. She and Mike liked starting a place from scratch. They had done that in other places. It was a challenge, it kept everything exciting, new.

Richard Hayes listened amazed as she spoke of Mike with this respect and love.

She was totally enmeshed with Mike in a way Richard had never understood. Her concern had nothing to do with a fear that Mike might be hurt or made to suffer. It was much more an involvement, a caring what he would do and decide and where he would want to go.

'But you don't love him!' he gasped.

'Of course I love him, I've never loved anyone else.'

'But why ... ?' He couldn't even finish the sentence.

'He couldn't give me everything I wanted. No one can do that for anybody. I love him because he lets me be free.'

Richard realised she spoke the truth. 'And does he know ... ?'

'Know what?'

'About me, about us. Do you tell him?' His voice grew angry and loud. 'Is this what gets him excited, your coming home and telling him what you and I did together?'

'Don't be disgusting,' she said.

'You're the one who is disgusting, out like an alley cat and then pretending that you're the model wife and mother.'

She looked at him reproachfully. He knew it was over.

In the years when he had wriggled out of relationships and escaped from affairs he had not been as honest as she was being, he had been devious and avoided face-to-face contact except when it was utterly necessary. His heart was heavy when he thought of Olive Kennedy, and the way he had disowned her in front of her parents.

If only he could have his time all over again. He hung his head.

'Richard?' she said.

'I didn't mean it about the alley cat.'

'I know you didn't.'

'I don't know what to do, darling Gloria. I don't know what to do.'

'Go away and leave this place, have a good life in Dublin. One day I'll meet you there, we will talk in a civilised way like you and the girl in Baggot Street, the one who was having the baby.'

'No.'

'That's what you'll do.' She spoke soothingly.

'And if you go to another town will you find someone new?'

'I won't go out looking for anyone, that I assure you.'

'And will he ... will he put up with it, turn the other way ... ?' He couldn't even bear to speak Mike Darcy's name.

'He'll know I love him and will never leave him.'

There was nothing more to say.

There was a lot to be done.

He would go back to the office and telephone some solicitors' offices in Dublin. He would ask his mother if he could go back to the basement flat in Waterloo Road. He would work day and night to clear his files, and leave everything ship-shape for Niall. He could shake off his years here and start again.

They tidied up the little house that they were visiting for the last time. As usual they emptied the cigarette butts and ash into an envelope. They straightened the furniture to the way it had been when they first found the place. They left by the window as they had always done. They rearranged the branches that hung to hide it.

She wouldn't bring anyone else here after he had gone, he felt sure of that. With a little lurch he wondered had she ever brought anyone before.

But that was useless speculation.

'Now that we're legitimate we can walk home together,' he said.

'Why not?' She was easy and affectionate, as she was with everyone.

'The long way or the short way?' He offered her the choice.

'The scenic route,' she decided.

They went up past the open ground that led to the Old Rock, and back through the woods, past Maddy Ross's house where she sat at her little desk, maybe writing letters to that priest who had gone to the missions, the one that she might have fancied. Richard felt a huge wave of sympathy for her. What a wasted love that must have been. Compared to his own great passion.

They came to the bridge, children still playing there as they had been the day Richard Hayes had come to town five long years ago.

Different children, same game.

Imagine, only an hour ago he had been planning for Gloria's children to go to school in Dublin. He thought he had taken over a family.

And now everything was over.

Now they were free to talk to each other there was nothing to say. His thoughts went up the road to the old schoolhouse, to the big beech tree which was covered with people's initials and their names.

In the first weeks of loving Gloria he had gone there secretly and carved 'Gloria in Excelsis'.

It didn't seem blasphemous, it seemed a celebration. If anyone saw it in years to come they would think it was a hymn of praise to God. They might think a priest had put it there. He would not go and score it out. That would be childish. He could finish the story, of course. He could say that the glory of the world passed by; *Sic Transit Gloria*

Mundi. Only a few would understand it and when they did they would never connect it with Gloria Darcy, loving wife of Mike Darcy, shopkeeper.

But that would be childish too.

Maura O'Sullivan and her son Michael passed them by as they stood on the bridge, Gloria and Richard who would never speak again.

'Good day Mrs Darcy, Mr Hayes,' she said.

'My daddy?' Michael ran up to him and hugged his leg.

Richard knelt down to return the hug properly.

'Go home, Gloria,' he said.

She went without a word. He could hear the sound of her high red heels tapping down the road towards the centre of Shancarrig.

'How are you, Michael? You're getting to be a very big fellow altogether,' he said and buried his head in the boy's shoulder so that no one would see his tears.

LEO

When Leonora Murphy was a toddler, her father used to sit her on his knee and tell her about the little girl who had a little curl *right* in the middle of her forehead. He would poke Leo's forehead on the word *right* to show her where the curl was. Then he would go on, *And when she was good she was very very good, but when she was bad she was HORRID.* At the last word he would make a terrible face and roar at her, *HORRID, HORRID.* It was always frightening, even though Leo knew it would end well with a big hug, and sometimes his throwing her up in the air.

She wasn't frightened of Daddy, just the rhyme. It seemed menacing, as if someone else was saying it.

Anyway it wasn't even suitable for her because she was a girl with much more than one little curl. She had a head full of them, red-gold curls. They got tangled when anyone tried to brush her hair. Her mother gave up in despair several times. 'Like a furze bush, like something you'd see on a tinker child.' Leo knew this was an insult. People were half afraid of the tinkers, who camped behind Barna Woods sometimes when they were on the way to the Galway races.

If Leo ever was bad and wouldn't eat her rice or fasten her shoes properly, Biddy would say that she'd be given to the tinkers next time one of them passed the door. It seemed a terrible fate.

But later when she was older, when she could go exploring, Leo Murphy thought that it might be exciting to go and live with the tinkers. They had open fires. The children ran around half dressed. They went through the woods finding rabbits.

She used to creep around with her friends from school, Nessa Ryan and Niall Hayes and Eddie Barton. Not daring to move they'd peep through the trees and the bushes and watch the marvellous free lifestyle of people who had no rules or no laws to tie them down.

Leo couldn't remember why she had been so afraid.

But then, that was when she was a child. Once she was eleven and grown up things could be viewed differently. She realised that there were a lot of things she hadn't understood properly while she was young.

She hadn't realised that she lived in the biggest house in Shancarrig, for one thing. The Glen was a Georgian house, with a wide hall leading back to the kitchen and pantry. On either side of the hall door were big beautifully proportioned rooms – the dining room where the table was covered with papers and books, since they rarely had anyone to dine – the drawing room where the old piano had not been tuned for many a year, and where the dogs slept on cushions behind the big baskets of logs for the fire.

There was a breakfast room behind where they ate their meals, and a sports room which had wellingtons and guns, and fishing tackle. This is where Leo kept her bicycle when she remembered, but often she left it outside the kitchen door. Sometimes the wild cats that Biddy loved to feed at the kitchen window came and perched on the bicycle. There was a time when a cat brought all her little kittens one by one and left them in the bicycle basket, thinking it might be a safe haven for them.

That was the day that Leo had watched stony-faced as her father drowned them in the rain barrel.

'It's for the best,' her father said. 'Life is about doing things for the best, things you don't like.'

Leo's father was Major Murphy. He had been in the British army. In fact, he had been away at the War when Leo was born. She knew that because every birthday he told her how he had been at Dunkirk and hadn't known if the new baby was a boy or a girl. Since there had been two boys already the news, when it did arrive, was great news.

Leo's brothers were away at school. They didn't go to Shancarrig school like other boys did, they were sent to a boarding school from the time they were very young. The school was in England, where Grandfather lived. Grandfather wanted some of his family near him and he paid the school fees, which were enormous. It was a famous school, where prime ministers had gone.

Leo knew that it wasn't a Catholic school, but that Harry and James did go to mass on Sundays. She also knew that, for some reason, she wasn't to talk about this to her friend Nessa Ryan, or to Miss Ross, or Mrs Kelly, or especially not to Father Gunn. It was all perfectly right and good, but not something you went on about.

She knew there were other ways in which she was different. Major Murphy didn't go out to work like other people's fathers did. He didn't have a business or a farm, just The Glen. He didn't go down to Ryan's Hotel in the evening like other men, or pop into Johnny Finn Noted for Best Drinks. He sometimes went for a walk with Niall Hayes's father, and he went to Dublin on the train for the day. But he didn't have a job.

Her mother didn't go shopping every morning. She didn't call to Dunne's or to the butcher's. She didn't get a blouse and skirt made with Eddie Barton's mother. She didn't get involved with arranging flowers on the altar for Father Gunn, or helping with the sale of work at the school. Leo's mother was very beautiful and gave the air of having a lot to do as she floated from room to room. She really was a very beautiful woman, everyone always said so. Mrs Murphy had red-gold hair like her daughter, but not those unruly curls. It was smooth and shiny and turned in naturally, as if it had always been like that. Once a month Mother went to Dublin and she had it trimmed then, in a place in St Stephen's Green.

Somehow Leo knew that Harry and James weren't going to come back to Shancarrig when they left school. They had been talking about Sandhurst for as long as she could remember. They were both accepted. Her father was delighted.

'We must tell everyone,' he said when the letter arrived.

'Who can we tell?' His wife looked at him almost dreamily across the breakfast table.

Father looked disappointed. 'Hayes will be pleased.'

'Your friend Bill Hayes is the only one who's heard of Sandhurst.' Miriam Murphy spoke sharply.

'Ah come on. They're not as bad as that.'

'They are, Frank. I've been the one who's always lived here, you're only the newcomer.'

'Eighteen years, and still a newcomer ...' He smiled at her affectionately.

Leo's mother had been born in The Glen, and had played as a child in Barna Woods herself. She had gone fishing down to the River Grane, and taken picnics up to the Old Rock, from which Shancarrig got its name. She had been here all through the troubles after the Easter Rising, and through the Civil War. In fact, because there were so many upheavals at that time, her parents had sent her off to a convent school in England.

Shortly after she had left it she had met Frank Murphy and, as two Irish amid the croquet and tennis parties of the south of England in the early 1930s, they had been drawn together. Frank's knowledge of Ireland was sketchy, but romantic. He always hoped to settle there one day. Miriam Moore had been more practical. She had a falling down home, she said. It needed much more money than they would ever have to turn it into a dream.

Miriam's parents were old. They welcomed the bright son-in-law with open arms. They hoped he would be able to manage their beautiful but neglected house and estate. They hoped he would be able to keep their beautiful but restless daughter contented.

They died before they could judge whether he had been able to do either.

'Is Sandhurst on the sea?' Leo asked interestedly. If Harry and James were going to a beach next year, instead of back to school, she was very jealous indeed.

Her parents smiled indulgently at her. They told her it was in Surrey, nothing to do with sand as in Sandycove or Sandymount or any other seaside place she had been to. It was a great honour to get in there. They would be officers of the highest kind.

'Will they be a higher rank than Daddy if there's another war?' Leo asked.

'There won't be another war, not after the last one.'

He looked sad when he said that. Leo wished she hadn't brought the subject up. Her father walked with a stick and he had a lot of pain. She knew this because she could hear him groaning sometimes if he thought he was alone. Perhaps he didn't like being reminded of the War, which had damaged his spine.

'You should write to them, Leo,' her mother said. 'They'd like to get a letter from their little sister.'

It was like writing to strangers, but she wrote. She told them that she was sitting in the drawing room, and that Lance and Jessie were stretched in front of the fire. She told them about the school concert where they all wanted to sing 'I've Got a Lovely Bunch of Coconuts' and Mrs Kelly had said it was a filthy song. She told them how Eddie Barton had taught her how to draw different kinds of leaves, fishes and birds, and said she might do them a special drawing for Christmas if they ordered it.

She said she was glad they were going to be high-class officers in the army, even if there was never going to be another war. She said they would be glad to know that Daddy was walking a bit better and Mother looking a lot less sad.

To her surprise they both wrote almost by return and said that they loved her news. It was strange not being one thing or the other, they wrote.

Leo had a big bedroom that looked out over the garden. It was one of four large rooms around the big square landing. Nessa Ryan was always admiring the upstairs.

'It's like a room in itself, this landing,' she said in admiration. 'It's so poky in the hotel, all the rooms have numbers on them.'

Leo said that when her mother was young in The Glen there was breakfast on the landing. Imagine, people bringing all the food upstairs to save the family going down. Sometimes they used to eat in their dressing-gowns, Mother had told her.

Nessa was very interested that Major and Mrs Murphy had different bedrooms; her parents slept in the same bed.

'Do they really?' Leo was fascinated. She broached the subject with Biddy.

Somehow, it didn't seem right to ask directly.

'Don't go inquiring about where and how people sleep. Nothing but trouble comes out of that.'

'But *why*, Biddy?'

'Ah, people sleep where they want to sleep. Your parents sleep at each end of the house, that's what they want. Leave it at that.'

'But where did your parents sleep?'

'With all of us, in one room.' So it wasn't much help.

When Harry and James came home for a very quick visit she decided to ask them. They looked at each other.

'Well, you see. With Papa being wounded and everything . . .'

'All that sort of thing changed,' James finished.

'What sort of thing?' Leo asked.

They looked at each other in despair.

'All sorts of things. No sorts of things,' Harry said. And she knew the subject was over.

Mother never told Leo anything about the facts of life. If it hadn't been for Biddy and Nessa she would have been astonished by her first period. Although she knew how kittens, puppies and rabbits, and therefore babies, were born, she had no idea how they were conceived. She very much hoped that it was nothing to do with the behaviour of the dogs and cats at certain times. She didn't see how such a thing would be possible for humans anyway, even if any of them would agree to do it. She hated Nessa Ryan being so knowing so she didn't ask her, and she knew that Biddy in the kitchen flushed a dark red when the matter was mentioned . . .

When Leo Murphy was fourteen such matters had been sorted out, if not exactly satisfactorily, at least she felt that she had mastered whatever technical information there was about it from reading pamphlets and magazines.

She had agreed with Nessa and Maura Brennan that it was quite impossible to believe that your own parents could ever have done it, but then the living proof that they must have was all around.

Maura Brennan was able to add the information that a lot of it happened when the man was drunk, and Leo said it was very unfair that the woman shouldn't be allowed to get drunk as well, because it was bound to be so awful.

Maura was very nice. She never pushed herself on anyone. In ways Leo liked her better than she liked Nessa Ryan, who could be moody if she didn't get her own way. But Maura lived in the poorest of the cottages. Her father Paudie was often to be seen sitting on someone's steps with a bottle in his hand, having been out drinking all night.

Maura wouldn't go on to the convent with them next year when she and Nessa went into town on the bus to secondary school. And yet at fourteen Maura seemed to know a lot more about life than the rest of them did.

It seemed very unfair to Leo that families like Maura Brennan's and Foxy Dunne's had to live in the falling down cottages by the river and had such shabby clothes. Foxy Dunne was much brighter than Niall Hayes, much quicker when it came to giving answers in school, but Foxy had no bicycle, no proper clothes, and had never been known to wear shoes that fitted him. Maura Brennan was much kinder and more gentle than Nessa Ryan but she never got a dress like Nessa got for her birthday and she hadn't a winter coat.

Leo knew she wasn't meant to go into the cottages and so she didn't. No one ever said not to, but it was something that was unspoken.

Only Foxy ever challenged it.

'Aren't you coming in to see the Dunne family at leisure . . . ?' he asked.

They had learned the word leisure at school today. Mrs Kelly had written it on the board and talked about what it meant.

'No thanks. I've got to go home today,' Leo would say.

'But *I'm* allowed to come and see the Murphy family at leisure,' he would say.

Leo was well able for him. 'Yes you are, and very welcome too, when you want to ...'

It was a stand-off.

They admired each other ... it had always been like that, since they were in Mixed Infants together ...

After the end of the summer term Leo and Nessa travelled on the bus to the convent school. They would meet the Reverend Mother, get a list of books and other items they would need, details of the school uniform and probably a string of rules as well. They thought that they would also be shown around the convent, but this did not materialise. They were tempted to spend the time idling round and sampling the pleasures of freedom of a place ten times the size of Shancarrig, but they felt that somehow they would be found out. It would be told back in Ryan's Hotel that they had been skitting and laughing on a corner with an idling lad, or licking ice creams in the street.

Better by far to get the early bus home and be shown to be reliable.

Nessa went into the hotel where she felt they weren't nearly grateful enough to see her.

'Are you back already?' Mrs Ryan said without enthusiasm.

'I hope you did everything you were meant to do,' her father said.

Leo grinned at her. 'It'll be the same in my place,' she said companionably. 'They'll have fed the dogs and won't have kept anything for me.'

She strolled up the hill, pausing to talk to Eddie Barton and tell him about the convent. He would be going to the Brothers. He said he wasn't looking forward to it. It was only games they cared about.

'In this place it's only prayers they care about,' Leo grumbled. 'There's statues leaping at you out of every wall.'

She trailed her shoulder bag behind her as she passed the old gate lodge that had been let once to people, who had left it like a pigsty. Now it was all boarded up in case any intruders got in.

It was a Thursday, and as soon as she was home Leo remembered that it was, of course, Biddy's half day. There would be food left under the meat safe. They usually had something cold for supper on a night when Biddy wasn't there. Leo knew that she should help herself because there was no one to greet her. Major Murphy had gone to Dublin that morning. He had caught the early train. Her mother must have gone walking in Barna Woods. Leo planned to take her food up to her bedroom and listen to her gramophone. She had written to James and Harry about the song 'I Love Paris in zee Springtime'. She could play it over and over. Some day she would go to Paris in 'zee Springtime or zee Fall' with someone who would sing that to her. She thought it would never go out of fashion. She closed herself into her room and before she even started on her milk and chicken sandwich she put on the record.

She threw herself on her window seat and was singing along with it when, to her surprise, she heard a door bang and footsteps running up or down the stairs, she couldn't tell which.

Thinking she might be playing it too loudly, she went to take off the handle of the machine and as she did so her eye caught sight of a young man fleeing across the grass and into the shrubbery. As he ran he was pulling on a shirt.

Leo was very frightened. It must have been a robber. Could there be more of them downstairs? She didn't know whether to shout for help or pretend that she wasn't there.

Her mind raced. They must know she was there if they had heard the music playing. Perhaps one was waiting for her outside her bedroom door. She could feel her heart thumping. In the silence of the house she heard a door creak open. She had been right. There *was* someone else lying in wait for her. She prayed as she had never prayed before.

As if in direct answer to her, God had managed to make her mother's voice call out, 'Leo? Leo? Is that you?'

Mother was standing outside her bedroom door, flushed-looking and confused.

Leo ran to her. 'Mother. There were robbers ... are you all right?'

'Shush, shush. Of course I am ... what are you talking about?'

'I heard them running down the stairs ... they went through the garden.'

'Nonsense, Leo. There were no robbers.'

'There *were*, Mother. I heard them, I saw them ... I saw one of them.'

'What did you see?'

252

'I saw him pulling off or putting on a shirt. Mother, he ran over there behind the lilacs, over the back fence.'

'What on earth are you doing home anyway ... weren't you meant to be on a tour of that school?'

'Yes, but they didn't show us. I saw him, Mother. There might be others in the house.'

Leo had never seen her mother so full of purpose. 'Come downstairs with me this moment and we'll put an end to this foolishness.' She flung open the doors of all the rooms. 'What burglar was here if he didn't take the silver, the glass? Or here, in the sports room, all your father's guns. Each one intact. Look, they didn't even take our supper, so let's have no chats about burglars and robbers.'

'But the feet on the stairs?' She was less sure of the figure now.

'I went downstairs myself and came back up to my room. I didn't know you were back ...'

'But I was playing the record player ...'

'Yes. That's what made me come out and look for you. To know what you were doing blasting it out and then turning it off.'

Mother looked excited. Different from the way she was normally.

Leo didn't know what made her think it was dangerous, but that is exactly what she felt it was. She had to walk just as delicately here as if there really were a robber hiding in the house.

She spoke nothing of the incident to her father, nor to Biddy. When Nessa Ryan asked whether Leo's welcome home had been any more cordial than the one that Nessa had got herself in the hotel, Leo said that she had made a sandwich and listened to 'I Love Paris'.

Nessa Ryan said that life was very unfair. She had been roped in to help polish silver, since she was back.

Imagine having all the freedom in the world in a big house like that.

Imagine. She didn't notice Leo shiver as she realised that she had denied the fright, and that somehow made the fright much bigger than it had been before.

Foxy Dunne came up the drive next day. His swagger showed a confidence that many of those twice his age might not have felt approaching The Glen.

But Foxy didn't push his luck; he went to the back door.

Biddy was most disapproving.

'Yes?' she said coldly.

'Ah, thank you, Biddy. It's good to get a real traditional Irish welcome everywhere, that's what I always say.'

'You and your breed never say anything except to make a jeer of other people who put their minds to work.'

Foxy looked without flinching.

'*I'm* different from my breed, as you call it, Biddy. I have every intention of putting my mind to work.'

'You'll be the first of the Dunnes who did, then.' She was still annoyed to see him sitting so confidently in her kitchen.

'There always has to be the first of some family who does. Where's Leo?'

'What's that to you?'

At that moment Leo came into the kitchen. She was pleased to see Foxy Dunne. She offered him one of Biddy's scones that were cooling on a wire tray.

'Will you like the place inside?' He was speaking about the secondary school.

'I think so. A bit Holy Mary, but you know.'

'A lot of people around here could do with being Holy Mary,' Biddy said.

Leo laughed. Everything seemed to be back to normal again.

'You'll work hard, won't you?' Foxy was concerned.

'Imagine one of Dinny Dunne's lads laying down the law on working hard,' Biddy snorted.

Foxy ignored her. 'It's important that you work as hard as I do,' he said to Leo. 'I have to, because I come from nothing. You have to because you come from everything.'

'I don't know what you mean,' Leo said.

'It would be dead easy for you to do nothing, for you to just drift about without doing anything, and end up just marrying someone.'

'Not for ages.' Leo was indignant.

'Not any time. You should get a job.'

'I might *want* to marry someone.'

'Yes, yes. But you'd be better off with a job, whether you married anyone or not.'

'I never heard such nonsensical talk.' Biddy was banging the saucepans around to show her disapproval.

'Come on, Foxy. We'll go out to the orchard,' Leo said.

They picked small gooseberries and put them in a basket that Leo's mother had left under a tree.

'It won't always be like this here, you know,' Foxy said.

'No. It'll be term time, and a list of books as long as your arm.'

'I meant this house, this way of going on.'

She looked at him, alarmed. The anxiety of the other night came back; things changing, not being safe any more.

'What do you mean?'

She looked very startled suddenly, and he didn't like the way her face got so alarmed, so he reassured her. He told her that if he could pretend to be sixteen or over he could get taken on by a man who was raising a crew for a builder in England – all fellows from round here, fellow countrymen ... he'd start just doing odd jobs, but he'd work his way up.

'I wish you weren't going away,' Leo said. 'I know it's crazy, but I have this stupid feeling that something awful is going to happen.'

It was three weeks later that it happened. On a warm summer evening. The house was quiet. Biddy had gone on her annual summer holidays back to her family's farm. Leo had finished her letter to Harry and James, she had written how Daddy's back seemed much better and that Dr Jims had said that walking couldn't do him any harm – it couldn't hurt him any more than he had been hurt in the War – and that if he sat in a chair like an old man with a rug over his knees then he'd turn into one.

So he went off for long walks with Mr Hayes, even up as far as the Old Rock. That's where they had gone today. Leo decided to walk down to the town to post the letter. Once it was written she liked it to be on its way. It could sit on the hall table for days, with Biddy dusting around it. She found a stamp and headed off. Mrs Barton was ironing, Leo could see her through the window. She never went out to sit in her little garden. Surely she could have brought some of her sewing out of doors on a beautiful evening like this. Leo looked up to see if she could see Eddie's face at his window. He wrote almost as many letters as she did. She met him sometimes at the post office and Katty Morrissey said that between them they kept the whole of P & T going.

But there was no sign of Eddie. Maybe he was off finding odd shapes of wood and clumps of flowers to draw. She did meet Niall Hayes, however, walking disconsolately up and down The Terrace.

'God, that school I'm going to is like a prison,' Niall said. 'It's like *The Count of Monte Cristo*'.

'The convent's all right. It's choked with statues, though, all of them with cross faces.'

'Oh, I wouldn't mind if it was only the statues. You should see the faces on these fellows. All of them in long black dresses, and looking desperate.'

'Sure doesn't Father Gunn wear a long dress, and Father Barry. You're used to them.' Leo thought Niall Hayes was making heavy weather out of it all.

'They don't have faces like lighting devils.'

'Did your father go to school there?'

'Of course he did, and all my uncles. And they've forgotten how awful it is. They keep telling me of all the fun they had there.'

'Your father's gone for a walk with my father.' Leo was tired of all the gloom.

'Well, it must have been a short one then. My father's back in the house there, making some farmer's will. Leo, I don't think I could *bear* to be a solicitor here in Shancarrig.'

'You could always go somewhere else,' Leo said. There seemed to be no cheering Niall today.

She was sorry her father's walk had been cancelled, but maybe he was sitting with Mother in the orchard. She had seen sometimes they had a big jug of homemade lemonade, and they looked as if they were a bit happy.

She met Father Gunn, who said wasn't it amazing the way the time raced by. There was another whole class ready to leave Shancarrig and go out into the wide world. It was extraordinary how grown-ups thought time raced by. Leo found it went very slowly indeed.

As she came in the gate of The Glen she heard cries coming from the gate lodge, and at the same moment she saw her father hastening as fast as he was able down the drive. Leo shrank away from the sound of crashing furniture and screams.

But she knew without a shadow of a doubt that it was her mother's voice she heard screaming, 'No, no! You can't! No,' and a great long wail.

'Oh, my God, my God. Miriam. *Miriam.*'

Her father was stumbling. He had dropped his stick, and had to bend down for it.

Leo watched as if it was slow motion.

Then they heard the shots. Three of them. And at that moment

Leo's mother came staggering to the door. Her blouse was covered with blood. Her hair and eyes were wild.

'My God ... he tried to ... he was trying to ... he would have killed me,' she cried. She kept looking behind her where they could see a shape on the ground.

'Frank!' screamed Leo's mother. 'Oh, do something, Frank. For God's sake! He would have killed me.'

Leo shrank still further away from the scene which she could see unfolding, but yet could not take in.

Her father walked in exaggeratedly slow motion towards the door and took her mother in his arms.

He soothed her like a baby.

'It's over, Miriam, it's over,' he said.

'Is he dead?' Leo's mother didn't want to look.

Horrified, Leo saw her father bend to the shape on the floor and turn it over. Leo could see a man with dark hair, lying on the floor of the gate lodge. There was a big red stain all over the front of his shirt.

It was the man she had seen running towards the lilacs in the shrubbery three weeks ago, the day that she thought there had been robbers.

And now both her father and mother were crying.

'It's all right, Miriam darling. It's over. He's dead.' Her father was saying this over and over again.

Later they gave Leo a brandy too. With a little water in it. But that was well after they had come back to the house.

The door of the gate lodge had been closed. They all walked up the drive arm in arm and Mother had gone up to wash herself.

'You might need to, you know, not change anything,' Leo heard Daddy say, but Mother looked at him wildly.

'You mean ... wear this? Wear *this* on my body? All this blood? What for? Frank, use your head. What for?' She was near hysteria.

'I'll wash you,' he offered.

'No. Please let me be on my own for a few moments.'

Mother had a wash basin in her room, with a mirror and a light over it, and little pink floral curtains.

Leo didn't want to be alone, so she followed her mother into the room. Their eyes met in the mirror.

'Are you all right, Mummy?' She rarely used that word.

Mother's face softened. 'It's all right, Leo. It's over.' She said Father's words like a parrot.

'What are we going to do? What's going to happen?'

'Shush. Let me get rid of all this. We'll put it out of our minds. It'll be like a bad dream.'

'But ...'

'That's for the best, Leo, believe me.' Mother looked very young as she stood there just in her slip and skirt. She rubbed her neck and arms with a soapy flannel and warm water, even though there was no trace of blood. That was all streaked and hardening on the yellow blouse she had thrown into the wastepaper basket.

Mother was brushing her teeth, and she shook her tin of Tweed talcum powder into her hand and rubbed it into her skin.

'Go on, darling. Go down to your father. I want to finish dressing.'

Leo thought Mother only had to put on a blouse. And of course a brassiere. She had only just realised that for some reason Mother hadn't been wearing one as she stood beside the hand basin. Just the slip. Her silky peach-coloured one.

Everything was so strange and unreal. The fact that Mother had asked her to leave the room now was only one tiny fragment more in the whole thing.

Leo went into the drawing room. She felt something like this should not be discussed in the breakfast room where they lived on ordinary days. Her father must have felt the same thing. He had put a match to the fire and the two dogs, Lance and Jessie, seemed pleased. They stretched their big cream limbs in front of the grate.

Leo thought suddenly that Lance and Jessie didn't know what had happened. Then she remembered that nobody knew – not Niall Hayes, whom she had been talking to half an hour ago – nor Mrs Barton, who had waved from her ironing – nor Father Gunn, who had said that time passed so quickly.

Father Gunn? Why wasn't he here?

The moment someone died you sent for the priest. And Dr Jims, Eileen and Sheila's father, he should be here. That's what happened when people got sick or died, Father Gunn and Dr Jims arrived in their cars.

Mother was at the door. She shivered and hugged herself.

'That's lovely of you to light the fire,' she said.

They both looked up, Leo and her father. Mother sounded so

ordinary – so normal. As if it all hadn't happened out there. Down in the gate lodge.

That was when Father poured the brandy for the two of them.

'Give Leo a little, too.' Mother sounded as if she was offering more soup at lunchtime.

'Come up here to the fire. Warm your hands. I'll phone Sergeant Keane. He'll be up in five minutes.'

'No.' It was like a whiplash.

'We have to call him, we should have phoned immediately.'

Leo was sipping the horrible and unfamiliar brandy. She didn't know how people like Maura Brennan's father wanted to drink alcohol all the time. It was disgusting.

'My nerves won't stand it, Frank. I've been through enough already.'

'Sergeant Keane's very gentle. He'll make it as quick as possible. It's just the formalities.'

'I won't *have* the formalities. There's no point in asking me to.'

'A man tried to kill you, he had one of my guns. He *could* have killed you.' Father's voice broke with emotion at the thought of it.

Mother became even more icily calm.

'But he didn't. What happened was that I killed him.'

'You defended yourself against him … the gun went off. He killed himself.'

'No. I picked up the gun and shot him.'

'You don't know *what* happened. You're in shock.'

Major Murphy made a move as if to go out to the hall to the telephone.

Mother didn't even need to raise her voice to make her seriousness felt.

'If you ring him, Frank, I'm walking out of that door and you'll never see me again. Either of you.'

He put out his arms as if to hold her again, support her as he had up the drive, console her as he had done when he was holding her, telling her it was over.

Mother really seemed to believe that it *was* over.

Leo kept moving the glass around between her hands as she listened to her parents talking about the man who lay dead in their gate lodge.

Her mother's voice was strange and unnatural. It didn't sound like a voice, it sounded like a noise, a thin even noise, with no highs and lows.

She spoke as one who is being perfectly reasonable.

Frank had told her it was over, finished. So let it be forgotten. Why drag heavy-footed policemen in, and go over it and over it, and ask questions and give answers? The man had threatened her. He had got killed himself. It was an eye for an eye. Justice had been done. Let it be left as it was.

At every interruption she gave her strange disembodied threat: 'Or else I will disappear from this house and you will never see me again.'

It was as if they had forgotten she was here. Leo watched mesmerised as her mother, by sheer force of repetition, began to beat down the rational arguments. She saw her father change from the strong man comforting his wife caught in a terrible accident and become someone hunted and unsure. She saw him bite his lip and watched his eyes widen with fear at every repeated threat that Miriam Murphy would walk out the door and never be seen again.

She wanted to interrupt, to ask Mother where she would go. Why she would leave them, her home and her family?

But she didn't dare to move.

It was when her father had said, 'I couldn't *live* without you, Miriam, you couldn't leave knowing that ...'

'Please ...' She looked across at her fourteen-year-old daughter, as if a lapse of taste had been committed. A man shouldn't speak of his need, of his weakness, not in front of a child.

Major Murphy came over to the window seat where Leo was sitting.
'Leo, dearest child.'

'What's going to happen, Daddy?'

'It's going to be all right. As your mother says, it's over, it's over. We mustn't ...'

'Will we get Dr Jims? Father Gunn ... ?'

'Leo, come with me. I'll bring you up to bed.'

'I want to stay here, Daddy, please ...'

'You want to help us, you want to be big and brave and do the right thing ...'

'No. I want to stay here. I'm afraid.'

Outside in the big garden darkness had fallen. The bushes were big shapes, not colours as they had been when the three of them walked back up, huddled together from the horrors they had left in the gate lodge.

He propelled her out of the door and to the kitchen where he warmed some milk in a saucepan. He took the big silver pepperpot and sprinkled some over the top of the milk when it was poured into a mug.

He walked up the stairs with her and led her to the room.

'Put on your nightie, like a good girl,' he said.

He turned his back as Leo slipped out of her green cotton dress and her summer vest and knickers, and pulled on the pink winceyette nightdress from the nightdress case shaped like a rabbit. Leo remembered with a shock that when she stuffed her nightie in there this morning nothing had happened. None of this nightmare had begun.

She got into bed and sipped the milk.

Her father sat on the bed and stroked her forehead. 'It will be all right, Leo,' he said.

'How can it be all right, Daddy?'

'I don't know. I used to wonder that in the War, but it was.'

'It wasn't really. You got wounded and you can't walk properly.'

'Yes, I can.' He stood up.

His face was so sad Leo wanted to cry aloud. She wanted to open the window in her room, kneel up on the window seat and cry out for someone in Shancarrig to help them all.

But she bit her lip.

'I have to go down now, Leo,' he said.

It was as if they were allies. Allies to protect a strange silent mother downstairs who wasn't speaking in her ordinary voice.

She used to play that game of 'if'.

If I get up the stairs before the grandfather clock in the hall stops striking then Mrs Kelly won't be in a bad mood tomorrow. If the crocuses come up in front of the house by Tuesday I'll get a letter from Harry and James.

Now she sat in the dark bedroom with her arms around her knees. If I don't get out of bed it will be all right. Dr Jims will come and say he wasn't dead at all. If he is really dead then Father Gunn will say it wasn't Mother's fault.

If I don't get out of bed at all and if I sit like this all night without moving then it'll turn out not to have happened at all.

She woke in the morning stiff and awkward. She hadn't managed to stay awake. Now the charm wouldn't work. It *had* happened, all of it.

There was no point in holding her knees any more. None of it was going to work.

How could it be an ordinary day? A sunny day with Lance and Jessie rushing around outside, with Mattie the postman cycling up the drive, with smells of breakfast coming from downstairs.

Leo got out of bed and looked at her face in the wardrobe mirror. It was grey white and there were shadows under her frightened grey-green eyes. Her curly hair stood upright over her head.

She pulled on the clothes she had thrown on the floor last night, last night when Daddy had been standing with his frightened face.

At that moment the door opened and Mother came in. A different Mother from last night. Mother was dressed in a blue linen suit, her hair was combed, she wore her pink lipstick and she looked bright and enthusiastic.

'I have the most wonderful news,' she said.

Leo felt the colour rushing to her cheeks. The man wasn't dead. Dr Jims had cured him.

Before she could speak Mother had opened the wardrobe door and started to take out some of Leo's frocks.

'We're going on a holiday, all three of us,' she said. 'Your father and I suddenly decided that this was what we all needed. Now, isn't that a lovely surprise?'

'But ...' Leo's voice dried in her throat.

'But we have to get going just after breakfast, it's a long drive.'

'Are we running away?' Leo's voice was a whisper.

'For a whole week we are ... now, where are your bathing togs? We're going to a lovely hotel on a cliff, and we'll be able to run down and have a swim before breakfast every day. Imagine.'

Her father didn't catch her eye at breakfast, and Leo knew that she must not mention the events of last night. Her father had somehow bought the right for both of them to run away with Mother. That's what was happening.

They heard a knock at the back door. All three of them looked at each other in alarm, but it was Ned, who did the garden. Leo heard her father explaining about the sudden holiday ... and giving instructions.

The glasshouses were in a terrible state – if Ned could concentrate entirely on clearing them, and sorting out what was to be done....

'And what about the rockery, Major, sir?'

'It's very important that you leave that. There's a man coming down from the Botanic Gardens in Dublin to have a look at it. He said nothing was to be touched until he came.'

'I'm glad of that.' Ned sounded relieved. 'Will I fill in the hole we dug?'

'Oh, we've done that already . . .'

If Ned was surprised that a man with war injuries, and his frail wife, had covered in a pit that it had taken him two days to dig, he showed no sign of it.

'I'll leave it as it is then, Major, sir?'

'Just as it is, Ned. No disturbing it at all.'

Leo felt a cold horror spread all over her.

The memory of last night, hugging her knees in the dark. The sound of footsteps, of low urgent voices, of dragging and pulling. But her mother was calm as she listened to the conversation at the back door, and even laughed when Daddy came back into the room.

'Well, I expect that was welcome news for our Ned. Anything that he hasn't to do must come as a pleasant surprise.'

Leo beat back the wild fears.

Often her dreams seemed real to her . . . more real than ordinary life. This is what must be happening now. There was another knock at the door. Again the look of alarm was exchanged.

This time it was Foxy Dunne.

'Yes, Foxy?' Leo's father was unenthusiastic.

'How are you?' Foxy never addressed people by title. He wouldn't greet the priest as Father and he certainly wouldn't call Leo's father Major.

'I'm fine thank you, Foxy. How are you?'

'Great altogether. I came to say goodbye to Leo.'

Suddenly her father's voice sounded wary. 'And how, might I ask, did you know that she was going away?'

'I didn't.' Foxy was cheerful. 'I'm going away myself, that's why I came to say goodbye.'

'Well, I suppose you'd better come in.'

Foxy walked easily through the scullery and the kitchen and into the breakfast room.

'How're ya?' he said, nodding easily at Leo's mother.

She smiled at the small boy with the freckles and the red hair, the one Dunne boy that poverty and neglect had never managed to defeat.

'And where are you off to?' she asked politely.

Foxy ignored her and addressed Leo. 'I'm off to London, Leo. I didn't think I'd ever be able to do it. I thought I'd be hanging around here like an eejit, dragging a brush around someone's shop.'

'You're too young to go to England.'

'They won't ask. All they want is someone to make tea on a site.'

'Will you be frightened?'

'After my old fellow and Maura Brennan's old fellow? Both of them coming home drunk and both of them trying to beat me up ... how could I be frightened?'

He talked as if Leo's parents weren't there. It wasn't deliberately rude, it was just that he didn't see them.

'Will you ever come back to Shancarrig again?'

'I'll come home every Christmas with fistfuls of pound notes, like everyone else on the buildings.'

Major Murphy asked whether Foxy would learn a trade.

'I'll learn everything,' Foxy told him.

'No, I mean a skilled trade, you know, an honourable trade, like a bricklayer ... It would be very good to serve your time, to do an apprenticeship.'

'It'll be that all right.' Foxy didn't even look at the man, let alone heed him.

'Will you write and tell what it's like?' Leo knew her voice sounded shaky and not full of interest as Foxy would have liked.

'I was never one for the writing, but as I say, I'll see you every Christmas. I'll tell you then.'

'Good luck to you over there.' Leo's mother was standing up from the breakfast table. She was bringing the conversation to a close.

Foxy gave her a long look.

'Yeah. I suppose I'll need a bit of luck all right. But it's more a matter of working and letting them know you can work.'

'You're only a child. Don't let them ruin your health, tell them you're not able for heavy work.' The Major was kind.

But Foxy was having none of it. 'I'll tell them I'm seventeen. That's how I'll get on. Seventeen, and a bit stunted.' He was going in his own time, not in Mrs Murphy's. 'I'll see you at Christmas, Leo,' he said, and went.

Leo saw him fondling the ears of Lance, and throwing a stick for Jessie.

Other people were in awe of the two loudly barking labradors. Not Foxy Dunne.

She thought of him a few times during their holiday, that strange time in a faraway hotel, where there was nothing whatsoever for her to do except read the books that were in the library. Sometimes she walked with her father and mother along the sandy beaches, collecting cowrie shells. But usually she left Mother and Father to walk alone, with the dogs. They seemed very close together, sometimes even holding hands as Father limped along, and Mother sometimes bent to pick up some driftwood and throw it out into the sea so that Lance and Jessie could struggle to bring it back.

She didn't sleep too well at night in the small room with the diamond-shaped panes of glass in the window. The roar of the Atlantic Ocean down below the cliffs was very insistent. The stars looked different here from the way they looked in Shancarrig when she'd sit on her window seat and watch at night – the familiar garden of The Glen, the lilacs, the shrubbery down to the big iron gates and the gate lodge.

She shivered when she thought of the gate lodge. She had not been able to look at it as they had driven past on the morning they had left home. She dreaded seeing it again when she went back, but she wanted to be away from this strange dreamlike place too, this holiday that never should have been.

Biddy would be at home now in The Glen. What might have happened? What might she have found? Yet neither Father nor Mother telephoned her or seemed remotely worried.

Leo felt a constriction in her throat. She couldn't eat the food that was put in front of her.

'My daughter hasn't been well. It has nothing to do with your lovely food.'

Leo looked at her mother in disbelief. How could she lie so easily and in such a matter-of-fact voice? If she could do that she could lie about anything. Nothing was as it used to be any more.

Leo was very afraid. She wanted a friend. Not Nessa whose eyes would widen in horror. Not Eddie Barton who would retreat into his woods, and his flowers, and his drawings. Not Niall Hayes who would say it was typical of grown-ups – they never did anything you could rely on.

She couldn't tell Father Gunn, not even in confession. Maura Brennan would be more frightened than she was herself.

For a moment she thought of Foxy Dunne, but even if he were at home he wasn't the kind of person you could tell. She wondered how he was standing up to life on a big building site in London. Did he seriously think that people would believe he was seventeen? But he was always so cocky, so confident, maybe they would.

She looked away to the other side of the car as they drove back in through the gates of The Glen. It was as if she was afraid that the door of the gate lodge would be swinging wide open and that Sergeant Keane and a lot of guards would be there waiting for them.

But everything was as it always had been. The dogs raced around, happy to be home and no longer cooped up in the station wagon. Biddy was bustling around full of interest in their sudden holiday. Old Ned, who was sitting smoking in the glasshouse, busied himself suddenly.

There had been no news, Biddy said. Everything had gone fine. There was a letter from Master Harry and Master James, and some other parcel that didn't have enough stamps on it and Mattie wanted money paid.

There had been cross words with the butcher because they had delivered the Sunday joint of beef as usual and been annoyed when told that the family were on holidays. Sergeant Keane had been up to know if there was any word of one of the tinkers who had gone missing.

Biddy had given them all short shrift.

She had told Mattie that enough money had been spent on stamps to and from this house for him to feel embarrassed even mentioning the question of underpayment. He had slunk away, as well he might. The butcher had felt the lash of Biddy's tongue as she told them that the new frontage on the shop had been paid for with money that Major Murphy and his family had spent on the best of meat, they should be ashamed to grumble.

She asked Sergeant Keane what he could have been thinking of to imagine that a tinker boy could even have crossed the lawns of The Glen.

At first Leo didn't want to meet anyone. She wanted to stay half sitting, half kneeling on her window seat, looking out to where the dogs played, and old Ned made feeble attempts at hoeing, to where her father walked with his halting movements out to meet Mr Hayes, and where Mother drifted, her straw hat in her hand, through the shrubbery and past the lilacs.

No man came from the Botanic Gardens in Glasnevin to deal with the rockery that they had planned on top of the great pit that had been filled in.

When Mr O'Neill, the auctioneer from the big town, came to inquire whether they would be interested in letting the gate lodge, Leo's father and mother said not just now, some time certainly, but at the moment everything was quite undecided – perhaps one of the boys might come home and live in it.

There had never been any question of Harry or James coming back. Leo realised it was one more of these easy lies her mother told, like when she had told the people at the hotel that Leo had been unwell and that was why she hadn't been able to eat her meals.

One day Maura Brennan from school came and asked for a job as a maid in the house. She said she had to work somewhere and why not for someone like Leo, whom she liked. Leo had been awkward and frightened that day. It seemed another example of the world going mad: Maura, who had sat beside her at school, wanting to come and scrub floors in their house because that was the way things were.

But as the days turned into weeks Leo got the courage to leave The Glen. She called on Eddie Barton and his mother. They spoke to her as if things were normal. She began to believe they were. There was an ill-written postcard from London saying 'Wish you were here'. She knew it was from Foxy, though it didn't say. And one Saturday at Confession Father Gunn had asked her was there anything troubling her.

Leo's heart leapt into her throat.

'Why do you ask that, Father?' she said in a whisper.

'You seem nervous, my child. If there's anything you want to say to me, remember you're saying it to God through me.'

'I know, Father.'

'So, if there is any worry . . .'

'I am worried about something, but it's not my worry, it's someone else's worry.'

'Is it your sin, my child?'

'No, Father. No. Not at all. It's just that I can't understand it. You see, it has to do with grown-ups.'

There was a silence.

Father Gunn was digesting this. He assumed that it was to do with a child's perception of adult sexuality and all the loathing and embarrassment that this could bring.

'Perhaps all these things will become clear later,' he said soothingly.

'So, I shouldn't worry, do you think, Father?'

'Not if it's something you have no control over, my child, something where it would not be appropriate for you to be involved,' said the priest.

Leo felt much better. She said her three Hail Marys, penance for her other small sins, and put the biggest thing as far to the back of her mind as possible. After all, the priest said that God would make it clear later; now was not the appropriate time to worry about it.

As she prepared for her years in the convent school in the town she tried to make life in The Glen seem normal. She had joined their game. She was pretending that nothing had ever happened on that summer evening when the world stopped.

Leo started to go down the hill to meet the people she had been at school with once more – her friend Nessa Ryan in the hotel, whose mother always found work for idle hands – Sheila and Eileen Blake, who were home from a posh boarding school and kept asking could they come and play tennis at The Glen. Leo told them the court needed a lot of work. She realised she was lying as smoothly as her mother these days. She met Niall Hayes, who told her that he thought he was in love.

'Everyone's doing everything too young,' Leo said reprovingly. 'Foxy's too young to be going to England to work, you're too young to be in love. Who is it anyway?'

He didn't say. Leo thought it might be Nessa. But no, surely not? He lived across the road from Nessa, he had known her all his life. That couldn't be what falling in love was like. It was too confusing.

She met Nancy Finn from the pub. Nancy was what they called a bold strap in Shancarrig. She was fifteen and had been accused of being forward and giving people the eye. Sometimes she helped serve behind the counter. It was a rough sort of place.

Nancy said she'd really love to go to America and work as a cocktail waitress. That was her goal but her father said it was lunacy. Nancy said her father, Johnny Finn Noted for Best Drinks, was fed up. The guards had been in every night for three weeks asking was there any brawl between tinkers and anyone, and her father said he wouldn't let a bloody tinker in the door. Sergeant Keane said that was a very unchristian attitude, and Nancy's father had said the guards would have another tune to play if he *did* let the tinkers in and took their money, so there had been hard words and the upshot was that the guards were watching Johnny Finn's pub night after night, ready to pounce if anyone was left with a drink in front of them for thirty seconds beyond the licensing hours.

The summer ended and a new life began, a life of getting the bus every day into school in the big town. The bus bounced along the roads through villages and woods, and stopped at junctions and crossroads where people came down long narrow tracks to the main road. Leo and Nessa Ryan learned their homework to the rhythm of the bus crossing the countryside. They heard each other's poems, they puzzled out theorems and algebra. Often they didn't even look out the window at the countryside passing by.

Sometimes Leo seemed as if she was looking out at the scenery. Anyone watching her would think that there was a dreamy schoolgirl looking out at the fields with the cattle grazing, the colours changing from season to season in the hedges and clusters of bushes that they passed.

But Leo Murphy's eyes might not have been focusing on these things at all. Her thoughts were often on her mother. Her pale delicate mother, who wandered more often through the gardens of The Glen no matter what the weather, with empty eyes, talking softly to herself.

Leo had seen her mother sit under the lilac tree picking the great purple flowers apart absently in her lap and crooning to herself, 'You had lilac eyes, Danny. Your eyes were like deep lilac. Your eyes are closed now.'

She spoke of Danny too when she half sat and half lay over the rockery. Every day, rain or shine, she tended it, and a weed could hardly put its head out before Mrs Murphy had snapped it away.

'At least I kept your grave for you, Danny boy,' she would cry. 'You can never say I didn't put flowers on your grave. No man in Ireland got more flowers.'

The first time Leo heard her mother speak like this she was frozen with horror. It was a known fact that the missing tinker was Danny. His family had told people that he must have a girl in Shancarrig. He used to be gone from the camp for long periods, and when he'd come back he was always smiling and saying nothing. There was the question he might have run off with someone from the locality. Sergeant Keane had assured the travellers that there were no unexplained disappearances of any of the girls of the village; he had made inquiries and there was no one missing from the area.

'No one except Danny,' said Mrs McDonagh, the sad-looking woman with the dark, lined face who was Danny's mother.

Leo heard all this from other people. Nessa Ryan heard it discussed a lot in the hotel, and reported it word for word. It was the only exciting thing that had happened in their lives. She couldn't understand why her friend Leo wasn't interested in it, and wouldn't speculate like everyone else about what might have happened.

The months went by and Leo's mother became less in touch with reality.

Leo had stopped trying to talk to her about school, and everyday things. Instead she spoke as if her mother was an invalid.

'How do you feel today, Mother?'

'Well ... I don't know, I really don't know.' She spoke in a dull voice. The woman who used to be so elegant and graceful, the mother who would plan a picnic, correct bad grammar or a mispronounced word with cries of horror ... that had all gone.

She barely touched her food, just smiled vaguely at Father, and Leo, and at Biddy as if they were people she used to know. She spoke to the dogs, Lance and Jessie, no longer the big gambolling pups, but more stately with years. She reminded them of how they had known Danny, and they would stand guard over his grave.

Biddy *must* have heard it. She would have had to be deaf not to have known what she was talking about.

But the conspiracy continued.

Mrs Murphy had been feeling under the weather, surely now the longer days, or the bright weather, or the good crisp winter without any damp ... whichever season ... she would show an improvement.

Old Ned had been pensioned off. Eddie Barton came and cut the grass sometimes, but there was nobody coming to do the gardens as they should have been done. Sometimes Leo and her father would struggle, but it was beyond them. Only the rockery bloomed. Mrs Murphy wandered outside The Glen with her secateurs in her pocket and took cuttings for it, or even dug up little plants that she thought might flourish.

In the increasingly jungle-like gardens of The Glen the rockery bloomed as a monument, as a memorial.

In her efforts to keep her mother out of anyone else's sight and hearing, Leo pieced together the story of horror, of what had happened in those weeks when she was fourteen and had understood nothing of the world. Those weeks before her world changed.

Mother remembered not only Danny's lilac eyes but his strong arms, and his young body. She remembered his laughter and his impatience and greed to have her, over and over. With a sick stomach Leo listened to her mother remembering and crying for a lost love. She hated the childlike coquettish enthusiasm in her mother's face when she spoke of the man she had welcomed on the mossy earth, in her bedroom on the rug, under the lilac trees, and in the gate lodge.

But it was when she mentioned the gate lodge that her face would harden and her questioning take a different turn. Why did he have to be so greedy? What did he need with silver? Why had he demanded to take their treasures? What did he mean that he needed something to trade, some goods to deal in as they went towards Galway? Had he not taken her, was that not the greatest treasure of all? Miriam Murphy's eyes were like stone when she went through that part of the story of the last time they had met ... of the silver he had wrapped in a tablecloth as he had roamed through the house, touching things, taking this, leaving that. She had begged him and pleaded.

'Say there was a robbery ... say you came back and found it all gone.' His lilac eyes had laughed at her.

'I told him he must not go, he had been sent to me, and he could not leave.'

Leo knew the chant off by heart, she could say it with her mother as the woman stroked the earth of the rockery.

'You wouldn't listen, Danny. You called me old. You said you had given me my fun and my loving and that I should be grateful.

'You said you'd take some guns, that we had no need of them, but in your life you'd need to hunt in the forest ... I asked you to take me with you ... and you laughed, and you called me old. I couldn't let you leave, I had to keep you here, and that was why ...' Her mother would smile then, and stroke the earth again. 'And you are here, Danny Boy. You'll never leave me now.'

Leo had known for years why her father had struggled that night, dragging and pulling with his wounds aching and his useless leg trailing behind. He knew why this woman had to be protected from telling this sing-song tale to the law. And Leo knew too.

At school they thought her a tense child. They spoke to her father about her since Mrs Murphy, the mother, never made any appearance.

Mother Dorothy, who was wise in the ways of the world, decided that the mother might have a drink problem. It had to be. Otherwise she'd have come in some time. Very tough on the child, a nice girl, but with a shell on her as hard as rock.

Leo told Father Gunn that Mother wasn't all that well, and that if they didn't see her at mass he wasn't to take any wrong meaning out of it.

Father Gunn asked would she like the sacraments brought up to The Glen.

'I'm not too sure, Father.' Leo bit her lip.

Father Gunn also knew the ways of the world.

'Why don't we leave it for the moment?' he suggested. 'And if there's any change in that department then all you have to do is ask me.'

Leo thought to herself that in Shancarrig it was really quite easy to hide anything from anybody.

Or maybe it was only if you happened to live in The Glen, a big house surrounded by high walls, with its own gardens and shrubberies and gate lodge.

It might be different trying to keep your secrets if you lived in the cottages down by the river, or in The Terrace with everyone seeing your front entrance, or in the hotel with half of Shancarrig in and out of your doors every day.

She felt watchful about her mother, but not always on edge. No long-term anxiety like that can be felt at the pain level all the time. There were many hours when Leo didn't even think about her mother's telling and re-telling the story. There were the school outings, there were the parties, the times when Niall Hayes kissed her and their noses kept bumping, and later when quite suddenly Richard Hayes, who was Niall's older cousin, kissed her and there was no nose-bumping at all.

Richard Hayes was very handsome, he had stirred the place up since he arrived. Leo felt sorry for Niall because deep in her heart she thought Niall still had a very soft spot for Nessa, and Nessa was of course crazy about the new arrival in town.

And it had to be said that Richard was paying a lot of attention to Nessa. There were walks, drives and trips to the pictures in the town. Leo thought he was rather dangerous, but then she shrugged. Who was she to know? Her views on love and attraction were extremely suspect.

Some of the girls at school were going to be nurses; they had applied to hospitals in Dublin and in Britain for places.

'Should I be a nurse, Daddy?' she asked.

They were walking, as they often did in the evening. Mother was safely talking to the rockery, and if you counted Biddy as the silent rock she had been for three long years, then there was no one around to hear the chant that had begun again.

'Would you *like* to be a nurse?'

'Only if it would help.'

Her father looked old and grey. Much of his time was spent persuading his sons not to come back to Shancarrig, and telling them that their mother was in poor mental health.

Naturally they had written and asked why was nothing being done about this. They had written to Dr Jims, which Major Murphy thought an outrageous interference. But fortunately Jims Blake had agreed with him that arrogant young men thought they knew everything. If Frank Murphy said there was nothing wrong with Miriam, then that was that. The doctor had seen the thin pale face and the over-brilliant eyes of Miriam Murphy, always a fairly obsessional person he would have thought, checking light switches, refusing to throw out old papers. This is what he had noticed on his visits to The Glen, and assumed that like many a nervy woman there was nothing asked and therefore nothing that could be answered. This was not a household where he would be asked to refer her to a psychiatrist in order to work out the cause of the unease. At least he wasn't being asked for ever-increasing prescriptions of tranquillisers or sleeping pills. This in itself was something to be thankful for.

Foxy Dunne came home every Christmas as he had promised. When he arrived on his first visit home, wearing a new zippered jacket with a tartan lining, at the back door of The Glen, he was surprised at the frostiness of his reception. Not that he had ever been warmly welcomed there, but this was out of that league ... 'Well, tell my friend Leo. She knows where I live,' he said haughtily to Biddy.

'And I'm sure, like everyone, she knows only too well where the Dunnes live and would want to avoid it,' Biddy said.

Leo had heard. She called to the Dunnes' cottage that afternoon.

'I came to ask if you'd like to go for a walk in Barna Woods,' she said.

Foxy looked very pleased. He was at a loss for words. The quick shrugging reaction or the smart joke deserted him.

'Well, I won't ask you into my house either,' he said. 'Let's go and be babes in the wood.'

He told her of living in a house with eleven men from their own country. He told her of the drinking and how so many of them spent everything they had nearly killed themselves earning.

'Why do you stay there?' she asked.

'To learn ... to save. But mainly to learn.'

'What can you learn from old men like that drinking their lives away?'

'I can learn what not to do, I suppose, or how it could have been done right.'

Foxy sat on a fallen tree and told her about the chances, the men who had made it, the small contractors who did things right and did them quickly. He told her how you had to watch out for the fellow who was a great electrician, a good plumber, a couple of bright brickies, a class carpenter. Then all you needed was someone to get them together and you had your own team – someone who had a head for figures, someone who could cost a job and make the contacts.

'And who would you get to do that?' She was genuinely interested.

'God, Leo, that's what *I'm* going to do. That's what it's all about,' he said.

She felt ashamed that she hadn't the confidence in him.

'Did you know my father was in gaol?' he asked defensively.

'I heard. I think Biddy told me.'

'She would have.'

She was torn between being sympathetic and telling him it didn't matter.

'Did he hate it?' she asked.

'I don't know, he doesn't talk to me. He should have been there longer. He hit a fellow with a plank that had nails in it. He's dangerous.'

'You're not like that,' she said suddenly.

'I know, but I didn't want you to forget where I come from.'

'You are what you are, so am I.'

'And do you have any tales to tell me?' he asked.

'No. Why?' Her voice was clipped.

He shrugged. It was as if he had been offering her the chance to trade confessions.

But he didn't know they were not equal confessions. What his father had done was known the length and breadth of the county. What her mother had done was known by only three people.

He looked at her for a while, as if waiting.

Then he said, 'No reason, no reason at all.'

She saw him looking at her, with her belted raincoat, hands stuck deep in her pockets. The wind made her cheeks red. Her red-gold curls stood out around her head like a furze. She felt he was looking straight through her, that he could see everything, knew everything.

'I hate my hair,' she said suddenly.

'It's like a halo,' he said.

And she grinned.

Every Christmas he came home. He called to The Glen and she would take him walking. For the week that he was home they would meet every day.

Nessa Ryan was very disapproving. 'You *do* know his father was in gaol,' she told Leo.

'I do,' Leo sighed. She had heard it all from Biddy, over and over.

'I'd be surprised you'd go walking with him, then.'

'I know you would.' Leo had heard the same thing from her father. But that particular time she had answered back. 'Well, if everyone knew about us, Daddy, maybe people wouldn't want to go walking with us either.' Her father looked as if she had struck him. Immediately she had repented. 'I'm so sorry, I didn't mean it ... I just think that Foxy is lonely when he comes home. I don't ask him in here. I'm seventeen, nearly eighteen, Daddy. Why can't we let people alone? We, of all people?'

Her father had tears in his eyes. 'Go and walk with whoever you like in the woods,' he had said, his voice choked.

That was the Christmas when Foxy told her that he was on the way to the big time. He was working with two others. They were setting up their own contracts, they would hire men, get a team together. No more working for cheats and fellows who took all the profit.

'I'll soon have enough saved to come back a rich man,' he said. 'Then I'll drive up your avenue in a big car, hand my coat and gloves to Biddy, and ask your father for your hand in marriage. Your mother will take out the sherry and plan your wedding dress.'

'I'll never marry,' Leo told him.

'You sure as anything didn't take my advice about getting trained for a career or a job,' he said.

'I can't leave The Glen.'

'Will you tell me why?' His eyes still had that power to look as if they could see right through her, and know everything.

'I will, one day,' she promised, and she knew she would.

This year at least she had an address for Foxy. She wrote to him, he sent a very short note back.

'Why don't you learn to type, Leo? Your writing is worse than my own. We can't have that when we're in the big time, neither of us able to write a letter.'

She laughed.

She didn't tell Nessa Ryan that she had just got a sort of proposal from Foxy Dunne.

She didn't tell her parents.

Her mother died on an autumn night. They said it was of exposure. Her lungs filled up with the damp night air and, added to a chest infection ... There was no hope for a woman whose health had always been so frail.

She had been found in her nightdress, lying over the rockery in the garden.

The church was crowded. Major Murphy asked people to come back to Ryan's Hotel for a drink and some sandwiches afterwards. This was very unusual and had never been known in Shancarrig. But he said that The Glen was too sad for him and for Leo just now. He was sure people would understand.

Then Leo went to the town every day on the bus and learned to type in the big secretarial college where Nessa had done a course.

'Why couldn't you have done it with me?' Nessa grumbled.

'It wasn't the right time.'

There had been no note from Foxy Dunne about her mother's death.

She didn't write to tell him. Surely some member of his awful family was in touch, surely there would have been a mention that Mrs Murphy of The Glen had been found dead in her nightdress, and that her wits must have been astray. Everyone else knew about it.

When he came back at Christmas it was clear that he hadn't known. He was sympathetic and sad.

276

She asked him in, not to the breakfast room but the drawing room. Together they lit the fire.

The old dogs lay down, pleased that the room was being opened up.

Biddy was beyond complaining now. Too much had happened in this house. That Foxy Dunne be invited into the Major's drawing room seemed minor these days.

He told Leo of his plans. He had seen so much in England of how places could be developed. Take The Glen. They could sell off most of the land, build maybe eight houses, and still keep their own home.

'I expect your father would like that,' he said.

Outside they could see the sad lonely figure of Major Murphy walking up and down to the gate and back in the darkening evening.

'We can never sell the land,' Leo said.

'Is this part of what you told me you'd tell me one day?'

'Yes.'

'Are you ready to tell me now?'

'No. Not yet, Foxy.'

'Does your mother's death not make it different?' Again that feeling that he knew everything.

'No. You see, Daddy still lives here. Nothing could be . . . interfered with.'

She thought of the big diggers, the excavators, the rockery going, as it would one day, when The Glen would disappear like so much of Ireland, and make way for houses for the Irish who were coming back to live in their own land, having worked hard in other countries.

People like Foxy coming back to their inheritances.

The body of Danny McDonagh which had lain so long under its mausoleum of flowers would be disturbed. The questions would be asked.

'We're over twenty-one. We can do what we like,' he said.

'I could always do what I liked, for all the good it did me.'

'So could I,' he answered her with spirit. 'And it did me a lot of good. I never wanted anyone else but you, not since we were children. What did you want?'

'I wanted to be safe,' she said.

He promised her that was exactly what he would do for her. They talked a little that night, and more the next day in Barna Woods. He left her at the gate of The Glen, and saw her look away from the gate house.

'Something happened here,' he said.

'I always knew you had second sight.'

'Tell me, Leo. We're not people to have secrets from each other.'

Through the window of The Glen they could see her father sitting at the drawing-room fire. He must have got the idea of sitting in that room after seeing them there yesterday. She told Foxy the story.

'Let's get the key,' he said.

She went through the kitchen and took it from the rack in the hall. Together, with candles, they walked through the gate lodge, a blameless place that didn't know what had happened there.

He raised her face towards him and looked into her eyes.

'Your hair is like a halo again. You're doing it to drive me mad,' he said.

'Don't you see all the problems, all the terrible problems?'

'I see nothing that won't be solved by a load of concrete on where that rockery stands now,' Foxy Dunne said.

A STONE
HOUSE AND
A BIG TREE

T he decision to close the school was known in 1969; National Schools all over Ireland were giving way to Community Schools in the towns. But still it was a shock to see the building advertised for sale in the summer of 1970.

FOR SALE

Traditional stone schoolhouse. Built 1899. School accommodation comprises three large classrooms, toilet facilities and outer hall. Accompanying cottage: two bedrooms, one livingroom/ kitchen with stanley range.
For sale by Public Auction June 24th if not disposed of by Private Treaty.
Auctioneers: O'Neill and Blake.

Nessa and Niall Hayes read it over breakfast.

From their dining room they could look over at Ryan's Shancarrig Hotel and see the early tour buses leaving on their excursions. Nessa worked flexible hours across the road in her family business. Neither of her sisters had shown any interest in hotel work.

'They will when they see there's money in it,' her mother had said darkly.

'Imagine the school for sale. We'd never have thought that possible.' Niall was thirty now. Nobody ever referred to him as young Mr Hayes any more, in fact his father took the back seat in almost every aspect of the business nowadays.

'What's not possible?' Danny Hayes was four, and very inquisitive. He loved long words and would pronounce them carefully.

'That you're not going to go to the same school we went to.' Nessa wiped his chin expertly of the runny bits of egg. 'You'll go on a big yellow bus to school. You won't walk over the bridge like we did.'

'Can I go today?' Danny asked.

'After Christmas,' Nessa promised.

'Won't he be a bit young?' Niall looked worried.

'If *your* mother had had her way you wouldn't have been allowed up the road to Shancarrig school until you were twenty.' There was a laugh in Nessa's voice, but also a tinge of bitterness.

It had not been quite as simple moving into The Terrace as she had thought it would be. Although her father-in-law had handed over the reins quite willingly to his son, Ethel Hayes had been less anxious to let go the gloomy rein over the family.

There were dire warnings of pneumonia, rheumatic fever, spoiled children, temper tantrums, all directed at Nessa. Danny and Brenda would suffer for it all later, was Mrs Hayes's prediction – the children were allowed too much freedom, too little discipline, and a severe absence of cod liver oil.

'Would we buy it?' Nessa asked suddenly.

'What on earth for?' Niall was genuinely surprised.

'To live in. It would be a great place for the children to play ... the tree and everything. It would be lovely.'

'I don't know.' Niall bit his lip. It was his usual reaction to a new idea, to something totally unexpected.

Nessa knew him well enough.

'Well, let's not think about it now. It's a month to the auction,' she said.

Deftly she forced Danny to finish his egg and toast by cutting it into tiny cubes and eating one alternately with him. She settled Brenda into her carrycot. Niall was still sitting at his place pondering the bombshell.

'It's only an idea,' Nessa said airily. 'But if you're talking to Declan Blake at all, ask him how much he thinks they'll get for it.'

Niall looked out of the window, and saw Nessa moving into her parents' hotel. The carrycot was taken from her at the door by the porter. Danny had run to the hotel back yard where Nessa and her mother had built a sandpit, and swings and a see-saw to entertain the children who came to stay.

It had been yet one more excellent marketing notion for Ryan's Shancarrig Hotel.

Jim and Nora Kelly read it in Galway. They were staying with Maria and Hugh. They had wanted to be away when it was announced and by wonderful chance it coincided with the very time they were badly needed. Maria's first baby was due. She wanted her parents to be with her.

'It's the end of an era,' Maria said. 'There must be people all over Ireland saying that.'

'Not only Ireland – didn't our people go all over the world?' Jim Kelly said.

He was fifty years of age, and had been re-employed in the school in the town. It wasn't the same of course, nothing would ever be the same. But he knew a great number of the children, and he came trailing clouds of respect. A man who had run his own show, even in a small village, was a man to be reckoned with.

Nora had taken early retirement. And taken many a train to visit Maria over on the Atlantic coast. They walked along the beach together, the pregnant girl and the woman who was as good as her mother, with so much to say. Jim was pleased that his wife had taken the closing of the school so well. It might have been too much of a change for her to have gone to teach in the town.

Maria patted her stomach. 'It'll be so strange that she won't know the place as a school,' she said wonderingly.

'Or he. Remember, you could have a boy.' Jim Kelly knew that none of them minded whether it was a boy or girl.

They were so happy that Maria had found the steady Hugh after a series of wilder boyfriends had broken their hearts. Hugh seemed to know how much Maria needed her background in Shancarrig; he was always finding excuses to bring her there.

'Still, when the baby's born I'll wheel her ... or him, up to the school and say that this is where Grandpa or Grandma used to live, where every child lived for a while.' Maria looked sad. 'Oh, come on. I'm being stupidly sentimental,' she said with a little shake. 'And anyway, aren't you better off by far living in that fine house near everything, instead of having to toil up and down the hill?'

The Kellys had settled in one of the cottages that had been vastly changed and upgraded. The row of houses by the Grane that had once held the most unruly Brennans and Dunnes were now what young Declan Blake called Highly Des Res material.

'I wish there were going to be children there,' Nora Kelly said. 'I suppose it's unlikely that anyone who has children could afford to buy it, but somehow the place cries out for them. Or am I the one being sentimental now?'

'There'd be nobody local who could think of it.' Jim was ticking off people in his mind.

'Maybe when Hugh makes a fortune we'll buy it ourselves ... and let little Nora play under the copper beech like I did.'

There was a lump in their throats. It hadn't been said that Maria was going to call her child after Nora Kelly.

'I thought maybe Helen after your mother.' Nora felt she should say it anyway.

'The second one will be Helen!' said Maria.

And the matter was left there.

Chris Barton read the notice out to her mother-in-law. She always called Eddie's mother Una. It was yet another bond between them, the fact that she thought of the older woman as her sister.

'Well, Una. Is this our big chance?' Chris asked. 'Is this the famous opportunity that is meant to present itself to people? A ready-made craft centre ... get Foxy to build a few more outhouses that we could rent out as studios ... is this it or is it madness?'

'You're the one with the courage. I'd still be turning up hems for people and letting out their winter skirts if you hadn't come along.' Mrs Barton declared that she said an extra decade of the rosary every single night of her life to thank the Lord and His Mother for sending Chris to Shancarrig.

'I don't know, I really don't know. I'll ask Eddie. He has a great instinct for these things. We might be running before we can walk, or we might regret it all our lives. I trust his nose for this sort of thing.'

It was true. Mrs Barton realised that her daughter-in-law really did defer to Eddie's instincts and tastes. It wasn't a case of pretending to take his advice like Mrs Ryan in the hotel did, and indeed her daughter young Nessa who was busy pushing Niall Hayes into some kind of confidence. Chris genuinely thought Eddie the brains of the outfit. It made Una Barton's heart soar.

She thought less and less about the husband who had left her all those years ago – a quarter of a century – but sometimes she wished that Ted Barton could know how well his son had done and how splendidly they had managed without him.

Eddie came in holding the twins by the hand. He laughed as he saw his wife and mother automatically reach to protect everything on the table that was in danger of being pulled to the floor.

'Can we leave them with you, Una? I want to talk to Eddie in Barna Woods.'

'The last time you did that you proposed to me. I hope this doesn't mean you're going to leave.' He laughed confidently. He didn't think it was likely.

The children were strapped into their high chairs, and fussed over by their grandmother. Chris and Eddie walked as they so often walked together, shoulders touching, talking so that they finished each other's sentences, at ease with each other and the world. There was nobody in Shancarrig who noticed that Chris had a Scottish accent now, any more than they saw that she had a lame leg and a built-up shoe. She had been there since she was eighteen or nineteen. Part of the scenery.

They sat in the wood and she asked him about the centre. Was it exactly the right time? Or was this folly? Her eyes looked at him for an answer and she saw his face light up. He would never have thought of it, he said ... to him it would always have been the school, the place that he had gone, rain or shine, where he had played and studied. Of course it was the answer.

'Would we live there, or just work there?' Chris wondered.

'It would be great for the children.'

'We could sell the pink house.' Chris had always called it that, since the moment she had arrived.

'But my mother?'

'She said she'd leave it to us.'

'Where would she go? She's so used to being beside us ...' Mrs Barton lived in her own little wing of the pink house, beside them but not on top of them.

'She'd come with us, you big nellie. We'd be building a whole lot of places and she could choose the kind of place she'd like. It's no bigger a hill for her to climb than the one that she's been on all her life.'

Eddie's eyes were dancing. 'We could invite people in ... like the pottery couple, or the weavers ...'

'We could have a small shop there, selling everyone's work. Not only ours, but everyone's.'

'Nessa would get them up here from the hotel for a start, and Leo's got all sorts of contacts all over the place.'

'Will we do it?'

They embraced, as they had embraced in these woods years ago at the thought of being married and living happily ever after.

Richard saw the advertisement.

He wondered would whoever bought it cut down the tree in the yard. What would they make of the things that were written on it? He was prepared to bet that his wasn't the only carving that told a story.

He thought about the school all day in the office.

It was a tiring journey home, a lot of traffic. He was hot and tired. He hoped that Vera hadn't arranged anything for tonight. What he really would like to do was ... he paused. He didn't know what he would really like to do. It had been so long since he had allowed himself a thought like that.

He knew what he would really *not* like to do, and that would be to go to the club. Vera might have set up a little evening, a few drinks at the bar, dinner. He would know when he got in. If she had been to the hairdresser this is what she had planned.

He nosed the car into the garage beside Vera's.

Jimmy the gardener was edging the lawn. 'Good evening, Mr Hayes,' he said, touching his forehead.

'That looks great, Jimmy. Great work.' Richard knew his voice was automatic; he didn't see what the man had done or what needed to be done. He thought that a full-time gardener was a bit excessive in a Dublin garden.

Still, it was Vera's decision. It was after all she who had bought the house, and filled it with valuable things. It was Vera who made the day-to-day decisions about how they spent the money which was mainly her money.

She was sitting in the conservatory. He noticed sadly that she had been to the hairdresser.

'You look lovely,' he said.

'Thank you, darling. I thought we might meet some of the others at the club ... you know, rather than just sitting looking at each other all night?' She smiled.

She was very attractive in her lemon-coloured dress, her blonde upswept hair and her even suntan.

She did not look in her late thirties any more than he did. But unlike him she never seemed to find their life empty. She filled it with acquaintances, parties given, parties attended, a group of what she called like-minded people at the golf club.

Vera had taken their childlessness with what Richard considered a disturbing lack of concern. If the question was ever raised between themselves or when other people were present she always said the same thing. She said that if it happened it did, and if it didn't it didn't. No point in having all those exhaustive tests to discover whose *fault* it was, as if someone was to blame.

Since Richard knew from the past, only too well from his drama with Olive, that there could be nothing lacking on his side, he wished that Vera would go for an examination. But she refused.

She had the newspaper open in front of her.

'Look! There's a simply lovely place for sale, in that Shancarrig where you spent all those years.'

'I know. I saw it.'

'Should we buy it, do you think? It has tons of potential. It would make a nice weekend place, we could have people to stay. You know, it might be fun.'

'No.'

'What do you mean, *no?*'

'I mean NO, Vera,' he said.

Her face flushed. 'Well, I don't know what you're turning on *me* for, I only thought *you'd* like it. I do everything that I think you'd like. It's becoming impossible to please you.'

He moved over to reach for her but she stood up and pulled away.

'Seriously, Richard. Nobody could please you. There isn't a woman on earth that could hold you. Maybe you should never have married, just been a desirable bachelor all your life.' She was very hurt, he could see.

'Please. Please forgive me, I've had a horrible day. I'm tired, that's all. Please, I'm a pig.'

She was softening. 'Have a bath and a drink and we'll go out. You'll feel much better then.'

'Yes. Yes, of course. I'm sorry for snapping.' His voice was dead, he could hear it in his own ears.

'And you really don't think we should pick up this little house as a weekend place?'

'No, Vera. No, I wasn't happy there. It wouldn't make me happy to go back.'

'Right. It will never be mentioned again,' she said.

And he knew that she would look for somewhere else, a place where they could invite people for the weekend – fill their life with even more half strangers. Maybe she might even pick on whatever town Gloria had settled in. He knew the Darcys had left Shancarrig not long after he had.

Leo sat in the kitchen of The Glen making a very unsuccessful effort to comb Moore's hair. He had inherited the frizz from his mother and the colour from his father. He was six years old and in the last pageant that Shancarrig school had put on he had been asked to play The Burning Bush. This was apparently his own choice.

Foxy was delighted. Leo was less sure.

Moore Dunne was turning out to be a bigger handful than anyone could have believed. Foxy had insisted on the name. While he worked in England he said that he had discovered it was very classy to use one family name added to another. Leo's mother had been Miriam Moore, this had been the Moore household.

Moore's younger sister, Frances, was altogether more tractable. 'We'll liven her up yet,' Foxy had said ominously.

Unlike many of the builders who had returned from England in the prosperous sixties with their savings and their ideas of a quick killing, Foxy Dunne had decided to go the route of befriending rather than alienating architects.

The eight small houses he had built within the grounds of The Glen had a style and a character that was noticeably missing in such similar small developments in other towns. A huge row of semi-mature trees had been planted to give the new houses privacy, but also to maintain the long sweep of The Glen's avenue.

Major Murphy had lived to see his grandchildren but was buried now in the graveyard beside his wife.

From the big drawing room of The Glen Leo ran the ever-increasing building empire that Foxy had set up. All his cousins in the town now worked for him, the cousins who had once barred his father from crossing the doors of their shops. His cousins Brian and Liam waited on his every word and his uncle treated him with huge respect.

Foxy's father was not around to see the fruits of having totally ignored his son. Old Dinny had died in the county home some years previously. Foxy's own brothers, never men to have held down jobs for any notable length of time, most of them with some kind of prison record, were now regarded as remittance men. Small allowances were paid as long as they stayed far away from Shancarrig.

The main alterations that had put Ryan's Shancarrig Hotel on the map for tourism had been done by Foxy Dunne. It was he who had transformed the cottages by the River Grane, his only concession to any sentimentality or revenge having been his own personal presence as they levelled to the ground the house he grew up in.

The church hall, which was the pride of Father Gunn's life, was built by Foxy at such a reduced rate that it might even have been called his gift to the parish.

Foxy kept proper accounts. The books that Leo kept were regularly audited. The leases to the property he bought and sold were handled by his friend Niall Hayes. Maura came up from the gate lodge every day to do some of the housework and to mind the children. As always, her son Michael came with her. Michael was growing up big and strong but with the mind and loving heart of a small child.

Moore Dunne was particularly fond of him. 'He's much more interesting than other big people,' Moore pronounced.

Leo made sure she told that to Maura.

'I've always thought that myself,' Maura agreed.

Leo and Maura had a cup of tea together every morning before both went to their work – Leo to cope with Foxy's deals and Maura to polish and shine The Glen. Together they looked at the advertisement offering their old school for sale.

'Who would buy it, unless to set up another school?' Maura wondered.

'I'm very much afraid Foxy wants to,' said Leo. He hadn't said it yet, but she knew it was on his mind. It was as if he could never burn out the memory of the way things used to be. Not until he owned the whole town.

They heard the sound of his car outside the door. 'How's Squire Dunne?' he said to his son.

'I'm all *right*,' said Moore doubtfully.

'Only all *right*. You should be tip top,' Foxy said.

'Well yes, but I think there's another cat growing inside Flossie.' Moore was delighted.

'That's great,' said Foxy. 'It'll be a kitten, or maybe five kittens even.'

'But how are they going to get out?' Moore was puzzled. Maura giggled.

'That's your mother's department,' said Foxy, heading for the office. 'I have to think of other things like planning permissions, son.'

'For the school?' Leo asked.

'Aha, you're there before me,' he said.

She looked at him, small and quick, eager as ever, nowadays dressed in clothes that were made to measure, but still the endearing Foxy of their childhood. She followed him into the room that was once their drawing room, where her father had paced, and her mother had sat distracted, and Lance and Jessie had slept uncaring by the fire.

'Do we need it, Foxy?' she asked.

'What's need?' He put his arms around her shoulders and looked into her eyes.

'Haven't we enough?' she said.

'Love, it's a gold mine. It's *made* for us. The right kind of cottages, classy stuff, the kind rich Dubliners might even have as a summer place, or for visiting at the weekends. Do them up really well, let Chris

and Eddie loose on them. Slate floors ... you know the kind of thing.'
He looked so eager. He would love the challenge.

Perhaps he was right, it *was* made for them. Why did she keep thinking he was doing everything just to show? To show some anonymous invisible people who didn't care.

Maddy Ross thought it was wonderful that God moved so mysteriously. Look at how he had closed the school just at exactly the right time for Maddy.

Now she could be quite free to spend all her time with the Family. The wonderful Family of Hope. Madeleine Ross had been a member of the Family of Hope for three years. And it had not been easy.

For one thing there had been all that adverse publicity in the papers about the castle they had been given, and the misunderstanding over the deeds.

There had been no intention at all to defraud or deceive, but the way the papers wrote it all up you'd think that the Family of Hope was some kind of international confidence tricksters' organisation.

And there had been the whole attitude of Father Gunn. Maddy had never really liked Father Gunn, not since that time long ago when he had been so patronising and so judgemental about her friendship with Father Barry. If Father Gunn had been more understanding or open and liberal about the place of Love in God's scheme of things then a lot of events would have worked out differently.

Still, that was water under the bridge. The big problem was Father Gunn's attitude today.

He had said that the Family of Hope was not a wonderful way of doing God's work on earth, that it was a dangerous cult, that it was brainwashing people like Maddy, that God wanted love and honour to be shown to him through the conventional channels of the church.

It was just exactly what you would have expected him to say. It was what people had said to Our Lord when he went to the temple to drive out the scribes and the Pharisees. They had said to him that this wasn't the way. They had been wrong, just as Father Gunn was wrong. But it didn't matter. Father Gunn couldn't rule her life for her. It was 1970 now, it wasn't the bad old days when poor Father Barry could be sent away before he knew his mind to a missionary place where they weren't ready for him.

And Father Gunn didn't know about the insurance policy that Mother had left her. The money she had been going to give to the people of Vieja Piedra before they had been abandoned and the work stopped in midstream.

Maddy Ross still walked by herself in Barna Woods and hugged herself thinking of the money she could give to the Family of Hope.

They wanted to buy a place to be their centre.

She had wondered for a long time if there might be anywhere near here. She wanted to live on in Mother's house and near the woods and river that were so dear to her, and held so many memories. And now at last she had found the very place.

The schoolhouse was for sale.

Maura showed the picture of the school to Michael that evening in their little home – the gate lodge of The Glen.

'Do you know where it is, Michael?' she asked.

He held it in both his hands. 'Is my school,' he said.

'That's right, Michael. It's your school,' she said and she stroked his head.

Michael had never attended a lesson inside the school, but he had gone sometimes to play with the children in the yard. Maura had often stood, lump in throat, watching him pick up the beech leaves as she had done before him, and all his uncles and aunts – the Brennans who had gone away.

'We might walk up there tonight, Michael, and have a look at it again. Would you like that?'

'Will we have tea early so?' He looked at her anxiously.

'We'll have tea early so,' she agreed.

He got his own plate and mug, made of Bakelite that wouldn't crack. Michael dropped things sometimes. His mother's china he never touched. Some of it was in a little cabinet that hung on the wall, other pieces were wrapped in tissue paper.

Maura O'Sullivan went to local auctions, always buying bargains in bone china. She never had a full set, or even a half set, but it didn't matter since she didn't ever invite anyone to dine. It was all for her.

They walked past the pink house and waved to the Bartons.

'Can I go in and play with the twins?' Michael said.

'Aren't we going to look at your old school?' They crossed the bridge where the children called out a greeting to Michael, as they had done for many years. And would always do. As long as Maura was there to look after him. Suppose Maura weren't there?

She gave a little shudder.

At the school she saw Dr Jims and his son Declan. The *For Sale* sign was there in the sunset. It would look big in other places; under the copper beech it looked tiny.

'Good evening, Doctor.' She was formal.

'Hello, Declan ...' Michael embraced the doctor's son, whom he had known since he was a boy in his pram.

'Changing times,' Dr Jims said. 'Lord, I never thought I'd see this day.'

'Don't be denying me my bit of business, Dad ...' Declan laughed.

They got on so well these days, Maura realised. It must have been that nice girl Ruth that Declan had married. Some people had great luck altogether out of their marriages. But hadn't she got as much love and happiness as anyone had ever got in the whole world?

Michael was looking at the names on the tree. 'Is my name there, Mammy?' he asked.

'If it's not it should be,' Dr Jims said. 'Weren't you here as much as any child in Shancarrig?'

'I'll write it if you like,' Declan offered.

'What will you put?'

'Let's see. I'll put it near my initials. There, see DB 1961? That's me.'

'You've no heart drawn,' Michael complained.

'I didn't love anyone then,' Declan said. His voice seemed full of emotion. The two of them had made a great production of getting out Declan's penknife and choosing a spot.

Dr Jims said to Maura, 'Are you feeling all right? You're a bit pale.'

'You know me, I worry about things. Nothing maybe ...'

'It's a while since you've been to see me.'

'No, Doctor. Not my health, the future.'

'Ah. There's divil a thing you can do about the future.' Jims Blake smiled at her.

'It's like ... I wonder sometimes in case something happened to me, what would happen ... you know,' Maura looked over at Michael.

'Child, you're not thirty years of age!'

'I am that. Last week.'

'Maura, all I can say is that every mother in Ireland worries about her child. It's both a wonder and a waste. Life goes on.'

'For ordinary people, yes.'

Michael gave a cry of pleasure, and came to tug at her.

'Look at what he's written. Look, Mammy.'

Declan Blake had drawn a heart, and on one side he had *M O'S*. On the other he said he was going to put *All his friends in Shancarrig*.

'See what I mean?' said Dr Jims.

Maddy Ross invited Sister Judith of the Family of Hope to come and see the schoolhouse. Sister Judith said it was perfect. She asked how much would it cost. Maddy said she had heard in the area of five thousand pounds. With her mother's insurance policy, Maddy explained, there would be that and plenty more. She would get the deeds drawn up with a solicitor. Not with Niall Hayes. After all, she had taught Niall Hayes at school; it wouldn't be appropriate.

Maria's child was born in Galway. It was a girl. She was to be called Nora. Nora Kelly telephoned Una Barton with the good news. The old habits die hard and they still addressed each other formally.

'Mrs Kelly, I'm so *very* pleased. I'll make the baby a little dress with smocking on it,' she said.

'Maria'll bring her back to Shancarrig on a triumphal tour, and you'll be the first port of call, Mrs Barton,' she cried. The Kellys inquired about the school and was there any word about buyers.

Mrs Barton paused. She didn't know whether the children wanted it known or not. Still, she couldn't lie to a woman like Mrs Kelly.

'Between ourselves, Eddie and Chris are trying to get the money together, with grants and everything. They hope to turn it into an arts centre.' There was a silence. 'Aren't you pleased to hear that?'

'Yes, yes. It's just I suppose we were hoping there would be children there.'

'But there will. They're going to live there with the twins, and me as well. That's the hope, Mrs Kelly, but it may come to nothing.'

'That would be great, Mrs Barton. I'll say a prayer to St Anne for you. I'd love to think of your grandchildren and mine playing under that tree.'

The Dixons were just driving through when they saw the schoolhouse. They were enchanted by it, and called in to Niall Hayes to inquire more about it.

They found him singularly unhelpful.

'There's an auctioneer's name and telephone number on the sign,' he said brusquely.

'But seeing that you are the local solicitor we thought you'd know, might shortcut it a bit.' The Dixons were wealthy Dublin people looking for a weekend home; they were used to shortcutting things a bit.

'There could be a conflict of interests,' Niall Hayes said.

'If you want to buy it then why is the board still up?' asked Mr Dixon.

'Good afternoon,' Niall Hayes said.

'Terrifying, these country bumpkins,' said Mrs Dixon, well within his hearing.

'We've never fought about anything, Foxy, have we?' Leo said to him in bed.

'What do you mean? Our life is one long fight!' he said.

'I don't want us to buy the school.'

'Give me one good reason.'

'We don't need it, Foxy. Truly we don't. It'd be a hassle.'

He stroked her face, but she got up and sat on the edge of the bed.

'Things are always a hassle, love. That's the fun. That's what it was always about. *You* know that.'

'No. This time it's different. Lots of others want it too.'

'So? We *get* it.'

'No, not just rivals, real people. Chris and Eddie, Nessa and Niall, Miss Ross, and I think Maura has hopes of it.'

'Miss Ross!' He laughed and rolled around the bed. 'Miss Ross is away with the fairies. It would be a *kindness* not to let her have it.'

'But the others! I'm serious.'

'Look. Niall and Nessa are business people, they know about deals. That's what Niall does all day. Same with Chris and Eddie, they'd understand. Some things you go for, some you get.'

Leo began to pace around the room. She reminded herself of her parents. They had paced in this house too.

She shivered at the thought. He was out of bed, concerned. He put a dressing-gown around her shoulders.

'I told you. Give me one good reason, one *real* reason, and I'll stop.'

'Maura.'

'Aw, come on, Leo, give me a break! Maura hasn't a penny. We practically *gave* her the gate lodge. Where would she get the money? What would she want it for?'

'I don't know, but she has Michael up there every evening, the two of them staring at it. She wants it for something.'

*

'Nessa, come in to me a moment, will you?'

'Why do I always feel like a child, instead of the best help you ever had in this hotel, when you use that tone of voice?' Nessa laughed at her mother.

Brenda Ryan poured them a glass of sherry each, always a sign of something significant.

'Has Daddy gone on the tear?'

'No, cynical child.' They sat companionably. Nessa waited. She knew her mother had something to say.

She was right. Her mother said she was going to give her one piece of advice and then withdraw and let Nessa think about it. She had heard that Nessa and Niall were thinking of buying the schoolhouse as a place to live. Now, there was no way she was going to say how she had heard, nor any need for Nessa to bridle and say it was her own business. But all Breda Ryan wanted to put on the table, for what it was worth, was the following:

It would be an act of singular folly to leave The Terrace, to abandon that beautiful house just because old Ethel was a lighting devil and Nessa didn't feel mistress of her own home. The solution was a simple matter of relocation, banishing both parents to the basement.

But not, of course, describing it as that. Describing it in fact as Foxy Dunne and his architect having come up with this amazing idea about making a self-contained flat for the older folk.

Nessa fidgeted as she listened.

'It's only a matter of time,' her mother told her. 'Suppose you went up to the schoolhouse and his parents were dead next year, think how cross you'd be. Losing the high ground like that. Keep the place, don't let them divide it up with his sisters. It's the best house in the town.'

'I wonder are you right.' Nessa spoke thoughtfully, as to an equal.

'I'm right,' said her mother.

Eddie came back from his travels. He had found enough people to make the whole centre work. Exactly the kind of people they had always wanted to work with, some of whom had known their work too. It was flattering how well Chris and Eddie Barton were becoming known in Ireland.

The next thing was to visit the bank manager.

And the projections.

Eddie had asked the potential tenants to write their stories so that he and Chris could work out the costings. He also asked them to tell what had been successful or unsatisfactory in the previous places they had been.

He and Chris together read their reports.

They read of places where no visitors came because it wasn't near enough to the town, places that the tour buses passed by because there was no time on the itinerary. They learned that it was best to be part of a community, not outside it. They sat together and realised that in many ways the schoolhouse was not the dream location they had thought.

'That's if we take notice of them,' Chris said.

'We *have* to take notice of them. That's our research.' Eddie's face was sad.

'Aren't we better to know now than after?' Chris said. 'Though it's awful to see a dream go up like that.'

'What do you mean a dream go up like that? Haven't we our eye on Nellie Dunne's place after her time? That place is like a warren at the back.'

She saw Eddie smile again and that pleased her. 'Come on, let's tell Una.' She leapt up and went to Eddie's mother's quarters.

'I don't mind *where* I am as long as I'm with the pair of you,' said Mrs Barton. She also told them that she heard that both Foxy Dunne *and* Niall Hayes were said to have their eye on the school.

'Then we're better off not alienating good friends who happen to be good customers as well,' said Chris. The two women laughed happily, like conspirators.

Father Gunn twisted and turned in his narrow bed. In his mind he was trying to write the letter to the Bishop, the letter that would get him a ruling about the Family of Hope. It now seemed definite that Madeleine Ross had given these sinister people the money to set up a centre in Shancarrig schoolhouse. They would be here in the midst of his parish, taking away his flock, preaching to them, in long robes, by the river.

Please let the Bishop know what to do.

Why had he made all those moves years ago to prevent a scandal? Wouldn't God and the parish have been far better served if that half-cracked Father Brian Barry and that entirely cracked Maddy Ross had been encouraged to run away with each other? None of this desperate mess about the Family of Bloody Hope would ever have happened.

Terry and Nancy Dixon called in on Vera and Richard Hayes's house on their way back home after their ramble.

'We saw the most perfect schoolhouse. I think we should buy it together,' Terry said. 'It's in that place you worked for a while, Shancarrig.'

'We saw it advertised,' Vera said, glancing at Richard.

'And?' The Dixons looked from one to the other. Richard's eyes were far away.

'Richard said he wasn't happy in Shancarrig.' Vera spoke for him.

'I'm not surprised,' said Nancy Dixon. 'But you wouldn't have to mix all that much. It would be just the perfect place to get away from it all. There's a really marvellous tree.'

'A copper beech,' Richard said.

'Yes, that's right. It should go for a song. We talked to the solicitor but he wasn't very forthcoming.'

'That's my uncle,' Richard said.

The Dixons looked embarrassed. They said it was a younger man, must have been his son. Not someone who was going to set the world on fire? they ventured.

Richard wasn't responding. 'They all wrote their names on that tree,' he said.

'Aha! Perhaps you wrote *your* name on the tree, that's why we can't go back there.' Vera was coquettish.

'No. I never wrote my name there,' Richard said. His eyes were still very far away.

'Is there much interest from Dublin?' Dr Jims asked his son.

'No, I thought there'd be more. Maybe if we advertised it again.'

The two men walked regularly together in Shancarrig. Declan and Ruth were having a house built there now. They didn't want the place in The Terrace. They wanted somewhere with more space, space for rabbits and a donkey, for the children they would have. Ruth was pregnant. They also felt that it was time to have a sub-office of O'Neill and Blake Estate Agents in Shancarrig. Many of the visitors who came to Ryan's Shancarrig Hotel now wanted to buy sites. Foxy Dunne was only too ready to build on them.

'What will it go for?' Dr Jims had the school on his mind a lot.

'We've had an offer of five. You know that.' Declan Blake jerked his head across at Maddy Ross's cottage.

'We don't want them, Declan.'

'I can't play God, Dad. I have to get the best price for my client.'

'Your client is only the old Department of Education, son. They're being done left, right and centre, or making killings all over the place. They don't count.'

'You're honourable in your trade. I have to be in mine.'

'I'm also human in mine.' There was a silence.

If either of them was remembering how Dr Jims had bent the rules to help his son all those years ago neither of them said it.

'Perhaps they'll get outbidden.' Declan didn't seem very hopeful.

'Has Niall Hayes dropped out?'

'Yes. And Foxy Dunne – that's a relief in a way. And so has Eddie. I wouldn't want them raising the price on each other.'

'There. You do have a heart.' Dr Jims seemed pleased.

'And nobody else?'

'Nobody serious.'

'Who knows what's serious?'

'All right, Dad. Maura. Michael's mother. She says that she wants the place to be a home, a home for children like Michael, with someone to run it. And she'd help in it too. People like Michael who have no mothers ... that's what she wants.'

'Well, isn't that what we'd all want?' said Dr Jims. 'And if we want it, it can be done.'

Nobody ever knew what negotiation went on behind the scenes, how the Family of Hope were persuaded that it would be very damaging publicity to cross swords with a community which wanted to provide a home for Down's syndrome children – and had raised the money for it. Maddy Ross was heard to say that she was just as glad that Sister Judith hadn't been forced to meet the collective ignorance, superstition and bigotry of Shancarrig.

Foxy and Leo had provided a sister for Moore and Frances – Chris and Eddie a brother for the twins – Nessa and Niall a brother for Danny and Breda – Mr and Mrs Hayes had decided of their own volition to move downstairs to the basement of The Terrace and had their own front door by which they came and went – Declan and Ruth Blake had built their house and called their son James – the Kellys' granddaughter Nora was walking – when the Shancarrig Home was opened.

There were photographs of it in all the papers and nice little pieces describing it.

But it was hard to do it justice, because all anyone could see was a stone house and a big tree.